Single by Saturday

D0047942

Also by Catherine Bybee

Contemporary Romance

Weekday Brides Series

Wife by Wednesday
Married by Monday
Fiancé by Friday

Not Quite Series

Not Quite Dating
Not Quite Mine
Not Quite Enough

Paranormal Romance

MacCoinnich Time Travels

Binding Vows
Silent Vows
Redeeming Vows
Highland Shifter

The Ritter Werewolves Series

Before the Moon Rises
Embracing the Wolf

Novellas

Soul Mate
Possessive

Erotica

Kilt Worthy
Kilt-A-Licious

CATHERINE BYBEE

Single by Saturday

BOOK FOUR IN THE WEEKDAY BRIDES SERIES

Published by Montlake Romance, Seattle

www.apub.com

ISBN-13: 9781477849262
ISBN-10: 1477849262

Cover Design by Crystal Posey

Library of Congress Control Number: 2013911841

Printed in the United States of America.

To David and Libby

When God needed to create two people to help others . . .
he created the two of you.
For all you do!

Chapter One

After a year of practice at being Michael Wolfe's wife, Karen didn't hesitate when he walked up behind her, slid his hands around her waist, and kissed the side of her neck.

"There you are."

She smiled up at his gorgeous face and sighed. He really was one of the most beautiful men she'd ever met. Too bad he was gay.

"I'm not hiding," she said and leaned into him for the benefit of those watching.

"The caterer is going to serve in thirty minutes."

They did the domestic part really well, better than most married couples who were actually into the vows for the long haul. "I'll go check and make sure everything is ready."

He kissed the top of her head before she excused herself from the small gathering of friends she'd been talking to and headed back inside the house. Karen circulated through her and Michael's one-year anniversary party and greeted Hollywood's royalty by name. She couldn't help but wonder if the same crowd would be present in six months at their divorce party. She knew, without a doubt, that her name would be removed from the automatic invite list while Michael's would remain in stone. That's what happened when you were scheduled to divorce one of the most sought after names in the business. Of course, only a handful of people in the room were expecting the divorce. Everyone else would hear about it via a tabloid or entertainment newscast when the time arrived.

The Spanish-influenced home sat in Beverly Hills with amazing views of the city. There were over two hundred guests at the party, testing the limits of the house. Thankfully, the Southern California weather graced them with a mild evening and allowed guests to mingle inside the home and out.

Karen weaved around the guests, paused to accept a fake Hollywood hug or two, and made her way into the kitchen. The catering manager stood in the center of the chaos giving orders and shuffling her staff around with quiet tones and an evil eye. "Vera, how is everything running?"

"Everything is set for the top of the hour, Mrs. Wolfe."

Karen never corrected the use of her husband's name, though she'd never legally changed hers to match.

"And the wine?"

Vera lifted her chin and offered a smile. "Just as your husband selected."

"Good."

"However, we had a slight problem with quantity."

Karen frowned. It didn't matter to her, but Michael's preferences were discriminating.

"Did you check the substitute with Michael?"

Vera kept smiling, but her eyes fluttered with what Karen thought were nerves. "He wasn't available. Perhaps you'd like to see what I selected?"

"Of course."

Karen walked behind Vera as they stepped out the back door of the house to the catering supply truck, where Vera instructed one of her staff to open a wooden crate. Inside sat six bottles of Pinot Noir all elegantly labeled and presented as expected. But if there was one thing Karen had learned after living with a wine connoisseur for a year, the covers of these books didn't always match the insides. She knew Michael's taste and didn't hesitate in making a decision for him on this account.

"I don't recognize the label."

Vera gave a quick shake of her head. "No worry." From her apron, she removed a corkscrew and made quick work of removing the plug from the wine. Vera made a grabby motion of her fingertips, and one of her employees handed her a glass.

With a flourish, Vera poured the wine and handed a small sample over for Karen to taste.

During the time Karen and Michael had spent in France, she'd learned enough about wine to pass a simple tasting. She swished the wine around the glass and didn't notice any problem with the color of the liquid. In truth, she had always felt this part of wine tasting was the second most useless. Red wines were red, and white were always white. Karen lifted the wine to her nose, scented a little citrus and berry, and then let the wine hit her tongue.

Full-bodied and sweet. No need to spit it out. Spitting out the wine was the most useless of wine tasting practices in her opinion. Spitting out perfectly good wine defeated the purpose. "This will be fine," she told Vera, who appeared to hold her breath as Karen gave her opinion. "Be sure that the first bottles served are what Michael ordered."

Vera gave a swift nod and a motion of her hand while others moved around them to place the wine inside the house. They both turned to walk inside when a lone figure approached from behind them. "Mrs. Wolfe?"

With a practiced smile, Karen turned around and forgot to breathe. The hair on her arms stood on end as a mixture of sensation traveled over her skin. There was something familiar about the six-foot-three man with dark brown hair and piercing blue eyes. His jaw was as rugged as Michael's and held a day's worth of stubble, something Michael sported for some of his roles but preferred to shave off at first chance.

Thinking of Michael brought his image to her mind, and the realization hit that the man in front of her could quite possibly be his double. Only this man didn't have the laughter in his eyes or the easy smile on his face. No, there was something hidden behind his gaze that made her pause. This man was gorgeous, and if she were one to believe in instant attraction, her body responded to him with a fierceness she didn't think possible. Maybe this was what the women gazing at Michael experienced that she did not. This wild thrill of discovery that led to possibilities only the big screen could fulfill.

Instead of letting her imagination get the best of her, Karen flattened a hand over her stomach and attempted to act unaffected. "Do I know you?"

The sex-personified blue-eyed man stepped toward her. It took effort for her to hold her ground.

Sensing her unease, he held still, looked around the both of them as if noticing the caterers running about and guests arriving behind him, and said simply, "Zach Gardner."

The smile on her face stayed. The name tickled at the edges of her consciousness. Memories flashed behind the veil of her mind until she narrowed her focus. "Michael's brother?" she whispered.

Zach gave a small nod and swept his eyes down her frame. When his eyes met hers again, he masked whatever he'd been thinking, then he smiled and said, "And you're the wife none of us have met."

Not a lot shook Karen. She'd managed the role of Michael's wife under the ever-present scrutiny of paparazzi, producers, actors, and fans . . . but the man standing in front of her did what no one else could. He made her question her decision to marry.

Karen stepped forward and ignored the frown suddenly on Zach's face. "We didn't know you were coming."

"So you do know Mike has a family."

"Of course." No one called Michael, Mike. Somehow, family always made you remember where you were from.

Karen fidgeted under his stare and something in his gaze hesitated. It was as if he knew he was coming across harsh and blaming her for his brother's absence. But Karen knew Michael wasn't as close to his family as he once was.

"He's had a grueling schedule this last year." She made excuses for Michael, knowing that part of the reason his family had not been brought into their marriage was because it wasn't scheduled to last. His deception was meant for Hollywood, not his family. In reality, Karen had half expected someone to show up before now.

"Everyone's busy."

Which Karen translated as Zach not giving a shit about Michael's schedule or his excuses. They were Michael's to excuse, and Karen didn't want to step between him and his family.

"I'm sure Michael will be excited to see you." She started to walk past Zach to show him the way inside.

"Looks like my timing is bad."

It would have been easy for her to suggest that unexpected and unannounced visits had a way of having *bad* timing, but she refrained. "Not at all." Since they'd never met in person, and she had no way of knowing if Zach knew her name, she presented her hand. "I'm Karen, by the way."

Zach took her hand in his and an unexpected hot current shot up her arm. Now *that* was *bad* timing!

A zip of chemistry was just fine, thank you very much, but not with her temporary husband's brother. Oh, no, that wasn't fine at all!

Surprise passed over Zach's eyes before he pulled his hand away rather abruptly. "And I feel as if I owe you an apology."

"What for?" *For coming off as an abrasive, albeit sexy, ass?* Oh, yeah . . . maybe he did.

"I'm a little shocked to find a real person behind the pictures we've all seen."

"A real person as opposed to what?"

Zach shrugged. "My brother is seen with someone new at every film premiere. I think we assumed you weren't real . . . but I can see now that you are. Doesn't excuse my rudeness. My beef is with my brother, not you."

Karen felt a warm smile fill her face and something in Zach's eyes softened. "Was that an apology?"

"Half-assed, but yes."

Seemed Zach and Michael had that in common, the ability to apologize without actually saying the words. Though Michael was getting better.

"Apology accepted. Now c'mon, Zach, let's go find your brother." She didn't leave any room for discussion as she walked around him and into the house.

A couple of heads turned as the two of them walked into the kitchen. She couldn't help but wonder if the help thought the man beside her was Michael's twin, or stunt double, which Zach could easily pull off. If Karen remembered right, Zach was Michael's older brother by at least a year. There was an older sister and two younger sisters. All of whom still lived in the small town in Utah Michael had grown up in and moved away from shortly after high school.

Samantha, Karen's friend and sometimes colleague, intercepted the path to Michael's side. "There you are. Michael's looking for you." Samantha eyed Zach with a slight smile.

"We're looking for him, too. Samantha Harrison, this is Zach Gardner, Michael's brother."

"Of course. The family resemblance is hard to miss." Samantha shook Zach's hand.

"A pleasure." His words were dry, as if he'd like nothing better than to disappear.

"Where did you see Michael last?"

"In the courtyard. C'mon, I'll show you."

Thankful for Samantha's presence, Karen offered her practiced smile to Zach and led him through the house and out the massive doors to the courtyard where even more guests mingled and eyed the new guest.

Michael stood with his back to them.

Karen tapped his shoulder and caught his eyes before he looked beyond her. "Michael. Look who I found."

In a split second, confusion mixed into recognition, and then the most surprising thing happened. Michael lost some of his polish. "Jesus, Zach."

Karen stood aside and watched the two brothers offer smiles, handshakes, and man hugs.

"It's been too long," Zach said.

"Too damn long."

Both men smiled at each other as if they'd never shared a cross word or years apart.

Samantha tucked beside Karen and whispered in her ear, "He's crashing the party?"

Karen kept smiling. "Just showed up."

"Well this is going to be interesting."

That was what Karen worried about.

Michael turned toward the small crowd. "Everyone, this is my brother, Zach." Michael took a moment to offer a few names to Zach, but it became quickly apparent the man wasn't going to remember most of them. Or if he did, it was because of their fame and not the brief introduction. "And you've met Karen."

Zach once again took her in with his blue gaze. "I've met your *wife*."

Zach allowed Mike to lead him around and introduce him to his friends, though Zach didn't think there were many people in the house his brother could actually count on. He wasn't sure what he thought it would be like walking into his brother's world. He knew the level of success his brother had achieved, but he'd never experienced it. The plastic Hollywood scene was light-years away from the life they'd grown up in. Maybe that was the appeal. Lord knew growing up in a small town in Utah had its drawbacks.

Like never finding a woman as stunning as the one Mike called his wife. Zach had seen pictures, right before their mother went on a tear about having never met Karen. None of the pictures did the woman justice.

Her eyes were the shade of blue seldom seen outside of an ocean. Her blonde hair was too pure to come from a bottle, and despite all the activity around her, she didn't seem to let any of it affect her. Zach understood his brother's attraction and that had happened exactly never. Not once could Zach remember them both of them having the same girl in their thoughts.

He pushed Mike's wife out of his mind and remembered why he took this little trip to his brother's.

It was their youngest sister, Hannah, who prompted Zach to jump on the back of his motorcycle and take the road trip to LA. Mike could be Mr. Hollywood with everyone else, but his family missed him. Their mother was pissed, their father ready to disown the youngest male in the Gardner line, and the girls were convinced that Michael Wolfe wasn't blood related after all. But Hannah had practically begged Zach to drag Mike home.

"Hon?" Karen captured Mike's attention. "The caterers are ready to serve."

Michael placed his arm over Karen's shoulder and kissed the top of her head. "Thanks."

Zach had seen the move from Michael before. It certainly appeared as if Karen and Mike's marriage was happy.

"Can you excuse us for a second, Zach?"

"It's your party, I'm just crashing."

Mike waved at the disc jockey, who turned down the volume on the music playing in the background.

Zach had found a beer and sipped it now as he watched his brother welcome his guests and thank them all for coming. When he drew Karen next to his side and thanked her for being his wife, Zach found himself looking away. He noticed Samantha, Karen's friend, watching him before she diverted her gaze.

A few guests started mumbling to his right, catching Zach's attention. "Wonder how long it can possibly last."

"It's hard to get sick of your spouse when he's never home. Hasn't he been on location nine of the past twelve months?"

Zach sipped his beer and continued to eavesdrop. "At least. And he's headed out next month for another three."

He spared a glance and recognized an anorexic actress he'd seen, but couldn't name, talking with an older woman who appeared to love her Botox.

"I hear he's scored over thirty million on his next film. I'd let my husband travel wherever the studio wanted him to for that."

Disgusted, Zach forced his attention away from the gossiping movie stars and circled the edges of the courtyard.

Samantha caught his attention and brought him into her circle of friends, who were all chatting after Mike and Karen started the line at the buffet.

"Zach, I'd like you to meet some friends of Karen and Michael's. My husband, Blake Harrison. His sister Gwen and her husband, Neil MacBain." Zach shook the men's hands, happy he didn't recognize any of them.

"Are you actors?" he asked.

Gwen laughed. "Not everyone here is in the industry." Gwen's British accent laced her words.

"I'm in shipping," Blake offered.

Samantha snuggled into her husband's side, obviously very in love with the man. "He's also a duke, but we refuse to call him Your Grace."

Blake rolled his eyes.

"We do when he pisses us off," Gwen said.

"A duke, seriously?"

Blake sipped his cocktail and shrugged. "Can't pick your parents."

Samantha indicated the linebacker that stood by Gwen's side. "Neil is in private security."

That, Zach could buy. The man was huge; his narrow gaze took in everyone around them, and Zach guessed he was armed to the teeth.

"There you are!" A voice rose behind them, twisting Zach around.

The couple coming at him didn't need an introduction. He leaned toward Neil. "Is that the governor?"

"Yeah."

"Damn, didn't think Mike knew everyone in this state."

"Actually, we've been friends with Karen longer than Michael. Hence the reason we're huddled together talking about everyone around us."

"Eliza, Carter, this is Michael's brother, Zach."

Zach shook the governor's hand and offered the same to his wife. It would have been easy to feel out of place, but the group offered explanations to Zach as they talked among themselves.

"I didn't know Michael had a brother," Carter managed.

"One brother and three sisters," Samantha blurted out.

Zach narrowed his eyes and noticed Gwen nudge the petite redhead.

"I think that's what Michael said." Samantha glanced at the ground. "Is that right?"

"Yes."

"Are we still on for the park tomorrow?" Eliza briskly changed the subject. "I haven't seen Delanie since the christening."

Samantha removed her cell phone from her purse and the women huddled around it in what Zach recognized as the ceremonial showing off of the baby pictures.

His older sister, Rena, had two of her own, and there was no escaping the latest digital photograph if Zach so much as missed a Sunday dinner with the family.

"Eliza! Carter! You guys made it." Karen stepped into the growing circle and embraced her friends.

"Of course we made it."

Karen offered a polite smile to Zach as she glanced between the ladies. "Why are you guys not eating? I slaved over the menu, and most of the women here are worried about gaining an ounce."

"I'm going to eat, don't worry," Eliza said.

A waiter approached the party and offered flutes of champagne. The group took up a glass each and started to sip.

Beside Zach, Neil whisked the glass out of his wife's hand. "Not for you, Princess."

Gwen's face lit up with shock. "Oh, my. I almost forgot."

The group went quiet.

"Forgot what?"

Gwen bit her lower lip. "Ah, nothing. This is Karen and Michael's party."

Then, as if the women were all talking to each other in their heads, Karen let out a squeal. "Oh. My. God. You're pregnant!"

When there wasn't a quick denial, the group became over-whelmingly animated with the obviously shocking news.

"We were going to wait to say anything." Gwen accepted a hug from Karen.

"That's stupid."

"But this is your anniversary party."

Karen rolled her eyes. "Please, Gwen. It's Michael and me." Then, as if Karen remembered Zach was there, she abruptly stopped talking and let the others crowd in to offer their congratulations.

Zach, not knowing what to say other than the obvious, offered his congratulations to the father-to-be.

"You're next." Samantha pointed a finger at the first lady.

"Gee, thanks. Talk about pressure."

Because something about this whole group was bothering him, Zach asked, "What about you, Karen? Are you and Mike going to have kids?"

Silence met his ears. For a brief moment, he wondered if maybe there was something terribly wrong with his question. Could she have kids? Could his brother? But there wasn't pain in Karen's face when she smiled at him, more of a resolve. "I don't think anytime soon."

With that, the group steered the conversation far away from Karen having children and on to other subjects.

The entire introduction to his brother's wife was laced with more questions than answers.

Chapter Two

"This is going to get very sticky," Gwen whispered in Karen's ear as the party started to wind down, and many of the guests had left.

The two of them, along with Samantha and Eliza, were nestled in the far end of the courtyard sipping wine, coffee, or in Gwen's case, tea, and watching the men as they talked around a fire pit.

"Why do you think he's here?" Eliza asked.

"I have no idea. If there is one topic Michael and I don't really discuss, it's his family," Karen said to her friends, who knew the situation between her and Michael.

The group of men erupted in laughter, making the women frown.

"They act as if they just saw each other last week." This came from Samantha.

"You're the one who did the background check. Did I miss something in the file?" Karen asked.

The file referred to the dossier on every client and prospective spouse that hired Alliance to pick a temporary partner for them. In Michael's case, he needed an agreeable wife for sixteen to eighteen months in order to throw Hollywood, the fans, and the producers off the scent that the leading man of action flicks, fetching multi-millions per movie, wasn't interested in women.

CATHERINE BYBEE

Sadly, though Hollywood was incredibly flexible with sexuality, the public didn't pay to see films where it was common knowledge the man on the screen would never be interested in the woman in his arms. Michael Wolfe was the hottest action film star of the millennium and had more films lined up than should be legal. Though no definitive rumors circulated about his sexuality, he sought out Alliance to find a temporary wife to circumvent any that might evolve.

Samantha, who had a list of contacts an arm long, had created Alliance and prescreened every client regardless of their wealth or standing in the community. She and Eliza had worked together in the beginning, yet as each of them married and found other activities, such as being a duchess, the first lady of the state, and parenting, they took on lesser roles with Alliance. Gwen had stepped in to help run Alliance along with Karen, who was the only one who had actually been looking for a temporary husband to begin with, and as it turned out, she acquired exactly what she wanted.

A year or so long commitment with a huge financial payoff. Michael had placed five million dollars in an account that would become hers the day they separated. In return, he kept his reputation as Hollywood's bad boy that every woman wanted, and continued making films.

So Karen had to give up sex for a year. No big deal.

She'd met and partied with Hollywood's finest and found a best friend in Michael. It had only been in the past month that they'd actually talked about their mutual sexual frustration playing the role of a married couple. Ironically, the itch was never there to scratch with her husband, and if Michael were to make any real moves on Karen it would gross her out.

She glanced over the courtyard to the black jeans gripping the back end of Michael's brother. Now his brother, Zach . . .

"Michael grew up in his hometown in Utah. Did the typical high school thing. Starred in the plays and attempted football. But

14

that was his brother's sport. He never lived up to it. He applied to colleges here in California and fell into the lure of the big screen."

"No bad blood at home?" Eliza asked.

Samantha shook her head. "None that I found."

Karen watched Michael and Zach from across the yard and blew out a breath. "This is going to get awkward."

"Is he staying here?" Eliza asked.

Karen froze. "I-I didn't ask. He should, right?"

"He's family. And they don't seem to be hating on each other," Eliza stated the obvious.

Karen set her cup of coffee on a table and stood. "I should find out and have Alice make up a room while she's still here." Alice was the only domestic help they brought in during the week. She didn't live in and had only been employed for a few months. Michael refused to have help for any real length of time. Hollywood's best-kept secret would never keep if the housekeeper stuck around for long.

Karen walked to Michael's side, and he smiled in acknowledgment. "Sorry to interrupt. But I was wondering if Zach is staying over?"

Zach looked between her and Michael. "It's OK, I—"

"You're staying here. Mom would kill me if you stayed at a hotel." Michael's tone was genuine.

"Mom's going to kill you anyway."

Michael nodded. "You're right. No need to add to the ammunition. We have plenty of room."

"I don't know."

Karen did what any wife would and took matters upon herself. "I'll have Alice set up a room before she goes home." She left their side and walked into the house.

Gwen met up with her in the kitchen. The caterers had left boxed-up food that would all be going to the Boys and Girls Club in the morning. The beauty of Hollywood parties was how well the kids ate once the festivities were over. The kids thought they got the leftovers. Only Karen and Michael knew that wasn't the case. They always ordered more than they needed and had trays of food to serve to the kids.

"I'm outta here, Karen," Tony, Michael's manager, said as he passed through the great room.

Tony was short, Italian, and louder than any man should be.

"Did you pour Tom into a limo?" Karen asked.

Tony chuckled. "His car is parked to the side of the garage along with a few others. You'll probably have assistants here bright and early to pick them up. Might just wanna keep the gate open."

Karen shook her head. "Not a chance." The last thing she'd do was leave the gate to Michael's estate open for maundering fans or paparazzi to help themselves to a photograph. "Thanks for the warning. I hope you managed to have a good time."

Tony always seemed to be working when he was in her and Michael's presence.

"I always do. G'night Karen, Gwen."

"Good night, Tony."

Before Tony made it out of the room, he turned and shouted, "Oh, and happy anniversary."

"Thanks." Somewhere in all the excitement of the party, the fact that she and Michael had been married for a year escaped her for the past few hours.

Michael loved flashy parties, where Karen was just as happy with a few select friends with honesty flowing between them. Because her friends knew the business of Alliance, they all knew the marriage was coming to an end.

They'd only recently started talking about the Hollywood breakup and how it would go down. Irreconcilable differences without anything messy. Complete with a divorce party at some point.

They'd go their separate ways and remain friends.

"Where do you think Alice is?" Gwen asked as she leaned a slender hip on the center island, picked a fresh chocolate-covered strawberry from a tray, and nibbled on the ripe fruit.

The house had some order to it. The waitstaff had left thirty minutes before with the majority of guests. Now there were only a few guests weaving out of the house, waving good-byes as they left.

She seldom used the home intercom system, but Karen went to it and called Alice through the speakers. "Alice?"

A few seconds passed and the woman's voice came through. "Yes, Mrs. Wolfe."

"Can you make sure the spare room on the east side of the house is prepared for a guest?"

"Of course, Mrs. Wolfe."

Karen plucked a strawberry off the tray and joined Gwen in her snack.

"How are you feeling?" Karen asked, letting her eyes drift to Gwen's slender waist.

"I feel great. Samantha was so sick with both her pregnancies, I expected nothing different."

Karen grinned. "Not everyone has morning sickness."

Gwen positively beamed. "I'm so happy, Karen. And Neil's beyond himself."

It was hard to picture Neil being anything but his big stoic self. But when he thought no one was watching, he looked at Gwen as if he would take a bullet to keep her safe.

"It's going to be great seeing a baby make Neil crazy."

Gwen laughed. "My poor husband won't stand a chance."

"He's going to be a good dad. And we already know you're going to be a fabulous mom."

Gwen discarded the stem in a napkin and placed it on the counter. "We should shop next week. How's your schedule?"

"I'll be at the club tomorrow. Graduation is coming up so the kids are prepping for finals. Then summer."

"So it will ease up?"

"A little." Karen's work at the Boys and Girls Club took up her extra hours in the day. She still worked with the client base at Alliance with Gwen. But with one more baby in the mix, it appeared as if Alliance would need to recruit more help, and soon.

Karen hid a yawn behind her hand.

Alice walked into the kitchen with her hands full of bulging plastic trash bags. "The room is ready for your guest. I'll take these out on my way."

"Thanks, Alice. And you can come in the morning to help with the cleanup?"

Alice gave an enthusiastic nod. "I'll bring my niece to help."

Karen remembered the niece. "That's fine. If I'm not here, just keep it quiet in the back of the house and don't bother Michael."

"No problem. Good night, Mrs. Wolfe."

As Alice moved out of the room, the rest of Karen's friends made their way inside the house.

"It's time for us to go," Blake told her at Samantha's side.

"If we play it right, we'll get home by the late-night feeding and then get to bed," Samantha told her husband.

"Or Delanie will decide it's time to play and we won't sleep at all."

They talked about baby behavior for a few minutes before the men grabbed the women's sweaters and moved toward the door.

Michael took to Karen's side while Zach stood back after saying his good-byes.

In Karen's ear, Eliza whispered, "Be sure and sleep in Michael's room tonight."

Oh, damn . . . she'd nearly forgotten. It wasn't like them to have overnight guests or have a need to explain the separate rooms for the newlyweds. "Thanks," Karen uttered.

Once the door closed behind her friends, Karen turned to Michael. "I'm going to do a quick check and make sure everyone is gone. Why don't you show your brother where he's sleeping?"

Karen made her escape and took her time walking along the hidden paths and walkways of the outside, picking up the occasional empty glass on her way.

The exercise of searching for guests had less to do with those who were invited, and more to do with those who weren't. Karen was about to give up on her search when she noticed the burst of light.

Behind her, the flash of a bulb from a camera blinded her as the shutter sped through shot after shot.

"Are you done?" Karen asked in the direction of the flash. Not that she could see crap after the blinding light. Another shot went off. Apparently not. "Michael?" she hollered across the yard, hoping he'd left the sliding door open and could hear her.

"C'mon, Mrs. Wolfe . . . how about a smile?"

Karen was tempted to let her middle finger fly, but held back.

"What the hell?"

Behind her, Michael and Zach both jogged to her side. "Get out of here!" Michael yelled at their uninvited guest.

"Damn, there's two of you," the paparazzo said from the shadows.

The camera went off again. This time Karen was between both brothers. Michael went after the photographer, and she twisted away from the flash, attempted to dispel the spark in her sight, and stumbled.

Zach's arm kept her from falling. "You OK?"

She glanced up. "Fine."

Then Zach was gone, and she saw the boys grab the paparazzo and manhandle him out of the yard. Karen kicked off her high heels and followed behind with her shoes dangling from her fingertips. While the men took their uninvited guest through the side yard,

Karen moved into the house, and then closed and locked the back doors.

When both men walked back inside they were patting each other on the back as if they'd just won a tandem wrestling match. They really could have been bookends.

"Welcome to my life," she heard Michael say.

"That happens all the time?"

"Often enough."

They settled into the sofa as if they were gearing up for a long talk. Karen decided a graceful exit was in order. She'd let Michael lay the groundwork about their relationship to Zach and tell her about it later.

"I hope you don't think I'm rude, but I've had a long day."

Michael watched her walk toward them with a smile. "And you're at the club tomorrow morning, right?"

"Yeah, Jeff wanted me early. I'm taking the Escalade to fit all the food." She turned toward Zach. "If you need anything, just ask."

Zach smiled and her stomach twisted. "Thanks, Karen."

Feeling strangely awkward, Karen leaned down and kissed Michael.

"I'll join you in a few."

She shook her head. "Take your time. I'm sure you have a lot to catch up on."

She felt eyes on her as she walked away, and when she glanced toward them, it was Zach who watched her.

Chapter Three

Michael did a double take when he caught his brother watching Karen walk down the hall.

A strange sense of jealousy ran up his back. His sipped his beer, but didn't really taste it. His entire life had been a balancing act. The role of brother, or of son, just wasn't one he cared to play for a while. Maybe it was because his family could see through him like no one else. Though Karen was quickly becoming someone close enough to see the subtleties of his personality. But damn he'd missed his brother, was reminded about his family by Zach's presence. If only he could be completely himself with them . . . he thought of his dad, the small town he grew up in. *No.*

"Your wife is beautiful," Zach told him.

How do I play this? He couldn't be a man completely in love . . . not when their divorce was only months away.

"She is," Michael told his brother, purposely not meeting his gaze.

"And she doesn't seem to be as plastic as a lot of your guests tonight."

Michael drank from his bottle. "She isn't." He kept his voice even, trying not to show any real joy or discomfort in his brother's words.

"So what's the deal, Mike? Why are you hiding her from us?"

He blew out a breath between his teeth. One he actually felt instead of inserting it for a moment of drama.

"Is that what I'm doing?"

"That's the discussion back home. You have to know she's part of the reason I'm here."

"Mom's pissed, huh?"

"Pissed? She's damn near manic. Then you only called when you were on location . . . never giving her a chance to talk to your wife. If it wasn't for Hannah following your every move, I wouldn't have known you were in town."

Hannah was his sister, the baby of the family. Michael had to think about how old she was now. *Sixteen? No, seventeen.* Damn. "I suck."

"Yeah, you do. You're busy. I get it. But what would it have taken for you to bring her by? To invite your own damn family to this little shindig?"

"Dad would hate this."

"Hannah and Judy would eat it up."

"Mom would have felt she needed to cook."

"So give her a job. Seems Karen was running around keeping things together."

Michael laughed. "Karen didn't cook anything."

"That's not the point, damn it, and you know it. I half expected your wife to be a complete bitch."

That shot Michael's gaze to his brother's.

"Well there has to be a reason you don't want her to meet us."

"Is that why you're here? To find the flaws in my wife?" Because there weren't any. Karen was fucking perfect. He couldn't keep the defensiveness out of his voice. No acting needed.

"I'm here to save you the unfortunate event of our entire family showing up on your doorstep."

"Is that right?"

Zach set his beer down. "Yeah. And if I don't give Mom and Dad an ETA when they can expect to see you both, they're going to show up unannounced. Might be here, might be in one of those crazy-ass locations you work in."

The thought of his father showing up when makeup was working on him made Michael actually shudder.

Michael pushed off the couch and walked into the kitchen. He tossed his empty beer bottle in the trash and grabbed a bottle of water. He didn't need his marriage questioned now. He was leaving in two weeks for a shoot in Canada and his agent was already working on a deal for the next year. His and Karen's divorce was scheduled to happen after the contracts were signed. The publicity of his divorce and him being on the market again would drive in fans. Nothing quite like "that poor boy is heartbroken, let me help him feel better" to drive the female viewers to his flicks.

Maybe this new twist could work to his advantage.

He'd always kept his private life private. Even from his family. In truth, he didn't want to involve them. But he didn't want them hating Karen when they divorced either.

Zach walked into the kitchen, tossed his beer next to Michael's. "So what's the deal, Mike? You going to tell me what's going on, or are you going to introduce your wife to the family?"

He ran a hand through his hair. "I have to talk to Karen. See if she can free up her schedule."

Zach snorted. "What, the country club requires advance notice if you *don't* go?"

"Screw you, Zach. Karen volunteers at the Boys and Girls Club. She doesn't belong to a country club."

Zach's smirk fell. "Oh."

"That attitude, by the way, is exactly why I haven't brought Karen around. I don't need people passing judgment on her or me for our life." His motivation for keeping her to himself solidified in front of him. But, like all well-played parts, this one required time to build.

"I'm sorry." Zach's apology was quick and to the point. No buts required. "I didn't come here to fight."

Michael placed a smile on his lips. "It's OK. I'll talk to Karen."

"Don't know what you're worried about, dude. From what I've seen, our folks are going to love her."

Yeah, damn it, they would.

As tired as she was, sleeping in Michael's bed just wasn't happening. She beat the pillow under her head and attempted to twist it into a comfortable position. Nothing worked.

Finally, she slipped out of his bed, padded through their joined bathroom, and grabbed the book sitting on her bedside table and returned to Michael's room.

Some of the kids at the club had to read the classic in her hand for finals. It was taking serious effort to read the book, and she was an adult. Why didn't high school English teachers figure out that reading outdated books put their students to sleep?

Sure enough, her eyes drifted closed after half a chapter.

The sound of the door opening brought her awake and the book slid to the floor.

"Hey?" Michael said as he walked over to the bed. The normal smile on his face wasn't there. Strangely, Karen was pleased he didn't pretend with her.

"Was it bad?"

He sat on the edge of the bed, toed off his shoes. "Not bad. Just complicated."

"We've avoided your family for a year."

"Yeah. A few months more would have been nice."

Karen leaned over, picked up her book, and put it on the nightstand.

"Wanna talk about it?" He hadn't in the past, but his hesitation made her push. "C'mon, Michael." She lowered her voice. "You don't have a lover, and you know you can trust me. Who else can you talk to?"

There was his smile. He reached over and laid a hand on her leg through the blankets. "It would be so much easier if women turned me on. I'd marry you all over again."

"You wouldn't have met me if women did it for you," she teased.

"Still would have been easier."

She couldn't argue that. "Tell me about your family."

Just like that, the gates opened. He leaned against the bedpost and kicked his feet up on the bed. "Rena is the oldest, married her high school sweetheart, has two kids. Zach is older than me by a year and a half. Total jock in school. Then there's me. After a few years, we didn't think there would be any more of us, then Judy arrived, and a handful of years later came Hannah. Jesus, Karen, I forgot how old my youngest sister was." He shook his head in what looked like disgust with himself.

"What about your parents? Happy?"

"June and Ward had nothing on my parents. Cookie-baking mom, dad worked hard, built his business."

Karen reached deep in her memory to what she'd read in Michael's profile before she agreed to meet him. "Hardware store?"

"Yeah. Zach runs a small construction crew now. It's a small town, didn't take a lot to be the *go-to guy* for a team. I think my dad wanted some of that for me. My dad was disappointed in me from the beginning."

Karen waited for him to elaborate. For a while, she thought he'd stop talking. "I tried, Karen. I can work alongside my dad, but never liked it. I like cars, but didn't want to work on them. Zach was always working on his car, trying to drag me under it."

"Other than Neil, I don't know one guy who willingly works on his own car."

"Yeah, but it was more than cars. It seemed everything that defined Sawyer Gardner didn't define me."

"Did you and your dad fight?"

"We didn't have to fight for me to understand his disappointment."

In that moment, Karen knew why Michael worked so hard to be America's bad boy on screen.

"It didn't help that Hilton, Utah, is about as backwater as it comes for small towns. The running joke is Hilton isn't big enough for a Hilton." He laughed at that, as if it brought him a pleasant memory. "And Utah . . . Jesus, have you ever been there?"

"You've seen where I've been." She'd not traveled outside of California before meeting Samantha and hooking up with Alliance. Since then, she'd traveled to Europe a couple of times, Canada, where Michael had shot more than one film in their brief marriage, and Aruba for one more wedding in their circle of friends.

"You can't get a drink in Hilton, Utah, on Sunday."

"Really?"

"Backwater. I'm telling you. Everyone knows everything about everybody."

"I'm starting to understand why you left." She did. Michael's sexuality would never have flown there. But it wasn't exactly flying here either.

"If it's so ass-backward, why does your family stay?"

He sucked in a breath. "I don't know. Good people. It didn't suck growing up there. Crime isn't off the charts."

"Small-town America." Where secrets are hidden and the kids run to the city at the first opportunity they get. Karen glanced at the hands in her lap and fiddled with the ring Michael had placed on her finger.

Damn. Michael was like one of her kids at the club. One that needed direction to find himself, to forgive himself for not being just like the other kids. She wasn't sure he would ever give himself permission to be himself, to give up his tough-guy image . . . but she wouldn't live with herself if she didn't try. "We should visit your family."

His silence made her look up.

"You'd do that?"

"Michael, I said I was in this with you, and I meant it."

He wore a strange expression on his face. It was laced with question and concern. "We'd stay with my parents."

"How bad can that be?"

"In a room the size of this bed."

"So don't snore and let me have the covers. We'll be fine. Remember the bed in France?" They'd had a "brief" honeymoon in France and ended up at a chateau in a small winery. Michael had asked and paid for deluxe accommodations. They ended up with a twin bed and a bathroom with only cold running water . . . and pictures of them spread through the tabloids the next day. They'd held hands and laughed like friends, and by the time they had to come home, Karen knew there was no possible way for her to hold any attraction to the man she called husband. There simply wasn't any chemistry.

Michael took her hand in his and kissed the edges of her fingertips. "Thanks, Karen."

As he walked into the bathroom, and the sound of running water met her ears, Karen's smile fell.

Small-town America. How bad could it be?

Chapter Four

Zach usually made it out of bed before dawn. Sleeping in would have been a luxury, and his brother's digs were beyond comfortable. The king-size bed was overkill for a guest room, but Zach wasn't complaining. He was tall, like his brother, and he always hung off beds in hotels. There were tile floors throughout the home, and in the bedrooms large colorful carpets warmed up the space. He couldn't help but wonder if Karen had anything to do with the decor of the home. She and Mike had only been married a year, and not everything he'd seen looked new. In fact, there were antiques throughout the house and various pieces of art scattered along the walls.

He liked it. The entire palette of colors and textures wasn't something he would have chosen, but he couldn't deny the warmth and comfort of the home.

Zach had to admit that their father would probably hate it. He'd think everything was too perfect, too staged. Even though the home appeared more casual than he expected for his hotshot Hollywood movie star brother, he understood what things cost. On the construction level, there was crown molding and carved paneling along the walls in the main hall. The massive fireplace in the great room was large enough for a child to walk into. With a little less Spanish influence, and a little more Western rustic, this house would be perfect for him.

The sun peeked through the windowed doors that opened into the courtyard. Across the yard, he noticed movement through the rooms on the other side. The *u* shape broke the home up into two sections. He assumed that either his brother or Karen was up and preparing for their day.

He pushed out of bed and walked naked into the adjoining bathroom. As he'd discovered the night before, the lights came on with movement. He wondered what that little trick cost Michael to put in place. No one in Hilton wanted those kinds of touches. No, Hilton wanted functional and cheap. The hardware store that provided them food and clothes growing up would have to special order nearly every fixture in the bathroom, every hinge on the doors.

"You did good, kid," Zach whispered to himself as he ran his hand over the marble countertop.

Zach showered and dressed before leaving his room in search of coffee. He rounded the corner and spotted Karen struggling with the front door with her hands full of catering trays.

"Let me get that." He relieved her arms of the load.

"Oh, thanks." She opened the door and led him out to the drive, where several cars were still sitting from the night before. "I should have had Michael load the car before we went to bed last night."

"No problem."

Today Karen was dressed in tight-fitting jeans and a simple pullover shirt she'd tucked in. Her face was free of makeup and her hair was pulled into a ponytail. There wasn't one ounce of polish on her like he'd seen the night before, no silk, no shiny jewelry dangling from her ears or her neck. Without heels, the top of her head barely made it to his chin. She wasn't at all what he'd assumed she'd be from the pictures he'd seen.

Karen opened the hatch of the SUV and moved around to the second set of doors to lower the back seats. "Just pile those up. I have a few more to bring out."

"What's all this for?" He set the trays down and shoved them up toward the seats to make room for more.

"The kids at the club."

"You feed them?"

Karen walked around him back to the house. "Not all the time. But they know after we've had a party to expect something special."

He followed her into a huge pantry off the kitchen, which housed another refrigerator. Inside were several more trays of food. "All of this is leftovers?"

"No. We have the chef make extra, more kid-friendly food. The kids will eat the fancy desserts but skip the caviar."

"I'd skip the caviar."

Karen laughed and the sound splashed over him with warmth. "Yeah, me, too. I find more fish eggs in crumbled up napkins after these parties than I can count." She started pulling the oversize trays out one at a time and loaded him up. When he kept nodding for more, she continued to pile until they met his chin.

She pulled the last one and walked with him back to the car. "If no one eats the caviar, why do you serve it?"

"Some things are expected. Have you met Tony?"

"No."

"Tony is Michael's manager. He takes great pains in knowing the personal tastes of many of Michael's co-workers, the producers, so that everyone feels taken care of when they visit."

"Do you know their tastes?"

"I have a hard time with their names. Knowing if they're a vegetarian, or Jewish to the point of only eating Kosher . . . not a clue. Tony, on the other hand, has it all down."

Interesting. "But you know what the kids at the club eat?"

She helped him with his load until the back of the car was stacked full. She pressed a button and the hatch closed. "They're kids. They haven't been told what to like yet. I just try to keep it healthy without being obvious. Dip the strawberries in chocolate and leave fresh ones alongside them, and they all disappear."

Zach leaned against the car since she wasn't working her way back into the house. "My mom smothered broccoli in cheese sauce."

"Exactly."

"It sounds like you take good care of the kids."

"They're good kids. We can afford to spoil them."

"So you like kids?"

"Yeah."

He crossed his arms over his chest. "But you don't want any of your own?"

She blinked a couple of times. The answer stuck somewhere between her brain and her lips. "I'd like kids . . . someday." She narrowed her blue eyes on him. "Well, I should go."

Zach pushed away from the car, giving her room.

She opened the driver's door and said, "Can you remind Michael that he promised to stop by at three today? He said something about taking you out to shop for your sister's birthday present."

He'd forgotten. "Shopping. Yeah." There was no joy in his voice.

"I'll ask the girls what's on the top of a seventeen-year-old's wish list. Maybe they can help."

"If it cuts out hours, I'm all ears."

"You sound like Michael."

Zach shook his head. "No, he sounds like me. I'm older."

Karen slid on a pair of sunglasses and dropped behind the wheel, a smile played on her lips. "I'll see you later then."

He watched her drive away and hated how much he would enjoy seeing her later.

Karen brought the food early so kids could jump in before school and grab a bite. Much like Pavlov's dogs, which salivated with the sound of a bell, every kid in the club knew when Karen and Michael threw a party, and whenever Michael himself was going to make an appearance. She had to admit, making Michael her temporary husband had been a complete windfall for the kids.

Last year the club had been struggling with finances, and she was dipping into her income to help. It wasn't as if she had a big account or anything. Oh, she could hit up Samantha, and didn't feel guilty about doing so once in a while. But this was *her* passion, and she didn't want to mooch off her friends, even if her friends had serious money.

Long after lunch when the rest of the party food was gone, Karen stood in the kitchen doing dishes. Her mind drifted to her handful of friends and she couldn't help but smile. How the hell did a girl like her end up with such an influential guest list of her own to add to Michael's at these parties? It was insane.

She'd barely made it through college because of funds, she'd only just managed to pay off her student loans before signing up with Alliance. The only reason she was driving around in new cars was because Michael insisted they lease her something new. As he put it, no one would believe that his wife would be driving around in a seven-year-old Mazda with a broken air conditioner. The car wasn't that bad, but she knew he was right. She did nix anything over the top. It had taken the kids a few months to settle down after her marriage, and if she'd parked some hundred-thousand-dollar sports car in the drive, it would be near impossible to get the attention of the boys. On days like today, she brought the Escalade, which wasn't an unlikely car to be parked in the lot. She usually knew when Michael showed up before he walked in the door. He had no problem bringing something flashy for the kids to drool over. It brought joy to the kids, and to Michael.

The man worked nonstop. Oh, he played hard, too. They'd returned to Europe together and taken the inside passage in Canada and Alaska the previous summer. There were parties and award dinners with passing friends and fake acquaintances. There were a few people that Michael called friends, but she didn't think there was even one he'd shared his true life with.

Karen put the last of the dishes in the massive machine, lowered the door, and turned it on.

After grabbing the last of the empty trays that were ready for the trash, she opened the back door and moved around to the front of the building where they housed the Dumpster.

As usual, the roar of an engine sounded like a mating call to teenage boys. She turned around, garbage in hand, and caught sight of Michael pulling into the parking lot. The copper metallic paint glistened off the low-profile sports car that she couldn't immediately identify. It wasn't his. Or at least, it hadn't been when she'd left the house that morning.

Kids started pouring from the club as he cut the engine, and he and Zach hopped out of the car with *cat ate the canary* grins on their faces.

Karen popped the garbage into the trash can and wiped her hands on her pants as she walked over to greet the boys, who looked as if they had just been on a joy ride. She knew he'd show up in something crazy expensive, but she assumed it would be the Ferrari parked in the garage that she'd all but refused to ride in because of the time the semitruck nearly ran them over.

With her best eye roll, she crossed her arms over her chest and stared Michael down. "*What* did you do?"

He delivered his sexy smile. Beside him, Zach dished out a grin that would devastate her if she allowed it.

"Is it new, Ms. Jones?" Dale, one of the regular kids from the club, asked.

"There aren't plates on it, moron, of course it's new," his best friend, Enrique, said as he hit him upside the arm.

"Is it yours, Mr. Wolfe?" one of the kids in the back asked. By now there were two dozen circling the car. When the bell to the high school next door rang, Karen knew they'd be mobbed with kids from the school, and the club, within seconds.

"What is it, Michael?" someone else asked.

Karen walked around the back of the car and noticed the logo.

"It's a McLaren, dude."

"Sweet!"

"Do you like it, honey?" Michael asked over the top of the car as he watched her approach.

"It's very pretty." It was, even if the cost of it could probably feed several villages in third world countries for a year.

"Damn, Ms. Jones, you don't call a car like this pretty."

Karen shot a nasty look at the boy talking. "Language, Peter!"

He had the good sense to lower his eyes. "Still can't call it pretty. Sweet, sick, fu—" he stopped himself. "Freaking amazing, but not pretty."

It is fucking amazing. There was no denying that, and from the grins on both Zach's and Michael's faces, it was a fun ride, too.

"I'm glad you like it. I bought it for my sister for her birthday."

The smile on Karen's face fell. "You what?"

"Hannah. Think she'll like it?"

Words escaped her. "You did not!" She twisted toward Zach, who happened to be closer to her than Michael was. "Tell me he's kidding!"

Zach was still smiling, but she couldn't read much from his expression because of the sunglasses covering his eyes.

"Michael Gardner Wolfe, tell me you're joking!"

"You don't think she'll like it?" he asked.

"You can't give this to a seventeen-year-old girl."

A gasp went over the kids. "Lucky sister."

"Wish he was my brother," someone from the crush of kids said.

"Why not? It only has two seats so she can't pile kids inside, and it's only a V-8." Michael was still grinning, completely oblivious of how stupid this idea was.

"She's a kid! She'll hit the gas and wrap herself around a pole. It's too much. The insurance alone is insane!" She wagged her accusatory finger in his direction, and then swung it toward Zach. "You're not giving it to her. Your mother will kill you!"

Michael finally stopped smiling. "I hadn't thought of that."

"Yeah, well you should have. Holy cow! What were you thinking? A day at the spa, a trip to the mall, those are the kinds of presents you give to your kid sister, not a car like this."

Michael leaned over the hood and rubbed his jaw. She was getting through to him and her heart started to slow down.

"You're right."

The kids had gone quiet as they listened and recorded their argument on their cell phones. Like every visit to the club, Michael's presence would be up on YouTube and Facebook before the hour was up.

"Of course I'm right."

Michael lifted his glasses off his face and set them on top of the car. He looked at the keys in his hands and then to her. He tossed her the keys, which she caught with one hand.

"Then it's yours."

She tossed the keys right back as if they burned. "I don't need this car."

Back the keys came. "You said it was pretty."

"I already have a *pretty* car." The keys sailed over the car again. Like a tennis match, the phones were swinging back and forth.

"This one is prettier."

She caught the keys again and stomped her foot. "Michael!"

He mimicked her, stomped his foot, and winked. "Karen!"

He started to laugh. "C'mon, honey. It's your anniversary present. One whole year of putting up with me."

"Take the car, Ms. Jones."

When she caught Zach's expression, she knew the whole ploy of giving the car to Hannah had been a joke. Michael knew Karen wouldn't drive this car without some kind of hook.

"It's not polite to give someone's gifts back," Peter said beside her. She heard the words she'd told them more than once.

Karen glanced down at the car and cringed on the inside. She dangled the keys in her hand. As she walked around the hood, kids parted a path. If there weren't cameras pointed at her, she'd likely stomp on his foot and shove the keys in his pocket, but instead, she leaned into him and whispered in his ear. "I'm going to kill you when I get home."

He just laughed.

"You're welcome," he said loud enough for the audience. He kissed her cheek briefly and offered his Hollywood smile.

Chapter Five

Damn it was a sweet-ass ride. When Mike had suggested they go to the dealership for exotic cars in Beverly Hills, Zach thought it was to window shop, maybe score a test drive. At first, he thought maybe Mike was showing off his clout to his big brother. When they'd driven off the lot with little more than a handshake and a signature, Zach was all kinds of impressed.

He and Mike had left the Boys and Girls Club after an hour. The kids took turns taking pictures of the car, the celebrity, and themselves pretending to drive. All the while Karen stood aside with a half smile on her lips as she watched. He couldn't believe that she'd instantly said no to the car. Who did that? Michael told Zach at the dealership that he would figure out a way for her to accept it, but that if he knew her, she'd nix it outright.

"You were right about Karen," Zach said as they pulled onto the street leading to Mike's home.

Mike shifted around the curve and the whole car hummed. *Sweet.* "I'm sure I haven't heard the end of it."

No, Zach didn't think so either. "It's obvious she didn't marry you for your money."

Mike laughed. Instead of professing her love for him, he said, "Lotta good that would do. There's a prenup."

"Really? She agreed to that?" Seemed prenuptial agreements were a sign of doubt on the end of the person who had something to lose.

"She insisted on it."

Mike slowed the car at the gated entry to his house and pressed a remote opening.

"She doesn't seem to be the kind of woman you'd have to worry about taking you to the cleaners."

Mike revved the engine, which didn't do well idling. "I don't think so either, but this is Hollywood, and nothing is ever as it seems."

"Wow, Mike, that's cold."

He pulled into the drive. "And true."

Without more discussion, Mike jumped out of the car, and at the same time, a short dark-haired man stepped out of house. "I thought that would be you. Damn, Michael, you're already trending on Twitter."

Trending on Twitter?

"Leave it to the kids to jump on social media. Tony, have you met my brother, Zach?"

Tony . . . ah, the manager. Zach shook hands with the man.

"Noticed you last night at the party, but couldn't get over to you," Tony said. "How long are you in town?"

"Leaving tomorrow."

Mike narrowed his eyes. "You just got here."

"And there's work piling up at home. Besides, you'll be there soon enough."

"You will?" Tony asked.

Before anyone could elaborate, the gate opened and in drove Karen.

Tony lowered his voice. "She looks pissed."

"How can anyone be pissed about a car like this?" Zach asked.

"Karen doesn't do extravagant."

She damn near kissed the bumper of the McLaren before pulling the Cadillac to a stop.

Tony sucked in a breath and shot his hands in the air as if to tell her to stop before she ruined a machine worth over a quarter million dollars. Even Mike cringed.

"What was *that* about?" Karen came out swinging.

"What, a man can't buy a wife a present?"

Karen exchanged a look with Tony, and skimmed over Zach, before resting on Mike.

"We've had the car discussion."

Tony stepped forward, surprising Zach as he jumped in the middle of the discussion. "Michael, your agent already called me; Paramount has put in a call thanks to those kids posting all over the net."

Karen swiveled her anger toward Tony. "What are you talking about?"

"The producers at Paramount?"

She offered a blank stare.

"You met them last night at the party." Tony switched his discussion to Mike. "Lavine wants to talk to you tonight. They loved the YouTube splash and want to secure your name."

Zach's head spun. He had no idea what they were talking about and how it played into this discussion about the car. Apparently, he was the only one in the dark.

"Wait." Karen shoved in front of Tony. "Are you saying today's display was about securing a role?"

Zach was about to tell her she was wrong, but realized no one was talking.

"I wanted to buy you a car," Mike said, but at this point even Zach doubted him, and he'd been at the dealership during the transaction. Never once did Mike say anything about a part in a movie.

"Really?"

"What could be better than my wife driving the car featured in my next film?"

Zach watched as the two of them argued. Mike's words swam in his head: *this is Hollywood, and nothing is ever as it seems.*

"Look at it this way. Do you want the guy selling you your Ford to be driving a Toyota? No, you want the guy to drive a Ford."

"Nobody cares what I drive, Michael. No one even recognizes me unless I'm with you."

"That's not true," Tony muttered. "You're all over the tabloids today, both with and without Michael."

"You don't have to drive it daily."

She glanced over at the car. "I don't even know *how* to drive it."

Mike tossed an arm over Karen's shoulders. "That's my girl."

"I didn't say I'd keep it."

"You didn't say you wouldn't."

She opened the gull-wing door on the driver's side and peeked inside. "How long do you have before you *can't* take it back?"

"Five days or two hundred miles."

Karen placed two fingers in the air. "Only on two conditions will I keep this car."

Mike crossed his arms over his chest. "OK."

"One, if I can't figure out how to drive it without looking like an idiot in two days, it goes back."

"You're a good driver."

She rolled her eyes. "And two, you agree to leave your agent, your manager, and your producers at home when we're visiting your family."

"They're not coming with us."

"I'm talking cell phones, Internet . . . everything. Tony can call me every forty-eight hours, and I'll relay the time-sensitive information. I'm talking a real vacation."

Mike glanced over at Zach. "See what I live with?"

"Those are the conditions, Michael."

Mike tossed the keys at her again.

"Zach, do me a favor, will ya? Teach her how to drive it. I have a meeting to attend."

Mike and Tony turned around and left the two of them standing in the driveway.

"Son of a bitch," Zach said. "He was always going at Mach speed when he lived in Utah, but I don't remember him being *this* intense."

"You're seeing the city boy. What I want to know is where the country boy went." Karen glanced at him briefly and ducked into the house. "I'll meet you out here in an hour. I don't want to attempt to drive this thing in the dark."

Karen didn't even try talking to Michael before he left. She knew from experience that he wouldn't be home anytime soon and not to count on him for dinner. She showered and slipped into a California-casual outfit for early summer, a.k.a. sandals, Capri cotton pants, and a short-sleeved shirt, and then walked through the kitchen, checking the time. In the driveway sat a zillion-dollar car for which she barely knew how to open the door, let alone drive.

She stared at the car and found it to be a symbol of her husband's life, over the top and flashy in every way. If there was any possibility of Michael getting his life in perspective, it hinged on Utah. Hinged on family.

Thinking of family, she realized she hadn't spoken with her aunt in at least a month. She didn't hear Zach in the house and decided she'd take the last ten minutes before her driving lesson to call her only relative.

The phone rang twice. "Sedgwick residence."

"Hi, Nita. It's Karen. Is my aunt home?"

"Hi, Miss Karen. Yes, let me get her for you."

Karen waited for her aunt's housekeeper to fetch her. Man, they'd both elevated in life a peg or two. Her aunt had married a wonderful man named Stanley only a few years before. Stanley had contacted Alliance in an effort to find him a young and temporary wife to tick off his money-hungry children and grandchildren. Although Karen never considered the proposition, she'd met with him at Eliza's request and decided that what he really needed was a strong woman willing to put his family in their place. The rest, as they say, was history. Stanley and Aunt Edie married, and after a little drama, the kids figured out that Aunt Edie didn't do well with slackers and freeloaders, all of which Stanley's kids were.

"Karen?"

"Hey, Aunt Edie."

"How are you, honey? Are you eating?"

Karen laughed. Seemed all Aunt Edie worried about was if she was eating enough. "Yes, ma'am. I haven't called in a couple of weeks."

"Well you're a busy girl. How's your Hollywood husband?"

"He's fine. Off doing the Hollywood thing. How's Stanley?"

"He's good. The doctor gave him a clean bill last month. All the blood work looked good." Her aunt went on for a while about medicine and tests, much like everyone seemed to do when they passed the age of seventy. She finished talking about their health with a pause.

"Michael and I are going out of town for a couple of weeks."

"Oh?"

"He has family in Utah he hasn't seen for a while."

Aunt Edie hesitated. "You've not met them?"

Karen knew her aunt already knew the answer to her question. "No . . . well, except for his brother. Not his parents."

"A man who doesn't introduce his bride to his parents . . ."

"Edie!"

"Don't Edie me. It's not normal."

This wasn't the time to bring Edie up to date on the future, or lack thereof, of her marriage.

"It's fine. I'm OK. I promise."

"I should have done something different—"

"Edie. Stop. I'm good."

"Your mother didn't deserve you."

They'd had this discussion before, too. "Tell Stanley I said hello."

"You're cutting me off."

"I'm saying good-bye. I have a driving lesson to get to."

Edie sighed into the phone. A heavy gesture meant to make Karen notice. "I love you."

"Love you too, Auntie. Big kiss to that studly husband of yours."

That got the laugh out of her aunt that she loved to hear.

Zach stood outside leaning over the car. He'd combed his hair back and changed his shirt. The black button-up linen gave him a mysterious edge and made him look like he belonged on the back of his motorcycle or in the driver's seat of the McLaren. She allowed herself one brief glance at his backside as he bent over the car. His sex appeal was effortless. She wondered if he knew how much. Michael wore his like a badge, but with Zach, he didn't seem to notice.

Ignoring the way her skin heated, she removed her eyes from the package known as Zach, and asked, "Are you ready?"

He twisted around. His gaze traveled her body and then rested on her eyes with a soft, approving smile. "Are you?"

"How hard can it be?"

"Have you driven a manual transmission before?"

"Learned on my uncle's Jeep when I was sixteen." She glanced at the floor of the driver's seat. "Where's the clutch?" She looked for the lever to change gears. "You sure this is a manual transmission?"

Zach warmed her with a laugh. "It's all on the steering wheel."

She peered closer. "Seriously?"

There were levers on the wheel and many other buttons that she didn't recognize. "I tell you what. You drive her first, and I'll watch."

Zach lifted his eyebrows. "Don't have to ask me twice."

The childlike look of joy on his face stuck as he rounded the car and opened the door for her.

"Damn, the doors don't even open like a normal car."

"This isn't a normal car."

"Tell me about it."

Settling into the low seat was much like sitting on the ground. Only this ground moved.

Zach's grin grew as he wrapped his long fingers around the steering wheel.

"I take it you haven't driven it yet."

"Mike did the driving." With a press of the button, the car fired to life. The raw power of the engine felt like she was sitting on a live rocket ready to catapult into space. "Ready?"

Someone had moved the Escalade while she showered, giving enough room behind the car to back up. Zach pressed another button to put the car in reverse. His hands maneuvered the levers at the steering wheel as if he drove the car every day. Instead of watching his hands, she watched the driver. Joy radiated off him in waves.

She directed him away from the house and off the main streets. "Traffic is heavy until we get out of the city."

"Where do you want to go?"

"Let's go up Pacific Coast Highway. Eventually it clears out. Then I'll try to drive it."

"It's not hard," he told her. "You press on the right shifter to accelerate, the left to shift down."

She leaned over the center console. "No clutch?"

"None. It's a dual clutch system."

She waved a hand in the air. "I just need to know how it works up here." The tachometer revved past five thousand rpm before Zach shifted. He brought the speed down just as easily when they came to a stop sign. Karen didn't realize how far in she leaned until the spicy scent of the driver wove its way into her system. She sucked in her lower lip and tried to act unaffected as she sat straight on her side of the car.

"It's a sexy car," Zach said as he eased into traffic.

"Yeah, sexy." Oh, this wasn't good. She couldn't ignore the tingling, his scent, let alone what this man was doing to her system.

"Are you really going to make him take it back?"

Oh, good, a safe subject without the word *sexy* in it. "I don't *make* Michael do anything."

"Then what was all that talk about putting down his cell phone when he comes home to Utah?"

She sighed. "He needs a break. He won't get that if Tony keeps calling and setting up the next thing."

Zach seemed to chew on that for a moment. "You really do look out for him."

"Isn't that what friends do?" She glanced out the window, noticed the stares and pointing fingers. She pushed her sunglasses higher on her face and pretended not to notice the attention the car was getting them.

"And wives?"

"What? Oh, yeah . . . take the next right."

He moved the car over and kept talking. "You're really not interested in keeping it, are you?"

She shook her head. "He'd be better off giving it to you. You'll appreciate it more than I would."

"Driving this is right up there with sex," he said with a laugh.

She groaned. She wouldn't know. She'd yet to drive the car, and Lord knew it had been ages since she'd engaged in anything sexual outside of a battery-operated toy.

"Like I said, you'd enjoy it more than me." *Is it warm in here?* She fiddled with the controls and lowered the air conditioner temperature.

"So, if cars aren't your thing . . . what is?"

Good question. "I'm not completely sure."

"Travel?"

She shrugged. "I'd like to see the world, but if I didn't it wouldn't be the end of my life."

"Big house, fame?"

"You're describing your brother. Not me."

"You don't like the stares?" He looked up at a car with a cell phone hanging out the window as the passerby took a picture.

"I've gotten used to them."

"But you don't like 'em?"

"It's hard living life in a fishbowl." She pointed toward the highway. "Go north."

For several miles, they inched through traffic and red lights before the road opened up.

"Mike told me money didn't mean anything to you."

She glanced his way, noticed his frown. "He told you that?"

"Said you signed a prenup."

"Oh?" Why would Michael give that information to his brother? What else had he told him? "I'm not interested in your brother's money." Well, not all of it anyway. Just the contracted amount set aside in their agreement.

"And as his *friend*, you want to see him slow down."

She had said that, hadn't she? "The best relationships start off as friendships. I will always consider Michael my friend first. It's hard to find friends when you're as loaded as he is. People flock to his side, but he can't always tell who to trust. That's where family comes in."

Zach looked back at the road. "He's ignored his family for a while now."

"Which is precisely why I think it would do him some good to reconnect. Underneath his monstrous ego he has a need for someone to not take his shit."

"Like giving expensive cars to people who don't want them?"

"Right. I don't know one person in his circle that says no to him. Ever. Family doesn't work that way. They remember your lowest moments, your most comical, and they remind you that you're human."

Zach pushed the gas on a long stretch with a grin. "He's lucky to have you."

Yeah, he is.

"What about your family?"

"Oh, I only have my Aunt Edie and her new husband, Stanley."

"No siblings?"

"Nope." *Thank God.*

"So who keeps you grounded?"

She thought about that for a while. "I do." It was hard to keep the sadness from her voice.

———

Mike was right. Karen was a good driver, and as much as she might not admit to liking the car the smile on her face proved she wasn't unaffected by the raw power of the machine. They'd found a place to turn around several miles up the coast where Karen took over the controls. By the time they'd made it back toward civilization, they were both hungry and she was pulling into the valet parking lot of a restaurant.

The kid who opened the door for Karen had wide eyes and was practically salivating when she handed him the keys.

Zach narrowed his eyes at him. "You know how to drive this car?"

"Yes, sir. They come in here all the time."

"It's Malibu, Zach," Karen reminded him.

They were seated in a booth in the back of the posh restaurant overlooking the Pacific Ocean. "I'm starving," Karen admitted when she dug into the bread basket before the waiter approached them to take a drink order.

"Me, too."

"So, when will you be going home?" she asked.

"Ready to get rid of me?"

She popped a piece of bread into her mouth and chewed. "No. But my guess is you have what you came for."

"Oh, what's that?"

"Recon mission. You're here to find out about me."

Busted. He looked away.

"Was I that obvious?"

"Let's see . . . you've asked me about my family, about my lifestyle. You've quizzed Michael on his marriage. So, yeah . . . you weren't subtle."

"Couldn't have been simple curiosity?"

"Was it?"

He sat back in the plush seat and stared across the table. "Some. But you're right. Hannah had seen some piece on you and Michael about having a Hollywood-style anniversary party and our mom was pissed."

"And you, being the good son, decided to come here and find out for yourself what was going on."

"You could say that."

"Have you always been the good son?"

Ever since he'd come home from college. His father didn't see the need for a higher education, but his mom insisted that all of the kids had a chance to experience life outside of Hilton. Rena was the only one who never left. And Hannah, of course, but she was still a year away from finishing high school. "My parents can't complain about me."

"But do they?"

What was with this woman and her ability to draw out answers where she shouldn't?

The waiter arrived with their drink order and told them about the specials.

Zach kept talking. "I'm sure Mike has told you that our dad isn't an easy man. He expected us to both go into business with him."

"Michael said something about that. Did you ever feel trapped by your father's expectations?"

"I like construction. I've built a good life in Hilton."

She sipped her wine and gave a coy smile. "You didn't answer my question."

"So who's on a recon mission now, Ms. Jones?"

The tractor beams of her eyes shifted away. "It's none of my business."

The waiter returned and took their order. For a petite woman, she ordered food like a lumberjack. A thick steak, baked potato with all the trimmings with a salad, and more bread, thank you very much. Zach told the waiter to double the order.

They kept talking as if their conversation had never been interrupted. "When Mike didn't come home, I knew it would be up to me to keep the family business going. Eventually our father will retire and need one of us to take over."

"Did you ever resent Michael for not coming back?"

His answer was instant. "No. Deep down I knew he'd stay in LA. It's hard to keep kids from leaving small towns when they're old enough to move on."

"Unless family is holding them back."

"Right."

"Then you have the kids that escape to the city, only to find it unyielding and ready to exploit them." Her voice grew soft and he was once again drawn to her. Damn but she was beautiful. With a few more inches of height, she could easily be one of those fancy models. Most blondes he'd met had soft blue eyes, but hers had a metallic quality that sucked you in.

"Sounds like you have experience with that."

"Th-The kids at the club come from different walks of life," she said with a stutter. "I hear all their stories."

"They seemed well adjusted."

"They're good kids."

There was a look in her eyes that bordered on sorrow. He wanted to dig, but didn't. "So why do they call you Ms. Jones?"

She sipped her wine again. "What would you have them call me? The good people of Hilton might know Michael as Mike Gardner, but taking that name would have meant nothing here. And you know Wolfe is a stage name."

"So you kept yours."

"It's just a name."

A generic name, he decided.

"I'll answer to Mrs. Wolfe and try not to correct anyone in Hilton if they call me Mrs. Gardner."

"That sounds like my mom."

She laughed and something behind him caught her eye.

"What is it?" He started to twist around and she shot her hand out over his.

"No, don't."

"Why?" Now he really wanted to know what was going on behind his back.

"Someone caught sight of us. They probably think you're Michael. If you look, they'll come over and ask for an autograph or something."

Zach felt the weight of someone's stare. "We don't look *that* much alike."

Karen stared at him now, as if analyzing his features, and slipped her hand away. "You can certainly tell you're related. But you're right. You're not identical."

"I'm the better looking one," he said with a grin and a wink.

She tossed her head back with laughter. "Oh, good Lord, two mountain-sized egos. No wonder Michael left Hilton, there wasn't enough room for the both of you."

"Yep, good thing." Their conversation bordered on flirtation, but he couldn't seem to stop it.

"So am I in trouble when I get there? Does your family hate me on principle?"

He couldn't dispel all her fears, but he could see it was important to her to know she'd be welcome. "I'll soften the blow."

She took a longer drink of her wine. "Oh, great."

"My dad will watch you and say very little. Hannah will talk your ear off. My mom will hold back for a little while, but my guess is you'll have her thinking you're a saint in no time."

"I'm not a saint."

He wasn't so sure. Something wasn't completely up front about Karen, but she certainly wasn't hell-bound.

"What about your other sisters?"

"Judy's been at school most of the year. Chances are she won't even realize you've not met until you show up. And Rena is busy with her own kids. Though she is curious."

Zach filled her in on a few stories that helped define the family throughout their meal. When the waiter offered another drink, Karen suggested he drive home when she ordered another glass of wine.

Maybe it was because Karen was family by default, but Zach's level of comfort in Karen's presence was as if they'd known each other for much longer than a handful of hours.

On the drive back home, he asked how she came to know the first lady of the state.

"I worked in administration at a place called Moonlight Villas right out of college. Samantha, you met her last night—well, her sister was in the care facility for years. Samantha and I became friends, and eventually I met Eliza."

"Did you work at Moonlight Villas when you met Michael?"

"No. I worked for Samantha with her company. Samantha and Eliza are best friends. They've known each other for some time. Before either of them married."

"Of all the people at the party last night, your friends seemed the most sincere." They were the only ones he noticed helping Karen with anything throughout the night. None of Michael's friends did that from what Zach had seen.

"I really am blessed to have such great friends."

He pulled into the driveway of the house, noticed a lack of cars. "Michael's not home?"

"I'd be surprised if we saw him at all. Producers are night owls and they expect many of the actors in their films to be as well."

He cut the engine. "The streets roll up at dusk in Hilton. Fair warning."

She played with the handle of the door, trying to figure out how to open it.

Karen was laughing at herself when he jumped out to get it from the outside.

"Why can't they make the doors normal? Everything else is over the top as it is."

He pulled it open for her and stood back for her to get out.

"It forces chivalry," she said.

He laughed. "Must have been made by a woman."

She shut the door and turned toward the house only to find her sweater closed inside. "Oh, man."

Laughing, he leaned over to grasp the handle at the same time she did. Their fingers touched and both of them stopped laughing.

The peach scent of the shampoo she used hit him first, and then the silver fleck of her blue eyes sparkled as she looked up at him.

There it was again, the chemistry he'd been denying since he met her bounced between them like fireflies. He heard her suck in a breath as her eyes drifted to his lips. The heat of her body, close to his, brought awareness of his desire for her over him like a tidal wave. He fisted his hands, and realized that he'd caught hold of her arm. For one brief second she swayed into him and she lifted her face toward his.

Then she twisted away, and the moment was gone.

Zach jumped back, shocked at what had nearly happened between them.

Acting as if nothing had transpired, he opened the door with more force than necessary and freed her sweater.

She mumbled a quick thanks, and fled.

Karen stumbled into her room, shaking. She'd run like a frightened child, and like a teenager, she had no intention of facing Zach again. Not without interference. She'd nearly kissed him. Could feel the weight of his lips against hers with only a thought.

What the hell is wrong with me?

Her head told her not to be attracted to Zach, but her body had other thoughts.

She could only imagine what must be going through his head about her. What wife kisses, or almost kisses, her husband's brother?

"You're a fool, Karen."

There wasn't protocol on how to deal with the situation now. There was no way she could avoid visiting Zach's family. Not without causing serious issues for Michael, and she couldn't tell Michael about her attraction to his brother. Damn, even though their marriage was as fake as most of the breasts in Hollywood, chances were Michael would feel betrayed by his brother . . . and by her.

Karen rubbed her temples and made her way into the bathroom to scrub away Zach's scent.

She glared at herself in the mirror. "You didn't kiss him." Maybe they could both just forget the moment ever happened.

If they didn't talk about it . . . and they didn't end up alone again . . .

It could work.

It was only two weeks in Hilton, and Zach didn't live with his parents, so she'd probably only see him with the rest of the family.

It could work.

She fell into bed and woke in the morning with a raging guilt-ridden headache that only became more painful when she realized that Zach had left before dawn.

Chapter Six

When Zach had straddled his motorcycle, turned over the engine, and headed west, he was reminded that he was young enough to make changes in his life whenever he wanted to. The past few years he'd been restless, ready to make a move in his life. But each time he'd considered what that move would be, another job would come up, another way to build his construction business, another reason to stay in Hilton.

Being on the open road, with the wind blowing him around and the sun shining on him like the lone freaking ranger, Zach wanted just to keep riding.

Driving around with Mike for the half a day he had with his brother made him want a different life even more. Not that he wanted Mike's life . . . just something more.

Then there was Karen.

Dammit. He'd almost kissed her, almost tasted the most forbidden fruit of all. His brother's wife. He'd seen the spark of passion in her eyes, felt the way her body had swayed into his. So he ran.

Ran back to what he knew. Utah.

Only as he steered his motorcycle down Main Street and parked it along the curb by the hardware store, he realized how ready he was to move on. Rena's life was in this small town, Mike had found a life in California, and he didn't think Judy would stick around when she graduated from college the next year. So why did he stay? *Family.*

His father had expected him to stay and he had. For a while, he told himself it was because he wanted the small-town life. But now he realized that wasn't true any longer. He wanted something more.

Zach slid his helmet off his head and shook out his hair.

Inside the store, he waved to the kid behind the counter. "Hey, Nolan, my dad here?"

Nolan nodded toward the back.

"Thanks."

Sawyer Gardner was a strong man full of hard edges and inflexibility most of the time. His disgust about Mike getting married and not bringing Karen home to meet the family brought heated conversations every time Mike ended up in the paper.

Sawyer tossed a box full of plumbing supplies onto a dolly when Zach walked into the room. "Hey, Dad."

Sawyer glanced over his shoulder and kept right on stacking boxes. "You're back quick."

"California isn't that far away." Even on the back of a motorcycle.

"Did you remind your brother of that?"

"Yeah. I did."

Zach grabbed a box alongside his father and helped him stack them.

"So, did you meet her?"

Zach swallowed, hard. "Yeah."

"And she's real? Not some made up TV version of a wife?" Sawyer never had approved of what Mike did for a living.

"She's real." *Very, very real.*

Sawyer stood now, looked Zach in the eye. "Are we going to meet her?"

"Yeah. Mike's arranging some time off and Karen insisted they finally visit."

The stoic expression on his father's face didn't change with the news. He simply turned on his heel, pointed toward a box, and said, "Grab that, will ya?"

No thanks for driving hundreds of miles on behalf of the family, not one word of happiness about Mike's impending visit . . . nothing else was said on the Mike subject.

Although his father's reaction didn't surprise him, it still pissed him off.

Michael cleared his schedule for ten days. Not an easy task when everyone wanted a piece of him. They waited until after graduation ceremonies for the seniors that Karen watched over at the club so they could attend, and then they boarded their chartered flight for a direct route to St. George and from there rented a car to drive the next hour to Hilton. Between the wait at the airport and the rental car delay, by the time they'd hit the highway, Karen was convinced it would have been faster to drive the distance instead of taking a plane.

Karen used the last hour to talk about their overall plan of attack with his family when it came to their relationship.

"I feel guilty enough duping your brother. It's going to be harder with your parents."

"My parents are going to love you."

"And we're planning our divorce."

"So?"

"Michael, these are people we're talking about here. They have feelings."

"I know. I would have avoided the interaction altogether if Zach hadn't shown up."

Hearing Zach's name had dread rolling over her. "You're the actor, Michael. I've been trying, but your family is going to be the hardest to convince."

He looked at her over the brim of his sunglasses. "Having second thoughts? Aren't you the one who insisted we do this?"

Yes, she had. She watched the landscape as they drove by at seventy miles per hour. "I don't want to blow it."

He reached over and touched her leg. "You're going to be fine. The whole world thinks we're a couple."

She rubbed her sweaty palms together. "Maybe I'm just nervous about meeting your parents." It was so much more than that.

He squeezed her leg until she glanced up at him. "They're going to ask you about your parents."

That thought left her cold. "I'll tell them what I tell everyone. They're gone and my aunt raised me."

Michael knew there was more to it, but even he didn't have the whole story.

Michael returned his hand to the steering wheel. "My father won't probe, but my mom might."

"I've had a whole year of passing off half truths about us. I've spent over a decade pretending they're dead. If I didn't know me, I'd think I was a pathological liar."

"Or a better actress than any I've been on screen with."

She laughed at that and used the mention of his work to switch the subject. "So when will you know about the final contracts for *Blue Street*?" *Blue Street* was the feature film he was signing on for the following year, which would line him up for production for the next two years. He didn't think the contracts would be drawn up until fall. With the push forward on contracts, it appeared that their marriage contract was ending faster than they expected, not that they had to divorce right away, but the option would be there.

"It could be a few months."

"Hmm."

"Are you thinking about the divorce?"

She shrugged. "Yeah, I guess. It was easy showing the world we were into each other. The breakup worries me."

He nodded. "How did you deal with breakups in the past?"

"I didn't. I was to the point and moved on. *Hey, dude, it's not working for me.* What about you?"

He tapped a finger on the steering wheel. "*Hey, dude, it's not working for me.*"

Laughter shook both of them. "We're both gonna suck at the breakup."

"We'll be all right. We don't need to think about that today. Might be different if either of us were into *someone*."

Just the mention of *a someone* brought her thoughts to Zach.

Inside, the car grew silent. She glanced over and saw Michael looking at her. "You need to tell me if there's someone."

"Oh, good Lord, Michael, the only men I've been around since we've gotten married are your costars, producers, and your management team. And most of them are either married or gay."

He grinned.

"Except that Philippe guy last Christmas." She shivered. "The creep."

"It felt good to put a fist through that guy's nose. Can't believe he propositioned you in my own house."

She fanned herself and offered a fake smile. "My hero."

"Damn right," he said with a quick nod.

"I might not say no to Ben Affleck, however. Or Bradley Cooper." *Yum!*

"Ben, really? I can see Bradley . . ." He lifted his eyebrows a few times showing his mutual admiration for the man.

They were sizing up the attributes of both men as Michael pulled off the highway. The sign said, HILTON, 4 MILES. "I'd drive you around and point out the sights, but you'll see all five of them fifty times while we're here."

"It can't be that bad."

She noticed the smile on his face as they drove down what must have been a familiar road.

"Excited?" she asked.

He gave a slow nod. "Yeah, I am. It's been a long time."

"What time are your parents expecting us?"

"Three."

The time on the clock radio said three fifteen.

The two-lane road housed farmland on both sides. The occasional cow glanced up from her afternoon grazing to watch as they drove by. Hilton itself was at the base of two mountain ranges. According to Michael, his family owned a cabin in one of them that the family visited and played in during the summer.

They turned left after the stop sign, and houses started slowly dotting the landscape. "There's another town eight miles behind us. A little bigger than Hilton with a hotel and a Walmart."

"Good times," Karen teased.

"Hey, it was a huge deal when the big box store moved in. Half the town was like, hell no. We don't need it. The other was all for having more options for shopping."

They dropped their speed to twenty-five miles an hour as they drove down Main Street. Kids were riding bikes without helmets and a few women were pushing strollers. Flowering plants hung in pots off the streetlights and there wasn't a sign of graffiti anywhere. "It's so clean," she told him.

"And my dad doesn't have to lock up the spray paint like they do in LA. The local sheriff would scare the shit out of us as kids with just a look."

"I'm sure there are still kids getting into trouble."

"Oh, yeah . . . they just don't get their kicks by defacing property. Stealing a tractor for a joy ride, bonfires, and beer parties. Deer hunting off season."

Karen couldn't imagine. "Did you hunt?"

"Been years. But yeah."

"Did you like it?"

He turned off the main road and out of town toward the residential portion of Hilton. "Didn't hate it. Might have enjoyed it more if I liked the taste of venison. My mom's a good cook, but I never did like the gamey taste of deer."

Karen smiled at a couple who stopped to watch them drive by. "Doesn't taste like chicken?"

"Not even close."

"Has to be better than snails."

Michael made a heaving noise. They'd both tried escargot and both decided the French laughed at every American who ate the crap. "Stupid Americans. They'll eat anything," she said with her best French accent. They both laughed at the memory of their time in France.

There were several cars parked on the streets outside of the houses. Unlike homes in California, here there was sufficient space between the homes, and each one looked different from its neighbor. He slowed down in front of a two-story traditional with room in the drive for their rental. "You ready?" he asked.

Karen had never had a home to go home to. Although her heart rate had kicked up a notch as he put the car in park, there was an excitement to meeting the people with whom Michael grew up. Regardless of their not truly married status, Michael was a friend, and she couldn't remember seeing a more genuine smile on his face in the past. That made her extremely happy.

"I'm ready. Are you ready?"

Michael no sooner twisted the key away from the ignition than the door to the house swung open and out poured a gaggle of people.

One step out of the car, and a young teenage girl ran to him with open arms. "Mikey!"

Here we go.

———

Zach held back and let his family welcome home the famous son. Hannah couldn't hold in her enthusiasm as she jumped into Mike's arms and he swung her around. Judy quickly followed while little Eli ran around their feet in his excitement. Eli couldn't really know Mike all that much, except for the pictures and explanation that Mike was his uncle.

"Is that her?" Zach's mom whispered to him as they stood on the porch and waited for the youngest girls to give Mike and Karen a chance to get out of the car.

"Yeah."

"She doesn't look like the pictures."

He stared at her now. "No, she doesn't." *She looks better in person.*

As if Karen sensed their stares, she looked directly at him.

He stilled and the air around him charged.

"She's hot," Joe whispered behind him, jolting him out of his thoughts.

"Aren't you married to my sister?"

Joe was Rena's husband, and had been since they married right after high school. They adored each other.

"I'm not blind."

His mom moved from her perch and the rest of them followed.

"Hey, Rena." Mike hugged the oldest sister and tickled the baby's chin. "She's grown," Mike said.

"Eighteen months next week."

Rena stood back and gave their mom her turn. Mike pulled her into a hug and lifted her off the ground.

"I was starting to think you forgot about us," Janice said.

"I've had a crazy year," he told them. Then as if he realized for the first time that his wife stood by his side, he lifted his arm to Karen and invited her into the circle of their family.

"Mom, this is Karen. Karen, my mom, Janice."

Karen smiled, her perfect teeth shining. "It's a pleasure, Mrs. Gardner."

"Oh, Janice. Please." Zach could see wonder in Karen's face when Janice pulled her into a hug.

The girls stood back and let Mike introduce his wife.

"We're so excited you're finally here."

"Michael has had a very busy schedule this year. I've heard so much about all of you."

"Where's Dad?" Mike asked as he looked around.

"Closing up the shop," Rena told him.

Zach felt Mike's disappointment. Not that he should have expected anything different. Their father put work first. Almost before his family. It's just the way it had always been.

"This is Joe, Rena's husband," Mike told Karen.

Karen was too close to do anything other than shake hands, which appeared awkward for her.

"And you know Zach."

If watching her shake hands with Joe felt awkward, it had nothing on the open arms she presented to him. It was as if she knew they should be on a somewhat more familiar basis . . . and she was, but their brief hug did nothing other than remind him of the peach shampoo she used and the overall intensity he felt in her presence.

The desire to hold her, suck her in, made him hold on a fraction too long.

She stepped back and didn't meet his gaze. Instead, she looked beyond him.

Zach twisted around and tried to focus.

He cleared his throat. "Mike, Karen . . . this is Tracey . . . my girlfriend."

Chapter Seven

The entire time Karen sat among the Gardners, all she could see was the one person in the room who wasn't related by blood or marriage.

Tracey walked around the home, occasionally placing her hand on Zach's shoulder to gain his attention, but otherwise acting as if she belonged. She did, and would much longer than Karen.

Zach had yet to keep eye contact with her for more than a second. Neither of them had forgotten or misinterpreted what had happened in the driveway back in Beverly Hills. As much as Karen wanted to forget that moment, she couldn't.

She had no right to feel misled by the fact that Zach had a girlfriend, considering she was the married one, but the feeling was there nonetheless.

Thank God, they hadn't kissed. There would be no way she could have walked in the door with Michael if she could taste his brother on her lips.

The Gardner family home held a spacious living room complete with a fireplace, worn and comfortable sofas, and reclining chairs. Rena had put her daughter down for a nap in one of the upstairs bedrooms, while everyone else gathered in the living room. Karen had yet to see where she and Michael would be sleeping. She never made it past the living room before someone suggested she and Michael sit and allow the family to quiz them.

As Zach had told Karen, Hannah talked obsessively. "I can't believe you're finally here," Hannah told them.

"I can't believe you didn't come sooner," Rena scolded.

"Leave the pestering to Mom," Michael told his sister.

All eyes moved to Janice. "I'll pester later. Right now I want to make Karen feel at home." Janice offered Karen a warm smile.

"Oh, pester away," Karen encouraged them. "So few people in Michael's life give him any grief other than me."

The comment managed a few laughs.

"Thanks for throwing me under the bus, hon." Michael winked at her.

"Your ego was always too big for this town," Zach said.

"When it gets too big at home, I just tell him to take out the trash and lower the lid to the toilet."

"That's gross, Mike," Hannah chided.

Tracey sat on the arm of the couch and placed her arm around Zach's shoulders.

Karen skirted her gaze away.

"How did you two meet?" Tracey asked.

"Haven't you seen the YouTube video?" Hannah pulled her cell phone out of the back pocket of her jeans.

"You met on YouTube?" Obviously, Tracey didn't understand the social media site or how it functioned. Zach's girlfriend had a set of soulful eyes and dark brown hair. She stood a couple of inches taller than Karen, and carried a few more pounds, but not in an unflattering way. She didn't wear a lot of makeup, but Karen could tell she had put some effort in her appearance. She kept watching Michael, and it was impossible to miss the slight blush to her cheeks when he smiled her way. Karen had seen that happen more times than she could count over the past year. It was one thing to watch a celebrity on the screen and quite another to meet them in person, and here Tracey was thrust into a room with a virtual superstar and expected to hold a normal conversation when it was obvious she was having her own fan-girl moment.

"No, silly. They met when Mike went to one of those after school places that keep kids off the streets." Hannah scrambled over toward Tracey and Zach while she expertly surfed the net with one finger, all the while talking about Karen and Michael's *chance* meeting.

Karen glanced at Michael and noted the smirk on his face. They both knew there was nothing *chance* about their introduction to each other. In fact, they'd both had an opportunity to look over each other's Alliance profiles and had already agreed they were compatible, at least on paper, for a short marriage.

Through Hannah's phone, Karen heard the familiar sound of the kids at the center chatting over each other as they were telling Karen that *Michael Wolfe was asking her out.* She'd seen the YouTube clip so many times and from many different angles in the weeks following. It had aired on two entertainment television slots and even showed up as a clip on the local evening news.

Michael really was gifted in his art. He'd convinced everyone in the club that day that they'd just met and he was enamored with her. She, of course, knew there wasn't a snowball's chance that their marriage would be anything but temporary even before they met. Gwen picked up on his sexual preference when she met him, so Karen knew he was gay from day one.

Gwen's gaydar had been legendary since. At many Hollywood parties, Michael would hang back with Gwen to get a heads-up on the sexuality of the men in attendance.

Tracey watched the footage from the Internet with interest.

Zach glanced at the screen on the phone briefly. "I seem to remember you pulling that line on Suzie Baker in tenth grade."

Karen shot a playful grin to Michael. "You fed me a line?" she asked with a wink.

"Me, the actor? Fed *you* a line? Never!"

They were laughing when the sound of a car pulling into the driveway caught Eli's attention. "Grandpa."

Michael sat taller, and his smile fell. She reached out and clasped his hand in hers with a squeeze.

He glanced at her. For whatever reason, Sawyer Gardner twisted Michael in knots, and she was determined to help Michael through whatever the man presented. As platonic as their relationship was, she really did love her husband.

The weight of someone's stare had her looking around the room. More than one set of eyes landed on her. Rena appeared to be deducing something inside her head as she stared at Karen. Zach seemed to be focused on her and Michael's clasped hands. When his eyes moved toward hers, Karen glanced back at Rena, who was now watching Zach.

Karen purposely closed her eyes and drew in a breath. When she opened them again, she forced her eyes to the front door.

Janice welcomed the patriarch of the Gardner family home, as did little Eli, who ran to his grandfather with open arms.

Both of the Gardner sons obtained their height from their father, Karen mused. Sawyer stood six two and looked as if he could hold his own with lifting heavy weights at his hardware store, or lugging two-by-fours on a construction site. His dark hair was peppered with gray but didn't seem to be thinning, which probably lent some hope to both Michael and Zach that they would each have a full head of hair throughout their lives.

Michael stood, and pulled her to her feet to meet his father.

"Look who's here," Janice said to her husband.

Sawyer's gaze took in the room and hesitated on Karen for a brief moment before landing on Michael.

What will it be, a handshake or a hug?

Michael stepped in front of her and the handshake won.

"It's good to see you," he told his father.

"We thought you'd forgotten about us."

Karen cringed. How many times had she heard that in the past hour? *Too many to count.*

Instead of offering an apology or an excuse, Michael turned to Karen. "Dad, I want you to meet Karen."

She offered her hand as she had Janice earlier. "Nice to meet you, Mr. Gardner. Michael has told me a lot about you."

"Is that so?" he asked as he shook her hand briefly. "He's told us virtually nothing about you." Sawyer's unnerving stare shot through her.

"Wow, Dad, way to make her uncomfortable," Hannah said.

"Yeah, hold back, will ya?" This was from Zach.

Michael simply shook his head as if he knew his father would be an instant ass. The man obviously ruled his home and he expected a different level of respect than he actually gave.

"Sawyer!" Janice started in.

"It's OK, Janice. Zach told us when he came to California that everyone was upset that we hadn't come to visit. I'm sure he underemphasized all of your feelings in an effort to save mine." She couldn't help but glance Zach's way, or notice the way he glared at his father. So far, Sawyer had yet to crack a smile, even with Eli at his heels and Rena attempting to pull the child back.

"As I told Mom," Michael said, "I've had a breakneck schedule since Karen and I met."

Karen placed a hand on his arm. "But I have to take some of the blame for the delay in meeting you."

Michael glanced at her.

"Michael knows I don't have a family of my own and he worried that I'd be intimidated by your sheer numbers."

Janice tilted her head to the side. "No siblings?"

Karen shook her head and offered everyone her practiced lie all at once. "My parents have been gone for some time, and they only had me. My aunt is the only family in my life."

Michael placed a hand on her back and sighed.

Not that Karen was going for the sympathy card, but her words seemed to change the mood in the room.

Hannah was the first to say anything. "Well now you have us. We're noisy, but we're not bad or anything."

For the youngest child, Karen was surprised that she took on the role of mediator. That was usually left to the middle child, which would be Michael, and right now he was staring down his father, almost daring the man to say something.

It appeared to Karen that Sawyer wasn't going to say anything else, and thankfully, Janice stepped between them. "I need to check on dinner in the kitchen. Karen, why don't you come with me and let the men have a chat?"

Ready to escape, Karen glanced at Michael, lifted her eyebrows as if to say *good luck*, and then followed Janice.

The traditional home had a divided kitchen, giving her and Janice some privacy.

"Please try not to be offended by my husband's demeanor," she said as soon as they were out of hearing range of the living room.

"I understand." Though she really didn't. The truth was, she hadn't been around a large family who said what they felt because they could. In Karen's world, when you didn't know someone you were polite until the stranger became a friend or an enemy. Of course, that could happen in a matter of hours, but it usually took more than a sentence or two to find a reason to dislike someone.

Sawyer named that tune in one sentence.

"I can see by your face you're upset," Janice said.

Rena walked into the kitchen at that moment. "Well of course she's upset. Dad's being an ass." She stepped over to the refrigerator, opened it, and removed a bottle of wine. With a wave in the air she asked, "Would you like some, Karen?"

God yes. "Please."

"It will take a day or two for him to warm up," Rena explained.

"Michael said as much." Karen slipped onto a high stool that was tucked under the kitchen island.

"We were all shocked to hear Michael had gotten married." While Janice spoke, she wrapped an apron around her waist and opened the oven to check what cooked inside. From the rich aroma coming from the kitchen, Karen guessed it was some sort of roast. She couldn't remember the last time she'd had a home-cooked roast. Aunt Edie was a pasta sort of woman, the by-product of her first husband being a full-blood Italian.

"It was a bit of a surprise to Michael and me as well," Karen told them.

Rena shoved a corkscrew into the bottle and began twisting the plug free. "You really only knew each other for a few weeks before you got married?" she asked.

"Yeah. When I think about it, I realize how reckless it was to get married so quickly." All the combined lines, some holding truth and others only skimming the surface of truth, started to fall from her lips. "I think he was charmed because I didn't give a crap about his fame. Threw him back a couple of notches."

Rena handed her a glass of wine and poured herself one.

Because there was no way Karen would escape the kitchen without more information about her and Michael, she told as much of the truth as she could without giving away their secret. "Michael started talking marriage almost from the first date."

Janice exchanged looks with Rena.

"And you thought that was normal?"

Karen sipped the wine, pushed past the taste, and called herself a *wine snob* before taking another drink. Michael would hate it. Good thing he'd be stuck drinking beer while he was in Utah. Part of the macho image he loved so much meant he only drank wine in public during Hollywood parties and fancy dinners. Karen tried to tell him that plenty of heterosexual men drank wine, but he wouldn't. He was the ultimate closet wine snob ... and it was rubbing off on her.

"I thought it was crazy. But why not? We knew there wouldn't be a lot of time to get to really know each other before he had to run off to shoot another film."

"So why rush it?" Janice asked.

Karen shrugged. "I can't really explain it, Janice. And as for not visiting with everyone here, I think some of that has to do with both of us realizing, after the fact, that we rushed." They were both staring at her now.

"You've been married for a year."

Karen nodded. "And I can count on one hand the amount of months we've spent together in that time. Michael wasn't lying when he said his schedule has been grueling. Your son works very hard."

"Are you suggesting you barely know each other?"

Karen shook her head. "No. I think we know each other better than anyone else in our lives. Michael will be the first to tell you he has a lot of superficial friends. Hard to avoid in Hollywood."

The women seemed to relax. Karen knew this was where she proved to the family that she wasn't using Michael, but she wasn't about to profess undying romantic love for him either, not with their divorce only months away. A little doubt would soften the blow of obtaining a daughter and sister-in-law in the same year as saying good-bye to her. This might very well be the only time Karen spent with the Gardner family. She needed to remember that and keep her barriers up. She drank more of her wine and set the glass down. Already the liquid was going to her head. She glanced at the clock and noticed it wasn't yet four thirty. *Oh well, it's five o'clock somewhere.*

The door to the kitchen opened and Tracey walked through. "Hope you don't mind me interrupting. I thought I'd bring the boys a beer."

"Is it bad in there?" Karen asked.

Rena found beer in the fridge and handed them to Tracey.

Tracey offered a polite smile. "Let's just say that I'm sending in liquid courage and then coming back in here as fast as I can."

Rena rolled her eyes. "You should do something, Mom."

Janice shook her head. "Your brother deserves a tongue-lashing. Even if he hadn't married without any of us around, he hasn't exactly been attentive since he became famous."

Karen had so many words on her lips but kept them inside her mouth. Janice Gardner may have been a calming effect on her husband, but she wasn't happy with her son's lack of contact. Karen just hoped that Sawyer didn't push Michael away before they unpacked.

Tracey ducked back in the room and returned just as quickly.

"Judy pulled Hannah outside with Eli."

"Oh, good. I just hope they don't start shouting and wake the baby."

"Janice, can I ask you something?" Karen asked.

"Of course, dear." Her temporary mother-in-law pulled a bag of potatoes from a bin and piled them into the sink before turning on the water.

"How many hours a week does your husband work?"

Janice glanced at the ceiling as if it held the answer to Karen's question.

"Well, he works plenty of twelve-hour days."

"And weekends?"

"The store is closed on Sundays."

"Everything is closed on Sundays," Rena said with a laugh.

Karen tapped her fingers on the counter. "So he works twelve hours a day, six days a week?" That sounded grueling even to her.

"Not all the time," Janice defended.

Karen swirled the wine in her glass before taking another drink. "When was the last time you took a vacation?"

As if catching on to Karen's line of questions, Janice slowed down her answers. "We went to Michael's first premiere."

Which meant at least eight years. "Anything since?"

"We go up to the cabin every summer. Take a couple of day trips."

"One or two days at a time?" Karen asked.

"The store doesn't run itself."

Rena poured more wine in Karen's glass. "You sound like Dad," Rena told her mother. "The truth is, Karen, my dad doesn't leave town very often, and he has always worked more hours than anyone I've ever known."

Karen offered a smile, picked up her glass, and stood to leave the room. "That's what I thought."

Armed with knowledge, she entered the Gardner battlefield ready to fight.

Chapter Eight

Zach had a strong desire to be drinking whiskey instead of beer. The tension in the room was growing by the second. Joe had taken a spot by the window and made a point of looking outside as if searching for a reason to run away.

"It can take three days to shoot five minutes of film, Dad." Mike was trying to explain to their father the work schedule he'd been under, but Sawyer wasn't listening. Not that Zach thought he would. Their father only saw what he wanted to.

"I don't care if it takes a month. You should have come home before now."

"I didn't get where I am by slacking," Mike told him.

Sawyer's retort was on his lips when the door from the kitchen opened again.

Zach finished his beer in hopes more was on the way.

Their father glanced beyond them and closed his mouth.

"Don't stop on my account." Karen's voice slid over Zach's skin. She calmly moved to the edge of the sofa, across the room from Mike and their father. She offered a smile to Joe, who shifted his eyes away.

"I was just explaining to my son how disappointed we are that he hasn't made time for his family." Sawyer made no apologies to anyone.

Karen stiffened her spine and crossed her legs before leaning back on the sofa.

"I would think you, of all people, Mr. Gardner, would understand."

Zach blinked, looked at his father.

"What do you mean?"

"You work hard."

His eyes narrowed. "I see my family daily."

"Convenient, seeing as how they all live in the same town."

"Living a couple of states away isn't an excuse."

Mike lifted a hand in the air. "Let it go, Karen. He'll never understand."

Karen casually sipped her wine. The only sign of any nerves was in the tapping of her foot against the air. Zach felt himself starting to relax.

"Oh, I don't know, Michael. I think I might have just realized where you get your drive."

"What?"

"Your drive? Mr. Gardner, you've owned your own business for how long?"

"Over thirty years."

"You must have sacrificed a lot in those years." Karen's eyes never left Sawyer's.

Zach glanced at Joe, who was sitting closer to Karen than any of them, as admiration filled Joe's face.

"Anything worth having is worth small sacrifices."

"Things like long hours, missing weekends, vacations?"

Sawyer caught on and narrowed his eyes.

"Michael works his butt off and he does most of it out of a trailer on a set far away from his own bed. When he does finally come home, he usually drops. Sound familiar?"

Sawyer glanced at Mike.

"Michael is just like you. He works hard every day, pushes himself to his limits, and sometimes forgets about his family. But we're here now. And my guess is you haven't arranged any time off to spend with us."

Zach knew for a fact Sawyer was planning to open the store in the morning. Saturdays were busy.

"I own the store. I can take off anytime I want."

Mike laughed and said, "When was the last time you did that?"

"Don't question me."

The smile on Mike's face stayed. "That intimidating tone worked when I was seventeen, Dad. But you're right. I don't have to question. I already know the answer."

"Michael cleared his schedule for the next week and a half to spend time with everyone here. He promised me he'd avoid calls from his agent and manager to make sure that time is quality time. How much of it will he see you?" Karen laid out her challenge and sat back.

Every eye in the room swung back to Sawyer.

Zach noticed his father's fist on the arm of his chair. "I don't know if I like you."

"Dad!" Mike yelled.

"I don't know if I like you either, Mr. Gardner." Karen bored holes in Sawyer's head with her stare.

"Maybe we should just go." Mike set his beer down and stood.

"Oh, screw that!" Zach jumped up. "Dad, you're out of line. You know Karen has a point or you wouldn't be so pissed." He placed a hand on Mike's arm. "If you wanna stay with me, you can."

"Over my dead body." His mom stood by the kitchen door and glared at their father.

Rena and Tracey were standing by his mom with wide eyes and dropped jaws.

Janice pointed what looked like a potato peeler at Mike. "Michael Gardner, you sit back down. You and Karen aren't going anywhere."

She swung the peeler at her husband. "Sawyer, a word, please!" She exited the room by route of the stairs and expected their dad to follow.

Zach couldn't remember the last time his mother forced his father from the room to talk. Had to be when he and Mike were kids.

Sawyer grumbled and followed Janice up the stairs.

Everyone in the room turned to Karen.

"You have some serious balls, Karen," Rena said.

Mike started to laugh. The sound became infectious, and eventually Joe followed and Zach found a smile on his face, too.

Karen shrugged. "What? He doesn't intimidate me. I'm the daughter-in-law; someone's bound to hate me."

"You could make him shit bricks, maybe, but not hate you."

"Mike's right." Zach patted his brother on the back. "Damn it's good to have you back."

Mike picked up his beer. "Well, if you don't see me again for ten years, you'll know why."

"Don't say that." Rena waved her finger in Mike's general direction. "He's not the only person here who missed you. Dad just doesn't know how to tell you."

Zach noticed Mike and Karen exchange glances. Both of them seemed reserved, making him question what Mike had told her to expect.

"Does Dad still keep the whiskey locked up?" Mike asked.

———

Karen tossed her tired limbs on the double bed and dropped her arm over her eyes. "*That* was painful."

"Don't say I didn't warn you."

Sawyer Gardner had perfected the silent treatment and used it most of the night. He eyed her at every turn and challenged Michael as if they were bitter enemies on a field of battle.

"I now know why you left. Was he always so . . . mean?"

Michael shook his head. "Seems he reserves that side of ugly for me. And only since I moved away."

Karen removed her arm from her eyes and watched him walk around the small room as he pulled his shirt from his pants and unbuttoned it. "I think Rena said it perfectly. He doesn't know how to tell you what he's feeling."

"He told me exactly how he feels. He doesn't respect my work, thinks us getting married the way we did is a joke, isn't happy we didn't visit sooner." He sat on the edge of the bed and kicked off his shoes.

"You know what I think it is?"

"What?"

"I think he's pissed you don't live in Hilton and that you're not working hard to please him." Yet something told Karen that Michael was actually trying to please his father or at least earn his respect by being successful in his chosen field of work. What would it take for Sawyer to be proud of his son for what and who he was?

"I don't miss him. I missed everyone else. Hannah's practically a woman and I missed most of her growing up."

Karen sat up and laid a hand on his back. "No one realistically expects their children to stay close to home their whole life. Don't kick yourself."

He stood, grabbed his suitcase, and placed it on the one chair in the room before opening it. "I'd just like it to get easier with him."

"You told me it would take a couple of days for him to warm up."

"I don't remember him being this cold."

The last thing Karen wanted was for Michael's relationship with his family to grow worse because of their visit. "If he doesn't thaw in a couple days, we'll make our excuses and leave."

He grabbed his toothbrush and pointed at her. "Deal."

"What time is Zach coming by in the morning?" Zach wanted to show Michael the latest build he was working on in the neighboring town. In truth, Karen thought Zach wanted to get Michael out of the house early so he didn't have to butt heads with their father again.

"Seven thirty."

She rolled off her side of the bed and mimicked Michael in the search for her overnight bag and pajamas. "Wake me when you get in the shower. I think I'll take advantage of the country air and run in the mornings. Might help ease the stress of the day."

He glanced at the small bed they'd be sharing. "I don't think you'll have to worry about me waking you. That's the same mattress I slept in when I lived here."

Karen gave the bed a push with the palms of her hands. There wasn't a firm spring left, guaranteeing they'd feel each and every movement the other made all night.

It was going to be a very long ten days if Sawyer did actually thaw.

———

Sleeping beside Michael was much like sleeping beside a girlfriend at a teenage slumber party. Karen held no shame in tugging the covers back over her when he rolled over with them clutched in his hands, or pushing on his shoulder to tell him his quiet snores were waking her up.

Karen gave up on sleep just after six thirty and slid from the room to dress in a casual pair of running shorts and slim-fitting top in the communal bathroom. After brushing her teeth and pulling her hair into a sloppy ponytail, she exited the bathroom and found Judy waiting outside the bathroom door.

"G'morning," Karen said with a shy smile. When was the last time she'd had someone at home waiting to use the bathroom? She couldn't remember.

Judy gave her a quick once-over. "Going for a jog?"

Karen nodded. "Thought I'd take advantage of the fresh air."

Judy's plump lips, which were a slight departure from the other members of the Gardner clan, crept into a smile. She had pale brown eyes, which stood in an exotic contrast to her dark hair. Karen was reminded again that the entire family was really beautiful.

"Mind if I join you?" she asked.

"You're a runner?"

"Not sure if you can say what I'm doing is running. I'm just trying to keep my butt from taking on any more than it did my freshman year."

"Aren't you going into your senior year?" Karen would swear that Michael had told her that Judy had just turned twenty-two. Or maybe Zach had told her that.

"I am. But the freshmen fifteen have to be removed every summer."

She remembered those days, where school, studying, and the ability to drink beer legally for the first time kept on those extra pounds.

"Meet you downstairs in five?" Karen asked.

"You're on."

After a five-minute stretch, they both took off in a slow jog, one where they could carry on a conversation without too much effort. The morning was still cool, but Karen could tell the day was going to be one where the heat snuck up on you in no time.

"Do you jog a lot at home?" Judy asked.

"I try. The road to Michael's home isn't the safest one for foot travel. I have a friend in Malibu and we get together a couple times a week. Sometimes I get the kids from the club to run with me after school. What about you?"

Judy had placed a trendy hat on her head and had her hair sticking out the back of it. She glanced under the brim and gave Karen a strange look, making her realize that she once again referred to Michael's house as his house and not theirs. Luckily, Judy didn't say anything about it.

"Last year, in the dorms, we had a runner's club. Seems like it only really stuck for a few weeks then everyone found an excuse to sleep late."

"Well, if it makes you feel any better, it doesn't look like you need to lose fifteen pounds." It didn't. She seemed to have a little fullness around her face, weight that might be considered baby weight, but Karen couldn't know for sure if it was new or not since she'd just met Michael's middle sister.

"I've always had a few more pounds than I'd like. Wish I'd gotten more of Hannah's height."

Hannah took after their father. She was at least five nine and might even gain another inch or two. Karen could understand Judy's admiration for her baby sister. Hannah could easily walk the runway and model just about anything. Her long legs and slender frame would fit right in with Michael's world.

"There are advantages to being shorter than your sister," Karen told her.

"Oh, yeah . . . what?"

They rounded the corner of the neighborhood and met with houses on one side of the street and grazing fields on the other. A scattering of cows was off in the distance, but not enough to fill the air with the scent of manure, which was a blessing for the homeowners.

"Your dates are almost always taller than you. You can wear heels and not look like you're from a world of Amazonian women, and you can buy jeans off the rack and never worry they'll be long enough."

Judy spat out a breath of air. "You've given this some thought."

Karen waved a hand between the two of them. "I'm not much taller than you, sister. And I've had a few more years to get used to the advantages of my height."

"How old are you?"

"Twenty-seven." Her muscles were finally starting to warm up. "Wanna pick up the pace or are you good?"

"I can kick it a little more."

They did.

"What are you studying?"

"I started as a business major." Something wistful in Judy's tone had Karen turning to look at her.

"What's your major now?"

"Business." Now Judy sounded depressed and Karen was confused.

"But it's not what you want."

Judy passed her a quick look and even quicker smile. "No, no . . . I can work with a business major."

Karen could tell this wasn't something Judy was going to come right out and talk about, not without a little nudge.

"What are your electives?"

"My electives?" Judy appeared lost in thought.

"Yeah, you know . . . the classes that have nothing to do with business but you have to obtain in order to leave college well rounded?"

"Oh, those. Design," she said without hesitation.

"Home design, fashion . . . graphic?"

"Architectural design, actually."

Karen hadn't seen that coming, but the gates were open now, and Judy was excited to talk about her passion.

"I'm fascinated with the crafting of buildings. How the designers make decisions about design based on the materials used. Homes that are built into the landscape, others that are there to contrast it. Have you been to the Disney concert hall?"

They'd picked up their pace even more as Judy talked. "No."

"Seriously? You live right there." She sighed. "It's amazing."

"Have you been?"

She shook her head. "No. When we were in LA for Michael's premiere, I hadn't been exposed to architecture. I thought my dad built houses, then Zach . . . I never thought there was much more to building a home or business other than two-by-fours and concrete." She took a few deep breaths and continued. "Growing up in Hilton where the tallest building is the movie theater, and the only thing close to architectural design concepts is when the football team religiously toilet papers the current quarterback's home the night before the first game, doesn't leave much for the imagination."

Karen giggled. "I didn't think TPing anyone's home could be considered design."

"The sheer enormity of the effort is worthy of a spot in a magazine," Judy teased.

They pushed past the houses and beyond Main Street.

"Why aren't you studying architecture?"

Judy glanced at Karen like she was crazy. "What will I do with that degree in Hilton?"

"Who says you have to stay in Hilton?" Yet even as the words left Karen's lips, she knew the answer. *Sawyer.*

"W-well . . . I just . . ."

She'd obviously frazzled the girl with her questions. "College is supposed to open your mind to the possibilities of life. Not shut you into a pigeonhole of what someone else wants it to be for you." Sawyer was just going to love Karen for this advice. But she'd be remiss if she didn't offer it. "It's your life, Judy. You get one shot at it. Don't let anyone tell you how to live it."

They ran in silence for a while, which was just as well since they started up a slight incline and Karen was breathing a lot faster than when they started out.

After a few more blocks she asked, "So, do we have a destination or are we going to run back to California?"

Judy laughed. "No. I run to Beacon's barn and then turn around. It's about four miles round trip."

Karen usually managed three, but four wasn't undoable. "I don't think one car has passed us."

"Traffic here is when two cars pass at the light."

"It's quiet. I'm not sure I could live here."

"My mom swears it's the best place to raise kids."

Karen slid her a glance. "Was it a great place to grow up?"

"Yeah. I can't complain. It's nice to come home and visit."

Karen heard an unspoken *but*. "But?"

"I'm not ready to settle down and raise kids."

"Of course not. You're not even out of college yet."

"But my dad expects me to come home and help with his business when I'm done."

The more Karen heard about Sawyer Gardner, the more she disliked the man. Talk about mapping out your children's futures without letting them have any say.

"Let me guess . . . the thought terrifies you."

She huffed out a strangled laugh. "More like strangles me."

"You should talk to your brother. Life is much more fulfilling when you're living it for yourself than for someone else."

Judy stared at her now; her tight lips were in a thin line. "You're deep."

"Naw . . . I'm as shallow as they come," she teased.

Judy slowed her pace and turned around. Karen glanced at the empty fields and followed. "I thought we were going to Beacon's barn?"

She waved a hand in the air. "Oh, Beacon's barn burned down over ten years ago."

"So why do you still call it Beacon's barn if it doesn't exist anymore?"

"It's a small town, Karen. Every street, every burned-down barn, every inch of this town is married to some memory from the past that no one ever forgets. The bench outside the sheriff's station is the bench where Millie Daniels told her daddy that she was pregnant right before she jumped on a bus and never came back. Everyone calls it Millie's bench."

"Poor Millie Daniels. How long ago was that?"

"Six years ago." Judy ran for a while without talking. They both ran a little slower and talking became less difficult. "There's a lamppost where Steven Ratchet was caught puking his guts out after an all-night binge."

"That's an unusual occurrence? Seems small towns are magnets for underage drinking just like anywhere else."

"Steven was from a long line of Mormon families. Drinking alcohol is right up there with having premarital sex in the eyes of the church. Poor Steven didn't have a chance to hide his indiscretion in this town."

"Puking in public is hard to hide."

"Especially when half the town is Mormon and the other half is quick to point out who the 'good Mormons' are and who the 'bad ones' are."

Karen wiped her forehead with her arm. It was starting to warm up as they crossed over Main Street a second time. "What do you mean good versus bad?"

Judy grinned. "How can you tell a good Mormon from a bad Mormon?"

"This sounds like a joke."

"You ask them if they drink their caffeine hot or cold. They don't drink caffeine, or at least, they're taught not to. Bad Mormons drink coffee, and the good ones drink soda. Most of the kids I grew up with didn't give a crap and drank what they want. Steven bucked his family most of his life. Left town the day he hit eighteen."

Karen frowned. "Where did he go?"

"I think he went to Vegas."

Karen couldn't help but cringe. An eighteen-year-old in Vegas was wrong on many levels.

"Oh, don't worry . . . he came home. Just took him a few years. He has a wife and three kids now."

That made Karen feel better.

"That's what's kind of crazy about this town. Seems a lot of kids run off only to come back when they have a family of their own."

Karen thought of Michael and how that would never be him.

They turned onto the Gardners' street just as Zach was pulling out of the driveway with Michael in the passenger seat.

Karen ignored the sweat that was running down the soft T-shirt and the way some of her hair had fallen out of its binding when the two pulled up alongside them and rolled down the window. "Enjoy your run?" Michael asked. He was dressed more casually than Karen could remember. He wore an old T-shirt she'd never seen before, and when she glanced inside the car, she noticed faded jeans. She leaned against the car and peeked inside. Zach gave a wave and then quickly diverted his eyes to his sister.

"Hardly know what to do with the fresh air."

He laughed. "Call if you need anything."

Judy looped her arm in Karen's as if they were old friends. After the run, she had to admit she knew Michael and Zach's sister a whole lot better. "We'll take care of her, Mikey. We're taking her to Petra's today, then showing her off in town."

"You are?" Karen sent a puzzled look to Judy.

"Yeah, we have to get you ready for the parade."

The smile on Karen's face slipped. "The parade?"

Judy shifted her face to Michael. "You didn't tell her?"

Michael squirmed in his seat. "You and Mom can give her the details. We're late . . . right Zach?"

Karen felt Zach's gaze before she confirmed with her own eyes that he was looking at her.

Karen pulled her sticky shirt away from her body.

"Yep, we gotta go. See ya later, girls." Zach pulled away.

She watched the car leave before turning to Judy. "What parade?"

Chapter Nine

"How was it after everyone left?" Zach asked Mike as they left Karen and her nearly bare shirt that acted as a second skin. He really did need to get this ridiculous attraction to his brother's wife out of his system. He had a girlfriend for crying out loud. He'd suggested Tracey return to her house the night before instead of staying over with him at his. Zach told her that he anticipated Mike and Karen coming over that night and didn't want to complicate matters. The excuse was lame, but it worked. He'd been dating Tracey for nearly six months. She lived in Monroe, the next town over, but nearly everyone knew her in Hilton before Zach started dating her.

They got along well enough, liked the same movies, and laughed at the same jokes. Yet neither of them had ever suggested the other move in or elevate their relationship to anything more than what it was. He cared for her, but there wasn't a zip of chemistry that ignited with a look.

His mom had asked once if he saw himself settling down with Tracey long term. He hadn't considered moving toward forever with Tracey. Somewhere in the back of Zach's head, a tiny voice kept asking three little words. *Is this it?* Is this the kind of relationship one looks for all one's life and can't imagine living without?

Zach knew his life wasn't on track. He woke up an hour before he was scheduled to and stared at the ceiling in his room. He'd lain there and contemplated life as if he were a fucking poet or something. At thirty-one, he had the routines of a much older man. He went to work every day, traveled the same roads, and took predictable vacations with the same people year after year. After he returned from California, he hadn't been the same. The drive alone across the desert on the back of a bike was enough of a James Dean moment to remind him of the days when he'd been young and felt as if the entire world was in front of him.

Now he was taking his brother to his latest job site to show off his accomplishments as much as to relieve his brother of the confines of their childhood home.

"Dad went to bed early." Mike answered his question. "Mom tried to help Karen understand him."

Zach offered a joyless laugh. "We've known him our entire life and we barely understand the man. I wouldn't expect Karen to understand the great and powerful Sawyer Gardner."

Mike's gaze traveled to Zach's side of the truck. "I always thought you got him more than any of us."

"Just because I worked with him more, doesn't mean I get him."

"Karen has his number. She has this way of figuring out what makes someone tick within an hour. And then if pushed, she has no qualms with pushing that person against the wall with whatever bugs them most to get them to have a light-bulb moment."

Zach had noticed that about her. He'd felt a strangely proud moment when she told their father that she wasn't sure if she liked him either. Rena had it right. Karen had balls. Zach heard the admiration in Mike's voice when he spoke about his wife. His sexy, smart, and ballsy wife.

Zach hated the itch inside him that made him acknowledge the deep roots of envy when it came to his brother. Never once had

Zach begrudged Mike any of his success or his fame. He knew Mike worked his ass off, and Karen was right . . . he did it because he was taught to. Both of them had learned a strong work ethic from their dad, not a bad trait to have, unless it kept you from enjoying life.

"Dad could have used a light-bulb moment long before now," Zach said as he pulled onto the highway and headed toward the next town.

"Does he still insist on staying at the hardware store like he's the only one who can run it?"

"Mom has him coming home for lunch most days, but yeah . . . he thinks he needs to open it up and close it down. Monroe has been expanding, bringing in more business. He can't compete for the big jobs. The builders order from St. George and have their shit delivered."

"The store has never been a cash cow."

"More a means of survival," Zach agreed.

Mike stared out the window as Zach pulled off the highway only a few off-ramps from where they'd gotten on.

"I've tried to give them money." Mike blew out a sigh. "Dad won't have it."

Zach thought as much. "Dad has a hard time if I'm buying lunch. Best way around that is to give them gifts."

"I don't think Dad will drive the McLaren."

They both laughed at the thought.

"You can always front Judy a little money. She's always hitting them up for more at college. And Hannah will be out in a year. Putting all of us through college had to have taken a hit on their retirement."

"Does Hannah know where she wants to go?"

"She's aiming for Colorado. Judy wants her to go to Washington."

"But Judy will be graduating next year."

"Maybe."

"Is she behind in her credits?"

"No. It's not that. I think she's considering a shift in her major."

"To what?"

Zach shrugged. "I'm not sure. The last time we really talked, she said she wasn't excited about going into business of any kind after college. The thought of moving back to Hilton to work with Dad was depressing her."

Mike glanced at Zach. "What did you tell her?"

"I told her to use her next year of college to study what made her smile and screw what Dad thinks."

"Seriously?"

It had pissed Zach off that Judy was afraid and lived her life as if she were still fifteen and in need of their parents' approval to date a guy. If any of them understood what it felt like to be held down by family obligations, it was him.

"Why didn't you follow your own advice?" Mike asked quietly.

The question stiffened Zach's spine. "What makes you think I didn't?" He couldn't keep the defensive tone from his words. "Having a contractor's license can take me anywhere."

"Yet you're still in Hilton."

Instead of defending why he was still in Hilton, Zach decided to be honest with his brother. "I'm considering a move." As the words escaped Zach's mouth, he realized how much he liked them.

A warm smile spread over Mike's face.

Hannah and Judy dragged Karen around town and introduced her to nearly everyone, or so Karen thought. Her mind fluttered with names and faces . . . none of which she remembered. Apparently, Sawyer Gardner had a sister who lived in Monroe, and she had a handful of children as well. Seemed everyone Karen met was someone's cousin, aunt, or uncle.

They were on their way to Petra's, one of only two hairdressers in town. The short walk down Main Street brought out many new faces.

Have you met Mike's wife? This is Mike's wife . . . Mike got married last year. This is his wife . . .

Karen was sure that no one in town would know her as Karen. No one here called Mike, Michael, and no one in Hollywood called Michael, Mike. Occasionally Hannah would use the pet name Mikey. The name had brought a smile to Michael's face the night before.

After several sets of introductions, Karen leaned into Judy's side and asked in a whisper, "What's with the wedge haircuts?" Every other woman they'd approached had a short bob haircut with the dramatic wedge in the back. The style had been popular a decade or so before, but very few women had kept with it. To Karen, the cut looked like someone screwed up, and she for one was happy to see hairstyles take a different turn. Not that she ever paid attention to new hair fashions. She kept her shoulder-length hair simple so she could easily put it up into a French twist or ponytail.

"It's awful, isn't it?" Judy laughed and they both attempted not to giggle when yet one more woman with the awful cut walked by. "Brianna is the other hairstylist in town. She returned from some hair show in Salt Lake in March and told all her clients that this was the *new look* of the year."

Hannah jumped into the conversation. "It's better than the perms she was giving everyone last year."

Karen wasn't so sure. "I take it you two don't use Brianna very often."

They looked horrified. "Never. Petra cuts as fast as she talks but she'd never cut your hair in a way that makes you look stupid. Even if you tell her to," Hannah insisted.

"And she doesn't gossip," Judy added.

"Isn't gossip a favorite pastime in a small town?" Karen asked. Next to bartenders, hair salons were notorious for clients unloading their emotional garbage on the stylist. Must have something to do with sitting in a chair and being told not to move for hours on end to bring out all of one's problems to a near stranger.

"It's the *only* pastime in a small town," Judy told her. "Unless you knit."

Petra's salon housed the familiar smell of hair chemicals and shampoo. There wasn't a hair salon in the world that didn't have the same distinct odor. Hospitals and salons . . . you'd know where you were if you were blind and in a different country just by the smell.

Much like any small salon, there were two workstations with swiveling chairs. A hair-washing sink sat off to one side where clients could lie back and tuck their necks into the most uncomfortable position ever.

"Oh, good, you're on time." The woman Karen assumed was Petra waved from over the head of a young woman who sat in the chair. "I thought you'd get sidetracked showing Mike's wife around town."

"I told you two o'clock," Hannah said. "Hi Becky." She waved at the girl in the chair. Becky looked to be Hannah's age. Her soft brown hair had been blown dry and was floating around her face like a cloud.

"Hi Hannah. Hi Judy. Home for the summer?" Becky asked.

"Can't avoid it," Judy told the girl. "Petra, Becky, this is Mike's wife, Karen."

Karen waved at the other women. "Hi."

Hannah approached her friend and lifted a strand of her hair. "I like the little bit of color."

Becky blushed at the compliment and looked at herself in the mirror. "I like it too."

"Like it?" Petra asked with a laugh. "It's perfect for you. Look at your eyes sparkle."

Hannah giggled, showing her age. "You sure that's not Nolan putting that sparkle in your eye?"

From Becky's shoulders, Petra removed the plastic smock that kept the bits of falling hair from soiling her clothing.

"You're dating Nolan Parker?" Judy asked with interest.

Becky stood and let her eyes slide to the floor.

Hannah gave Judy's arm a playful push. "He took her to prom."

While the girls talked and giggled about what was obviously an exciting subject, Karen sat back and observed as she often did while at the club. She could learn a lot about the kids by watching them interact. There was always a pecking order among teens. The popular girls tended to lead the pack and the conversations. In this trio, it seemed that Hannah had the upper hand with Becky, but Judy was obviously a rival. Probably because of her age.

When Becky stepped out of the chair, she leaned forward to catch a hair clip before it hit the floor. When she did, the shirt she wore gapped at her waist. An angry red welt mark peeked below her shirt, which she quickly tucked down as she stood.

Karen skirted her gaze away from the girls, who didn't seem to notice, and over to Petra, who had noticed the mark as well.

"I can't believe your parents are letting you date Nolan."

Becky's shy smile fell. "Daddy doesn't like him."

"Because he's not Mormon?"

Becky shrugged.

Karen felt her insides start to twist. *How much did Daddy dislike Nolan?*

"That's stupid," Judy said. "Nolan's a good kid. Best employee my dad's ever had."

Petra moved around her shop and listened, something that struck Karen as strange. *Didn't Judy say that Petra talked obsessively?* Seemed she was doing a lot of listening.

Becky placed an unconscious hand to her abdomen and offered a coy smile. "My dad isn't going to like anyone I date."

"Dads are like that."

"Who's first?" Petra asked as their conversation started to fade.

Judy stepped forward. "I am. I can't find anyone in Washington to do my hair right."

Karen sat in a chair and picked up one of those gossip magazines that always seemed to litter the baskets in salons. Between those and magazines dedicated to hairstyles, hair salons were well-known for ten-minute reading material. Though she pretended to read the latest Hollywood gossip, she watched Becky from the corner of her eyes. She rubbed her stomach several times, and when she reached for her purse, Karen noted another mark on her upper arm.

It killed her to watch the girl leave the salon. Alarms were going off in her head and blaring loud enough to keep her from hearing what Judy and Hannah were talking about after the other girl left.

"Nolan, really?" Judy asked Hannah after Becky walked away.

"Someone caught him kissing her after the Homecoming game. After that, they were always holding hands in the halls at school."

"I bet her dad is pissed."

Hannah practically fell into the chair at Karen's side. "Probably. She's really come out of her shell since she hooked up with Nolan. He's good for her."

Out of her shell? Becky seemed as shy as they came.

"He always said he was leaving this shit town when he graduated, but he didn't. I think it's because of Becky." Hannah turned to Karen and clarified. "Nolan graduated this year."

"Oh."

"I bet they run off together after Becky's out of school."

Judy lay back in the salon torture chair with her head in the sink.

"Are you good friends with Becky?" asked Petra.

"We've been friends since third grade. But we don't hang out very much." Again, Hannah turned to Karen to explain. "Her family is Mormon and they don't like it when Becky hangs out with those of us who aren't."

"You're making it sound like a cult," Judy chastised.

"It's true. Did you ever get invited to your Mormon friends' slumber parties?"

Judy didn't comment.

"Exactly. Becky and I hang out at school."

"And she's dating one of your dad's employees?" Karen asked while flipping the pages of *People* magazine.

"Nolan Parker. He's supersexy. Becky 'bout died when he started flirting with her in chemistry. The whole school was talking about them most of the year."

The desire to learn more about Nolan Parker and Becky's family was a constant pull. Karen had seen her share of scared teenage girls. Though Becky wasn't crying and visibly frightened, there were a few unmistakable signs that she was in some sort of trouble. Girls held their stomachs for two reasons, and Becky didn't seem sick to Karen.

"Oh my God, that's you." Hannah grabbed the magazine from Karen's lap and twisted it around to Judy and Petra. "And that's Mike and Zach. Wow, how cool."

"Let me see that."

Sure enough, the magazine had a picture of her sandwiched between the Gardner brothers the night of her anniversary party. Michael was glaring at the camera, Zach had his hand on her arm, and they were looking at each other. The hair on Karen's arms stood up. They looked good together.

"It must be cool always being in magazines like this."

Karen rubbed her forehead. "It's highly overrated. Your brothers had to chase that guy out of Michael's backyard."

Hannah sent a puzzled look. "Don't you mean *your* backyard?"

"Isn't that what I said?"

"No. You said Michael's backyard."

Karen swallowed. "Well, you know what I mean."

Hannah returned her eyes to the magazine and searched through it again. This time asking who Karen had met within the pages.

Petra had gone silent again. Only this time she eyed Karen.

Damn.

Chapter Ten

Apparently, Petra went from *stealth information gathering* mode to *I'm the queen of this salon and you will do what I say* mode.

Petra was originally from Germany. She'd moved to the States when she met and married a military man. As Karen learned after a brief and *to the point* explanation, Petra's husband had gotten a stomach bug and ended up at the VA hospital shortly after she'd given birth to their son. The stomach bug had turned out to be cancer and he died six months after his diagnosis.

"What was I to do?"

Before Karen could answer, Petra went on. "Richard's family was here, and they wanted to help me with Alec. My English wasn't good back then."

"Back then?"

"It's been eighteen years now."

"Wow, that's really sad."

"It was awful. But I survived. Alec was a pain in his teens. So wild my boy."

Now this was the fast-talking woman Judy and Hannah described. She had Hannah's hair in one hand, the scissors in the other, and she snipped, pointed into the mirror, and combed. It was as if she had three hands.

Judy sat off to the side with her new do. Although if Karen had to guess, it was her old do just redone.

Apparently happy with the cutting, Petra tossed her scissors aside, picked up the bottle of mousse, and sprayed the white foam in her palm before rubbing it all over Hannah's head.

"Alec wasn't that bad," Judy said from behind her magazine.

"For a single mother, he was awful. Stayed out late, didn't call. Gave me a heart attack when he told me he wanted to leave town and not graduate."

"Did he graduate?" Karen asked.

"Nope. Moved to Florida."

"How did that work out?"

Petra turned on the hair dryer and picked up a brush. She talked over the noise. "He's OK now. Got his GED and joined the coast guard. I visit him a couple times of year in Key West."

"See, told you he wasn't bad. It's this town. Makes you wanna leave before society tells you it's OK."

Judy had a point.

Within minutes, Petra was flipping off the smock around Hannah's shoulders and saying, "Your turn."

"I really don't need a haircut," Karen protested.

Petra paused for a minute and tilted her head. "I've seen your pictures for months now. Everyone coming in pointing to pictures of Mike and his new wife. Every time your hair is up as it is now, or flat on your head."

"I don't like anything that requires work."

Petra made a clicking noise with her tongue and pointed to the torture chair. "Trust me."

Judy raised one brow. "Might as well give in. She's relentless."

"It's only hair," Hannah said. "It grows back."

"I won't do anything that requires more than five minutes to prepare. I bet you have a headache once a week at least."

Karen felt her limbs untangling from the chair and walking in Petra's direction. "I do actually. It's stress."

"Not stress. It's the rubber band. All that stress on your scalp is tension, gives you a headache."

Karen allowed Petra to wash her hair and watched as the hairdresser combed out the layers and ran her fingers through the ends with thought. "Shorter. With a few long layers around your face. Yes!"

Twenty minutes later Karen left Petra's feeling five pounds lighter. Not that her hair had been terribly long, but with this shorter style and the addition of the right mousse and appropriate hairbrush, Petra had changed her appearance.

"I like it." Hannah played with the ends of Karen's hair and smiled.

"She's good."

A familiar-looking truck was parked on the opposite side of the street. Karen glanced up to see the words Hardware Store above the building. "Is that your dad's store?"

"Yeah." Hannah grabbed her hand and tugged her. "C'mon. Let's show Zach your new style."

That's right, the truck was the one she'd seen Zach and Michael leave in that morning. Although the road was void of any cars driving by, it was strange for Karen to walk down the middle of it without feeling like a car would scream around the corner any second. Hannah's endless energy was weighing on her as the day moved on.

They pushed through the store with a ringing of a bell at the top of the door.

Like the inside of a hair salon held familiar smells, so did hardware stores. Sawyer's life's work was laid out on aisles of shelves holding boxes of everything a household could need. The narrow rows of merchandise stood eight feet tall and ran the span of the room. At the front of the store, there was a register without anyone standing behind it.

"Dad?" Judy called out the minute the door closed behind them.

"He's not here," a voice called from the back.

Hannah rushed to the sound of the boy's voice.

Judy set her purse on the counter and started toward the back room. "I have to use the bathroom."

Abandoned at the counter, Karen looked around and noticed a few plaques behind the register. The local Boy Scouts thanked Sawyer Gardner for his donation to a kid's eagle project, and another one was a framed newspaper clipping of news of the business expanding.

The bell behind her had Karen turning. "Can you get the top one, Nolan?"

Zach's hands were full of boxes that kept him from seeing her standing there. Karen set her purse down and grabbed the surprisingly heavy box on the top of Zach's pile.

"Got it," she said as she relieved Zach of the extra weight.

His gaze caught hers. "Hey." He blinked a few times, standing there holding boxes. "Wasn't expecting you here."

"We were at the hairdresser's. Hannah ran me over here." She shifted the box in her hand.

Zach's eyes looked her hair over and his smile grew bigger. "I like it."

Karen couldn't help the blush in her cheeks. "Petra's hard to say no to."

"It suits you."

"Thanks."

With their hands full, they stood there staring at each other until Hannah stepped around them with a teenage boy at her side.

"Here, let me get that," the boy said, taking the box from Karen's hands.

Zach and the boy Karen assumed was Becky's boyfriend, Nolan, walked to the back and out of sight.

"That's Nolan. Cute, right?" Hannah asked.

Karen chuckled. "Little young for me."

Hannah rolled her eyes with a laugh. "Not to mention you're married. Becky's lucky."

Karen waved a finger in Hannah's face. "It's the boys that are lucky to find a nice girl."

She didn't look convinced. "I'd like to find my Nolan."

Karen draped an arm around her. "You will. I think the boys are going to be terribly shy because you're so beautiful."

"Am not."

"Are too." Karen gave her a quick hug.

Judy ran down the aisle with her cell phone waving in the air. "Oh, my God, Hannah, we're supposed to be over at the rec hall working on the float."

"The float?" Karen questioned.

"More like a trailer that will be pulled by a truck, but it's for Mike and we're in charge of decorating it. I forgot all about it." Judy grabbed her purse and pulled on Hannah's hand.

"Wanna come?" Hannah asked before they made it to the door.

"I'm good. I know the way back to your parents'."

"You sure? I feel like we're abandoning you."

She made shooing motions with her hands. "Go. You two are exhausting me," she said with a wink.

Judy pulled her sister away. "C'mon, we're thirty minutes late."

Within a blink of an eye, the girls were running out and down the street.

There weren't any customers in the store, and Zach and Nolan still hadn't returned from what she assumed was the storage room. Karen picked up her purse and walked to the back of the store.

Before she saw them, she heard their conversation and paused.

"I can really use the hours, Zach. I keep telling your dad that he can work me full-time. It's not like I'm in school anymore."

"What does my dad say?"

"Says I should be in school. Not everyone is cut out for college," Nolan told Zach. "Some of us don't have the money to go to college anyway."

Karen peeked around the corner and noticed the two of them talking over the boxes they had placed on the floor. Zach placed a hand on Nolan's shoulder. "I'll see what I can do."

A look of relief swept over Nolan's young face. "Thanks, Zach. I appreciate it. I really need the money."

"Is everything OK?"

Nolan ran a hand through his too-long hair. "Yeah. My old man isn't about to help with much is all. It's time I figure out how to make it on my own."

Zach folded his arms in front of his chest. "Have you ever considered working construction?"

Nolan's face lit up. "Like building stuff?"

"Yeah. You know the store, but do you have any idea how any of the stuff in here works?"

Nolan nodded. "Yeah. A little anyway. But I can learn what I don't know."

"Let me talk to my dad. If he can't work you in, maybe I can find something for you with me."

Karen's heart swelled. It was obvious that Nolan was struggling, and she had a pretty good idea as to why, and Zach had caught on to the intensity of his need as well and reacted with solutions. Nothing put a smile on her face faster than someone willing to help when they didn't have to.

She cleared her throat and stepped into the room. "Sorry to interrupt," she said. "The girls ran off and I was going to walk back to the house."

Zach swung around. "I can take you. I was just dropping off a few things."

"It's not far."

"It's all right. I'm going by that way."

There was a protest on her lips, but she let it die. It was hot outside and she felt as if she'd walked the entire town five times since she woke that morning.

Nolan smiled at her and Karen extended a hand. "You must be Nolan Parker."

"Oh, I'm sorry. Nolan, this is Karen Jones," Zach introduced her. For the first time since she'd arrived someone didn't introduce her as an extension of Michael. She smiled.

"I met Becky an hour or so ago."

Nolan's face lit up with the mention of her name. *Yeah, he has it bad.*

"She stopped by after she had her hair cut." He glanced at Zach. "She only stayed a few minutes."

Zach grinned. "Where's the fun in that?"

Nolan offered a cocky grin and reached for the boxes of inventory. "Nice meeting you."

Karen followed Zach out of the store and waited as he opened the door of the truck for her.

He jumped in his side and turned over the engine.

"Nice kid," Karen said.

"He is. Kind of surprised he didn't leave town the day after graduation." Zach switched the air conditioner on high.

"He's not leaving town without his girl," she said with confidence.

Zach was about to pull from the curb and glanced at Karen. "How can you be so sure?"

If there was one thing Karen hated it was outright gossip, but if her suspicions were anywhere near correct, Nolan was going to need a real job with real money coming in or Hilton was going to have two more runaways to add to the list.

"Do you know his girlfriend?"

"I've seen her a couple of times. Nice girl." He moved onto Main Street after a car passed them.

"I think she's pregnant."

Zach swung his head to Karen, disbelief on his face. "You think?"

"I'd love it if I was wrong, but my gut says I'm not."

"Oh, damn. Do my sisters know?"

Karen shook her head. "No. My guess is the only ones that know are Nolan and Becky."

"How are you coming to this conclusion?"

"Side effect of what I've done most of my life. I work with teenage kids, and I've seen my share of knocked-up girls who are trying to hide it from the world. Do you know her parents?" Karen said.

"I've seen them, but can't say as I've ever met them."

"Unplanned teenage pregnancy isn't easy for anyone. Even worse if the parents don't approve of the boy responsible."

"Nolan's a good kid."

"I keep hearing that. But apparently Becky is Mormon, and Nolan isn't."

Zach shrugged as they turned down his parents' street. "Not sure why someone's religion is supposed to dictate falling in love."

"I didn't either, until I talked to Judy and Hannah. They think it's a huge factor for Becky and Nolan."

Zach released a long sigh.

"I know. Anyway can you talk your dad into giving him more hours?"

"You heard that, too?"

"Didn't mean to eavesdrop."

"It's all right. I'll push my dad. And if he won't add hours, I'll see if Nolan has any ability with swinging a hammer."

He pulled up to the Gardner family home. "There's always the possibility that I'm wrong."

Zach met her eyes. "He seemed desperate to have more money coming in. If it's not because she's pregnant, it might be something just as important."

Karen wasn't about the mention the marks on Becky's body. That would require more investigation. Walking away from a hurting kid wasn't in her.

"Please don't say anything . . ."

He waved her off. "Of course. You don't even have to say that."

She reached for the door. "Are you coming in?"

"No. I'll be over tomorrow." His eyes once again took her in, and that crazy current that sat in silent moments buzzed between them.

"Till then."

———

"So what do you think of Karen?" Judy asked Hannah while the two of them hot glued bits of colored paper to Mike's float.

"I think she's great!"

Judy did, too . . . almost too good to be true. "Don't you think it's odd that she and Mike didn't visit sooner? I mean, she seems perfect yet Mike doesn't want to show her off."

Hannah leaned over the edge of the bench Mike would sit on while riding down the parade route. "You know our brother better than I do. I was just a kid the last time he lived in the house. I remember him being kinda shy about girls."

"I thought so, too. Not like Zach. He always seemed to bring his dates around."

"Maybe we notice that because Zach lives in Hilton now. Kinda sucks that we don't know Mike as well as we should."

The memory of Karen's conversation while they jogged brought a smile to Judy's face. "I think we'll be seeing a lot more of our brother now that he's happily married."

"I hope you're right."

Sunday dinner with the Gardners was a lot like a family reunion with the Brady bunch after the kids had all grown up and given birth to their own. Janice and Sawyer's home couldn't contain the clan that showed up to celebrate Michael's visit. They set up shade tents in the park and commandeered several grills to barbeque a smorgasbord of meat.

Zach hadn't seen Karen since he dropped her off the day before. That didn't mean he hadn't thought about her. In fact, he hadn't stopped thinking about her, and it was really starting to piss him off.

Tracey was going to meet him at the park later in the day. He'd skipped out on their normal Saturday night date, which usually didn't end until Sunday morning, and he couldn't give himself a good reason as to why.

It was a lie, but he had no problem lying to himself. He was an ass for wanting to know what it felt like to press his body up against his brother's wife, but he wasn't so far gone as to sleep with Tracey and picture Karen in her place. He wondered if Tracey noticed that they'd not slept together since he returned from California.

She was starting to look at him in that strange way women did when they had a thousand words on their tongues but only sighed or shook their heads instead of expressing them. It just wasn't working with her anymore. Even if his eye hadn't wandered to Karen, the fact that it did told him he couldn't lead Tracey on much longer. He asked himself why he was waiting to break it off, but he knew that answer, too. Having a girlfriend kept him on a strange leash, adding to the walls that kept his gaze from lingering on Karen more than was appropriate.

Zach found a parking spot and went around to the back of his truck to grab the volleyball net and ball for the family game. He wondered how much his brother had slacked since being Mr. Hollywood.

Several faces lifted and hands waved as he walked through his family crowd. He greeted everyone by name and noticed more than just family at this gathering. Some of Mike's old friends and their families joined in the fun.

Unable to help himself, Zach peered over the heads of everyone, searching for a certain blonde who stood out like a white swan in a pond full of ducks.

She stood over a picnic table with his niece, little Susie, on her hip. She was laughing at something, and the sound traveled above everyone there and met his ears.

Larry, one of Mike's high school buddies, met him as he walked across the grass and grabbed the ball from his hand. "Hey, Zach. Haven't seen you in a while."

"I haven't gone anywhere. Is Kim here?" Kim and Larry had married a few years before. There was already a little Larry toddling about somewhere.

"Of course. Probably talking to your brother. She about shit herself when I told her he was in town."

"Another starstruck female to add to the pile. Mike's ego will be impossible to live with."

Larry nodded toward the pack of females surrounding his brother. "They'll get used to him before he leaves."

"I doubt that."

Zach dropped the bag with the net away from where the food was being served. "Wanna grab a couple of kids to set this up?"

Larry tossed the ball in the air and walked away as he called a few of the teenage kids over to do the busy work.

Zach stepped over to the buffet table and snagged a handful of chips. He kissed his mother on the cheek and tickled Susie under her chin. "Hey everyone."

He tried to act unaffected when Karen smiled at him, but his insides went to mush.

"There you are. We were beginning to wonder if you forgot." Rena was opening up large plastic containers and setting them on the table with the others.

"I couldn't find the volleyball net."

"Likely excuse. You just didn't want to get stuck on the grill."

Zach glanced over and noticed his father over the flame. Joe stood by him and Uncle Clyde beyond them both. "Looks like that's all taken care of."

Susie made grabbing motions with her fingers and reached to jump into his arms.

"Done with me already?" Karen said as she handed the baby over.

"She loves her Uncle Zach," Rena said with pride.

"Picking the good-looking boys over the girls is just smart," Karen said with a grin.

Zach caught Karen's smile and handed his niece a cheesy chip. "I think it has more to do with what I let her eat, and less to do with my looks," he said with a wink.

Karen blushed.

Rena grabbed the chip out of her daughter's hand. "She'll be wearing that all day if you give it to her."

Susie's little lip puffed out.

"Spoilsport."

He grabbed another one when Rena turned away and moved to the grills to greet the men. Susie smacked her lips against the messy chip when he gave it to her.

"Nice of you to join us," Joe said. "Show up late and hold the baby so no one will put you to work." He waved a spatula in Zach's direction. "I have your number, buddy."

"Why don't you drag Mike over here?"

"Naw, we'll make him do the dishes."

That got them all laughing.

Zach moved away and handed Susie off to Aunt Belle, who sat among the older members of the Gardner clan. He kissed an aunt, hugged a grandmother, and moved toward his brother to help drag him away from his adoring fans.

"C'mon bro. Time to see if all those crazy moves you do on the big screen are smoke and mirrors or if your body is still in shape."

Zach ignored the protests of the women surrounding Mike as he removed him.

"Thanks," Mike whispered in his ear as they both walked over to where the teens were setting up the net.

Zach patted him on the back. "I always have your back." Yet even as the words left his mouth, his gaze reached for a set of eyes he felt on his back.

He turned and caught Karen looking toward them.

Damn!

The teams were divided by the usual pecking order: age, family obligation, and skill. Not exactly in that order. Zach and Mike started on the same team along with Joe and three more guys, which left the jocks from their days in school. Larry, Ryder, and Keith were the star athletes who'd stuck in Hilton, or at some point returned. They stacked their team with old football friends.

With six men on each team, the ball made it through the air and it was game on.

After a couple of sets, Zach knew his brother's acting wasn't softening his body in the least.

The crowd grew around the game, some picking sides while others just cheered. They'd been playing a good thirty minutes before Mike pulled their team into a huddle. "Larry is totally dogging. If you can aim toward him, we have this game."

Zach served the ball to have it volley over the net twice before Mike took the opportunity to spike it in Larry's direction. Even Zach was shocked to see it back on their side of the net. Zach set the ball and Mike hit it toward Larry again for the game point.

The match was close and everyone shook hands. They tossed the ball to the younger kids, who took time picking teams to make their own match.

"Show-off." Rena punched Zach's shoulder with a smile.

Karen rolled her eyes but the grin on her face matched the smile in her eyes. "Men!"

His mom brought the first tray of cooked steaks from the grill and placed it on the table.

Zach and Mike stood back as the women hustled around the table, uncovering dishes and getting ready for the onslaught of takers.

His dad brought over another tray and smiled at Zach and Mike before returning to the grill.

Zach glanced over at his brother. A soft smile accompanied Mike's gaze as he watched their father walk away.

"He's hard on your ass because he misses you."

Mike patted him on the back before he grabbed a plate, filled it with food, and then allowed one of his old friends to drag him off across the park.

Zach piled a plate full of food and sighed over the perfection of the steak. Joe took a seat beside him and soon Rena followed. There were people everywhere. Rena waved Karen over to sit beside them. Zach scooted over so Karen could sit and tried to ignore her closeness.

"Where did Mike run off?" Joe asked.

Rena motioned away from their table. "Keith and Larry have his attention."

"Friends from school?" Karen asked.

"You've not heard about them?"

Karen shook her head as she bit into her corn on the cob. Zach watched her lips wrap around the corn and had to force his gaze away. *Lucky-ass corn.*

"Larry and Keith were his best friends their senior year. Busted his ass when he took the lead in the high school play."

"Until the chicks started to swarm," Joe told Karen. "Then they changed their tune."

Karen chuckled and kept eating.

"I can't believe Mike hasn't told you about them."

Karen swallowed her lucky corn and wiped her mouth. "High school was a long time ago."

"Don't you keep up with any of your high school friends?" Rena asked Karen.

A quick shake of Karen's head gave her answer. "Not really."

"That's too bad. High school friends are the ones who knew you when. The kids that keep you grounded."

Karen glanced at Mike and the smile on her face fell. "I'm glad Mike has friends like that. He needs them."

Zach looked beyond Karen, then back to his sister. "Really? Why do you say that?"

Karen looked away and then stabbed the meat on her plate with her fork. "It's different in LA. Everyone wants him to be something different." She placed the steak in her mouth and chewed.

Before anyone could ask more, Karen spoke around her food. "It's different here. Yeah, there are a few groupie types watching him, but he's more relaxed than I've ever seen him."

Zach and Rena swiveled toward Mike at the same time. They passed a knowing look then focused their attention back to Karen. "I'm glad you made him visit," Rena said.

Karen shook her head. "Don't thank me. Zach was the one who made that happen."

He smiled at her and continued to finish the food on his plate.

"Where's Tracey?" Joe asked when they were nearly finished eating.

Zach did a quick look around. He hadn't realized that she hadn't shown up. Where was she? He reached for his cell phone but it didn't show any missed calls or text alerts. "Maybe something came up."

"Is everything OK with you two?" Rena asked.

Zach noticed Karen look away.

"Yeah. Fine."

Joe huffed out a small laugh. "Fine? Fine doesn't describe a woman, ever."

Rena elbowed her husband.

Before Zach could reply, Eli ran to his father and pulled on his arm. "Daddy, play ball with me."

Joe pushed his plate away and untangled from the picnic table to play with his son. In his place, Aunt Belle made herself comfortable.

"Is this the kids' table?"

Rena picked up her red cup. "The kids' table doesn't have alcohol, Aunt Belle."

Belle tossed back her head with a laugh and her gaze fell on Karen.

"So, you're Mikey's wife?"

Zach couldn't help but feel Karen's discomfort.

Karen swallowed. "Yes, ma'am."

"Humph! Funny how none of us were invited to the wedding."

Zach couldn't look at Karen when she spoke of her marriage. He would leave the table if it didn't look so damn obvious that he was uncomfortable.

"It was a sudden thing."

Belle narrowed her eyes. "When did marriage become a *thing*?"

Karen drank from her red cup and didn't answer the question.

"Well, I guess that answers that question," Belle said.

"What question was that?" Rena asked.

Belle had always had a mind unique to herself and didn't often hold her words in. So what she said next shouldn't have come as a shock, but for some reason, they blew Zach out of the universe.

"I always thought our Mikey was gay."

Rena sucked in a laugh.

Zach forgot to breathe and Karen sputtered the beverage from her glass and choked on the liquid.

Chapter Eleven

Karen's attempt to keep the white wine contained within her mouth resulted in choking the liquid down her lungs. The alcohol burned up into her nose until her eyes watered. Zach's strong hand rubbed her back as she fought to catch her breath. Rena was staring at her with a smile on her lips, and Aunt Belle lifted an eyebrow. When Karen glanced over as she tried to gain her breath, she saw concern in Zach's eyes. "You OK?"

Karen coughed into the napkin and reached for the water. As soon as she was able to speak, she pointed a finger at Aunt Belle and laughed. "That's a good one."

Karen hid her face behind the glass of water and kept coughing into the napkin even after the urge to do so had passed.

"Well, I did," Aunt Belle continued once it was clear that Karen was going to live.

"I think it's safe to say that's not the case," Zach said.

All Karen could do was nod behind her cup and hope to hell her face wasn't giving anything away.

She searched for the topic they'd been discussing before Aunt Belle sat down and uprooted what felt like an easy role of duping Michael's family, but whatever they'd been talking about had escaped her brain.

Across the field, she heard Michael laughing. As much as she wanted to go to him now and let him in on the conversation that was taking place at their table, she didn't.

"Well what about babies?"

"Aunt Belle!" Rena chastised. "They've only been married a year."

"You had Eli nine months after you were married," Belle pointed out. "Or was it eight and a half?"

Rena's jaw dropped. "It was eleven."

Karen felt her cell phone buzz in her back pocket. Happy for the distraction, she pulled it out and checked her text messages.

Is Aunt Belle behaving?

The message came from Judy. Karen glanced around and noticed Judy watching from another table.

Could use a graceful exit. Help!

Karen shoved her phone back in her pocket and waited.

"Well you're not exactly young," Aunt Belle pointed out. "Babies are easier before you're thirty."

"I'll take that into consideration," Karen told Michael's aunt. The woman was too sharp for her own good.

"Aunt Belle, give Karen a break, will ya?" Zach asked.

She offered him a grateful smile right as she felt a tap on her shoulder.

"Hey, Karen? Can you help us settle the debate over who's sexier, Brad Pitt or Bradley Cooper? We figured you've met them both and would know firsthand."

The smile that spread over Rena's face was poetic. Even Zach sighed as Karen swung her leg from beneath the table.

"Love to." Karen grabbed her cup that didn't hold nearly enough wine and saluted Aunt Belle. "Fabulous talking with you."

Karen tucked her arm into Judy's and let her voice travel. "Isn't it crazy how two men with the same name can be so different? What kind of name is Brad anyway?"

Judy laughed and glanced into Karen's cup when they were too far away for Aunt Belle to hear her words.

"She's a crazy old lady."

"I think she was about to ask me if I was ovulating."

Judy busted out a laugh. "She's convinced that Eli was conceived before Rena and Joe were married."

"I heard that. Are there any other crazy aunts I need to be alert for?"

"No, she's the only one."

"Thank God."

Karen tucked into the table with Judy and her friends.

"Have you really met Brad Pitt?"

Karen shook her head. "No. But Bradley Cooper is crazy hot."

The girls squealed and Karen enlightened them with details that would fuel their conversation for days to come.

When she was relatively certain that no one was watching her, she made her way to Michael's side. She could tell by the slight sheen in his eyes that he had a little buzz going, which wasn't something she'd seen very often, at least not when they were with a crowd.

"Hey, babe." He draped his arm over her shoulders. "Have you met the guys?"

"You introduced her to us hours ago, moron," Larry said as he tipped his cup back.

"Hey." She waved at Keith and Ryder, who were watching her a little too closely.

"Can I talk to you a minute?" she asked Michael.

"Sure. Be right back," he told his friends.

She pulled him away from the ears of others.

"What's up?"

Karen turned toward him so his back was away from the Gardner crowd.

"Your Aunt Belle is on to us."

Michael narrowed his eyes. "On to us?"

"She told me she always thought you were gay," she whispered.

He stiffened and the playful smile on his face fell.

Karen caught his arm to keep him from turning around. "No, don't."

"Is that *all* she said?"

"She asked about babies. The usual stuff. But if I had to guess, I'd think she's the one to watch out for."

A muscle in Michael's jaw twitched.

Michael leaned over as if he was picking something up from the ground, and when he stood, Karen had to turn her back to the crowd to continue looking at him.

He tucked a strand of her hair behind her ear and glanced over her head.

She wasn't sure what was going on inside his head, but there was a fierceness in his gaze she'd not seen before.

"Michael?"

Something flashed behind his eyes as he looked beyond her, then without any warning he gripped the back of her head and forced his mouth on hers.

She stood motionless, her body rigid as Michael fought some of his demons and used her as a battering ram. He tried to pull her close and she pushed against him. He'd never kissed her like this. Not for the cameras, not for his family. This was feral and dangerously close to abuse.

Oh, Karen knew he was doing it for effect, but it didn't make her any more forgiving of the line he was crossing. When his free hand dug into her side, she was close to kneeing his groin to make him let her go. Tears sprang to her eyes as she felt her lips bruise.

It was almost impossible to grab hold of any flesh through his clothes, but she managed to twist the skin under his arm and pushed him with the other.

Michael gasped and let her go.

They stared at each other, shell-shocked.

Karen lifted her hand to her lip and worried that he'd split it.

"Oh, God, Karen." Instant remorse filled Michael's face.

She stepped out of his reach. Memories of other unwanted hands on her broke through her memory and had her trembling.

Never again.

"If you ever touch me like that again, our divorce will be anything but friendly." Without waiting for his reply, Karen nearly ran away from him and his family.

Zach caught Mike looking over Karen's shoulder as they stood apart from the family having a private conversation. He cautioned himself for staring, but something in the way Karen was standing, her fingers flexing her sides, or the nervous and shifting gaze of his brother kept Zach watching.

When Mike reached for his wife to kiss her, Zach started to look away. Then he noticed Karen push against him.

Let her go, Mike. Only Zach's mental message to his brother didn't work.

The longer the kiss went on, the more apparent it became that Karen wasn't a willing party.

Wife or not, no one deserved to be manhandled. Before Zach could take one step in their direction, Karen stumbled away from Mike and then ran out of the park. Zach waited to see if his brother would follow.

When he didn't, Zach did.

He caught up with her as she turned down the road to Beacon's barn. Her pace was so fast, he was out of breath when he ran up behind her.

She swiveled her head long enough for him to see the tears in her eyes.

He considered grabbing her arm to make her face him, but he pictured her punching the next man who touched her. Instead, he jogged in front of her and stopped.

"Hey?"

She simply stepped around him and kept walking.

This time he kept her pace at her side. "Where are we walking? Back to LA?"

"Maybe."

He decided silence would be his friend at this point. Eventually she'd get past whatever had pissed her off and talk . . . right? They passed Beacon's barn and continued down what he knew was a dead-end road. He doubted Karen knew this or she probably would have taken another route.

A half a mile of silence later, Karen asked. "Why are you following me?"

Zach made a show of opening his arms and looking around. "Wouldn't want you to get lost."

"Hard to get lost in a one-horse town."

"So you know where you're going?"

She walked another block before answering. "Thought I'd go and see if old man Beacon wanted to have an affair with a younger woman."

Zach liked the fight in her voice. "Old man Beacon would have loved that. Too bad he died a few years back."

Karen snorted, but didn't smile. "Just my luck."

He laughed, hoping she'd follow suit.

She didn't. "Really, Zach. You don't need to follow me."

He didn't slow his pace and didn't make excuses as to why he stayed by her side.

The farther away from the park they walked, the less he heard her sniffling. He never could deal with a woman's tears. If that woman was as strong as he felt Karen was, those tears weighed even more on him. Strong women didn't crack easily, and when they did, whoever or whatever made them crack deserved to pay. Even if that someone was his own damn brother.

The inevitable end to the road approached, and he saw Karen looking around for a path or some escape route. She twisted around and he noticed her dismiss the idea of going back.

"C'mon," he said as he led her though the long weeds and forgotten trail behind Beacon's property.

Karen followed as he ducked into the woods behind Beacon's old abandoned house. The trees thickened and the brush at their feet thinned out. Eventually the trail widened so they could walk side by side. Even if it was in complete silence.

They stepped over fallen trees and around overgrown brush as they moved steadily uphill. Zach felt his heart rate shoot up, even though their pace slowed. He was ashamed to say that his legs started to burn with the strain of Karen's pace.

When Beacon's pond, which was more lake than pond, opened before them, Karen finally stopped. Zach wanted to sing.

"Wow." Karen gazed over the majestic pond and quiet landscape.

Zach leaned forward and caught his breath. "Don't think anyone gets up here anymore."

He diverted his gaze from her breasts as they pushed against her shirt with each deep breath she took.

"It's beautiful." She paused. "And quiet."

"No crazy aunts to be found."

Karen glared at him. "Mention her again and I'm going for another five miles . . . uphill."

Zach lifted his hands in surrender. "Did I say something?"

She moved closer to the oversize pond and sat on a fallen log. He parked himself beside her and picked up a handful of rocks from the forest floor. He tossed one into the water and watched the ripples flow from the center of impact. After a few pebbles made it to the water, Karen picked up her own and joined him.

She grunted with a particularly forceful throw and Zach decided it was time for a diversion. Whatever weighed on her mind was getting worse and not better.

"When we were kids," he started, "my friends and I would sneak up here to fish."

After a couple more tossed pebbles, she asked. "Why did you have to sneak?"

"Old man Beacon didn't like kids in his pond. He'd stock it every few years but wanted the bounty all to himself."

"Seems like a long way to walk for an old guy."

"That's what we'd thought until he came at us with a shotgun." Karen's horrified expression made him laugh.

"He'd fire a round in the air and we'd shit ourselves getting away. I'd lay money on finding all our old fishing poles in his barn."

"The burned-down barn?"

Zach tossed another rock. "You heard about that?"

"Judy's my history teacher for Hilton."

Zach wanted to ask what Mike had told her about the town, but mentioning the man who drove her on her aimless walk would rank up there with bringing up crazy Aunt Belle.

"After Beacon died, a few of my friends and I came up here and toasted the old man."

"Toasted the man who came at you with a shotgun? I'm surprised he didn't get arrested."

"He was harmless. Probably laughed when he collected our fishing poles and the buckets of fish we'd caught." He scratched the stubble of his beard. "Come to think about it, we were never run off until after we'd spent half the day here and had a crap-load of fish."

Karen smiled now, and the effect on her face was this side of magical. "Sneaky bastard."

"Smart."

"Too bad he's not around for that affair."

Zach laughed at that.

This time when Karen laughed, her smile grew and she winced. She brought her fingertips to her lips and that's when he noticed the swelling.

He couldn't stop his hand from reaching toward her and touching. She lowered her eyes and didn't look at him as his thumb lightly swept over her lips.

His heart rate sped up again, only now it was with a strong desire to lay a fist into his brother's face.

"He should never have kissed you like that."

Karen easily backed away from his hand but kept silent.

Although Karen didn't seem like a woman who would put up with abuse, Zach had to ask. "Has he done that before?"

She shook her head. "No. And he won't be given a chance to do it again." Her words were bitter and full of anger.

What does that mean? It killed him not to ask.

Karen changed the subject. "Did you ever bring girls up here and give Beacon something interesting to watch?"

"Oh, no . . . Hilton's inspiration point is up by my family's cabin."

She stood and grabbed a handful of rocks. Leaning over, she attempted to skip a rock over the flat surface of the water only to see it fall into the pond without a bounce.

"Isn't the cabin several miles away?" The next rock she skipped bounced once.

"Far enough away to not get caught."

"Is there such a place in this town?" The next three rocks dropped into the water.

Zach stood up behind her. He took her hand in his and slowly guided her in the right motion to skip the rock. "It's in the wrist."

He demonstrated and skipped it four times before it gave up and fell in.

Karen tried again, failed. Zach placed one hand on her shoulder, the other on her arm. Her next attempt skipped the rock three times.

He kept a hand on her shoulder, unable to move away as she skipped a few more.

She straightened her spine and he expected her to move away. Instead, she leaned back into his arms and sighed.

He held her and they both stared out over the water in silence.

Zach looked down when her hand reached up to caress his arm. The simple touch spoke volumes.

He placed his lips next to her head and indulged in the peachy smell of her hair. He closed his eyes and savored the moment.

"If I turned around right now," she whispered, "I'd want you to kiss me."

Zach forgot to breathe. His arms tightened around her as he soaked her in. Her honesty humbled him. "I'd want to taste you, too."

Instead of acting, they stood there and enjoyed their embrace.

When Karen moved away, Zach let her.

Chapter Twelve

The house was quiet when Zach walked her up to the steps.

"Looks like everyone is still at the park."

"Sunday dinners go well into the night," Zach explained.

The walk back from Beacon's pond wasn't nearly as intense as walking toward it. Karen and Zach had come to a strange understanding. The attraction was there, but neither of them planned to act on it. Yet she knew, without a doubt, that if she needed him, he'd be there. She wanted to cry when she realized that Michael used to be that for her.

Her hike to Beacon's pond reminded her of a different time in her life. Where the murky waters of reality darkened her life and made her question everything. If Michael hadn't been a friend to her, she would have used every means necessary to bring him to his knees for what he'd pulled at the park. But because she knew, on a deeper level than most, that he acted out of fear, she allowed him his indiscretion. Not that he wouldn't pay for his abuse, he would. But she didn't feel he needed to give up everything.

If he did it twice, however . . . he wouldn't do it twice. Karen was certain of it.

"Are you going to be all right?" Zach asked.

She'd survived her parents. She could do this. "I'll be fine."

He held out his hand.

She looked at it, not sure what he wanted.

"Your phone."

She fished it out of her back pocket and handed it to him. He punched in his number and handed it back to her.

"I'm never more than ten miles away."

A strange laugh escaped her. "This is such a freaking small town."

He laughed with her. "Yeah. It is."

Laughter faded and she gave him a wistful grin. "Thanks for keeping me from getting lost."

He tucked his hands in his pockets. "You're welcome."

Then, like a schoolgirl, she turned and walked into a parental house and closed the door. She leaned against it for several minutes before she worked her way upstairs.

She fell back onto the bed she'd been sharing with Michael for the last few days and draped an arm over her eyes.

Her mind drifted, probably because of the stress of the day, to her parents.

The pain she'd tried hard to forget for years bubbled to the surface and threatened tears. She'd be damned if she'd allow one more wasted tear on them.

Her mother had abandoned her when she needed her most.

If it wasn't for her Aunt Edie, Karen would have gone the way of many homeless teens.

Michael and his millions were her ticket to helping others, but she wasn't willing to sell herself out to obtain them.

In her back pocket, she felt her phone buzz. She'd considered ignoring it, but looked to see who called.

There were three missed calls from Michael with messages. She didn't bother listening to what he had to say.

Then there was a text from Judy.

Where are u?

She didn't need the entire Gardner family searching the small streets of Hilton looking for her. Karen tapped her chin, then texted.

Have a splitting headache. At the house.

She waited until the next buzz.

You're FOS. Mike is frantic. Did u fight?

Judy might be several years younger than Karen, but damn if she wasn't in tune with life.

U R right. Tell your brother to screw off.

Karen hit Send as she picked herself off the bed and walked down to the kitchen. She found a bottle of wine and pulled the cork before the buzz came in from Michael's sister.

Ohhh, someone's sleeping on the couch tonight!

Karen saluted Judy in an empty kitchen. "Good idea, sister."

Karen sent one last text.

Xoxo

She sat on the sofa and waited for Michael. Because blood was thicker than water Judy would tell Michael that she was at the house, and if he held any remorse, he'd show up as fast as his feet could carry him.

When the door swung open ten minutes later, Karen kept her eyes focused on the ridiculous crocheted plant hanger that went out of style sometime in the seventies.

Michael approached her with slow steps. He sat on the coffee table in front of her when she refused to meet his gaze.

"I'm so sorry."

She blinked. Debated what she'd say to him. Because she did love him as a friend and felt he'd violated that friendship with his own drama, she told him something she'd never uttered to another human being.

"When I was thirteen my father stepped into my room one night and kissed me as no father should ever kiss his daughter."

Michael's eyes grew wide. His skin paled.

"I pushed him away but he came back and forced himself on me again. When I told my mother, she called me a liar. The day after I told her, they both left. I sat in the house for almost a week before I realized they weren't coming back."

She refused to cry.

She met Michael's gaze. "You crossed that line today, Michael."

There was no reason to sugarcoat his actions, and she needed to make him understand the intensity of her feelings so he wouldn't ever feel he had the right to do this again.

"I'm so sorry, Karen."

He rested his forehead on her knee, but otherwise didn't touch her.

"If you want to be my friend when this is all over, you'll listen and agree to what I'm going to say."

He looked up and waited.

"From today on you will not kiss me. Not touch me in any intimate way. As far as the world is concerned our irreconcilable differences began today."

He swallowed with a nod. "I can live with that."

She sipped her wine, set the glass to the side.

Outside she noticed the lights of cars pulling into the drive. The last thing she wanted tonight was to deal with any of the Gardner clan.

She stood and started toward the stairs. When Michael followed, she shot him a look.

"Not sure where you're going, buddy. That couch looks mighty comfortable."

That stopped him in his tracks.

———

Zach walked to the park before jumping into his truck and driving home. He was twisted in so many knots he didn't know which way was up.

Loyalty to his brother hung over him like a suffocating blanket, and his attraction to Karen threatened to undo him every time they were in the same room. Not that he needed her to confirm what he'd already felt coming from her, but now that Karen had brought to words her desires, Zach wouldn't be able to pretend their chemistry wasn't there.

He was seriously screwed.

What had Karen meant when she said that Mike wouldn't have the opportunity to hurt her again? There had been one warning bell after the other going off in Zach's head since his trip to California. It was as if he was looking at one of those pictures within a picture and not seeing the intended image. If only he could sweep away all the garbage and peer inside Karen, he could determine what was going on.

Two blocks from his single-story two-bedroom home, he noticed Tracey's car parked outside his driveway.

Once again, with his attention focused on Karen, he'd forgotten all about Tracey. What a bastard he turned out to be. His temples started to throb when he realized it was time to end things with her. She deserved someone's full attention, not his half-assed consideration.

Tracey sat on one of the deck chairs on his front porch.

"Hey?" he greeted her as he walked up his drive.

She said nothing, and gave a sad smile.

"I didn't see you at the park."

She looked beyond him and blinked a few times. "I was there. I saw you."

"Why didn't you . . ."

"Someone else had your complete attention, Zach."

He wanted to play dumb but didn't want to insult Tracey's intelligence. "There was some family drama to deal with."

She closed her eyes and shook her head. "You haven't been the same since you went to California."

Zach leaned against the pillar supporting the overhang on the porch and studied his shoes. "I've considered uprooting my life," he told her. "Maybe moving out of Hilton."

She paused then asked, "Does this have anything to do with her?"

He froze, not willing to admit to anyone his thoughts about Karen.

"I don't know what game you're playing, Zach. Or why you've picked your brother's wife to play it with, but I do know you're playing with fire."

She was right, but he felt like a man stuck in quicksand who desperately reached for a faraway branch even though he knew his movements were going to hasten his death. The draw to Karen was that powerful. It defied reason and threatened everything he'd ever believed in.

"I'm not playing a game." No. It was more like someone was playing a game with him. "I do know that I've not been fair to you."

Tracey's eyes met his and waited. She wasn't going to make this easy on him, and why should she?

"I don't think it's been working with us for a while. I thought with time my feelings would deepen, but they haven't." That was the honest truth. With or without the presence of Karen, he and Tracey weren't meant to be.

"So that's it?"

Please don't make this ugly.

"What do you want me to say?"

"Nearly a year of my life and you don't have feelings for me?" Her tone grew short.

"I care for you, Tracey. Just not on the level I think I should."

"Great." She pushed off the chair and stood in front of him.

He glanced into her hurt eyes. "I'm sorry."

Her jaw tightened. "I'd like to say something kind, like have a nice life, or it was fun while it lasted . . . but I don't really have it in me."

She marched across his yard, jumped in her car, and slammed the door before driving away.

He rubbed the tension from his forehead and opened his eyes to find his neighbor across the street staring at him.

Zach acknowledged him with a wave and ducked into his house for some much-needed peace and quiet.

Chapter Thirteen

Michael had seriously fucked up and deserved any possible rage Karen bestowed upon him. He didn't think it was possible to act with such complete and utter neglect of another person's feelings, but that was exactly what had happened.

Michael punched his pillow a few times, turned it over, and tried to get comfortable on the worn-out sofa his parents had purchased sometime in the 1980s.

When Karen had approached him in the park, he'd been on a reunion high with his old friends. Seeing the only lover he'd taken in Hilton in the mix added just the right amount of nostalgia to help him lower his guard. He never worried that Ryder would open his mouth about their sexuality. To do so would be to put a target on his back as well, and since he now taught at the high school, Michael knew there wasn't a threat of his secret leaking.

Michael had felt like he was eighteen again. No stress of the studios breathing down his neck, no one telling him how he was supposed to act and when, and then Karen enlightened him on Aunt Belle's observation.

He'd seen red. After all the trouble he'd gone through to keep his secret he wasn't about to let the ramblings of his crazy aunt blow it. When he noticed several sets of eyes on him, he pulled Karen into his arms and kissed her. Fuck if he'd be found out by his own family. Fear of being found out and anger over his inability to control other people's thoughts fueled his actions. When Karen pinched him and thrust herself from his arms something inside him died.

He knew he'd hurt her. Saw the raw pain in her eyes before she ran away.

He wanted to run after her but knew in doing so he'd just draw more attention to them. What could he say to her to make it OK? Nothing. He knew he'd crossed a line.

Michael replayed the scene in his head, tried to fix the outcome so that he didn't come out to be such an ass. It didn't work.

He *was* an ass.

Giving up on sleep, he sat up and rested his head in his hands.

Heavy footfalls walked down the old stairs in his childhood home. He didn't need to turn to know who it was.

His father released a dramatic sigh as he stepped around the couch to take up space in what had always been *his* chair. After clicking the light to his side one time, the room took on a slight glow.

Michael wasn't sure if there was a lecture in store, or painful silence. Perhaps both.

"I've tried getting your mother to replace that couch for twenty years," Sawyer said as he placed both his hands over his overweight abdomen. He wasn't obese by any means, but he'd always carried a good twenty extra pounds. When Michael was a kid, the weight intimidated him. Now it just looked unhealthy. "You know what she says to me when I suggest we go shopping?"

Michael shook his head.

"Says the couch is fine for sitting. Leaves a lot to be desired for sleeping, and I should work hard to avoid making her angry so I'm not forced to use it as a bed."

Michael felt a smile on his lips despite the fact he didn't deserve to grin. "Mom's a smart woman."

They sat in silence for a while, then Sawyer started talking. "When you, Zach, and Rena were still either in diapers or just in school, I spent more nights on that couch than I care to admit. Maybe it was the stress of taking care of little ones, or maybe I worked too much away from home, but I couldn't go a month without visiting that spring in the middle."

Michael had only been trying to sleep there for an hour and already he knew the spring his father spoke of intimately.

"Think Mom will let me buy her a new couch for her birthday?"

His dad laughed. "She'll probably put the new couch in our room and keep this lumpy thing out here."

After a few quiet moments, his dad asked, "Are you and Karen going to be OK?"

Karen's words swam in his head. *As far as the world is concerned, our irreconcilable differences began today.* No use pretending otherwise.

"I screwed up pretty bad, Dad."

"All marriages have ups and downs."

Michael shook his head. "This is different."

Sawyer's confidence fell. "Do you wanna talk about it?"

Sure Dad . . . how about I just tell you I'm gay? My marriage is a farce, and I may have just fucked up my only real friend in my life.

"Not particularly."

Sawyer removed himself from his chair. "You know where I am."

Emotion clogged Michael's throat. He couldn't remember the last time he'd shared this many civil words with his father.

Before Sawyer walked up the stairs, he turned and delivered one more piece of advice. "There's no shame in a little groveling."

Michael smiled. "I'll keep that in mind."

The dream took hold and didn't let go.

"If I turned around right now I'd want to kiss you." Please . . . kiss me. Take away the question of what you taste like from my mind and swallow me whole.

Zach's hand clasped her shoulders as they stared over Beacon's pond, and then . . . as if he couldn't control himself, he turned her around, shoved a hand into her hair, and took her lips. She pressed into him, let his pine scent seep into her every pore. His desperate kisses were wet, indecent, and so filled with need Karen didn't want them to ever end.

Zach backed her up against a tree, leaned into her.

On some level, Karen knew she was dreaming. Lingering thoughts of Michael drifted in her brain . . . made her heart ache. She shouldn't be kissing his brother.

Or letting Zach touch her.

You're dreaming, *her mind screamed.*

But I want this, *her conscience reminded her.*

Need quickened. Her breath lodged in her throat, and when Zach reached between her legs . . .

Karen shot up in bed, her heart pounded behind her rib cage.

A dream.

Damn!

She flopped back on the squeaky childhood bed once occupied by Michael, kicked off the hot covers, and tried to go back to sleep.

There was a back staircase to the Gardner family home, which gave Karen the perfect escape the next morning for her run.

She needed the peace as well as time alone to make a much-needed phone call to someone who knew the hell she was going through.

She slipped from the house wearing running shorts and plugged her ears into her music on her cell phone. With a brisk pace, she made her way to Beacon's barn and went ahead and turned down the road to the abandoned home she'd passed the day before with Zach.

Once she was sure there wasn't a soul for miles, she speed-dialed Gwen's number and hoped she was up and ready for Karen to unload.

Gwen's cheerful voice brought a smile to Karen's face. "Karen? How are you?"

"I suck. That's how I am. Oh, God, Gwen . . ."

"Oh, no. What happened?"

"Coming here was a mistake." On so many levels.

"Is Michael's family awful?"

Karen rubbed the back of her neck. "No. They're actually really nice. His sister Judy and I really hit it off. Even his younger sister, Hannah, is crazy fun."

"And his parents?"

She couldn't even complain about them. "I thought at first his dad and I would fight the whole time but even he seems to have mellowed. And his mom, Janice, is the quintessential mother."

Gwen cleared her throat. "And Zach?"

Karen groaned.

"Ah! So Zach is the problem."

"I'm an awful person, Gwen. Tell me how horrible I am to be dreaming of the man."

Gwen didn't deliver the much-needed reprimand. "Sorry, my dear, but you won't be getting that from me. I noticed him watching you at the party. I'm guessing he is still looking."

"He's looking. I'm looking."

"I knew this would become sticky," Gwen said. "Does Michael know you're having horizontal dreams about his brother?"

"Who said I'm having sex dreams?"

Gwen laughed. "I don't believe I said sex dreams. But thank you for clarifying."

"Ah! No! Michael doesn't know. Not that he deserves to, the asshat." She went on to tell Gwen about the previous day and the line Michael had crossed.

"That doesn't sound like our Michael at all."

Karen plopped down on the edge of a rock as she talked into her phone. "No, it doesn't. Which is the only reason I'm still here. I think he's having his own identity crisis. Having his family and old friends around has been good for him. He hasn't even asked if Tony has called."

"I never have envied him. Seems his entire life is a farce."

"Yeah, well, right now so is mine." Maybe Karen was having an identity crisis of her own.

"How much longer will you stay in Hilton?" Gwen asked.

"A week. There's a parade tomorrow and then we're going up to the cabin for a couple of days. Even Sawyer is taking time off work, which apparently is a rarity."

"You lost me at parade."

Karen laughed. "Hilton celebrates its Founder's Day with a parade and fireworks. Hannah and Judy have been putting together a float of some sort for Michael to ride in. Hilton's claim to fame will be waving to the crowd."

"Oh, that's rich. Will you be on the float with him?"

"Hell no. He can have the spotlight all to himself. Besides, it's not like I want this town to know me more than they do right now. I won't be Mrs. Michael Wolfe or Gardner . . . or whatever next year at this time."

"I suppose that's for the best. Unless of course your sex dreams about Zach manifest into something more than a fantasy."

Karen squeezed her eyes shut and ignored the heat that rushed to her face with the mention of intimacy with Zach. "You're not helping, Gwen."

She giggled and Karen imagined Gwen tossing her long hair over her shoulder. "I'd apologize but we both know I'm not sorry. Taboo sex is the best sex of all."

"I haven't had sex in so long I forgot the mechanics of it."

They both laughed. "It's like riding a bike and all that. One never forgets. Though the longer you go without the better it's likely to be when you're back in the game. And Michael's brother is rather sexy."

"Aren't you married?"

Gwen couldn't stop laughing. "And satisfied on more levels than is proper to say into a phone, but we both know your paper marriage has left you frustrated for over a year. And if I'm not mistaken you didn't have even a one-night anything for months prior to slipping on Michael's ring."

Karen didn't need to be reminded. "I really did need you to tell me to keep my distance, Gwen. If anything happened between Zach and me, we'd both feel remorse on colossal levels. I may know that I'm not cheating on my husband, but Zach wouldn't. What kind of woman sleeps with her husband's brother? And what kind of brother goes after his sister-in-law?" No matter how she looked at the situation, the outcome was bad.

"Matters of the heart are not dictated by societal restrictions, Karen."

She didn't need Gwen to tell her that. She'd been married to a homosexual man for a year because of societal views.

"Doesn't change the facts. If I did anything right now to jeopardize Michael's secret, I'd never forgive myself. I love him too much."

"What if Michael were to give his blessing?"

"That isn't going to happen unless he tells his family about the entire arrangement. After yesterday, I don't see that happening."

Gwen sighed. "I suppose you're right."

"I know I am."

"Can you promise me something?"

Karen glanced toward the white fluffy clouds in the sky and cursed such a perfect day. "Sure."

"Promise me if anything does happen between you and Zach that you won't hate yourself for it."

"Nothing is going to happen."

"Good intentions aside, if something did—"

"I can't let it happen." God knew she'd already gone there in her head and the experience had been fabulous. The fallout, however, was a bitch . . . even in her dreams.

"Be true to yourself, Karen. You know where I am should you need me."

Karen counted her blessings for having such a great friend. "Thanks. Say hi to everyone."

Nolan had shown up ten minutes early and eagerly jumped into whatever Zach wanted him to do. Zach hadn't bothered approaching his father for more hours for the kid. Working retail was fine if you owned the business or had another source of income. It wasn't something that would sustain Nolan in life. With Zach, Nolan would learn a trade that could support a family.

After listening to Karen's concerns about Nolan and his girlfriend, Becky, he couldn't walk away from these two kids' problems. Not that Zach needed to invite any more issues into his life.

After breaking up with Tracey and fantasizing about Karen all night, Zach only managed a few hours' sleep. He had to put in a full workday considering the entire job site would shut down for the Founder's Day festivities on the next.

His second-in-command, Buck Foster, was going to keep an eye on things over the next several days in Zach's absence. The Gardner family routinely vacationed together up at the cabin after Founder's Day. Sometimes they spent an entire week up in the forest. Other times they'd scrape together only a handful of days. With Michael joining them for the first time in years, it should be something to celebrate.

Only Zach was dreading it.

He knew that if he witnessed Michael so much as lay a finger on Karen in a harmful way, he'd flatten his Hollywood profile to teach him some manners. Zach wanted to believe Karen when she told him that Michael had never treated her poorly in the past. But he couldn't be too sure. Something about his brother was off and he had yet to figure out what.

Then there was Karen herself. How the hell was he going to sleep in the same room with her only feet away? The cabin was communal. There was a huge loft upstairs where for years they'd all dropped into their bunks at the end of the day. The only bedroom was on the main floor and that was his parents' sanctuary. Up until Zach had obtained his contractor's license, there had been only one bathroom. But with so many women under one roof, he wasn't about to leave the cabin with one shower. They owned over a hundred acres at the top of the mountain and Zach had considered more than once to build a second structure. Now that Rena and Joe's family was expanding, the cabin felt smaller and smaller.

Maybe he'd bring a tent . . . just in case.

"Where did you find this kid?" Buck asked as the two of them were visually inspecting the latest supply shipment that had come in that morning.

"He works for my dad. Just graduated from high school."

"I thought I recognized him. He's eager."

Zach glanced over and noticed Nolan lugging an armload of two-by-fours. "I can see that. What we need to see is if he has the ability to learn."

"I paired him with Sean. We'll figure out how he is with framing."

Zach nodded. "Good idea. Let me know if there are any problems. He still has hours he has to work at my dad's, so see if we can keep him going here part-time."

Zach checked the invoice order numbers against the pallets of kitchen hardware.

"How is it with your brother in town?" Buck asked.

Zach tried to separate his brother and Karen in his head in order to answer the question.

"I'm looking forward to getting him away from his adoring fans in town." And he was, he decided.

"Gotta get him off his own personal float first. I hear the mayor has the road sign ready to unveil tomorrow morning."

He'd forgotten all about that. All across the country, small-town America celebrated its stars with freeway signs that boasted things like HILTON, UTAH, HOME OF MICHAEL WOLFE, hoping to draw in tourist dollars. Hilton was taking the opportunity to bestow such a sign on Mike.

"His ego can handle it." At least Zach hoped it could.

Buck pushed into another pallet to check his set of numbers. "I hear his wife is hot."

Did he have to mention Karen?

"She is beautiful." He rubbed the back of his neck.

Buck cut through the cellophane that kept the boxes on the crate together with a grunt. "You know ... when he started doing those plays in high school several of us laid bets that he was gay."

Zach froze.

"Guess we were wrong about that." Buck ripped the packing slip away with a curse. "Dammit, I ripped off the number. What do you have?"

Zach shook his head, looked on his invoice, and repeated the numbers Buck asked for.

"Close enough."

Zach scratched his head, lost in his thoughts. "Yeah, close enough."

Chapter Fourteen

The flowers started arriving shortly after Karen stepped from the shower. She'd arrived back at the Gardner home to find Michael gone. She shouldn't have been surprised, but with his family eyeing her every move . . . all of them no doubt wondering what had transpired between them to warrant a night on the couch, she felt a little abandoned. The brat.

"Karen?" Judy yelled from downstairs.

She was just about to switch on the hair dryer when she heard her name called.

"You have a delivery."

She set the hair dryer aside and walked downstairs with the hairbrush in her hand. "Delivery?"

Judy stood beside a kid in his early twenties wearing a goofy smile and holding a bouquet of two dozen long-stemmed white roses. "Are you Karen?"

Flowers? Really Michael? "I am."

He offered a shy smile in Judy's direction and handed the roses to Karen.

"Oh, wow!" Hannah ran down the stairs.

If Michael thought a couple of dozen roses would sway her, he hadn't been paying attention. "You like 'em?" Karen asked Hannah while she plucked the small envelope from the stems to read later.

"I don't think I've seen that many roses in one vase."

The delivery boy turned to leave.

"Let me get a tip."

He waved her off. "It's all taken care of."

"Thank you," she said to the kid.

Before the door could close behind him, Karen turned to Hannah and thrust the roses into the teenager's hands. "For you."

Hannah gasped.

Judy said, "Whoa."

The delivery boy managed, "I haven't seen that before."

Karen skipped up the stairs and continued her morning routine.

Thirty minutes later the same delivery boy arrived again, this time with pink roses . . . again two dozen. Karen plucked the card, shoved the flowers in Judy's hands, and returned to her room.

When the doorbell rang a third time, Karen called to Janice, who was in the kitchen cooking food to last the family for a week. "Janice? You have a delivery." White lilies made a wonderful display on Janice's table.

By noon, Judy was on a first-name basis with Myles, the delivery boy who was apparently driving three towns over to the florist where he worked part-time in the summer. The house smelled like the floral house at the LA County Fair.

"Ms. Karen?" Myles said as he handed her his eleventh delivery that day.

"Yes, Myles?"

"I was kinda hoping to hook up with my friends tonight. But my instructions are to keep delivering flowers until *you* accept them." He shuffled his feet. "And I'm running out of gas."

Karen hid a laugh behind her hand. She glanced at the orchid bouquet she held and buried her nose in them for a sniff. "Well Myles, you can tell your boss that the orchids worked."

He sighed with relief. "Thank you."

Three sets of eyes watched her set the orchids next to Sawyer's chair. She pulled one stem from the bouquet and grinned.

"I think Mike is sorry for whatever he did," Hannah said.

Janice watched her with narrowed eyes.

"You're not going to keep any of them, are you?" Judy asked. "You just said that to Myles so he didn't have to keep coming back."

Karen pointed the flower in Judy's direction. "You're right."

Hannah puffed out her lower lip. "But why? I think if a boy sent me one bouquet I'd press each flower into a book forever."

"They're just flowers, Hannah."

"Thousands of dollars' worth of flowers," Judy pointed out.

Hannah glanced around the room. "Thousands? Really?"

"A dozen roses on their website are a hundred bucks." Obviously, Judy had used the time between deliveries to look stuff up. "Without delivery."

It was time to impart some older sister advice to the younger generation. Advice Karen had told more teens than she could count. She dropped into the couch and looked between Judy and Hannah. "Let me tell you how the male brain works. Men think sending flowers to a girl when they've done something to make you mad is their *get out of jail free* card. Lots of girls fall for it. So what does that tell the guy?"

Judy spoke first. "Means he can do whatever he wants and send flowers later and everything is good."

"Exactly. Apologies are only words until they are backed up with actions."

"But the flowers are nice," Hannah argued.

"I don't care if he sent diamonds. Though let's face it, diamonds don't die. It's still only words until time proves that Michael doesn't screw up again."

Karen caught Janice's smile from the doorway.

"What are you going to do with all the flowers if you don't keep them?"

A slow smile crept over her face. "Ever heard of the Rose Parade?"

———————

Karen held no guilt sitting on Millie's bench while licking an ice cream cone. Especially when she realized while on approach to said bench, it already had an occupant.

She made a quick sweep of the area around the bench to see if there was a bag big enough for a change of clothes. Confident that wasn't the case, Karen tucked in beside Becky with a smile.

"Hey."

"Hi," she said, lowering her eyes to the grass at her feet.

"It's Becky, right?"

The smile on Becky's face said she was pleased that Karen remembered.

"Yeah. I'm sorry. I don't remember your name."

Karen licked her ice cream to keep it from dripping in the hot Utah sun. "Karen. Though everyone in this town calls me Michael's wife. It's like I don't exist without him." Years of experience at getting kids to talk told her to open up with something personal to make the teen feel like he or she was special.

"Well, everyone here knows about Michael."

"Honey, I have news for you . . . everyone everywhere knows about Michael."

Becky released a small laugh, but the smile on her face didn't last long.

"It must be hard being married to someone so famous."

Karen pointed her ice cream in Becky's direction. "You know what? You're the first person in Hilton that's said that. Everyone keeps telling me how lucky I am, or how cool it must be. But you know what? It *is* hard. We can't go anywhere without someone taking pictures or poking into our personal life." Karen offered a not-so-fake laugh. "It's kinda like being in a small town where everyone knows what's going on with everyone. But you don't want every secret out there, so you try really hard to hide them. Eventually all the secrets come out."

"Some secrets stay hidden."

Karen thought about Michael. "I guess that's true. I guess that's why it's so important to have close friends . . . or maybe just one person you can tell your secrets to. Otherwise all those hidden facts clog up inside of you until they burst out in one big ugly mess."

Becky looked lost in her own thoughts.

"Just yesterday I told Michael something I hadn't told one other person my whole life. And you know what?" She didn't wait for Becky to answer. "It felt good."

"What if your secrets affect other people?"

Karen held her dripping ice cream away from both of them and gave up trying to eat it.

"Well, I guess it depends on the secret. I think if your BFF tells you she likes some guy, or she's kissing on him or . . . other things, then it might be a good idea if you kept that secret. But if you knew the BFF's kissing partner is really bad news, then keeping that secret might not be the best thing to do."

"But if you tell someone, then that BFF might not be your friend anymore."

Karen nodded. "That's the chance you take. But if she was a BFF in the first place, eventually she'll come around."

Karen wasn't sure how they'd gotten sidetracked on a conversation about keeping a best friend's secrets, but it seemed that Becky was thinking really hard and didn't look quite as depressed.

"Is there someone you can tell your secrets to?" Karen asked her.

Becky really was a pretty girl when she smiled. "Nolan. He listens to everything."

"That's nice." It made Karen feel better that the boy she was obviously in love with didn't elicit a flash of pain when Becky talked about him. "Where's Nolan now?"

"Oh, he's working. He got an extra job working for your brother-in-law . . . I mean Zach Gardner."

Oh, damn . . . he actually did it. How sweet was that? She needed to remember to thank Zach when she saw him.

"That's great."

"Yeah." Becky picked herself off Millie's bench and offered a smile. "Well, it was nice talking to you, Karen."

"You, too, Becky."

After the teenager walked away, Karen dropped her forgotten cone into the trash and ducked into Petra's salon.

"Mind if I wash my hands?"

Petra was sweeping hair from the floor. "Not at all."

Karen soaped up her hands and ran them under the faucet in the bathroom.

"How do you like Hilton?" Petra asked.

Karen stepped from the bathroom with a paper towel. "It's a little maddening, to tell the truth. I can't get over how small it is or how everyone knows everybody."

"That does take some time getting used to." Using a dustpan, Petra swept the hair up and into the trash. "I saw you talking with Becky."

"She's a sweet girl." Karen remembered Judy's observation about Petra not gossiping. That didn't mean the local hairdresser didn't know exactly what was going on. "Do you know her parents?"

"Her mom comes in a couple times a year. The father keeps to himself. Sees a barber in Monroe."

Just the facts.

Time to address what they'd both observed. "I wonder how she got those welts."

Instead of dismissing Karen's words, she said, "I asked her outright the first time I noticed them. She said she fell. Then she didn't come in for six months."

"How long ago was that?"

"Two years ago."

Long before Nolan.

Karen crossed to Petra's appointment book and grabbed the pen that was sitting there. "I have a feeling that Becky is going to need a couple of older and wiser women looking out for her very soon. If you see anything, please call me." She tapped on her phone number. "Day or night."

"You're planning on staying in Hilton for a while?"

Karen looked directly into Petra's eyes. "Some conditions are time sensitive."

The hairdresser shook her head. "That's what I thought, too."

Neither of them had to voice their assumption to know they were on the same page.

Karen abandoned Hannah and Judy to their task of decorating a float worthy of the Rose Parade and took a stroll down Main Street. The patriotism of the town was on display everywhere. Flags with the names of the young men and women who'd dedicated themselves to a branch of the service were flown over every light post. American flags hung from every business, and not one storefront said it would be open on Founder's Day.

Hilton took *their* day seriously. *Wonder what the Fourth of July is like?*

She passed on the other side of the street from Sawyer's hardware store but didn't bother stopping in. Remembering Nolan's new job, Karen removed her cell phone and sent Zach a quick text.

Thanks for giving Nolan a job.

Her phone buzzed in her hand a few seconds later.

He's a good kid.

"Hey?"

Karen turned to see Michael jogging across the street to catch up with her. "Hey yourself."

He glanced around them. "I-I went by the house."

Karen spread her arms wide. "I'm not there."

The worry on his face started to soften hers. "I'm not good at this part, Karen."

"Well let me give you a hint. Flowers don't fix anything."

"I shouldn't have sent flowers?"

"I didn't say that. I said they don't fix anything." She noticed a couple walk out of the soda shop and turn to stare at them. Karen started to walk in the opposite direction of the gawking eyes.

"So I should send flowers?" Poor guy was growing more confused by the second.

"Flowers, fancy gifts . . . jewelry doesn't suck. But none of that fixes."

He walked beside her and asked, "What does?"

"Time without a repeat performance."

"I can tell you that it won't. But those are just words."

"Now you're catching on."

"My dad advised me to grovel."

Karen chuckled. "Smart dad."

"What does groveling look like to you?"

She stopped walking. He took two steps in front of her before he realized she wasn't beside him. His eyes met hers. "Well?"

Karen rolled her eyes. "Flowers, fancy gifts, and jewelry, helloooo?" It was hard to keep her expression stoic, especially when Michael started to grin.

Karen stepped around him and continued down the street in silence.

He tucked his hands into his pockets. "I'm still sleeping on the couch, aren't I?"

She patted him on the back. "You know, Mikey Gardner, you're a real fast learner."

He grumbled and now she did laugh.

"That couch is uncomfortable."

"Sucks to be you."

They walked to the end of town and turned to make their way back to the Gardner home.

"I really am sorry," he whispered. His eyes never left the road in front of them.

"I know you are."

Chapter Fifteen

Founder's Day was serious freaking business in Hilton. Families staked their claim on Main Street a couple of hours before the parade with chairs that spilled out onto the road. Watching the town set up for a parade wasn't so much the shock as the amount of people who started to pile in.

Karen leaned over to where Janice was setting up chairs in the space in front of the hardware store. "Where are they all coming from?"

Janice glanced up into the crowd. "Twenty miles in all directions. You'd be hard-pressed to find anyone from Hilton staying home today, unless they're sick."

Karen felt more than one set of eyes on her. A common occurrence whenever Michael was around. Only here the kind people of Hilton tried to hide their curiosity.

Rena waved while pushing a stroller carrying Susie, while Joe had Eli on his shoulders to see above the crowd. "Hey, Mom."

"Hey, honey."

Rena and Joe both said hello to Karen as they tucked the stroller between the folding chairs. Rena and Joe both took turns offering hugs in greeting.

"Where's Zach and Tracey?" Janice asked her daughter.

Karen glanced down the street, trying not to pay too close attention to the mention of Zach.

"Not sure where Zach is, but don't expect Tracey."

"Oh? Why not?"

"You didn't hear?" Rena asked in a way that attracted Karen's attention.

"Hear what?"

"They broke up."

Janice's shoulders slumped with the news and Karen felt three shades of awful for feeling a lift in her chest. Not that she had any reason to be happy for Zach's breakup . . .

Oh, who was she kidding?

Tracey wasn't right for him.

Like I know the woman enough to make that judgment.

You're awful, Karen. Awful!

She knew, on some level, that she was part of the reason for the split. Zach didn't seem like the kind of guy to lead one woman on while being attracted to another.

What must he think of her? The fact that she could even be drawn into someone else's orbit while being married must make her look horrific.

"Karen? Karen?"

She shook the fog and questions from her head and realized Rena was talking to her.

"Yeah?"

"I asked why you're not on the float with Mike?"

She lifted both hands in acute denial. "Not my gig. Hannah and Judy were more than happy to jump on board."

"It's better down here anyway. I think I've marched in this thing at least a half a dozen times," Rena said.

Janice sat in the chair closest to her granddaughter and corrected Rena. "You marched for six years in a row with the Girl

Scouts, then again with the high school marching band, and at least two more times with either Zach or Mike."

"Is there anyone in this town who hasn't marched or rode?"

"Nope. Even Sawyer has driven the route a time or two, and I was the den mom for Rena's troop for a couple of years and had to ride with them."

Who knew participating in a parade would be a family affair?

"There you are." Joe's voice had Karen swinging around to see who he greeted.

Zach offered her a warm smile and shook Joe's hand. "Didn't think I'd miss it, did you?"

Joe rolled his eyes.

Zach hugged his sister, leaned down, and kissed his mother's cheek. When he turned to Karen and said hello, she stepped into what might look like an impersonal hug, but it felt like so much more. His arms were strong, the pine scent of his skin would linger if he could hold her for just a moment longer, but he pulled away nearly as quickly as he entered her arms. Though a soft squeeze of her arm let her know that he wanted more.

"Where's Dad?"

"He'll be along," Janice said. Then she lowered her voice. "I'm sorry to hear about Tracey."

Zach drew in a breath and looked directly at Karen. "Stuff happens."

Janice continued. "I thought you two were . . ."

"We weren't." Zach blinked his gaze away.

Karen twisted in the opposite direction and waved at Petra, who watched them from the other side of the street.

"Are you all packed for the cabin?" Joe asked.

"If that's your way of asking if the liquid is ready for the red cups, then yes."

"Hey, I'm asking about the bikes. But good thinking."

They settled into the chairs and talked about the trip to the cabin while the parade route began to clear.

Children lined up with bags in eager anticipation of the candy that would be tossed to them from those in the parade.

There was a PA system set up along the parade route, which crackled out patriotic music. "Do you guys do this all over again on the Fourth of July?" Karen asked.

"We sure do. Any reason to party." Rena laughed at the insaneness of it. "Pathetic, isn't it?"

"I don't know. It's wholesome and not completely commercial." There were a few vendors running around selling Founder's Day merchandise, but most of the vendors were charity organizations raising money to support themselves.

The PA squeaked and the music abruptly turned off.

A rough voice called into the crowd. "We're about to begin, can everyone please stand for the Pledge of Allegiance."

Flags flew everywhere, and soon the formalities were out of the way and the trucks pulling flatbed trailers started the slow pace down the two miles of Main Street.

Rena tugged Susie from the stroller right as Sawyer emerged from the crowd and took the seat next to Janice. Karen sat at the end of their group and Zach took the seat next to her.

Don't look at him. Don't look at him.

But damn he was gorgeous to look at. He always had just a hint of stubble on his face, which gave him an edge of uncertainty. It said, *I know it's sexy and wouldn't you love it if I roughed up your skin with mine?*

Zach shifted his eyes to hers and she quickly looked away.

Don't stare, Karen!

A line of tractors made its way through first. One was as tall as most of the buildings along Main Street, while the others ranged from a glorified riding lawn mower to the standard issue seen on most farms.

Zach leaned over. "There are a lot of farms in the area."

"I can see that."

People waved and kids chased candy into the streets.

Rena's old Girl Scout troop marched by, followed closely by the Boy Scouts. Now it was Karen's turn to impart wisdom. "I see the boys are all chasing the girls."

Zach acknowledged with a wink that shot straight to her belly.

After the third flatbed rolled by Karen called out her observation. "I take it American made trucks are the only ones allowed in the parade." There were Fords, Dodges, and Chevys but not one Toyota anywhere.

"You got it," Joe called from the other side of Zach.

The next Ford that passed had a sticker on it from the dealership. In the window was a sign that read: GET A FREE GUN WITH PURCHASE OF THIS TRUCK. If that wasn't a testament to the small town, she didn't know what was. There were Junior Miss Monroe floats, Junior Miss Hilton floats, and Class of 1993 with the high school colors on the truck drove by, too.

In the center of the parade, Michael's "float" slowly made its way.

Karen removed her cell phone from her pocket to snap a picture. Hannah and Judy had outdone themselves with spreading all the flowers he'd had delivered the day before. The crowd cheered on the famous son, and Michael tossed candy and waved with his huge Hollywood smile.

Surrounding his float were a handful of what Karen assumed were friends of Hannah's and Judy's who walked around handing out roses to the older women lining the streets. There were plenty of *isn't that sweet*, and *how nice* comments as his float puttered by.

Hannah and Judy jumped off the float and hand delivered flowers to both Janice and Rena. Then Judy handed Karen a gift box and laughed.

The whole family glanced at her as she opened the velvet-lined jewelry box. Inside was a white gold bangle with two rows of small diamonds. It really was pretty but nothing at all like something she would wear. She did, however, know someone who wore exactly this kind of jewelry. Karen glanced at Michael and offered a little wave.

"Hey, Rena. Michael has something for you." Then with a grand gesture, Karen handed the box over Zach's and Joe's laps and gave Rena Michael's gift.

Michael gave her a playful smile and shook a finger in her direction before the float continued on.

"My God, Karen, I can't take this."

"Sure you can."

Zach was watching her, as was Joe. Janice just smiled and acted as if Karen giving away Michael's gifts was an everyday occurrence. Sawyer, if Karen wasn't mistaken, was trying to hide a laugh.

Rena tried to hand it back. "I can't."

Karen brushed against Zach as she pushed it back. "If you don't take it, I'll just give it to someone else. I think Hannah's a little young for it . . . Judy might want it, though."

"But Mike . . ."

"Michael knows I won't keep it. Trust me. He'd want you to have it."

Rena gave up on the argument, placed the pricey *I'm sorry* gift on her wrist, and stuck her arm out in front of her to admire it.

Once their party tuned back in to the rest of the parade, Zach's lips hovered close to her ear. "What was that all about?"

"Gifts to say you're sorry don't work with me."

Zach craned his neck to see the tail end of Michael's float. "Is that what all those flowers were about?"

"Yep."

Karen couldn't help the smile on her face.

———

Zach kept a slight distance from Karen the rest of the day.

Mike, Hannah, and Judy joined them after the parade was over, only to usher them all to the courtyard outside the park. There, the mayor of Hilton presented the road sign that would go up on the highway a quarter mile before the exit.

Zach actually thought his brother looked uncomfortable when they unveiled the sign. HILTON, UTAH . . . CHILDHOOD HOME OF MICHAEL WOLFE . . . stood out in bold letters.

Someone from the school newspaper snapped a couple of pictures, then Karen asked that the entire family gather around the sign with Mike so she could get a shot.

"You should be in here, too," Hannah said to her.

Karen wouldn't have it and insisted that Mike and the rest of them scoot in close.

They walked around the town and shopped with several local vendors who painted or did some kind of artsy craft. Every so often, Zach would feel a set of eyes on him and he'd turn to find Karen watching him.

What he found interesting was how Mike was seldom by her side. He'd laugh beside her and then easily be drawn away. Zach had overheard Mike tell Rena that the bracelet looked good on her, reinforcing Karen's words about how he hadn't expected Karen to keep it. After watching the two of them with each other for over an hour, Zach then focused on Joe and Rena.

They juggled the kids between the two of them, but would often hold hands or sneak in a little kiss now and then. Even his father dropped his arm around his mother's shoulders from time to time.

Zach guessed that maybe the fight between the Mike and Karen had caused the rift, but the more he thought about it, the less he remembered if they *ever* interacted like a loving couple.

They didn't, but they also didn't act as if they were a bickering couple.

So what did that leave?

Zach wasn't sure, but he'd figure out what was going on between the two of them while they were up at the cabin. Observing from the sidelines was one thing . . . living with them would be completely different.

Chapter Sixteen

The road to the cabin wasn't paved. In fact, it seemed to Karen that the next several days of her Utah vacation were either going to be organic to the point of dust-filled hair or in traction from the ride alone. In comparison to the vacations she'd had in the past couple of years, this was just this side of backpacking it in the high country of the Sierras.

Joe drove Rena and the kids up in one truck while filling the back of his rig with most of their luggage and food supplies. Zach drove another truck pulling a trailer with a couple of quads and motorcycles. Hannah and Judy tagged along with their older brother while Karen and Michael rode with Sawyer and Janice.

"Did you ever camp as a kid?" Janice asked Karen once they turned onto the dirt road.

"No."

"This isn't camping," Sawyer pointed out. "It's a cabin with a roof and a bathroom. Not exactly roughing it."

Michael glanced at her. "Compared to LA, it's like pitching a tent."

"I'm not a shrinking violet," she reminded him. "I've pitched tents with the kids at the center more than once."

"That's kind of like camping," Janice snuck in.

Karen gave her mother-in-law a doubtful look. "Not really. A full kitchen, bathroom . . . everything was only feet away. It was more of a change of venue for the kids."

"You spend a lot of time with the kids at the Boys and Girls Club?"

Michael snorted. "If Karen was paid for her time, she'd be rich."

Karen giggled and Sawyer watched the two of them through the rearview mirror.

"I love it. At some point I want to open a center for runaways."

Janice turned from the front seat. "Why not do that now?"

Karen glanced at Michael. "It's not quite the right time. But someday. There are plenty of kids who need help that slip through the system because they don't have a place to sleep at night. Many of them travel to a place like LA thinking they're going to walk down Hollywood Boulevard, meet a producer who says they have the 'perfect look' for the part in the next blockbuster, and strike it big. But it takes a hell of a lot more than that to make it in LA."

Michael huffed out a breath. "You can say that again."

Karen tapped her fingers on his knee. The gesture so normal for her it was like breathing.

Michael smiled in her direction. "Poor kids need to worry about predators, con artists . . . any number of shitty personalities."

"Not to mention drugs and sex for hire."

Janice actually cringed. "We worried about all that when you were in college," Janice told her son.

"I wasn't a runaway," Michael reminded his mother. "And I'd had over a year and a half of college before landing my first role."

"You were still young," Sawyer said.

Michael nodded and seemed lost in his own thoughts. "I guess I was."

"But you were so confident in what you were doing. And once

that first movie came along, your father and I knew you'd never go back to school."

"School wasn't going to help me in what I wanted to do," Michael said.

Karen couldn't help but feel that the conversation was a first for Michael and his parents. Had they ever really talked openly about his choice in profession? Maybe on some disjointed level over the phone . . . but not this, not cooped up in a car on a dusty road up to a cabin.

"We worried Mike would end up like those kids you talked about. Such a stressful time for us," Janice admitted.

"My first film made me a ton of money, Mom."

"And for all we knew there was someone there taking it from you. Being a parent is hard work. Letting your children make their own choices . . . it's not easy."

"I've always thought you were disappointed." The words seemed to escaped Michael's lips before he realized what he said.

Janice swiveled in her seat. "We were scared, Mike . . . not disappointed."

Karen made a point to look at Sawyer's face when Janice spoke. He didn't say anything, but she could tell by his tiny glances in the rearview mirror that he felt the same.

Karen squeezed Michael's knee and felt his hand cover hers.

The cabin nestled between a backdrop of pine trees and a massive meadow in front. A crystal blue lake stretched out several hundred feet from the cabin and meandered beyond the road.

"It's beautiful up here," Karen observed aloud.

"We don't get up here nearly as much as we should," Janice said.

"Zach and I made it up here a lot when we were teenagers."

"What a fabulous escape." Karen would love to have had a place like this to run to when she was a kid.

Sawyer pulled his truck alongside the others and everyone piled out. The crisp air was at least fifteen degrees cooler than that down in Hilton. Karen couldn't help but toss her arms wide and suck in the freshness of the open space. "My lungs aren't going to know what to do with all this clean air."

"Maybe we can convince you both to visit more often." Janice's words reminded Karen that this would probably be her one and only visit, a sobering thought.

The inside of the cabin smelled as all closed-in wooden structures do. A mixture of moisture, dust, and oak made Karen think of spiders and possible unwanted four-legged vermin.

Janice and Rena strode into the cabin and began opening all the windows to let the light in and the air out. Hannah took the stairs to what Karen assumed was the sleeping loft, and soon the mountain breeze could be felt in the middle of the giant open room.

"Girls are on the right and boys are on the left!" Hannah yelled from upstairs.

Eli ran up the stairs with his backpack and Joe set up a playpen for Susie on the front porch. After a few trips back and forth to the trucks, each one with armloads of supplies, food, and luggage, Karen finally made it upstairs to see where they'd be sleeping. It was like sixth grade camp all over again. Only instead of the boys being in cabins across the lake, they were in the same room with only a curtain separating the sexes.

Eli had tucked a personal blanket around what looked like a stuffed alligator into a small bunk and sat next to said alligator to talk to him.

"Eat spiders, Nate."

Hannah ran downstairs and Karen found herself alone with Eli. Not that she minded. She'd always loved kids, even the small ones.

Karen sat on the edge of the bed closest to Eli's and asked, "Does Nate eat the spiders?"

Eli's eyes grew wide when he gave an enthusiastic nod. "Yeah."

"Oh, well when he's done eating the spiders can he eat them on our side of the room? I don't like spiders either."

Eli's big deer-in-the-headlight eyes blinked several times before he shoved his chubby little hand into his backpack and removed another stuffed friend. This one was a small cat. He looked at the cat, then to Nate and apparently decided that the alligator would do a better job of protecting him from spiders so then he handed the stuffed animal to Karen.

She couldn't help but think poor Eli was giving up his backup plan; she decided to make a game of the spider worry.

"That's a very nice cat. What's his name?"

"Kitty."

"That's a great name. Appropriate, too."

Eli smiled.

Karen stood and wandered to her side of the huge room and looked around as if inspecting the most likely place for a spider to hide.

Truth was she had seen those awful B movies when she was a kid about giant spiders, or those who killed with one bite . . . or covered the entire house just dying to get in to kill the humans . . . spiders rated up there with birds, and she didn't really want to think about birds right now and freak poor Eli out more than he already was.

"Where do you think Kitty will do the best job?"

Eli jumped off his bunk while hugging Kitty to his chest. He looked behind the bunks and mimicked whatever Karen did. She searched around the curtains, noticed a few dead eight-legged prey, and quickly lowered the shades back to their original place.

She made a show of scratching her head and moving back to Eli's side of the room.

"I think maybe it would be best to keep Kitty close to the stairs," she told the toddler. The stairs were close to his bunk and her words brought a smile to his lips. "Cuz everyone knows that spiders love to climb stairs, but he can get 'em before they make it to the top."

Eli shook his head as if Karen was the wisest person on the earth and looked around for the perfect spot to place Kitty.

Once he was happy with Kitty's placement, he jumped back over to his bunk and removed several toys from his backpack. Noise from downstairs drifted up, but it sounded as if the majority of the family was outside.

Karen glanced over and found Zach standing on the top step watching the two of them.

Their eyes locked. Chills ran up her arms and her breath quickened.

The soft smile Zach bestowed threatened to break her. The want, which reached much further than desire, pulled at her with his eyes.

The magnetic pull of Zach threatened to undo her resolve of indifference. She forced her eyes away from his and focused on the pint-size occupant in the room.

From nowhere, moisture gathered behind her eyes. She sucked in her bottom lip and bit it gently to force the tears away. This week was going to be the hardest one of her life.

"Wow, Eli . . . great thinking putting that cat up here. I saw a spider running down the stairs on my way up. Must be halfway to Hilton by now." Zach made his way into the loft space.

Eli forgot his other toys and ran over to where Uncle Zach stood and stared down the stairs. Then he picked up his chin and walked . . . hugging the wall, down to the main floor and out of sight.

"He really doesn't like spiders."

"That makes two of us," Karen admitted.

She moved to her bunk and tried to put distance between her and Zach.

"You're really good with kids."

"Kids are great. Full of innocence and wonder at Eli's age . . . discovery and questions when they're older."

From the corner of her eye, she noted Zach's questioning gaze. Instead of leaving the quiet between them for long, she said, "Thanks for giving Nolan a job."

"You already thanked me."

She remembered the text. "Well, thanks again."

The room grew quiet. Downstairs was void of noise, and outside she heard the sound of a quad, or maybe it was a motorcycle, turning over.

"We should probably go outside . . . join everyone." Yet her legs stuck in place and her eyes found his again. She drank him in with one long gulp and then forced herself around him and down the stairs.

Note to self. Don't stay in room alone with Zach for more than two sentences.

This was going to be a very long week.

———

Zach watched her run away.

First he'd found her pining over Eli like a woman with a ticking biological clock without a mate, and second he'd seen the vulnerability in her eyes when she noticed him watching her. He'd seen the unease in her eyes when it was only the two of them in the room, knew she felt the energy between them that would register on a Geiger counter.

Then she ran.

As if she didn't trust herself.

Damn if he wasn't willing to test her. As every hour ticked by with her in the same county, he felt the chemical draw.

He'd learned from his younger sisters on the way up the mountain that Mike had been sleeping on the couch, but neither sister saw one bit of animosity between the newlyweds.

In Zach's brain, he'd contemplated one possibility. Could his brother be gay?

The first reaction was hell no. He was married, which proved he wasn't gay.

Or did it? As much as the deception of it bothered him, Zach decided to watch the interaction between Karen and Mike with the thought of his brother not having any sexual interest in his wife.

There were differences between people who were attracted to each other and those who weren't. Which were they? Close friends or lovers?

Zach jogged down the stairs and out the front door of the cabin and focused on his target. Karen walked alongside Hannah and Judy as they both made their way down to the water's edge. Mike knelt down next to the little 50 on which they had both learned how to ride motorcycles when they were Eli's age.

"Zach?" Mike waved him over. "I seem to remember there being some kind of trick to turning this thing over."

The bike brought back a swarm of great memories. Sticky clutch and all. Zach fiddled with the clutch, went through a couple of attempts before the 50 roared to life. Eli came running with his little head stuffed into a helmet. Joe walked up behind his son with a huge smile.

With a little instruction to Joe about the clutch, Zach and Mike stepped back and watched Joe instruct his son to ride for the first time.

Rena stepped up to them while Joe jogged beside Eli as he puttered off. "I remember the first time you got on that thing," she told Mike. "Zach was more excited for you to ride it than Dad was."

"I can't believe Dad still has that thing," Mike told them.

"He'll never get rid of it."

Zach glanced behind them and noticed their parents holding Susie and watching the activity from the porch.

Rena slipped her arm through both Mike's and his. "I'm so happy we're all here. Maybe in a couple of years you can show your kids how to ride that bike," Rena directed her comment to Mike.

Mike offered a playful nudge. "Why don't you bother the older brother about kids?"

"Cuz you're the one who's married."

"It wouldn't be right for me to be a father right now," he said. "My production schedule is booked for the next eighteen months."

"That's not forever," Rena said.

Zach kept quiet and watched Mike as he squirmed around the conversation about having children of his own.

"I'll have kids someday," Mike assured their sister.

Funny how he said *I'll have kids* and not *we will have kids*.

Zach dislodged his arm from his sister and nodded toward the bikes to Mike. "Do you still have it?"

Mike removed his sunglasses from the front of his shirt and pushed them onto his nose. "If there is one thing I don't let stunt doubles do, it's my bike shots."

Like old times, Zach and Mike jumped on the backs of the bikes and skidded out of the drive and down the old trails they knew better than the backs of their hands.

———

"It's called the 'OR' game," Judy told them as they sat around a campfire two days into their vacation. Sawyer and Janice had turned in, and Hannah was up in the loft with a sleeping Eli and Susie texting her friends.

The rest of them sat under a blanket of stars while sparks from the fire drifted into the sky. Their red cups had been full for a couple of hours and none of them could claim sobriety.

Zach had to admit, watching his baby sister tip back the margaritas felt strange, but he had to remind himself that she wasn't a kid anymore.

"I remember that game," Karen said from across the fire. "Played it in college all the time."

Judy pointed her cup in Karen's direction. "There is only one rule. You have to answer the question honestly . . . I'll start . . . Rena, margaritas or martinis?"

"That's easy. Margaritas." Rena sipped her beverage and looked at Karen. "Karen, Coke or Pepsi?"

"Coke. Michael . . . the McLaren or the Ferrari?" Karen asked.

Mike shifted in his seat. "Oh, that's hard. I have to go with my first love and say Ferrari."

"I don't know, Mike, that McLaren is an orgasm on wheels," Zach told his brother.

"You have to drive the Ferrari next time you visit," Mike told him. "OK, Joe . . . explore outer space or the deep ocean?"

Joe lifted his glossy eyes to the sky. "I'd be all over what's up there."

The questions kept rounding between them, most innocent until Karen decided it was time to up the stakes. "OK, Judy . . . hot college guys or hot college professors?"

Judy's smile made Zach think maybe she'd attempted both. "Professors."

Zach closed his eyes and tried not to picture his sister with an older man.

Joe nudged Mike's arm. "All right Mike . . . kissing Marilyn Cohen or kissing Jennifer Ashton?"

Everyone in the group knew that Mike had the opportunity to kiss both women as they'd costarred in his films.

"Jennifer."

"Really?" Joe asked. "I think Marilyn is more beautiful."

Mike laughed. "She is . . . but Marilyn and I are friends. When I kissed her, her husband, Tom, was on set."

Karen giggled. "Well let me know the next time you have to kiss her and I'll come by and kiss Tom, make the whole ordeal even."

"Tom is so hot!" Judy fanned herself while Mike and Joe shook their heads. "Karen," Judy said. "Brazilian wax or total leg wax?"

The image of Karen having anything waxed shot Zach's temperature to the sky. Good thing it was dark and no one would notice how Judy's question affected him.

"What's a Brazilian?" Rena asked.

Mike started to laugh. "It's wrong on many levels that my baby sister knows something that my older sister doesn't."

Judy puffed out her chest. "That damn college education is sneaking in. A Brazilian is when a woman has all her hoochie hair removed."

Rena blushed scarlet and giggled into her cup. "Sounds painful."

"It is," both Karen and Judy said at the same time.

Zach was equally mortified that his sister knew this . . . and turned on that Karen did as well. He poured straight tequila into his cup and took a swig while he waited for Karen's answer.

"Well?" Mike nudged his wife.

Karen blushed. "I have to go with Brazilian, but for the record . . . it's only because there's more torture with a leg wax."

"Yeah, sure," Mike said, laughing.

Zach smiled into his cup and barely heard his name being called by Karen. "Zach . . . a hooker in Las Vegas, or a hooker in Bangkok?"

Joe and Mike tossed their heads back and Judy high fived Karen. "Good question," Judy said.

Zach squeezed his eyes shut and tried to picture either one.

"What's the matter . . . I think I'd go with the foreign woman," Joe said.

Rena swatted his arm. "Eweh."

Zach lifted a hand in the air. "No, wait . . . I'm thinking that Las Vegas has plenty of twenty-dollar tricks, where Bangkok probably gives 'em away for five bucks . . . I think there would be more chances of disease in Bangkok. I have to go with Las Vegas."

Karen met Zach's gaze across the fire and held. This little game of get to know you was more than he thought it would be. Seemed Karen might not be the complete saint after all.

"What about you, Mike . . . which would you pick?" Judy asked.

"I'm with Zach. I'd stick with Vegas."

Karen fluttered her gaze away, and kept the questions going. "OK, Judy . . . broad shoulders or tight butts?"

Once again, Zach had to close his eyes.

"Oh, that's hard . . ." Apparently, his baby sister had a preference for big shoulders. Zach just hoped that no one asked her about penis size or he'd have to excuse himself.

Chapter Seventeen

"No, Tony...he isn't doing anything that might land him in the hospital."

Karen stood several yards from the cabin where the cell reception was the best for talking. Seemed texting up in the mountains proved a better source of communication than actual phone conversations.

"I know he's gotta be off-roading up there."

"Nothing he doesn't do when he's shooting a movie."

"Production starts in two weeks, Karen. Keep him whole."

Karen shook her head. What she really wanted to tell Michael's manager was that there was more to life than a production schedule. She'd not seen Michael smile as much as she had since they arrived in Hilton. Up here with the clean air and family memories, he was more at ease than ever.

Even after their divorce, she'd encourage him to visit his family as often as possible. They were good for him on many levels.

"He'll come back to LA whole and ready to deliver the best movie ever. This really has been good for him, Tony. Trust me."

A long-suffering sigh escaped Tony through the phone. "Tell him I called."

"I will. And thanks for calling me and not him. I know it's killing you."

Tony chuckled. "Hey, it's what he pays me for."

"Talk soon," Karen said before hanging up.

The sky was clear on their fourth day at the cabin. They'd eaten under the stars at night, and sat around a campfire roasting marshmallows playing word games. Karen couldn't wait to do it all again.

Sawyer, with all his roughness when they'd first arrived, really was a softer man up in the mountains. He bounced his grandson on his knee, and when he thought others were watching him, he'd shout some order to keep his edge. In the end, Karen thought the man simply wanted his family around him all the time. Even if his desire wasn't practical. She made a note to try to find a moment alone with the man before they left in order to encourage him to give his kids room to grow. That way when they all did come together it would be like this . . . loving and full of everything good, not resentment for having to stick within a mold he'd set up for them. Karen wasn't sure why she always wanted to fix the relationships of those around her. Maybe it was a by-product of not having anyone step in for her as a child . . . she wasn't sure. She simply knew it was in her blood to try to do something to make things right between parents and their children. Even if their children were adults.

The now familiar roar of a motorized off-road vehicle kicked up behind her. Back at the cabin, she noticed another person arriving. From the distance, she thought it was one of Michael's old friends.

She started back toward the Gardner family but Michael headed her off and swung her around in the opposite direction.

"Would you mind if I took off for a few hours?" The grin on Michael's face held mischief.

"Of course not. But . . ." She glanced over her shoulder, noticed his friend watching them. His single friend . . . "Oh, my God. You're going to get laid!" she whispered with a playful smack to his arm.

Michael lifted his eyebrows a couple of times. "I just might."

"You bitch!" Yet Karen understood the need. They'd both had nothing for so long and Michael had to be so careful with his lovers. "Go."

"You sure? I was going to show you how to ride the motorcycle today."

She rolled her eyes. "Go ride your own bike . . . I'll have someone else teach me."

Mike winked, gave her arm a little squeeze, and strode off.

She tapped the book she'd been reading before Tony's call against her thigh and walked closer to the lake. After settling against a tree, she opened the book only to look up and wave as Michael and his friend rode by with a wave.

Brat.

But she was smiling and truly happy for Michael.

She let her mind slip into the pages of the story while the sun warmed her skin. The story wasn't catching her, and her eyes slid closed. The nights had proved less than restful. Between the small bed, the unfamiliar room, and the overall restlessness of the others in the communal room, sleeping wasn't easy.

"Good book?" Rena's voice woke her, causing the book to slide off her lap.

"Not really."

Rena dropped to the ground and leaned against her elbows to stare out at the lake. "How are you liking it here?"

"A lot more than I thought I would."

"It's a great place to recharge."

Karen could tell by how Rena fiddled with the grass at her side that something was on her mind.

"Do you think you'll be back?"

Karen hesitated, knowing full well she wouldn't return. Unless the Gardners were up to inviting Michael's ex-wife along for their family vacations.

"Uhm, yeah."

Rena didn't look at her, just nodded slowly. "You love him, don't you?"

She was being led, and set up if she wasn't completely clueless, but didn't have an earthly idea how to get away from this conversation. "Of course." She did love Michael, for the friend he'd been since they met.

"But you're not *in love* with him."

Karen opened her mouth to deny her words, but Rena stopped her.

"No. Please don't reply to that."

Karen swallowed her words and waited.

"One summer when Mike was sixteen we sat close to where you and I are right now. He was miserable. He'd tried to explain to our parents his desire to jump into the plays at school . . . how he didn't mind working with his hands but didn't see it as something he wanted to do to earn a living. Our dad didn't get it. He sat right here and told me everything in his life was confusing and that none of us understood."

"Sixteen is a hard age," Karen added.

Rena nodded. "Coming of age is a lot easier if you're not struggling with your sexuality."

Karen froze. Through tight lips she asked, "Don't all teens struggle with their sexuality?"

Rena caught her eyes. "Some more than others."

Oh, Michael . . . your sister knows.

"You know what I think?" Rena asked.

Here it comes. She waited for the bomb to drop and couldn't do anything other than watch.

"What's that?"

"The reason you both haven't come sooner is because Michael didn't want any of us to get to know you. I also think the reason you and Michael aren't talking about having kids . . . and you hesitate about discussing your return to Hilton, is because the two of you are planning to divorce."

Karen opened her mouth.

Rena shook her head.

"I'd even lay money on the table to say the two of you could appeal for an annulment even after a year of marriage."

"You have an interesting imagination," was all Karen could come up with.

"Yet you're not denying anything."

How could she? Flat-out lying to Michael's sister would make her look stupid when they filed for a divorce. "What do you want me to say, Rena? My loyalty to your brother is stronger than most family bonds."

"I can see that. My guess is you'd even sacrifice yourself . . . for a while anyway, to help him."

She hesitated . . . then said, "Your brother deserves his family's love and respect."

Karen glanced toward the cabin, the lake . . . anywhere but Rena's eyes.

Rena offered another slow nod. She gazed over the lake again. "You're going to tell Mike about this conversation, aren't you?"

"Are you ready for any conversation the two of you might have as a result?" Karen asked.

"I miss my younger brother. We'll all miss him. I can't speak for everyone, but for me, I'll take the real Mike Gardner any day over Michael Wolfe."

"He needs to protect Michael Wolfe." Karen hoped the message behind her words was clear.

"I've protected him my whole life," Rena said. "I won't stop now."

Karen pushed to her feet before Rena achieved any more revelations. "It's a cool enough day for a jog."

Rena glanced around with a frown. "You should take Judy with you."

Karen patted her back pocket. "I have my phone." She didn't even bother going back to the cabin to change clothes before taking off into a run.

There wasn't a real trail around the lake, but Karen kept close to it anyway. She needed some alone time, but didn't need to get lost.

In a way, she hoped she could be gone long enough for Michael to return, and maybe Rena could talk to him herself. Who else knew about him? Not Judy . . . or Hannah. They were clueless.

Zach had kept his distance over the past few days, but she always felt his eyes on her, across the campfire, or as she helped Janice and Rena with their meals. His eyes often lingered on his brother, too.

Karen jogged until she couldn't see the cabin any longer then slowed her pace to a brisk walk. She checked her phone, noticed a lack of service, and shoved it back in her pocket. Calling Gwen for some sisterly advice wasn't an option. She'd have to figure this one out herself. Part of her wanted to warn Michael before he returned to the cabin, but the other part wanted him to enjoy his alone time. Then at least he could go into any pending confrontation sated and ready for battle.

Maybe he'd always worried that spending time with his family would reveal his secret.

A long stretch of an even path appeared before her so she took off into a run. She cut through the trees that sat along the bank, and back down to the lake several more times before she realized how far she'd run. She removed her phone from her pocket and attempted to find a signal. Nothing. It was still midday, but she didn't know exactly how far or how many miles it would take to get around the lake to come back alongside the road so she turned around. She walked for another mile or so before resting on the water's edge.

After a good thirty minutes of sitting there contemplating life, she heard the buzz of a motorcycle moving toward her.

Sure enough, Zach made his way to her with a frown on his face. He skidded to a halt and killed the engine. "I've been searching for you for an hour." His accusatory tone brought the hair up on the back of her neck.

"I'm right here."

He glanced around, flung his arms wide. "You don't even know where *here* is."

"I'm not lost, Zach. I was on my way back."

"You shouldn't run off alone. There are hunters out here, trails that lead to nowhere."

"I might be a city girl, but even I know not to wander off in the woods alone."

He lowered the kickstand and climbed off the bike. She noticed his lack of helmet and wondered how fast he had left the cabin.

"What if you got hurt, twisted an ankle or something?"

"I have my phone."

He glared at her. "A phone that doesn't work most of the time."

He had her there.

"Dammit, Zach. I needed some time alone, OK?"

Her outburst stopped his. His arms fell from his hips.

She turned to the water, and tossed the rock she had in her hand at a nearby bush. As soon as the rock hit, the bush rustled and started to move. Before Karen could move away, more ducks than she could count took flight and aimed directly at her.

She screamed and scurried from her rock, slipped on the bank, and found herself knee-deep in muck before scrambling up and out of the water. Her cry didn't stop as she covered her head and lunged toward Zach.

Birds . . . all of them, scared the crap out of her. Always had.

Zach caught and held her still. "Hey. It's OK."

She heard another flap, but refused to open her eyes. "Get 'em off."

"They're gone."

She stood perfectly still, eyes closed and ears opened. She had one hand protecting her head, and the other one latched to Zach's waist. His arms sucked her into him.

Once the noise of the birds flying away drifted, she opened one eye, fully expecting at least one bird to have held back to make her panic all over again.

Only the two of them stood there. "Gone?"

"Yeah." Zach started to chuckle.

"It's not funny."

"I've never seen a woman move so fast in my life."

She shoved out of his arms and looked down at herself. Her knees were covered in mud, the side of her leg caked with the stuff. "I don't like birds."

"I gathered that." He still laughed. "Ducks haven't been known to attack humans, though. I think you're safe."

"Stop laughing."

He sucked in his bottom lip but his eyes still mocked her.

"Birds are unpredictable," she made her argument. "They have claws and beaks."

Zach's eyes swept her wet frame. He laughed again.

"Oh ... you ..." she reached down, took a handful of muck and tossed it directly at his chest.

He stopped laughing. "Oh, you didn't just do that."

She lobbed another handful of mud at him before she slapped a hand on her hip. "Stop laughing."

He swiped the mud from his chest, and leaned over to grab a handful for himself. When he rose to his full height, his playful smile met hers. "I think you missed a spot."

The mud hit her chest and it was game on.

Her position close to the bank gave her the most ammo. She took two handfuls to his one and had him dripping in mud in a few throws. He started to duck away from her assault.

She slipped on the bank, grabbed handfuls of mud, and flung it in his direction several times. When it became apparent she was going to be over her head in the water, she retreated from the water's edge.

He chased her around the bike, and missed a shot that was aimed for her butt. She was leaning down to grasp more dirt when he grabbed her from around her waist and took them both to the forest floor.

She was laughing so hard she couldn't breathe, the birds forgotten.

Zach rolled her onto her back and covered her body with his. Karen took one last shot and smeared mud on his face with a free hand. They were laughing and Karen was moving her head from side to side to avoid him smearing mud on her face, too.

He grabbed her hands and pinned them above her head, then leaned down to rub the dirt from his cheek against the side of hers.

"Eweh!"

They were both laughing, chests heaving, before either one of them realized where they were.

The deep blue pools of his eyes watched hers as everything around them calmed except the pounding of their hearts.

Her head told her to move, push him away. She saw the indecision in his eyes as well.

The forest closed in and the chemistry they'd been denying since they met zeroed in on this very moment. Zach's heated gaze lingered over hers.

"Make me stop," Zach whispered over her lips.

The brisk staccato of his breath raced against hers.

His lips were so close and the need to feel them too strong to deny. "I-I can't."

His eyes searched hers. "I can't either."

Zach's warm breath was nothing compared to his lips. Soft, sensual, and searching. His kiss was so caring and careful she closed her eyes and allowed herself to feel. It had been so long since she'd lost herself in something so basic she'd forgotten how wonderful it was to just be kissed. She moaned and kissed him back, opened her lips against his to play and deepen the feeling they both had wanted for so long.

Zach released the hold on her arms and they fell behind his back to hold him close while his tongue slid beside hers for a solid taste. He was testosterone, and pine . . . strength and desire all rolled up in one.

His body pressed her into the soft earth and her leg wound around his to bring him closer. She broke contact briefly, then rushed back in for more. The taut muscles of his back narrowed to his waist and tight ass. When was the last time she felt anything so perfect?

They went on like this until breathing became a serious effort and a warm fire pooled just south of her stomach. Zach's thumb pushed against her breast, and her nipple hardened.

Reason started to leak back in. If Zach was anyone other than Michael's brother, she'd welcome everything. His kisses, his caress, the erection she felt even now as it pressed through his clothing and against her leg.

She couldn't do this. Maybe in six months, when she and Michael were divorced . . . but now? The deceit to Zach, the disloyalty to Michael . . .

Karen forced her emotions back in and ended their kiss.

Zach watched her under a hooded gaze.

"We can't . . ."

He closed his eyes, rested his forehead against hers. "I know."

She swallowed and tried to catch her breath.

"I should run from you as fast as my feet can take me away," he confessed.

Remorse laced his words. She wanted to tell him he wasn't an awful brother and she wasn't a cheating wife, but that could only lead to an explanation that would ruin Michael.

"Don't hate yourself Zach."

"How can't I? I think about you. Dream about you." He opened his eyes and found hers again.

"Maybe after this kiss, that will all fade."

He smiled through the pain. "I'd like to believe that."

The thought left her cold. She'd dream of nothing but him.

"We should go. Before someone else comes looking for us."

He nodded, looked as if he were going to kiss her again, but then pulled away and helped her to her feet.

When he turned around, she noticed the muddy handprint on his ass and cringed. She looked down at herself and noticed his print on the side of her waist and breast.

"Zach?"

He turned around and she pointed to her clothing. "Oh, that's not good."

"You have a little . . ." She pointed to his butt. He noticed the damage and smeared a patch of fresh dirt to cover her prints. Karen followed his lead and did the same to herself. After the two of them were satisfied with the hiding of evidence, Karen slid behind him on the motorcycle and he drove her back to the cabin.

Chapter Eighteen

Michael rode up to the cabin, killed the engine on his bike, and jumped off with a smile. He couldn't remember feeling more relaxed. He really did need to thank Karen for insisting they travel to Utah.

His mother stood in front of the sink washing vegetables when he walked inside. He snagged a carrot from her stash and popped it into his mouth. "Hey."

"Hi, honey."

"Where is everyone?"

The cabin was unusually quiet this close to dinner hour.

"Hannah and Judy took off with some friends hours ago. Your dad and Joe are teaching little Eli how to fish . . . though I'm guessing they just didn't want to stick around here for me to put them to work. Rena is putting Susie down for a nap in our room, and I think Zach went looking for Karen."

"Looking for her? Where did she go?"

"Rena said she went for a run. But that was a few hours ago and we started to worry so Zach headed out on a motorcycle. I'm sure she's fine," Janice offered. From the expression on her face, she didn't seem at all concerned.

"There you are," Rena exclaimed as she walked into the kitchen. She slid an arm around his waist and Michael kissed the top of her head.

"Miss me?"

"Fishing for a compliment?"

"Maybe." Their banter had always been like this . . . playful and easy.

Rena gave him a hug. "Can I talk to you a minute?" She nodded toward the door.

"Sure." He grabbed a couple more carrots and followed his sister outside. They moved away from the cabin and she laced her arm through his.

"What's up?" He asked between bites.

Rena sucked in a deep breath and didn't answer right away. When Michael smiled down at her, his stomach churned. "What is it?"

"You know I love you . . . right?"

He narrowed his eyes and tossed the carrots to the ground. Did any conversation ever start out like that and end well? "Of course. I love you, too."

She tugged on his arm and kept walking.

"I wanted to talk to you before Karen came back."

The suspense was killing him, but he kept listening and tried not to jump to conclusions.

"Before she could tell you about our conversation."

"What conversation?" he asked.

"It wasn't a conversation so much as me talking to her. She really cares for you, Michael."

His palms were actually sweating. So much for his perfect day. "I care for her, too."

"Last year when we all heard about your marriage I remember watching the coverage on TV and thinking it was all a Hollywood stunt. A prank for a movie or something like it. Then after you talked with Mom and Dad and you told them you really were married I still didn't believe it."

"We really are married." He tried to laugh but it came out strangled.

"Yeah, I get that. But you're not going to stay that way."

He stumbled, but kept walking.

"That's what I told Karen. She didn't seem surprised by my observation."

Was that what this was about? A divorce? "We have had some problems," he said. "Being married to me isn't that easy." He tried to put the blame on him.

Rena released an exasperated sigh. "Please, Mike. I know you're not divorcing Karen because it isn't working out between you. You're divorcing her because that was in the plan all along."

The pounding in his temple started to throb. "Did she tell you that?"

"Of course not. And stop looking at me like that. You did have a life here before you moved away, Mike. You might not remember all the conversations you and I had when you were a kid, but I remember them."

They stopped now, feet from the lake, and were watching each other.

"I think you married Karen because your image needed it. The blockbuster superstar Michael Wolfe needed a wife. So poof! Here's a wife."

He swallowed. "Does anyone else think this?"

"Mom and Dad? No. And I don't think Hannah and Judy . . . or even Zach realize this either. Not yet anyway. Though I think Zach suspects something isn't right."

"But Joe?"

"Joe's my husband. We talk about everything. As I suspect you and Karen talk about everything."

He wanted to tell his sister she was wrong . . . he couldn't.

"Please . . . please don't say anything to them."

Rena tilted her head to the side and offered a sad smile. "I won't."

A sense of relief washed over him. At least there was one person in his family that understood his marriage arrangement. One ally when the divorce took place.

Michael hugged his sister.

Before she pulled away, she whispered, "I also know you're gay."

When the cabin came into view, Zach felt Karen straighten on the back of the bike. Her arms loosened around his waist and her breasts no longer sat snug against his back. He missed her instantly. He had no idea what he was going to do about his attraction. She was equally torn, desperate even. There were times in his life when he heard about someone having an affair, and he always thought how stupid could two people be? Why would someone risk so much for a fuck? But damn, that wasn't Karen. This was more than physical and they both knew it. If it were only physical, they'd have probably given in by now, jumped in full force and not danced around with conversation.

No, Zach wanted to explore the woman riding behind him on his bike, and not just in bed. He wanted to understand the sad look in her eyes when she talked about the kids she took such loving care of at the club. Why did she say she didn't want kids, yet act like they were the most precious thing in the world?

If there was one thing their brief intimate moment proved, it was that he wasn't sated. He wanted more. So much more.

Zach helped Karen off his bike, held on to her elbow a little too long. Their eyes met briefly.

"Wow! Looks like you two went one-on-one with Loch Ness herself."

From the porch, Rena sat with Mike, both of them watching them with smiles.

Trusting smiles.

The situation was making him sicker by the hour.

Karen lifted her arms in the air. "There was a flock of birds . . . I fell in the lake."

Mike's smile fell. "Oh. Are you OK?"

"Scared the crap out of me." Karen offered a coy smile to Zach. "Then Zach started to laugh."

"Ah, now I understand the mud all over Zach. She hates birds, big brother. With a passion. Telling her they aren't out to peck her eyes or claw her hair won't make her believe it."

"I'm right here! And they do those things all the time." Karen shuddered. "After last year with Gwen . . ." She hugged herself, lost in thought.

"What happened with Gwen?" Zach asked.

"There was a guy stalking her, leaving dead ravens at the house, by our cars . . ." Karen's voice drifted off and Mike finished for her.

"The guy wasn't after Gwen, but using her to get to Neil. You met them at the party."

"Big guy and British woman, right?"

"Right. Well, Neil is an ex-Marine. The guy after him was one of his men back when he served. He took out Gwen and Karen's neighbors while we were in France."

"Took out?" Rena asked.

"Murdered," Michael elaborated. "Thank God Karen wasn't there when that happened. He left ravens everywhere, apparently."

"It was awful." Karen's voice dropped to low tones.

Zach reached out and rubbed Karen's arm. He actually felt bad for laughing at her now that he heard the story.

"What happened to the stalker?" Rena asked.

Zach glanced at his brother.

Mike gave a quick slicing gesture to his neck, his explanation clear.

"My fear of birds happened long before last year. It's just the way I'm wired," Karen told them.

Thinking nothing of the move, Zach gave her a quick hug. His arm slipped away when he looked up to find Rena staring at him. Mike, on the other hand, was staring at Rena.

"I need a shower," Karen announced as she ducked away from Zach and up the short stairs into the cabin.

Mike followed Karen into the cabin, and Zach watched them go.

He dragged his hands over his chest to rub off some of the caked on mud before he made his way to the second shower of his day.

"Oh, boy," Rena mumbled before Zach could walk by.

"Excuse me?"

Rena shook her head, and didn't meet his gaze. "Nothing. Think I'll go find the girls for dinner."

No sooner did Karen step from the shower than Michael confronted her.

"We need to make our excuses and leave." He whispered his words and kept glancing over his shoulder to the voices that carried from outside the cabin.

"Rena spoke to you."

He nodded. "She knows everything."

"I didn't—"

He placed a finger to her lips. "I know you didn't. But I need to get out of here before someone else figures it out."

His need to leave gave her the opportunity to detach herself from Zach. She'd proved a massive lack of willpower in regards to the oldest Gardner son.

"I've already called Tony," Michael said. "Told him to call an hour from now. As it turns out, production is starting early."

Michael would run off, and she'd be walking around his house alone once again. "I think I should start transitioning back to the Tarzana house."

The home in Tarzana was the one she shared with Gwen before she married Neil. The home belonged to Samantha and Blake, and Neil's friend Rick occasionally occupied it, but with the scheduled divorce approaching, it was always understood that Karen would move back.

"We don't have to think about that now, do we?"

Karen looked over Michael's shoulder, then back to him. "I don't know why we'd wait. You signed contracts. You're ready for the next couple of years."

"Let's talk about this later."

"All right."

The smell of charcoal from the barbeque drifted from the grill, reminding Karen that she'd not eaten since before lunch.

Karen soaked in Michael's family for the next hour. Eli sat beside his grandfather asking him why the sky was blue. She hadn't really thought kids actually asked those questions, but apparently, she was wrong.

Judy and Hannah were highly animated with the conversation about how far . . . or in the case of their conversation . . . how unfar, the football players of Hilton actually got in life.

"C'mon, Rena, who played football when you were in school?"

"Mason Reynolds was the quarterback senior year."

"Mr. Reynolds?" Hannah cringed when she said the man's name. "He's fat . . . and slow."

"And bald," Judy added.

"And living in his daddy's old home," Hannah pointed out. "See . . . another football player doomed to go nowhere and do nothing."

"Hey, I played football," Zach protested.

"You're different," Hannah said.

Karen laughed and cut into the steak on her plate right as Michael's phone rang.

He made a show of looking at who was calling. "I have to take this. Sorry." He jumped up from the table and moved away from the family to talk to Tony.

Zach and Rena watched him walk away while the rest of the family continued with their meal. Karen put down her fork, no longer hungry.

"Most football players peak in high school," Judy said between bites. "Unless they play college ball."

Joe laughed and pointed to Eli. "Guess that means you get to play baseball."

They were laughing when Michael made his way back to the table.

Janice took one look at her son and said, "What is it?"

He released a Hollywood sigh that Karen picked up on but didn't think his family did. "Production on my next film is moving up by two weeks." He offered Karen a sympathetic look. "We have to get home . . . tonight."

"No," Hannah protested.

"Do you have to?" Judy asked.

"Oh, honey." Janice looked devastated. "Can't you make them wait?"

Michael rested a hand on his mother's shoulder. "Doesn't work that way. There's a huge crew being brought in . . . it's complicated."

Nice vague answer, Michael.

The only one at the table who didn't seem to buy it was Rena. Her gaze skidded past Karen's only to drop to her plate. She probably blamed herself for his early departure.

Karen scooted out from the table and dropped her napkin onto her plate.

"You can finish your meal," Janice insisted.

"I'm nearly done anyway. I'll run upstairs and pack."

Judy jumped up. "I'll help."

Before they reached the cabin, Karen heard Zach say, "I'll drive you back to the house."

Karen shoved her cosmetic bag into her suitcase, and rolled her dirty clothes into a plastic bag before pushing them on top of her clean clothes.

"I can't believe you guys have to run."

"It's the nature of Michael's business. Always on the run."

"Doesn't seem fair."

Karen sat on the edge of her bunk and rested an arm around Judy's shoulders. "I'm sure he'll be back more often now that he's spent time with everyone. And you're always welcome to visit."

"I'd like that."

Karen squeezed Judy and stood to zip up her bag.

Michael made his way to his bed with a tearful Hannah trailing behind him. "You better not fall off the face of the earth again," she scolded.

"Talk about dramatic, Hannah-banana. I'll be back." Michael exchanged looks with Karen as they passed in the loft.

Halfway down the stairs, Zach met her and took her bag. "Let me."

She mumbled a soft thanks as he jogged her luggage out the door. The lump in her throat was growing as the minutes passed. Having grown up with only her aunt, Karen had missed big family gatherings and good-byes. At this moment, she was happy for that loss.

Their quick exit was probably best all the way around, or so she told herself.

Outside the cabin, the family had abandoned their meal to help Karen and Michael leave.

Rena stood off to the side, holding Karen's muddy shoes. "Hey, Karen?"

She walked to where Rena stood and gathered them.

"I'm sorry," Rena said under her breath.

"Don't be." Karen glanced around, noticed there wasn't anyone standing close. "He just needs time, Rena. Be patient."

She smiled with tears in her eyes. "We're not going to see you again, are we?"

Karen shrugged, pushed back tears of her own. "Michael and I will always be friends."

Rena hugged her then with another apology.

Judy hugged her good-bye next, told her to expect a call soon.

Hannah was practically sobbing. Karen knew there wasn't much she could say so she encouraged her to text often, which she knew didn't need to be said. Teenagers and texting went together like a highway and asphalt. Joe gave her a hug, and Karen kissed Susie's little cheek and thanked Eli for saving her from the spiders.

Behind her, Michael was making his rounds of good-byes.

Janice hugged her the longest, then held her arms as she stood back. "Thank you for bringing our son back to us."

"Thank you for your hospitality."

"You're family," Janice said. Karen forced herself not to cringe. "You're welcome anytime."

"Thanks."

When Karen turned to Sawyer, he watched her. "You know something, Karen?"

A hint of a smile met his lips.

"What's that?"

He sized her up for a moment and said, "I think I like you."

She remembered their first conversation and held back the huge smile she wanted to spread. "You know, Sawyer, I think I like you, too."

When Michael's father hugged her, she knew he was a whole lot of bark and very little bite.

Swiping tears from her eyes, she said a quick good-bye and moved toward the truck where Zach waited to take them back.

Michael continued with longer good-byes while Karen jumped into the backseat.

"No need to cry," Zach said. "You'll see everyone again."

Karen looked directly at him. "No, Zach. I won't."

Chapter Nineteen

Karen kicked herself the minute the words escaped her lips. But there was no pulling them back. She just couldn't lie to Zach anymore. It was as if each lie was sucking her soul deeper into an abyss.

Thankfully, Michael made his way inside the truck and Zach didn't ask her to elaborate. Maybe like Rena, he'd figure it out all on his own. Or maybe Rena would slip?

"Thanks for driving us," Michael told his brother.

Karen waved out the back window, thankful at least to have their good-byes behind her. She looked forward to getting home and clearing her mind.

Weren't vacations supposed to be relaxing?

"Not a problem."

Zach looked in the rearview mirror and met Karen's gaze. He had questions in his eyes.

"Are you booked out of LAX tomorrow?" Karen asked Michael, hoping to keep the ruse of an early departure going.

"Yeah. We have ten p.m. tickets out of St. George waiting for us tonight."

It was only five. They had plenty of time to get to the Gardners' home and grab their rental car to drive to the nearest airport.

"Where are you filming this time?"

"Montreal."

"How long will you be there?"

"Couple of months."

"Don't you get a break? Come home?" Zach asked.

"I take a few long weekends when I can."

Karen sat back and listened to Zach's questions.

"Do I even want to know what they're paying you?"

Michael slouched in his seat. "Thirty-two million."

Zach's jaw dropped. "Fuck."

"Yeah, right? I'm sure you understand my need to run."

Zach met her eyes again. "Just don't forget about the important things on your quest for the big money, little brother."

"That's why we came here. Right Karen?"

"Yep."

Karen watched the vistas as they drove the mountain in silence. When they arrived at the Gardner family home, they shoved their suitcases into the back of the rental and picked up a few remaining things from inside.

She wanted this to go quickly. Didn't want any long-winded good-byes with Zach. Her heart couldn't take it.

Her phone buzzed in her back pocket. Several text messages had piled up. One number didn't look familiar and Karen nearly disregarded it before clicking.

Call me, Petra.

Karen's body chilled. *Becky.*

Karen hit redial and walked into the Gardner front yard.

"It's Karen."

"I thought you'd like to know," Petra said.

"Know what?"

"Becky's been missing for two days."

"No."

"I didn't see her leave. She sat on Millie's bench every day, then her mother came in crying asking if I'd seen her."

"What about Nolan?"

"He's opened Gardner's store every day. Saw the sheriff's car there yesterday."

Karen ran a hand through her hair, glanced toward the house to see Michael and Zach talking. "That doesn't make sense. Nolan wouldn't just let her leave."

"Another Hilton runaway."

"Thanks for calling, Petra. I'll be in touch."

Karen clicked off the phone and ran over to the boys. "Becky's gone."

Zach's eyes grew wide.

"The girl you think is pregnant?" Michael asked. She'd told him her suspicions about the girl when they'd first evolved.

"Yes, her. Only Nolan is still in town."

"You think they broke up and she ran off?"

She shook her head. "I think where she goes, he goes. If he's still in town, she's still in town . . . or close by."

Zach had his phone to his ear. "Hey, Buck . . . yeah, been great. No, just wondering how it's working out with Nolan?"

Zach shook his head for both her and Michael. "No. It's good. I'll be back in a few days. Yeah, thanks." He hung up. "Nolan is showing up, working hard."

Karen swung in a circle, as if looking around this suburbia in Utah was going to show her anything. "I'd bet money she's here somewhere."

A hand met Karen's shoulder. "You can't save every kid."

She shrugged Michael's hand off. "No. But I can help *this* one. I just need to find her."

Having made up her mind, she walked to the car and removed her bags.

"What are you doing?"

"I'm not leaving till I know where that girl is and that she's OK."

"Karen?"

She placed a hand on her hip and glared. "You have your job. I have mine."

"It's not your responsibility."

"Stop. OK." Then because he just didn't understand, she reminded him of what she'd told him early in their vacation. "A week, Michael. I was in that house for a week, cold, tired . . . distraught. And I wasn't a teenage pregnant girl. Becky needs someone looking out for her."

His shoulders fell. "I can call Tony—"

"No. You go. I can skirt around unnoticed better than you can. If I find her, and she needs to stay hidden, I can manage that. You'll cause attention."

He sighed. "I feel like I'm abandoning you here."

"This big mean city doesn't scare me," she joked. "But think of her alone in LA, or Salt Lake?"

"It's hard to think of her when I've not met her."

"She's a good kid. Karen's right . . . her boyfriend was all over her. She's probably still in town," Zach told his brother.

Michael rubbed his hands over his face. "You sure?"

"I'm sure. Go. Call me when you land."

Michael held out his hands and she hugged him, felt his lips on the top of her head. He didn't even try a kiss to her lips.

"Take care of her," he told Zach.

She noticed Zach's Adam's apple bob a couple of times. "I will."

She stood beside Zach as Michael pulled out of the driveway and down the street. They returned her bags to the house and closed the door.

"Do you know where Nolan lives?"

"Yeah. I drove him home a couple of times when he first started working for my dad. Before he started driving."

"I think the fastest way to find Becky is to find Nolan."

She opened her suitcase, removed a cardigan sweater, and threw it over her shoulders.

Zach was staring at her when she stood.

"Are you going to explain what you said before Mike got in the truck?"

Rena already knew about Michael and her pending break-up . . . the rest of them would find out soon enough. Karen didn't want Zach to hear this from anyone else. "Michael and I are getting divorced."

Zach held his breath. "What . . . when?"

"We'll file in a few months, maybe sooner. We haven't discussed the details."

"Discuss the details?"

She turned her back on him, closed her suitcase. "It's all very friendly."

He took her arm and turned her to face him. "Why didn't you tell me? Before I kissed you? After?"

"Because it doesn't change anything. I'm still married to your brother and Michael has no idea of our attraction. He would hate it."

"But you don't love him." She heard the relief in his voice, saw the confusion in his eyes.

"I will always love your brother . . . as a friend."

Her words did something to him. Zach pulled her close and placed his palm on her cheek. Without words, he kissed her. There wasn't any hesitation this time, just pent-up passion as he possessed her lips. Apparently, her concerns about still being married to Michael didn't affect Zach in the least. One hand ran down her back and pulled her close while the other slipped into her hair. Her will started to slip and the need to kiss Zach deeper, feel him everywhere, crawled up her spine like tiny pinpricks.

Michael wasn't even out of the city and she was in the arms of his brother.

With her body trembling with sensation and heat, she pulled away, and kept Zach from reaching for her again.

"Zach, please. I can't . . ."

"But you want to."

"I'd think that was obvious."

She turned away, hoping he wouldn't see her hesitation. "We need to find Nolan. See where he stashed his girlfriend."

Karen didn't ask if Zach would help. She just assumed he would and walked out the door.

———

They were driving to the edge of town to where Nolan lived, searching for a teenage pregnant girl, and Zach couldn't stop smiling.

They were getting divorced.

The words were music, in Technicolor, inside his head. *It's friendly*, she'd said . . . *we'll file in a few months*, she'd said. He knew Karen and Michael weren't right. He had questions still, but Karen wasn't answering any of them. Fine. He could wait.

Michael would hate it.

He would but it wasn't going to keep him from pursuing Karen. There was no use pretending otherwise.

"What's Nolan's last name?"

"Parker."

They drove into the trailer park just off the freeway and crawled to Nolan's space number.

"Why are mobile home parks always off a highway?" Karen asked.

"Cheap land."

"Do you think Nolan would keep Becky here?"

"If I remember right, Nolan's dad is an alcoholic. I doubt Nolan would expose Becky to that."

"Eweh. Not good."

Zach pulled his truck to the side of the road in front of Nolan's childhood home and cut the engine. "Wait here. I'll see if he's home." He glanced behind the truck. "I don't see his car."

He jogged up the short steps of the singlewide and knocked on the door. It wasn't quite dusk, but the sun was low enough on the horizon for the lights of the TV set to flicker through the windows. When no one answered the door, he knocked longer and harder.

"Coming. Damn!"

Zach backed up and waited.

The man Zach assumed was Nolan's father swung the door wide and glared with glossy eyes at him. "Yeah?"

The man reeked of whiskey and stale cigarettes.

"I'm looking for Nolan."

"You and everyone else. He's not here." Instead of offering anything else, the man attempted to close the door.

Zach stopped him by putting his hand on the door. "When did you see him last?"

Mr. Parker glared at Zach's hand and wobbled on his feet. "You a cop?"

"I'm his boss."

"Tell you the same thing I told the pigs. He comes and goes as he pleases. And there ain't no girl here."

"Do you expect him back?"

"What about comes and goes as he pleases did you misunderstand, boss-man?"

Zach figured that Nolan's dad didn't know if he'd be back.

"Thanks." Zach noticed Karen's anxious gaze as he rounded the front of the truck. He shook his head as he climbed back into the cab.

"He's not here."

"Where do you think he is?"

He shrugged. "We could wait until morning and see if he shows up for work. Talk to him then."

Karen squeezed the bridge of her nose. "But if I'm wrong and Nolan stayed in town, and Becky ran off . . . the longer we go without that information the farther away she'll get. Who knows what will happen to her."

Zach shifted in his seat and looked at Karen full on. "If you're right and Nolan is keeping her safe, we'll find out in the morning."

"I could be wrong."

He didn't think she was. Instead of arguing, he asked, "Where would he stash her then? Not here." He noticed the streetlight blinking on and a few teenage kids starting to eye his truck.

"Where's the nearest hotel?"

"Monroe, but I'd think the police would have looked there."

"Then the next-closest hotel?"

Instead of answering, he pulled his truck away from the Parker home, drove to the freeway, and headed north. He bypassed his job site and drove into Bell ten minutes later. "There are a few motels. Nothing fancy."

"I'd think Nolan would have to avoid using a credit card."

"I doubt he has one."

They drove to every motel, each one seedier than the last. They were told that no one had checked in matching the descriptions of Nolan or Becky.

It was completely dark, but they continued to drive around Bell on the off chance they'd find Nolan's car parked somewhere. The outskirts stretched for miles, however. Nolan could have Becky anywhere.

"Do you think they could have gone farther?" Karen asked as she looked up the highway.

"The next real town is thirty miles away."

"That doesn't feel right."

"Buck assured me Nolan is showing up for work. If he knows where Becky is, I don't think he'd stick her miles away."

"I think we're going about this all wrong," Karen said. "If you were eighteen and your girl was knocked up and in need of running away, where would you take her?"

If he'd knocked up a girl at eighteen, he'd have moved her in with his parents, but that obviously wasn't what Nolan would do.

"If I was Nolan, I'd hold on to my job until I had enough money to split. I wouldn't spend it at a motel."

"And if the girl's parents thought you were hiding her, they'd be watching to see if you left town." Karen scratched her head. "Is there a back room at the hardware store?"

Zach shook his head. "The storage room is crammed full. But you might be on to something."

He pulled back onto the freeway and turned off several exits before Hilton. If Nolan was in need of shelter . . . why not hide in front of everyone?

"Where are we going?"

"Nolan shows up for work, early. The question is how early? Or does he even leave?" The small housing development was dark and quiet as he pulled into the gravel, past the nearly complete houses.

"This is your project?" Karen asked.

"Yeah."

"Nice. How big are the houses?"

"Smallest model is twenty-three hundred square feet, the largest is twenty-seven-fifty."

Karen smiled as she looked up at a passing house. "You do nice work, Zach."

A strange sense of pride filled him. He hadn't brought her there to show off his skills, but the fact that she'd taken a moment to compliment him made him smile.

He drove beyond the first phase of houses and parked the truck. "If Nolan's here, he wouldn't leave his car in plain sight. There are several finished garages to hide a car."

"He probably saw us driving in if he's here."

"Or Becky did."

They jumped out of the truck and walked around the back of the first row of houses. The moon helped light the way. When Karen tripped over an exposed drainage pipe, Zach took her arm and kept her upright. After she almost fell a second time, he just kept her arm in his hand. He liked it there anyway, he decided.

"We should see a light, or something?" Karen whispered.

"I'd cut the light if I were Nolan."

Karen stopped walking. "Listen."

Zach held his breath and closed his eyes. The trickling of water brought his attention to the houses on the other side of the street.

They stayed close to the shadows of a house and peered into the darkness for several minutes. Then he saw a shadow in an upstairs window of the third home in. He pointed for Karen's benefit. She watched and the shadow reappeared.

"How many doors lead into the house?" she asked.

"Front, back, and garage."

"I'll go in the front, since I don't know my way around. You watch the back door in case they try and run off."

"Are you always this sneaky, Ms. Jones?"

"I am when I'm on a mission. Now get moving before they spot us."

He gave a mock salute and kept to the shadows as he rounded the side of the house and around the back. He turned the knob quietly and slid into the dark interior. The house was nearly complete, all that remained to be done was carpet, some painting, and finishing work.

He heard Karen open the front door.

Instead of doing this in the dark, Zach flipped the switch next to the door and illuminated the kitchen. The door to the garage was in his line of sight, and there weren't any kids running away.

"Becky?" Karen's voice sang in the empty house, echoing off the bare walls. "Honey, I know you're here."

Zach went ahead and opened the door leading to the garage and saw Nolan's car. "Nolan?" he called out.

"It's OK you two. We just want to help." Karen's voice sounded closer.

Zach walked from the kitchen and noticed her standing at the foot of the stairs.

Above him, the floor squeaked.

"Nolan, buddy, you're not in trouble here. We just want to talk to you two." When silence met them, he said. "I saw your car."

Karen kept her eyes on the stairs and waited. Finally, footsteps sounded above them until Nolan stood holding Becky's hand at the top of the landing. "She's not going back to her parents."

Zach noticed the dark bruise alongside Becky's face at the same moment Karen gasped.

Karen ran up the stairs and hesitated when Becky flinched at her approach. "Oh, baby. Who did this to you?"

Becky looked at Nolan then back to Karen.

Zach waited at the foot of the stairs and listened.

"You should tell them," Nolan said. "Maybe they can help."

Becky nudged closer to Nolan, whose arm slid around her shoulders. When the girl started to cry Zach noticed Karen's body tense.

"Let's sit down," Karen suggested.

Nolan nodded. "We have a couple of chairs up here."

Zach walked toward them and followed them into the master bedroom where Nolan had blown up an air mattress and had two folding chairs sitting beside a suitcase. There were food wrappers and a few bottles of water sitting off to the side.

"I clear everything out before anyone shows up," Nolan explained. "I'm sorry, Mr. Gardner. I didn't know where else to go. I've saved up some money, but not enough."

Zach waved a hand in the air. "Don't say another word." The bruise on Becky's face and the marks on her arms proved Nolan had more to protect than just the knowledge that his girlfriend was pregnant. If in fact she was. "I meant it when I said you're not in trouble. We just want to help."

Nolan and Becky sat on the mattress beside each other, holding hands and looking as scared as mice in a kitchen full of cats.

After Karen took a chair, Zach grabbed the remaining one, turned it around, and straddled it.

When it appeared that the kids weren't going to talk, Karen let out a heavy sigh.

Chapter Twenty

Karen's hands shook as she waited for the couple sitting in front of her to talk. The bruise on Becky's face made her want to hit some-one . . . preferably whoever had struck the teen. The determined but slightly scared expression on Nolan's face made her want to whisk them both away without any questions at all.

If this was going to be her life's work, helping kids, runaways . . . then it started right here, with painful silence and patience.

Zach zipped his lips shut and waited right along with her.

She felt his eyes on her and she offered a smile. He lifted an eyebrow toward Nolan and she shook her head as if asking him just to wait.

"She can't go back," Nolan said for the second time.

Becky sat with her head tucked into Nolan's shoulder, the bruise was still visible for Karen to see and question.

"Is that where the bruises came from? Your parents?" Karen asked softly.

Becky's reply was a tiny nod.

"Have they hit you before?" Zach asked.

Again, Becky nodded, but said nothing.

"How long have you known about this, Nolan?" Zach's direct question caught Karen off guard.

Nolan snapped his gaze to Zach. "I didn't know." Nolan's defenses came up like a shield in battle. "Becky told me she fell."

"No one is blaming you," Karen told him and glared at Zach.

"I didn't tell anyone," Becky mumbled. "It didn't happen all the time. Just . . ." Her voice trailed off.

"So you ran away."

"I had to." Becky looked at Karen now, her eyes swollen and red.

Karen nodded. "I would, too. Much easier to run away than allow yourself to be hit."

"I wanted to go to the police," Nolan told them.

Becky shook her head. "No. Please . . ."

Karen held back her own thoughts on the subject of the police for now. "How old are you, Becky?"

"Seventeen."

"Nolan?"

"I'll be nineteen in three months."

Karen glanced at Zach. Concern marred his brow.

"So what's your plan?" Best to figure out what the kids thought they knew and help them come to the right conclusions instead of telling them they weren't thinking at all.

Nolan sat up straighter. "Becky and I are getting married."

Karen nodded, as if contemplating that route.

"That way she'll be emancipated from her parents. Then they can't make her do anything."

She scratched her head. "Well. It's true that a married minor is emancipated from their parents, but in order for a minor to get married they need a parent's permission."

Nolan scowled. "But Becky's pregnant—"

"Nolan!" Becky turned on him quickly and Nolan snapped his mouth closed.

"It's OK. Zach and I already figured that out," Karen assured the teenagers.

Their wide eyes watched both of them.

"How?"

"I work with a lot of teens back in California. I know the signs." She waited for the knowledge that everyone in the room understood the situation to sink in before she popped Nolan's bubble. "Unfortunately, Becky's pregnancy doesn't give her the right to get married without her parents' consent."

"But—"

"It's the law. Meant to keep kids from making lifelong mistakes."

"But we love each other. And now with the baby . . ."

Becky went back to staring at anything but her or Zach.

"You want to do the right thing, Nolan . . . we understand that," Zach said. "Marriage is a big step."

"So is having a baby."

"Yep. Huge," Karen added. "The baby will come whether you're ready or not. Marriage on the other hand doesn't have to happen today."

"But—"

"If you did manage to lie and get a license, Becky's parents could void the license because of her age. Worse, they could try and bring charges against you because you're considered an adult."

Nolan's blank expression made Karen pause.

"Nolan hasn't done anything wrong," Becky muttered.

"I didn't say he did. I'm just pointing out possibilities. Here's another one. There isn't a court out there that would make Becky live with her dad if he's hitting her."

Becky shook her head and a tear ran down her face. "It's not my dad."

"Oh?" Karen wasn't expecting that.

"It's my mom. My dad hits her if she doesn't punish me."

The blood rushed from Karen's face. If she wasn't sitting she probably would have fallen with Becky's admission. How many ways can a parent fuck up someone's life?

"They can't stay here," Zach told her ten minutes later when they broke away from the teens to talk about the situation.

"No. Becky needs a real bed and some much-needed rest. I'll bet she hasn't even seen a doctor yet."

"I can take them back to my house—"

"Too risky. And until we can convince Becky that she's the sole victim in this situation, she'll avoid the authorities. You harboring a runaway wouldn't be the smartest idea."

"You harboring a runaway isn't any better."

"I don't live here."

"What does that matter?" Zach asked.

"It doesn't," she said with a chuckle. "But I can't ask you to do more than you have."

"You're not asking. I'm volunteering."

She smiled. "I appreciate that. But this is what I do. I have a few ideas and need time to think about this situation. Taking Becky closer to her parents is going to cause her a lot of anxiety, which can't be healthy for the baby . . . or for her."

Zach gazed at the floor. "Yeah. You're right. I can't believe her parents. Mothers are supposed to protect their kids." Zach's voice had a bite to it.

"Not all mothers are the same. You're lucky to have Janice."

He brought his arm up and glanced at his watch. "Oh, damn . . . I'll bet they're worried that I didn't get back up the mountain."

"You should call them."

"I will."

Karen heard Becky and Nolan whispering in the room and turned her head their way.

Zach placed his hand on her shoulder and gave a gentle squeeze. "They're going to be OK."

"I know. I'm just sick for them."

"You and me both."

"There's something we haven't considered."

"I'm listening," Zach said.

"If Becky's parents realize that they could be brought up on charges, they might just let her go."

"You mean let her run away, or give their permission for them to get married?"

"Either . . . both. Although I'd love to convince them to hold off on marriage right away. It's their decision, but they're both so young."

Zach was rubbing her arm now and leaning close enough for her to absorb his heat, his strength.

"Let's get them out of here."

They packed all their stuff into the back of Zach's truck and drove to Bell. There, Karen rented a room with two beds, hiding Nolan and Becky in Zach's truck until they pulled around the back of the motel.

Karen tossed her suitcase on one of the two beds. Zach stood by the door and once again, Becky took the space beside Nolan.

"So here is what I think we should do," she began, looking at Nolan. "Tomorrow Zach can come back here and pick you up, take you to work . . . unless you want to go home with Zach tonight."

"I want to stay with Becky." Nolan's voice was firm.

"Fine. But if you don't show up at work and someone's watching, they're going to know you two are together. We need a couple of days to figure out how to get you both what you want. And unless I'm wrong, I don't think you've seen a doctor yet . . . right, Becky?"

The girl shifted her eyes to the floor. "No."

"So tomorrow I'll rent a car, and I'll drive Becky over to St. George. We'll find a doctor and get you and the baby checked out. St. George should be far enough away to avoid anyone recognizing you, don't you think?"

Becky glanced between Nolan and Karen. "Yeah, I guess."

Karen glanced at Zach. "I'll call you from St. George. I have a few contacts back home who might be able to advise me on what to do next." Karen knew it would be easier to blend into a bigger city than the town they were in now, but she didn't want to worry Becky or Nolan about the possibility of staying in St. George until the legalities could be worked out.

"Karen?" Becky asked with a timid voice.

"Yes, honey?"

"Why are you doing this? You don't even know me."

All eyes in the room were on her.

"I'm incapable of walking away from good kids in shitty situations."

Becky diverted her eyes. "I'm not a good kid. I ended up pregnant—"

"Whoa!" Karen made a cutting motion to her neck. "Enough of that. Yeah, maybe you two could have done something to prevent a pregnancy, but that doesn't make you a bad kid. You have hormones just like everyone else. They're really powerful when you care for someone and damn hard to resist. A bad kid would have their baby in a bathroom and toss the infant in the trash . . . you plan on doing that?"

"No!" The horror on Becky's face was exactly what Karen was aiming for.

"Good to know. Now enough of the *bad kid* talk."

"Yes, ma'am."

"So we're all in agreement about tomorrow?"

Nolan and Becky offered slow nods and Zach asked to talk to Karen outside before he left for the night.

"Are you sure you want me to leave you here?" Zach asked as they walked across the parking lot and out of hearing range.

"Do you have a better idea?"

Zach chuckled. "Not a one."

Karen leaned up against his truck and rubbed the back of her neck. This was not how she thought this day was going to end. "I'm afraid if we left them here alone they'd run off. If Becky's parents pressed charges, Nolan would end up in jail."

"I thought about that. What a shitty world. The kid doing the right thing is screwed while the messed-up parents get away with everything." Zach leaned against the truck. "Are you going to tell me why you're really doing this?"

"I really can't walk away from a sad story." She tried not to look in his eyes and feel him looking deeper.

"There's more to it than that."

It had taken her over a year to tell Michael about her parents, but Zach was different.

"My parents are still alive, Zach. My father didn't use his fist to abuse his power over his child." She remembered her father walking into her room, and the wave of discomfort that swam over her in the moments leading up to . . . "I was barely a teenager, just in a training bra, and he started looking at me different." The entire memory was clouded . . . as if she could make it different just by looking the other way.

Zach's body tensed, and the playful smile fell from his lips, his fist clenched at his side.

"He came to me one night, kissed, and touched me." Destroyed her trust . . . made her feel dirty just by existing. "It was awful."

The familiar hurt sat in her chest and threatened tears.

Zach pulled her to him and wrapped his arms around her as if he could protect her from her memories.

"Good God, Karen."

She was in the kitchen, helping her mother clean the dishes. A rare moment since her mother wasn't much for household chores.

Karen took the moment alone with her mom to open up.

"Mom?"

"Yeah?" Her mom slapped another dish into the drainage rack for Karen to dry.

She stared to shake . . . more nervous than ever about the words that threatened to escape her lips. Her mom worked at a local bar, lived on the tips she'd earned. She left her alone with her dad a lot. Something that started to bother Karen more and more as the years moved on. Now she understood why.

The plate in her hand fell to the floor with a resounding crash.

April, her mother, turned off the water and scolded her. "Dammit. That's the third dish you broke this month."

"Sorry."

"You should be more careful."

"I'm sorry. I didn't mean it."

April squatted to the floor and started to clean up the mess.

Karen stood there and watched her mother.

"Well, aren't you going to help me?" April yelled.

Karen removed the trash from under the sink, picked up the big pieces, and tossed them inside. The last bit caught her finger and gashed the end. She sat there on the floor watching her finger bleed. So much pain for such a small cut.

"What's wrong with you? Get that in the water. Stupid girl."

Karen stood and turned on the faucet and let the water run over her finger for several minutes.

"What is your problem?"

Tears started to fall before Karen opened her mouth. "Mom . . ."

"What?"

"Dad . . . he . . ."

April stood perfectly still. Waiting. As if she knew what was coming. "What?" Her voice was gruff, making it even harder for Karen to force the words from her lips.

"He . . ." Tears were flowing now. Each syllable harder than the last to produce. "He . . ."

"Spit it out."

Part of Karen told her to shut her mouth. Keep it inside. The other part, the one that told her it was wrong that her own father had touched her in the ways that her sexual education class in fifth grade had taught her, kept her lips moving. "He touched me."

April waited. The water ran in the sink and neither of them gave it any attention.

"On my privates."

April shut the water off, nearly taking the faucet with her. "You're a liar. Always embellishing the truth. Last Saturday you said I came home at three . . . I was home by two thirty."

Karen's lip trembled. It was three. And her mom was drunk.

"I'm not lying."

Karen's head spun with the slap her mother delivered. Her mom hadn't struck her since she was a toddler.

"Go to bed. Think about what you're saying."

Karen turned, left her mom . . . and never saw her again.

She wrapped her arms around Zach and pushed back her rising emotions. "I told my mom but she called me a liar. Then they both just left."

He cradled her head in his hands and pulled away enough to look into her eyes.

"What do you mean they left?"

This story didn't get any easier. "They packed their bags and left. I sat in the house for a week before I realized they weren't coming back. I was scared, alone. Worried about how I was going to live, eat. My aunt lived on the other side of the country and there wasn't any other family. Eventually my school notified the authorities and my aunt stepped in."

"How old were you?" he asked with a hoarse whisper.

"Th-thirteen."

He pulled her close again, held her tighter.

She rested her cheek on his chest and inhaled his scent and the protection his arms created around her. "So you see . . . I can't walk away. I can't."

"We won't. We'll figure this out."

When he looked her in the eye again, he lowered his lips to hers. The kiss was caring, soft, and brought on a different kind of want inside of her. Sharing herself with someone intimately had always been separate from sharing herself with someone emotionally. Never did the two actually happen with the same man.

Until now.

For a brief moment, Karen didn't think about Michael or about the fact they were married or that Zach was Michael's brother. She simply fell into Zach's touch, his kiss and let herself enjoy the tender moment.

Zach nibbled on her lower lip before ending their kiss. "I'll be back in the morning."

"I'll call if something changes."

He kissed her once more before pulling way.

Chapter Twenty-One

Karen ended her night texting Michael.

We found them.

Is everything OK?

No. Everything sucks. But I have it handled. Let me know when you're in Canada.

I will.

She thought about Zach . . . the kissing.

We really need to talk.

I know. Maybe you can meet me up north?

Maybe.

Be safe.

Michael's last message as it always was. Thoughtful, friendly . . . Michael.

Karen glanced at the young couple as they settled beside each other in the bed next to hers and listened as the night sounds invaded the room. Sometime around one, she felt her eyes drift asleep.

The first door that slammed outside the motel at five woke her.

Nolan and Becky still slept soundly.

Karen twisted around, found the cool spot on her pillow, and drifted off again.

Then a knock sounded on the door. "Karen?"

Zach!

"Yeah. Hold on."

Becky was stirring next to Nolan as Karen opened the motel door.

Zach lifted a small tray with steaming cups of what smelled like coffee.

"Oh, God . . . thank you!"

Zach smiled. The stubble of his chin lifted with his lips and gave him the sexy edge she couldn't help but love.

He stepped in the room and noted the sleeping lot of them. "Taking the day off, Nolan?"

"Sorry." Nolan swiped a hand over his eyes and slid from beneath the covers. "Just need a quick shower."

The teen walked to the shower in a pair of sweatpants, and before anyone could grab a cup of java, the sound of the pipes rattling filled the room of the cheap motel.

Karen held the door open as Zach moved inside. "I wasn't sure what to get. I managed doughnuts and bagels, figured that would please someone."

Becky scooted up in her bed, a timid smile on her lips.

"And milk for you."

When he handed Becky a paper container with milk Karen felt tears in her eyes.

Her eyes weren't even open and Zach was already working the room.

"Thanks, Mr. Gardner."

Zach winked at the teen and focused his attention on Karen. "How did you sleep?"

Karen shrugged. She could only guess how she looked. Like a woman who'd managed only a few hours of sleep, much of it filled with unwanted memories and dreams. "I'm OK."

He didn't buy it, she could see by the worry etching his face.

She accepted his offering of coffee and adorned it with cream and sugar before sampling its flavor. Perfect.

She sighed and opened her eyes to find Zach watching her with a smile.

"What?"

"It's *that* good?"

"Long night."

Zach handed her a paper from his back pocket. "Here's the only rental car company in town. If you run into a problem, call me."

She accepted the paper and thanked him.

The water from the pipes in the walls made a squeaking noise before turning off.

When Nolan stepped from the bathroom he strode to the side of his bed, sniffed a shirt he'd tossed there the night before, and then pulled it over his head.

Karen laughed, but tried to do so quietly.

Becky sat in the center of her bed sipping her milk and nibbling on a doughnut.

"Did you call your parents?" Karen asked Zach.

Zach nodded. "Told them I had some issues I needed to deal with on site. That I'd try and get back to them later today."

Karen gave a sad smile. "Guess your vacation is over."

He looked through her. "Some people make it better. Without them, it's just idle time."

Like the last year of her life. Idle time spent pretending to be something she wasn't. Not that it was terribly difficult living with a great friend in a fabulous home. Only in the past month did her decision to put much of her life on hold cause any real emotional turmoil. In the end, it would be worth it to help people like Becky and Nolan, or so she told herself.

"Is one of those for me?" Nolan asked when he eyed the cups of coffee.

"Yeah." Zach pulled one from the tray and handed it to him.

Nolan mumbled thanks and took a big drink from the black coffee. He sighed with satisfaction. "That's good."

"We should get out of here. Before anyone sees us."

Zach was right.

Karen sat on the end of her bed and watched as Nolan packed his small bag. Then he hesitated before he leaned over and kissed Becky's cheek. The motion was sweet, and so full of innocent love that Karen had to look away. "You need anything . . . call me."

Becky nodded with a smile. "I'm OK."

Then when she didn't think anyone watched, Karen noticed Becky mouth the words *I love you* to Nolan.

Nolan kissed her again, then took a bite of Becky's pastry and strode past Zach and out the door.

"Coming?"

Zach lifted an eyebrow and then glanced at Karen with a smile. "Call me."

Karen saluted him with her coffee cup as he closed the door behind him.

Alone with Becky, they both smiled at the closed door.

"Nolan is a good guy," Karen told her.

When her comment was met with silence, she turned to see Becky's blank stare. "He's the best."

Her lower lip trembled.

Karen set her coffee on the table between the beds and moved next to Becky. With her closeness, the girl started to cry.

Karen enveloped her in her arms and Becky clasped on. "I'm so scared."

"I know, baby. I know. It's OK." Karen stared at the stained ceiling of the tacky motel and thanked God she had been in Hilton when this girl needed her most.

Becky's hand clutched Karen's shirt. Her sobs filled the room. "It's OK. You're going to be OK. You're not alone."

———

Zach pulled Nolan aside and shoved a bag with a double cheese-burger, fries, and a Coke at him for lunch. They both sat on the tailgate of his truck and bit into their burgers in relative silence.

"How do you like construction?" Zach asked him between bites.

"I like it. Much better than filling orders and inventorying your dad's shop."

Zach understood that. "Do you think you and Becky will stay here in Hilton?"

"I need to work."

That wasn't the answer Zach was looking for.

"But I don't think Becky's parents are going to walk away. And people will talk."

"People are going to talk anywhere."

Nolan shoved several fries in his mouth and talked around them. "But less people know us in Bell . . . or even St. George."

"That's a long commute."

"Whatever. I have to think about Becky. I don't think she's safe here . . . ya know? And if I run into her dad, I'm bound to rearrange the man's face. Bastard."

Zach was half-ready to do that himself and he didn't even know what the man looked like.

"You have a lot to think about." Zach sipped some more of his soda. "And you're thinking. That's good. Best for both of you."

"I love her. Not just because of the baby either."

"Are you saying that for my benefit or yours?" Zach watched him now, searching for doubt.

"Yours. I already know how I feel. Yeah, I would have waited until she was out of school . . . until I'd saved some money and we could find a place of our own. But shit happens. Go with the flow and all that. Life happens whether you want it to or not."

Zach's thoughts shifted to Karen and her honey blonde hair and pink lips she licked right before he kissed her. The way she made him feel alive. Hell, he hadn't realized how dead he felt inside until she walked into his life.

He shook thoughts of Michael from his head. Life happens, whether you want it to or not.

———

The clinic provided an anonymous setting for Becky and Karen. Karen had called ahead and arranged for them to be taken into a room quickly. Becky gave them the name Rebecca Parker and answered all her medical questions on the history form while Karen sat beside her in support. They'd covered up the bruise on her face with some makeup, but only a blind person wouldn't notice the marks.

"Do you want me to stay in here when the doctor comes in?" Karen asked.

When Becky didn't immediately say no, Karen took the decision away. "I'll stay. If you want me out, just nod."

"OK."

One of the nurses stepped in the room and retrieved the form. She scanned it with a smile and then handed Becky a plastic cup. "We need a urine sample. And you can put this on, open in the back." Becky took the blue and white hospital gown and crumpled it to her chest.

The nurse directed her to the restroom and then moved back into the exam room and waited.

"Is she your sister?"

Karen smiled. "No. I'm a friend."

"Poor kid. She's scared."

"Aren't they all?"

The nurse nodded. "At least she's not fourteen."

Karen didn't even want to think about those kids. At least at seventeen, Becky was close to adult age. Fourteen-year-olds shouldn't be having sex. Even Karen had her limits. She thought of her own father and closed the image from her mind. Some kids didn't have a choice about sex.

Becky slipped back in the room holding her gown closed with one hand, her clothes and the plastic urine-filled cup with the other.

Karen helped her with her clothes, while the nurse took the sample away. "The doctor will be here in a minute."

Becky wiggled up on the small exam table, her legs dangling.

On the walls were posters showing the different stages of pregnancy. There were hotline numbers to help lines, runaway shelters, and adoption agencies.

"Have you been to a gynecologist before?"

Becky shook her head. "No."

Her parents really hadn't done their job in preparing this girl for life. "Well, it's not that bad. And remember, the doctors do this all day."

They stopped talking when the door opened and a petite brunette stepped in wearing a lab coat.

"Hello, Rebecca," the woman said with a smile. "I'm Dr. Grayem." The doctor held out her hand for Rebecca to shake.

"Hi."

Karen waited for the doctor to turn her way. "And you are?"

"A friend."

"Not her mother?"

Karen shook her head and noticed Becky stiffen.

"No."

Dr. Grayem sat on a rolling stool and dropped the questions about who Karen was.

She looked at the chart and asked questions. "Your last period was twelve weeks ago?"

"Yes, ma'am."

"You have normal periods?"

"Yes."

Dr. Grayem made a few notes on her paper. "Any morning sickness?"

"A little."

"How much did you weigh before you realized you were pregnant?"

Becky told her and the doctor nodded. "Do you know who the father is?"

Becky sucked in a breath. "Yes. I-I've only been with him."

Dr. Grayem stopped writing notes and glanced up at Becky. "I'm not suggesting you sleep around, Rebecca. I want to know what risk factors you might have. Is your boyfriend involved now?"

She nodded.

Karen snuck her hand next to Becky's and the girl grasped on.

The doctor asked several more questions, mostly confirming what Becky had already indicated on the history form, but in doing so, Becky was growing more anxious.

Dr. Grayem snapped the paper in her hand closed and set it on the table behind her. "I'm going to examine you now and tell you everything I'm doing before I do it, OK, Rebecca?"

"Is it going to hurt?"

The doctor smiled. "No."

Karen backed away from the table but stood close enough to assure Becky that she was there. Becky closed her eyes during the pelvic exam and winced at the coldness of the doctor's hands. All the while Dr. Grayem talked about what to expect over the next month, about what to watch for, cramping, bleeding . . . the usual suspects of complications. The exam was brief, after which the doctor washed her hands and walked toward the door. Instead of leaving, she called for a nurse to bring an ultrasound machine into the room.

"Is everything OK?" Becky asked.

"Everything is fine. You're already into your second trimester. Do you want to see what your baby looks like?"

Becky blinked, tears started to gather behind her eyes.

"If you think you want to give the baby up for adoption, I can—"

"No! I'm not giving my baby away."

Karen smiled and stepped aside when the nurse rolled in the ultrasound machine.

"All right then. Let's take a look."

Dr. Grayem rolled the chair beside Becky, and the nurse dimmed the light in the room to see the monitor better. Karen stood at Becky's side and held her hand.

After they applied a thick layer of gel on Becky's abdomen, the sound of the machine picked up a heart rate.

"That's you," Dr. Grayem told them. "Notice the slow pace . . . well it's a little fast, but too slow to be your baby."

Becky was watching the monitor with wide eyes as the black-and-white images swam past.

Then the room filled with a much faster heart rate.

"There we are."

The doctor kept the wand on Becky's belly stable and pointed to the monitor with her other hand. "See there. Just a flutter."

Then the image on the screen twitched.

"Baby's waving. Saying hi." Dr. Grayem clicked a few buttons and moved the wand, then clicked a few more.

Becky was squeezing Karen's hand and smiling like a mother should.

Dr. Grayem pointed out the big head, the heart, and the little legs. So tiny, so precious.

Karen fished her phone out of her pocket. "Want me to take a picture, send it to—"

"Yes," Becky interrupted her before she mentioned Nolan's name.

"I'll print one for you here, too."

Karen watched the joy on Becky's face when the doctor told her when she wanted to see her again, and how in a couple of months they could determine the sex of the baby if they wanted.

Karen attached the ultrasound picture to a text to Zach with a message.

Tell Nolan mom and baby are fine.

Karen stepped out of the room with the doctor so Becky could dress.

"She's lucky to have a good friend," Dr. Grayem said.

"She's a good kid. Gonna be a great mom."

"Where did she get the black eye?"

Karen had no problem relaying what she'd been told. "Her parents weren't happy with the news of the baby. And they won't be involved from here on out."

Dr. Grayem shook her head and cussed under her breath. "If Rebecca needs a statement from me, call."

Dr. Grayem fished a business card from her pocket and handed it to Karen.

"Thank you."

Karen paid for their visit in cash, added a donation for those who couldn't pay along with it, and walked with Becky to the rental car. Once there, her phone buzzed.

Zach's reply to her text was, Wow. Didn't think I'd see a grown man cry. Call when you get a minute alone.

I will.

"You made Nolan's day," Karen told Becky.

Becky just stared at the picture of her baby. "I'm really having a baby."

"Yep. You're really having a baby."

"I'm going to be a mom."

Karen laughed at the wonder in her voice. "Well let's get you and the baby fed. You have to be hungry."

"Starving. And the doctor wants me to gain weight."

Karen giggled and drove away from the clinic.

Chapter Twenty-Two

Karen convinced Becky that staying in St. George was safer than driving back to Bell. Not to mention the hotel options were much better.

Karen booked a couple of rooms, knowing that Becky and Nolan would probably like their privacy. She no longer thought Becky wanted to run away . . . not from Karen and Zach anyway.

With a full stomach and having had a busy emotion-filled day, Becky crawled into bed for a late-afternoon nap.

Karen slipped into her own room to make some much-needed phone calls. She started with Gwen, in hopes of pushing a few mommy buttons to get some help.

"Hey baby mama," Karen teased when Gwen picked up the phone.

"Well it's about time you called. We were starting to think you're never coming back," Gwen scolded.

"I'd have made it back already but I got hung up." Karen told her about Becky and the entire messed-up situation.

"Oh, the poor thing."

"She's sleeping now. Much happier since she saw the baby."

"It's a wonderful moment. Neil cried."

"No way!" Neil was the poster child for stoic.

"He'd deny it if you called him on it. But he teared up and spent the rest of the night with his head in my lap as if he could hear the baby's heartbeat through my stomach."

Karen couldn't imagine it. Neil was simply too fierce and big to do something so gentle.

"Becky's more at peace now that she's seen the doctor and the baby. But we need to get her parents to back off. She's still considered a runaway, and I have no doubt they'd bring Nolan up on charges for God knows what if given the chance."

"What can I do?"

"I need some facts checked. I don't know how the laws are different here than in California. Becky still won't be eighteen when the baby is born, but close to it. She could just stay hidden until she's eighteen, but that's no way to live."

"If Neil and I were there, I'd have my husband knock on her parents' door and tell them to leave her alone or go to jail."

"I thought about that, actually. We should look into the resources for abused kids who want to escape their parents."

"Is Becky willing to go to the police?"

Karen cradled her head in her hands. "Not yet. But I think if it was that or risk the health of her baby . . . she'd rat her parents out. And rightfully so."

"It would still be hard on her."

"I'd like to find a way to keep Zach and Michael's family out of the drama as much as possible. Hilton is a freakin' small town. So if it comes down to it, I might ask for some help here."

"We're here for you. Or I can ask Rick to go."

Rick was a good friend of Neil's, a fellow retired Marine and nearly as big as Mr. Stoic himself.

"I might take you up on that."

Gwen sighed. "So how is everything else? I saw that Michael came home long enough to pack and leave again."

Neil and his security team, including Rick, monitored the house and probably knew more about the two of them than was necessary.

It was Karen's turn to sigh. "Michael's sister figured out what we've been up to . . . and why."

"Oh, my."

"She called Michael on it. But he's not ready for the rest of his family to know what's going on."

"Oh . . . and what about Zach?"

"He doesn't know."

"That's not what I'm asking, Karen. What about *you* and Zach?"

"I don't want to have feelings for him."

"But you do."

Karen nodded though no one could see the gesture. "I do. He's kind and thoughtful. He makes me laugh . . . makes me feel safe."

Gwen hesitated. "Have you . . . ?"

"No. Well, we've kissed. The guilt was so awful I couldn't do more than that. But the guilt is fading, Gwen. It's like the more time we spend together the harder it is to see why we're trying to stay apart. And he knows that Michael and I are getting divorced."

"Oh?"

"Yeah. I didn't see keeping the lie. Not when the sister already knows, and Michael and I weren't planning on visiting again. Not together anyway."

"Does Michael know about Zach?"

"No. Which is killing me."

Gwen clicked her tongue. "This is so easily solved."

"How can you say that? I'm falling for my husband's brother. There's nothing easy about that."

"Tell Michael."

"Michael will hate it."

"Oh, Karen. Michael might have his faults but he does love you. I'm sure he'd want to see you happy. So long as his secret doesn't get out, he can't fault you for falling for his gene pool."

Karen played with the diamond on her finger. "I don't know."

"You've given up your life for a year to help keep Michael's secret hidden."

"And I'm getting paid to do it."

Gwen snickered. "You know what's funny about that? I wouldn't put it past you to sacrifice yourself for a friend without the pay. Look what you're doing for those kids. You've known them less than two weeks and you're hiding runaways, sleeping in motels . . . Karen, my dear, you're a bleeding heart to the highest degree. Yes, Michael came to us, but had you known him, the real him, before meeting through Alliance you might have offered to marry him just to help him out."

Karen wanted to deny her friend, but couldn't.

"I have to tell him about Zach."

"Yes. You do," Gwen agreed. "Call Michael. I'll make some calls here and see what we can do for your runaways."

———

Thirty minutes later Karen connected with Michael. Her hands shook as she held the phone but Gwen was right. The longer this secret stayed inside her, the harder it was to let out. If she told Michael about her feelings for Zach, and he hated her for it, then at least she was the one to tell him and he wouldn't find out from someone else.

"Hey? How's Canada?"

"Cool and wet. Are you still in Utah?"

"Yeah. St. George." She brought him up to date on the kids, and the progress.

"How's my brother handling all the drama?"

She thought of the milk and doughnuts. "Really well," she said with a smile. "You two really are a lot alike."

"In some ways."

"Listen, Michael . . . I told Zach that you and I were getting a divorce."

Silence hung for a moment. "I guess that was coming. Has he told my parents?"

"No. I don't think so."

"I think my mom would have called had she heard."

"They're all still up at the cabin." So Karen thought. By now, who knew?

"We knew the breakup would be hard." He sounded so at ease with their divorce.

"Uhm, Michael . . . remember when we were driving to your parents and we were talking about wanting to be with someone?"

Again, there was silence. "Yeah?"

"Well, you told me when you hooked up with Ryder."

"Yeah? There's someone you wanna see?" She knew his playful tone would soon change.

"There is . . . but . . ."

"Go for it, Karen. Just be discreet. We had an agreement. We're good."

"Michael. It's not that simple."

He laughed. "Sure it is. Relaxing, too."

"Michael! Just . . . oh, God this is hard."

He stopped laughing. "Karen, sweetheart. I get it. You're horny. No one gets that more than me."

"Stop, Michael. It's not just sex. I mean . . . it might be, but . . ." The farther she got into the conversation the harder it was to say his name. "It's Zach. OK. I have it bad for Zach."

Complete silence hung over the phone.

The smile Michael wore while he joked with Karen about the need for sex slowly slid from his face while he dropped into the chair of the executive star trailer he lived in while on set.

Fuck. Oh, Fuck.

"I didn't want it. I've tried to deny it." Karen's voice wavered as she spoke; her words ran into each other like a freight train piling up cars. "I'm sorry. I'll just keep ignoring it. Forget I said anything."

He couldn't forget this.

Karen started to cry. "I'm sorry, Michael. I'll call you later."

"No! Wait. This takes a few minutes to absorb."

"I'm sorry," she whispered. "So sorry, Michael."

"Zach? Really?" Michael ran his free hand over his face and glanced at the ring he'd worn for over a year.

"Yeah."

"Damn. I think I saw this coming."

"You did?" She hiccupped into the phone.

"Yeah. I saw him watching you. Noticed the tension between you both." He understood more than most what it felt like to have feelings for someone he could never have. Not openly in any event. "Has he . . . have you?"

"No. Well. I kissed him, we've kissed, but that's all. And he doesn't know about you," she said quickly.

"You can't tell him." Yet Michael knew that it would only be a matter of time before something slipped from Karen. It wouldn't be her fault. When two people were intimate, certain truths had a way of revealing themselves. Even Ryder knew that he and Karen only had a paper marriage.

"Of course not. I would never do that to you, Michael. Ever." She wouldn't mean to. Damn, he had to figure out a way to tell Zach himself about his sexuality. He owed it to Karen so she didn't have to lie.

"If he figures it out, you need to tell me."

"I will."

He chuckled. "I have a strong desire to kick his ass," he confessed.

"Being territorial?"

"Yeah. Which is kind of sick. I have no right." No right at all. Karen was his best friend, not his lover.

"Of course you do. We're married."

He sighed. "In name only. I'd be even more upset if he wanted to bang Ryder."

Karen laughed. "I don't think Zach plays for that team."

The thought of Zach and Ryder made him laugh. "No. I'd think I'd have figured it out if he did. Wow."

"I'm sorry, Michael."

"Why do you keep apologizing? I doubt you set out to have the hots for my brother." As they spoke, some of the earlier tension eased. His friendship with this woman was too important. Besides, he loved his brother, and Michael couldn't think of a better person for Karen than Zach.

She choked on her one-word answer. "No."

"I still wanna kick his ass." He was playing with her now, and hoped it made her smile. The thought of her crying over him left a heaviness in his chest he didn't like. His thoughts quickly twisted to the paparazzi and the press. *Oh, damn . . . this is going to get ugly.*

"Just be careful, Karen. The media would have a field day with this . . . with you."

She paused before saying, "I don't have to act on anything with Zach."

Not act on it? He heard the guilt in her voice and needed to remind Karen of their honesty commitment to each other. "No. Karen . . . we wouldn't be having this conversation if you were in complete control here. My brother's a good guy. The fact you're both holding back means you give a shit about my feelings. He's still a complete dick for hitting on my wife . . . but how can I blame him? You're hot."

She laughed.

He kept talking. "And if you and I were happily married I doubt you'd be giving out the vibe of availability. Goes to show we needed to work on ending this charade before now." Yet selfishly he liked having Karen around. No one drove away the loneliness like her; no one knew him better . . . and loved him despite all his faults.

The reality that they were splitting up hit him.

"I've loved being your fake wife, Michael."

He felt moisture behind his eyes. "I've loved being your fake husband." He swallowed, hard, and said the only thing he could. "I'll file when I get home."

She started crying again, making it damn hard to avoid joining her. "I can move out when I get back."

"No need . . . not right away. I'm going to be up here for a while." He cleared his throat and looked around his lonely trailer. "Are you crying?" He wanted to dry her tears.

She hiccupped. "Yeah. Stupid huh?"

He swallowed the knot in his throat. "Naw . . . liberating. I'd cry but people might think I'm gay. Gotta go get pissing drunk and beat on someone. Wanna fly my brother up here to help a guy out?"

Her laughter caused the knot to untie and he leaned against his seat. Then she sobbed again. "OK, you have to stop the waterworks. The piece of paper is going to be ripped up. That's it. I still love ya. And I'll always have your back. Us Gardners are loyal that way." *Zach will be, too.*

Karen sucked in a deep breath he heard all the way in Canada. "So how is the producer? Asshat or hottie?"

"That's my girl." He ignored the moisture in his eyes and kept talking . . . kept laughing. "He's hot, but a complete asshat."

She laughed, and Michael felt it deep inside his heart.

"Isn't your leading lady Angie McMillian?"

"Yeah. Anorexic and just this side of a bitch."

"Really? She always seemed so sweet on TV."

They talked as they always had for a little while, and Michael knew they were going to be fine.

Chapter Twenty-Three

Zach drove Nolan down to St. George, and followed his GPS to the hotel where Karen said she and Becky were staying. The last time he'd been in St. George had been with Tracey to visit her family. Nolan had been a beaming ray of sunshine ever since the picture of his kid ended up on Zach's cell phone. He went from a nervous, unsure kid to a proud daddy before Zach's eyes. The transition was so unexpected he couldn't help but stare. He actually felt sorry for Becky's parents if Nolan ever had a moment alone with them . . . or if they tried to stand in their way of being together.

Zach found himself admiring the young man as he pulled off the freeway an hour later and zigzagged through the crowded streets of the larger Utah city.

"I could have driven myself," Nolan said as they pulled into the hotel parking lot.

"Your car will lead the authorities to Becky."

"I don't think anyone is looking for us here."

Zach pulled into a parking space. "Let's not take any chances right now. You have the weekend off, and Karen and I will figure something out over the next few days."

They walked to the outside balcony of the hotel room.

Nolan knocked on Becky's door. She opened it only after Nolan whispered that it was him. The teenager slipped into the room and Zach moved on to Karen's door.

She looked as if she'd just stepped from the shower, something he and Nolan had taken care of back at his house before he shoved an overnight bag in his truck in case he ended up stuck in the city. Then they hit the road to St. George.

"Hey?"

Karen opened the door wider and he stepped inside.

Her skin smelled like flowers, and her hair was a cloud around the edges of her face. She was so damn beautiful. He shoved his hands in his pockets, even though he wanted to touch her.

"Hey."

"I dropped Nolan off with Becky. He wanted to stay here with her."

Karen smiled and the room lost oxygen. "They probably want to stare at the ultrasound picture all night."

Zach grinned. "Yeah. That was something."

"Makes it real. It's not just a blue line on a pregnancy test anymore."

He couldn't imagine everything Nolan was going through. One thing he did know, the kid was in for the long haul.

Zach nodded toward the door. "Wanna go grab a bite to eat? Bring them back some takeout?"

"That would be great."

They told the kids they were leaving, and Zach led Karen to his truck and opened the door for her to get in.

They found a quiet Italian restaurant and Karen insisted on ordering a bottle of wine. The wine was surprisingly good but the company was what kept him smiling.

"I talked to Gwen. She had a suggestion that I think we should consider."

"What's that?"

Karen was ripping through a bread stick and washing it down with the cabernet.

"Talking to Becky's parents. Let them know we're aware of their abuse. Tell them that Becky will go to the authorities if they don't let her walk away."

"Isn't that an empty threat at this point? Becky didn't seem interested in pressing charges."

"I think if she felt threatened, that would change."

"To protect the baby?"

"Or Nolan. She's scared, but with each passing day, she's getting stronger. They're going to be OK. We'll get them over this hurdle."

"You're an incredible woman, Karen."

She sipped her wine and shook her head. "No. Just a sucker."

Their food came and she dug in with an appetite that rivaled his.

"I think Nolan is being watched. The police drove by the site three times that I saw."

Karen paused midbite. "Did they follow you here?"

"No. And Nolan's car is still in the garage. The sheriff goes to church with Becky's parents. Knows them really well according to Nolan."

"That can complicate things. She can always petition the court to emancipate her, but she has to prove she can care for herself and prove to the court that her parents aren't fit."

"To do that she'd have to reveal their abuse."

Karen sat lost in her own thoughts for a minute. He reached out and touched her hand.

"That's hard to do. So many people don't believe the victims." She shook her head. "We'll figure it out. I suppose it's time for me to investigate all the legalities of helping out runaways."

"You keep saying that. What exactly do you envision when you think of helping out kids like Becky and Nolan?"

Karen sat back and the shadows of her past drifted from her face when she spoke.

"I always saw a big house . . . you know, one of those colonial, or maybe even Victorian jobs with lots of bedrooms. Like those used in bed-and-breakfasts?"

"Yeah."

"It would have to be remodeled for extra bathrooms of course . . . and probably a larger kitchen than those old houses normally have. But I want something that feels like a home. I'd have it on some kind of registry for runaway safe houses. There would be rules of course. No drugs, no violence . . . that kind of thing. No bullying. And the kids would have to work part-time, be in some kind of continuation school, or be studying for the GED. If they're really young, and this is the part where I'd need legal guidance, they'd be registered in school."

"It sounds like you've thought a lot about it. Why hadn't you put your plan in motion before now?"

Her blue eyes left his. "Timing. But that's changing."

"You know what you're talking about is a full-time job, right?"

"I'm not afraid of hard work. And I've made some crazy rich contacts over the last few years. Plenty of them have expressed interest in helping me fund-raise and pilot my idea."

Zach could see her rallying an entire village on behalf of disadvantaged kids.

"You won't be able to save them all."

"But I can save a few . . . even one is worth it."

Zach's eyes fell on their clasped hands. He stroked the inside of her wrist, that's when he noticed she'd taken off her wedding ring. He bit his lip to keep from asking why. Maybe the timing she spoke of was her pending divorce. With the pressures of being Michael Wolfe's wife behind her, she could concentrate on what made her happy. Though he didn't see his brother standing in the way of anything she wanted.

The waiter stopped by and refilled their wineglasses. Karen ordered a couple of pasta dishes to go for the kids and pushed her plate aside.

"I don't think we're going to find out what we need to do for Nolan and Becky this weekend. But we're going to have to consider where they'll live."

"They can't stay in hotels forever," Zach said.

"Exactly."

"Nolan talked about finding a place here in St. George and commuting."

"Sounds stressful."

"Lots of people commute. And the cost of living here isn't as high as California." Which, if Zach had to guess, Karen would suggest they move to so she could help them.

"An hour commute in LA is standard operating procedure."

Zach laughed. "We can look into affordable apartments here. I'd be happy to cosign and advance Nolan some money."

"You don't have to do that."

"I want to." He turned his hand around hers and laced their fingers together. A small smile played on her pink lips and she squeezed his hand.

"I-I talked to Michael today."

The mention of his brother's name made him pause and look away. "Oh."

"Zach?"

God he loved hearing his name come from her lips. He looked up to find her still smiling.

"I told him . . . about us. About our attraction."

He waited for the boom.

"What did he say?"

Her smile was weak. "He asked me to fly you to Canada so he could kick your ass."

She was still smiling and he couldn't really tell if Mike's words were a joke.

"He was shocked. I think. I had to tell him."

Zach brought her fingers to his lips and kissed their tips. "It's the right thing to do."

"We've always been honest with each other."

"How did he really take it?"

She glanced at the ceiling as if it held the answer. "Gracefully. But he thinks the world of you and we already knew about our divorce. So it isn't as if there's a wedge between him and me because of you."

He kissed the place on her finger where his brother's ring once stood. "You took off the ring."

"It didn't feel right wearing it."

He sat there for several minutes just watching the color of her eyes and the sparkle from the dim lights reflect within them. He wanted to kiss her, hold her . . . make sure she was OK after what had to have been a difficult conversation.

The waiter dropped off their check. Zach quickly tossed a few bills on the table and led her out to his truck.

The parking lot was dark, and before he tucked her into the passenger seat, he took a moment and gathered her into his arms. She went willingly and tilted her head and lips toward his.

Her arms slid up and over his shoulders as he kissed her. She tasted like wine and smelled like passion fruit and flowers. Exotic flowers that made him think of vast beaches and warm sunshine. Her tongue sought his and he pressed her against the side of the truck. They were breathless when he pulled away. "I want to make love to you," he whispered.

She shivered and clawed at his back. "I have my own room at the hotel."

He chuckled against her temple. "Then why are we necking in a parking lot like kids?"

"Because it's fun?"

Laughing, he pulled her away from the truck long enough to open the door for her. The trip back to the hotel steamed up as she slid across the bench seat of his truck and tucked next to him, her hand resting on his thigh and keeping his cock on high alert.

They said very little as she led the way to her room. She stopped at Becky's door, knocked, and then handed them the food she'd ordered. The kids thanked both of them and shut the door.

Karen's hand shook as she slid the key card through the slot.

As soon as she closed the door behind her, Zach set the deadbolt, pressed her back to the door, and kissed her with an urgency he'd never felt before.

He couldn't touch all of her fast enough. Their lips were on fire. Her breath came in staccato pants that matched his. He'd dreamed of being with Karen from the moment they met. Now, she was reaching under his shirt and fanning her hands over his chest, touching him with the promise of more. When she lowered her hands to his butt and pulled him closer, he groaned, lifted her from her feet, and swung her around to the bed.

They fell onto it together, his leg pressed between hers. "I should slow down, but I don't think I can," he said between kissing her and playing with the buttons of her shirt.

"This is crazy," she said as she tugged his shirt from his shoulders.

"Reckless." He managed to pop a button free and worked on the next while Karen's hand slid into the waistband of his jeans.

"Sinful."

The creamy white of her breasts pushed from the maroon bra.

He lowered his lips to her flesh, pressed his tongue against her for a taste.

"Oh, Zach. Yes."

Finally, the last button was free, and he sent her shirt next to his on the floor. He filled his palms with her breasts, buried his head between them, and inhaled. He knew without a doubt her scent would stay with him forever.

Karen arched her back as he slid a hand behind her to find the clasp of her bra. His fingers slipped once, twice. "I used to be good at this," he told her.

Her warm laughter worked its way up his spine, or maybe it was her fingernails that were walking up his back and down over his ass.

When her bra popped open, they both laughed.

The dusky rose of her nipples puckered and asked for attention.

Karen stopped laughing when he filled his mouth with her. Her hips ground against his. "So good," she whispered.

"Perfect." He moved to her other breast, licked, and sucked his way over every inch of her. He hesitated only when she reached one hand to the bulge in his jeans. "Damn."

"Please tell me you have condoms."

He laughed at the stress in her voice. "Of course."

She sighed and pushed him until he lay on his back, and she straddled his legs. Her blue eyes were heavy with desire as she leaned over him to kiss his chest, his neck. When she nibbled on his jaw, she told him, "I've wanted this sexy chin on my skin since the first time I saw you."

He held her head when she slid her lips over his again. Wet kisses drove him past reason.

She sat up, her swollen breasts shoved in front of her, and reached for the button of her pants. Zach watched, fascinated as she released the button, and lowered the zipper. She spread her hand over her own stomach and let her fingers drift below the level of her panties that peeked at him through her jeans. His eyes snapped away from her little show to find her eyes on him, her lip caught between her teeth.

"Jesus."

He rolled her over and tugged her pants from her hips, made quick work of his own until they were both bare. Zach slid his hands over her thighs and along the edges of her mound.

She squirmed and moaned with frustration. "Zach, please. We've waited long enough."

The condom was out of his wallet, and in her hands seconds later. The feel of her fingers around him was something he could get used to.

The feel of her foot sliding along his leg, and the scent of her desire as she opened for him had him settling between her legs. Warm heat met him as he moved close and kissed her.

Her eyes fluttered open as he sat at her entrance. She was so damn tight as he sought to fill her. If not for the look of pure ecstasy on her face, he would have worried about splitting her in two. His control was ready to snap as she clenched around him.

"Damn, Karen."

"Everything. Please, give me all of you."

He pushed all the way in and saw stars. He had to close his eyes and push back the wave of release. He'd not been so ready to explode so quickly in his life.

"Zach?"

He opened his eyes, found her watching him.

"Make love to me."

Her sweet request moved his hips, sliding alongside her, within her. Her slick body opened for him and he whispered her name as he made her his.

She matched his every stroke and clung onto him as if her body depended on his for survival.

The moment her breathing changed, he angled her hips closer, moved faster, and stared deep in her eyes as she shattered in his arms. He followed her over the edge and knew his life was forever changed.

Chapter Twenty-Four

Up until Zach, sex came in two categories . . . memorable and forgettable. The forgettable exercise held very little space in her brain, and now that Zach dominated the memorable section, Karen was hard-pressed to remember any other man than the one in her arms. She wiggled a leg around one of his and settled into his side like a content kitten lying in the sunlight streaming through a window.

"Wow."

He chuckled, and the noise rumbled in her ear followed by the faint sound of his heartbeat as it slowed to a safer pace.

"I should feel guilty about that," Zach said as he wrapped his arms around her.

"Don't you dare." She couldn't feel guilty about something that felt so right. "Too amazing to feel guilty."

"You can say that again."

She couldn't help but wonder what thoughts were running through Zach's head. Was he thinking about Michael? Was he sated and the itch was gone? The question about Michael she couldn't ask for fear of opening questions she wouldn't answer . . . but the other one . . .

"Karen?"

"Zach?" They both called each other's name at the same time, and then laughed.

"You go." Zach kissed the top of her head.

She couldn't look in his eyes for fear he'd tell her what she wasn't prepared to hear.

"Is this . . . you and I . . . a onetime thing?"

The hand he used to hold her against him moved to her face and he urged her to look at him. Even in the dark, she saw the concern in his eyes. "Is that what you want?"

She hated the vulnerability in her heart. Karen shook her head. "No," she whispered.

Zach sighed and traced her cheek with his thumb. "I don't know how this is going to work, but I want you . . . this."

Her heart flipped in her chest. "It's going to be messy and complicated."

"My life has been too neat and easygoing for too long." His eyes sparkled.

"And if the adventure fades?" Damn, where had this insecurity come from? She looked away and swallowed hard.

"Karen." His voice was only a breath. "Look at me, sweetheart."

A soft smile met her gaze.

"I have never felt more drawn to a woman in my life. We've not been easy and I predict things won't sail in calm waters, but I'm willing to give this a go if you are."

What more could she ask of him? He didn't know their future any more than she did. At least she knew that her marriage was no more than a piece of paper. A *soon to be ripped up* license that would set her free.

"I want to see where this goes, too," she told him.

He leaned down and kissed her briefly.

When he pulled away she said, "You were going to ask something."

Now it was his turn to look uncertain as he opened up. "When are you getting divorced?"

She rested her hand on his chest and leaned her chin on her arm. "Michael is filing when he gets back to LA. The media always manages to get a hold of personal information like that and he wanted to be around to keep the press from hounding me."

"Isn't he working in Canada for a few months?"

"Yeah, but he'll come home in a couple of weeks, file immediately, then fly back to Canada when things die down." They'd talked about the scheduled day and choreographed it. "Without any contesting, it should be final in six months."

"You're sure that's what you want?" he asked.

She leaned up on her elbows, stared down at him. "Zach?"

He looked at her now.

"If I wasn't sure I wouldn't be naked in your bed."

Her own vulnerability stared back at her.

She kissed him, trying to tell him with her body that he had no reason to worry.

Later, after making love to him again, Karen drifted off to sleep nestled in his arms.

The sound of angry voices outside the hotel door jolted her awake, and the door to their room was kicked open.

"Police. Hands up."

———

Zach covered Karen with the blanket and placed himself between her and the flashlight peering in on them. From beyond the door, he heard Becky screaming, Nolan cussing.

"What the hell?" he yelled.

"Hands up."

The black barrel of a gun stared down at them, a uniformed police officer held it.

"Karen Jones?"

Karen held the covers to her chest with one hand while the other was half in the air. Zach kept his hands visible as he shielded Karen the best he could.

"Yes?"

"Zach Gardner?"

"Yes?"

The officer spoke behind him. "It's them."

Another officer pushed into the room and swept his arm in an arc with his pistol pointed at them.

"What's this about?"

"You're under arrest."

Zach's heart kicked in his chest. "For what?"

"Kidnapping."

"Kidnapping?" Karen yelled. "What are you talking about?"

The second officer walked through the small room, appeared to conclude there wasn't any threat, and holstered his gun.

"No! Leave him alone!" Becky's frantic voice outside the door reached Zach's ears.

"Becky?" Karen yelled from beside him. "Oh, God . . . her parents. Zach?"

The realization that those rough waters they'd talked about earlier were crashing all around them settled over him. "You have this all wrong!" he told the cops.

"Save it for the station."

"Out of the bed," one of the cops said.

The closest cop waved his gun between Karen and him. "Step out of the bed slowly," he instructed Zach.

The fact they were both naked and clearly not a threat didn't seem to dawn on the officer.

Zach didn't move. "Can you give Karen her clothes?"

One of them picked up her shirt, held it in his fingertips. "You, out."

With his hands in the air, Zach slid from the bed. "We'll straighten this all out," he told Karen.

Only Karen didn't seem to be listening to him. Her attention was beyond the door of the hotel and on Becky's receding voice as someone obviously led her away. The sheets had fallen along Karen's waist, her breasts exposed to the men in the room.

The primal need to shelter her rose up in him.

"Give her the shirt!"

His words snapped the cop out of his thoughts, and Karen's shirt sailed through the air. She swept it on. "How about my pants?"

"Step from the bed."

Their guns were still drawn, which made Zach's brain itch.

"We're not armed. Jesus."

"That's not what we were told. Step from the bed Ms. Jones."

"Dammit."

"It's OK, Zach." Karen kicked the sheets away and stood before the police half-naked. Her cheeks flushed. "Happy? Can I have my pants now?"

Nerves fired over every inch of Zach's skin.

To the cops' credit, they weren't staring at Karen, and one was already reaching for her pants and patting them down. Once he was convinced there weren't any hidden weapons in the clothing, he tossed the pants to Karen.

Only when she was clothed did Zach address his naked state. He pulled on a pair of jeans, stood by, watched as the officer twisted Karen around and slapped her wrists with metal cuffs. Never mind that they were doing the same thing to him. It was Karen and the look of horror on her face that would stay with him.

A third cop entered the room and started stripping the bed, dumping the overnight bags. "Where's the gun?"

"What gun?" Zach asked. "We don't have any weapons. You have this all wrong."

"Don't let Becky's parents take her. She's not safe with them." Karen's voice wavered.

The police exchanged glances.

The police officer closest to Zach grabbed his arm. "You have the right to remain silent..."

He didn't hear anything the man said. His focus was on Karen.

Karen's focus was on the door. "Her parents beat her. Please. Don't let them leave with her."

Becky screamed from outside.

Handcuffed, Karen started for the door. The officer closest to her grabbed her arm and swung her against the wall. The crack of Karen's face against the hard surface had Zach pushing against the cop holding him.

"Karen? Fuck, leave her alone."

"Get him out of here."

Two cops grabbed each of Zach's arms and shoved him out the door and into the night. He struggled against them, looking over his shoulder to witness them leading Karen out behind him. A small trickle of blood ran down her face from a cut above her eye.

Outside, police cars were parked everywhere. He saw Nolan in the back of a squad car.

Bystanders were surrounding the scene, flashes of light filled the night as someone took pictures.

His eyes saw stars as he tried to adjust to the flashing.

Karen continued to yell at the police to keep Becky safe, even as they were shoving her in the back of a waiting car.

Right as someone pushed Zach in to a separate car, his eyes fell on a lone, familiar figure in the crowd.

Tracey?

A strange satisfied smirk played on her face.

———

Her head throbbed, and her heart ached. How had this happened?

Nolan was in a holding cell, probably separate from Zach, and the police were shoving her fingers on a computer screen and telling her to hold still for the camera, and Becky wasn't anywhere in sight.

A female officer handled her from the time she entered the police station. With her, Karen thought maybe she could get through. "I don't care what you do with me, but you have to keep Becky away from her parents. She's not safe."

"Ms. Jones. Right now, you need to think about yourself. Kidnapping, resisting arrest, harboring a criminal."

"Harboring a criminal? What are you talking about?" As for resisting . . . well, she couldn't argue that without a lawyer.

"Turn to the right."

Karen did, the flash was evidence that she now had a complete mug shot. "Her parents beat her. Please. Just don't let her leave with them. She's scared."

Officer Carmen hesitated.

"Please."

"You can give a statement to my partner."

Karen closed her mouth. Why was no one listening to her? "I get a phone call. I'm not talking to anyone until I have a lawyer."

"Your choice."

Nearly an hour later, they gave Karen a phone.

The phone rang several times, making her worry that maybe her friends weren't home. Neil finally picked up. "Yeah."

"Neil? Jesus, Neil . . . I need you guys."

"Karen?" His voice was surprisingly awake for such a late hour.

The fact that she was calling from jail hadn't hit her until that moment. "I'm in jail."

"Jail?"

Her words tumbled on each other as she tried to explain the situation. "Listen. The police are saying Zach and I kidnapped Becky. We need a lawyer. We need to make sure Becky is safe. Her parents beat on her, Neil. And she's pregnant." The thought of Becky's parents getting her alone sickened her.

Karen heard Gwen's sleepy voice from beyond Neil on the phone. "What's going on?"

"Karen's in jail."

Karen's mind ran to the next obstacle. "Someone needs to call Michael. Oh, God. Becky's going to need protection, Neil." If anyone could know what needed to be done it was Neil.

"Where are you?"

"St. George."

"OK . . . hold on."

"Please hurry. The police aren't listening to me about Becky. I have no idea where she is."

Gwen's voice picked up from a second line. "Karen? Are you OK?"

Tears swelled in her eyes and she choked on her words. "I'm going to need Samantha and Blake's fancy lawyers."

"Oh, honey. We're on our way. Stay strong and don't say anything."

Karen's hands shook as she hung up the phone. All she could do now was wait and worry.

Chapter Twenty-Five

If someone had told him he'd be calling his parents to tell them he was in jail by the day's end, Zach would have told them they were on crack. Unfortunately, the call went to voice mail and Zach had little choice but to leave a message.

After the booking portion of his evening, he was placed in a holding cell with several other men, including Nolan.

"How are you doing?"

"They won't tell me where they took Becky."

"I'm sure she's safe." He wasn't sure of anything, but he needed to say something to ease the kid's pain.

"They're accusing me of raping her."

"It will all be worked out, Nolan. Just keep your mouth closed until the lawyers arrive."

"I can't afford a lawyer."

Zach nudged him. "Don't worry about that. I have you covered."

Nolan shook his head and stared at the floor. "I should have just run off with her. Then you guys wouldn't be here and she'd be safe."

"You don't know that."

Nolan slammed his fist against the bench he sat on in frustration. "Dammit."

There wasn't anything Zach could say to ease the kid's frustration. To add to his own, when Zach closed his eyes all he saw was Karen standing in front of the police with nothing on from the waist down. The humiliation of not being able to stop anyone from viewing her slapped him in the face. Where was she now? Was she scared?

Her father's phone pinged as they drove down the mountain. Hannah had decided to stay behind for another day with Rena and her family, while Judy shoved into the backseat of her parents' truck and rode with them back to Hilton.

The confidence Karen had infused into her during her brief visit gave her the incentive to discuss changing her major. To do that, Judy needed alone time with her parents.

Judy's phone buzzed in her pocket as they reached cell service. She saw several messages from one of her college roommates and opened up her texts.

OMG is this your sister-in-law? Was followed by a picture of Karen shoved up beside a police car.

Judy gasped and read the next text.

Your brother? Not the one she's married to?

Zach stood shirtless, hands behind his back.

"Oh, God."

The next picture showed the two of them kissing in a parking lot. "Oh, God!"

"What is it, dear?" Janice said from the front seat.

"Daddy, pull over."

Sawyer looked at her through the rearview mirror.

"Are you sick?"

"Just pull over."

The last thing she wanted was her father to see any of this while driving.

Her mother was turned around now and staring. "Judy?"

There had to be a mistake . . . *Zach would never, Karen would never.*

Her dad pulled over, not that there was much room on the road to do so, and put the truck in park.

With a shaky hand, Judy handed the phone to her dad and let the images sink in.

"This has to be a joke."

Janice took the phone next and Sawyer looked at the screen on his cell phone. He clicked a few things and put the phone to his ear.

"Oh, my." Judy's mom's face turned white.

"This can't be true," Judy said. "A tabloid ploy."

"Son of a bitch," her dad said as he tossed his phone to the seat beside him and shoved the truck in gear.

"What?"

Sawyer's hands gripped the steering wheel and his expression turned stone cold. "Zach's in jail. So is Karen."

It wasn't a joke.

"There must be a misunderstanding," Janice said quietly.

"He said he needed a lawyer, and that Nolan was with them."

"Nolan?" Judy asked. "What does Nolan have to do with Zach?"

"I have no idea," Janice said. "I know he's been working with him on his job site, but can't imagine why they'd be in jail."

"Unbelievable!" Sawyer grumbled.

They rode down the mountain in silence, and instead of driving toward home, they took the highway and drove toward St. George.

The sun streamed through the windows in the early morning hours as they pulled into the police station. The three of them filed into the sterile county building and walked past several people waiting in metal chairs before approaching the desk. Behind the counter sat a female officer who had one ear on the phone and her hands on a computer keyboard.

Judy stood behind her parents and glanced around the lobby of the station. She felt the eyes of someone fall on her from across the room. Trying to be careful of who she looked at, Judy removed her phone from her pocket and pretended to read a text as her eyes found those who watched her.

Light green eyes followed her every move. The man who possessed them had military short hair and a neck that was thick enough to bounce baseballs off it. His broad shoulders sat under a jacket that looked too small . . . or maybe the man was simply too big.

Judy couldn't stop her eyes from rolling down his frame any more than she could stop the sun from rising. He filled up the small space of the chair he sat in and long legs stretched out in front of him. As her gaze traveled back up his frame, she noticed those green eyes laughing above his dimpled smile.

She jumped and forced her eyes away.

"We're here for Zach Gardner," she heard her father tell the officer when the woman managed to hang up the phone.

"Two of you can come back."

Her mother looked at her and smiled. "Will you be OK here alone?"

"Mom, please. It's a police station."

On the other side of the glass, Zach's parents sat with their backs perfectly straight and their expressions full of shock.

Even though he knew the charges against him were bullshit and that they'd be dropped as soon as light was shed on the entire situation, talking to his parents from jail had to be one of the lowest points in Zach's life.

"Hey, Dad."

"What the hell is going on?" Sawyer jumped right to the point.

"I know it looks bad."

"Do you? Jesus, Zach . . . you're in jail."

Zach glanced behind him at the officer guarding the door. "I'm aware of that."

"Karen and Nolan are in there with you."

He nodded. "I know. We need a lawyer."

Sawyer shook his head, disgust sat deep in his eyes.

"What's this about, Zach? What did you do?"

The back of Zach's jaw grew tight. "Nothing. We did nothing wrong. Becky Applegate ran away from home. Karen and I found her and Nolan hiding out and we put them in a hotel until we could get to the bottom of the situation. The kidnapping charge is bogus."

"You should have just taken Becky home. Kidnapping . . . they're charging you with kidnapping."

Zach glared at his father now. "Am I capable of that, Dad? Do you really think for a fucking minute that is part of my character?"

How dare his father look at him with such accusatory eyes?

When his father didn't instantly agree that he wasn't capable of being the monster the police were pointing him out to be, Zach lost it.

"All my life I've done everything in my power to please you. Stuck in fucking Hilton, scraping together a construction business . . . all so I could be there for you and Mom . . . for everyone." Behind Zach, he noticed the officer stand taller. His hand reached for the door behind him.

Zach lowered his voice but felt his face heat up. "I've always done the right thing. Keeping Becky and Nolan away from her parents was the right thing."

"Zach, honey . . ." his mom grabbed the phone from his father's fingers. "We know you're not the man they're accusing you to be. It's a shock . . . for both of us to see you here."

Zach kept glaring at his father. "We need a lawyer, Mom."

Behind his parents, a man walked in wearing a suit and carrying a briefcase. "Mr. and Mrs. Gardner?"

Sawyer turned in his seat. Zach heard some of the man's words through the phone. "I was hired by Blake Harrison to represent Zach."

The name sounded familiar but he didn't understand what was going on until after his parents told them they'd speak with the lawyer after he talked with Zach.

"Mr. Gardner . . . I'm Ron Bernard. Blake flew me and two of my colleagues in from California to represent you, Karen, and Nolan."

"Blake who?"

Mr. Bernard sent him a puzzled look. "The duke and duchess?"

Oh, that's right . . . Karen's friends.

"If you're willing to let me represent you, I'll have the officer set up a conference room so you and I can talk privately."

Mr. Bernard looked more capable than any lawyer his parents could possibly come up with, and he saw no need to question Karen's high-powered friends.

Right now, his main priority was getting them out of jail and to make sure Karen was safe.

"Let's talk."

Mr. Bernard smiled and motioned for the officer.

Behind the lawyer, his parents dropped their gazes and walked from the room.

Five minutes later, Zach sat in a conference room explaining what had happened from the moment he left the cabin to the moment the lawyer showed up.

Now all he had to do was wait for a judge to be called in and an arraignment to be set up.

What a day!

———————

Judy found an empty chair away from the massive hottie of a man who watched her.

Unlike any lobby she'd ever sat in, this one had flyers from bail bond agencies and *dial a lawyer* pamphlets spread on the small table. A middle-aged woman and teenage boy sat at one end of the room, both looked as if they'd slept in the chairs all night.

Green Eyes stood when the door her parents had just walked through opened and an even larger man with a stunning blonde woman walked through. "How is she?" Green Eyes asked.

Judy tried not to listen, but the small lobby made it difficult.

"Worried sick about Becky and Nolan," the woman said.

With the mention of Becky's and Nolan's names, Judy looked at the three people with renewed interest. Were they friends of Karen's?

"Shouldn't she be concerned with her own fate?"

"She's not concerned about herself at all." The blonde's polished British accent had Judy sitting forward. Hadn't Karen told her about her British friend who was married to a retired Marine? The man at her side was certainly large enough to fit the description of ex-military. So was Green Eyes. "I received a message from Samantha. They'll be here within the hour."

Judy stood and walked over to the small party. "I'm sorry . . . are you friends of Karen's?"

The blonde fixed her eyes on Judy and smiled. "Yes."

"I'm Judy. Mike's sister."

The woman smiled brighter. "I'm Gwen," she said as she stuck a hand out for Judy to shake. "This is Neil, my husband, and a friend of ours, Rick."

Green Eyes placed his full wattage of a smile on her. At his side, she had to look up to see him. This close, she felt like a pixie in the presence of a dragon.

"Is Karen OK?"

"Oh, she's fine. We'll have them all out of here in a couple of hours."

"I don't even know why they're here. My parents just went back to talk to my brother, Zach."

Gwen and Neil exchanged glances.

"Why don't we step outside and talk?"

Judy followed them outside and away from anyone listening.

"From what I'm told," Gwen began, "a girl named Becky ran away from home with her boyfriend."

"Nolan?"

"Right," Gwen said. "Zach and Karen found them hiding and put them up in the hotel for a couple of days until they could figure out how to keep Becky safe."

"What's wrong with Becky?"

Gwen sighed. "According to Karen, her parents abuse her. They accused Karen and Zach of kidnapping . . . and her boyfriend of other nefarious acts."

The picture was clearing before Judy's eyes. "Becky's always been so shy."

"You know her?"

Judy nodded. "Hilton is a small town. Everyone knows everyone."

Gwen glanced at the men. "Do you know where Becky lives?"

"Of course. Why?"

As the question escaped Judy's mouth, a news van pulled into the driveway.

Neil moved between the newly arrived media and his wife.

"Karen believes Becky is in grave danger. She'll not be allowed to go anywhere near Becky until these ridiculous charges are dropped. And if I know Karen, she'll ignore the court to help the girl."

From behind them, a man with a microphone approached, his eyes narrowed on Judy.

"Aren't you Michael Wolfe's sister?" the reporter asked.

Rick moved between Judy and the reporter. "No comment." His deep voice made the reporter pause, but not for long.

"Is it true Michael's wife is being detained?"

"What about no comment did you misunderstand?" Rick's voice lowered and the smile on his face fell.

Neil ushered Gwen back into the station.

"Is it true Mrs. Wolfe was found naked in the hotel with Mr. Wolfe's brother?"

Judy froze. Her eyes grew big.

Rick placed his large hand on her back and gently pushed her through the door and away from the reporter.

The reporter didn't follow them inside right away.

"Is that true?" Judy asked Gwen.

The soft expression on Gwen's face confirmed the reporter's accusation. "It's not what you think."

What is it then?

The reporter took that moment to push inside the station.

Rick turned toward the door and once again blocked Judy from their annoying presence. "Dude, you're starting to piss me off."

Gwen grabbed Judy's arm and pulled her away. "I know you're confused. I can assure you that everything is going to be OK. I've already spoken with Michael. He's on his way here now."

Her stomach turned thinking of her brother. "Poor Mike."

"Mike is more concerned for Karen and Zach's safety right now than for himself. Listen, Judy . . . Karen told me that Becky is pregnant."

The rest of the air in Judy's lungs left and her head felt dizzy. "Really?"

"Yes. If her parents abuse her, she could be in danger."

Judy glanced at the police officers that were intervening between Rick, Neil, and the reporter.

"Then tell the police and let them handle it."

"Karen has. But they've given no indication that they are following up on her accusations. To them, Karen is the criminal."

That Judy didn't believe, and she knew Zach would never kidnap anyone. "The entire situation is ridiculous."

"Agreed. Would you be willing to check on Becky for Karen?"

Judy nodded. "Of course."

Gwen glanced around. "Can you go to her home now and make sure she's safe? Rick can go with you . . . keep you both safe."

Judy glanced at the broad back of the man blocking the reporter.

Her parents wouldn't like it, but she couldn't say no. Judy nodded.

Gwen tapped Rick on the back and spoke to him in hushed tones. Green Eyes glanced Judy's way and smiled briefly.

Rick stepped around the officers and met Judy by the desk. He smiled at the female officer. "Is there a back door we can use to escape the media?"

The woman nodded and ushered them around the counter and through another door. A small corridor later, Judy and Rick were running to a rental car and tearing out of the parking lot.

She stared out the back window, expecting the reporter to give chase. Only no cars or vans pulled behind them. "Take the freeway north."

Rick switched lanes, maneuvered the car onto the freeway. Only when she was sure no one followed did Judy twist in her seat and pull on her belt, and she felt the green-eyed stare of the most gorgeous man she'd ever seen in her life fall on her . . . again.

Oh, boy!

Chapter Twenty-Six

An officer led Karen into a large room and sat her on a bench to wait for the judge. They brought Nolan in next, then Zach.

"Are you OK?" Zach asked.

"I've had better days," she told him truthfully. Beyond them, the room filled up with their family and friends. Janice and Sawyer wouldn't meet her eyes. She could only imagine what was going through their heads.

Samantha, Blake, Neil, and Gwen offered smiles as they took their seats.

"Did you talk to the lawyer?" Karen asked.

"Yeah. We're all set," Zach told her.

"Are we getting out of here?" Nolan asked.

"We should."

A commotion brought everyone's attention to the back door of the room.

Several people walked into the room with handheld recording devices, their eyes swung toward the three of them.

"Great, reporters."

Zach shook his head. The three of them sat with their hands behind their backs in handcuffs. Humiliation crawled up Karen's spine.

The lawyer who'd visited Karen earlier walked into the room followed by two more men dressed just as well. Three-piece, fifteen-hundred-dollar suits were a sure bet of highly paid lawyers. All of whom Blake and Samantha brought in. Leave it to a millionaire duke to have the best.

"All rise for the honorable Judge Stanhope."

The occupants of the room stood and a hush fell over the crowd.

Gray peppered the hair of the judge who appeared to be somewhere in his sixties. His stoic expression said nothing as he took his seat and told everyone to sit.

"It's a little early for this kind of a crowd," the judge said as he shuffled papers on his desk and looked at the three of them.

A reporter in the back of the room lifted a small tape recorder and whispered into the device, drawing the attention of the judge.

"You! In the back."

The reporter snapped his attention to the judge.

"Yes?"

"Turn that crap off in my courtroom. If I see it again I'll have you and all your colleagues removed."

The reporter shoved the recorder into a bag and sat up.

Judge Stanhope glanced around the courtroom. "I've been called in on this fine Sunday, a day I'd much rather be spending with my family . . . so this had better be good."

Karen wanted to moan. *Great, a pissed-off judge.*

"Nolan Parker?" the judge called out.

Nolan stood. "Yes, Your Honor?"

"Do you have counsel?"

The attorney assigned to Nolan stood and walked over to the bench.

"Yes, Your Honor."

Judge Stanhope glanced at his papers, then to the attorney.

"Nolan Parker you're being charged with statutory rape, kidnapping, and resisting arrest. How do you plea?"

Nolan glanced at his attorney and said, "Not guilty."

The judge looked directly at Nolan, then at Zach. "Zach Gardner?"

Zach stood along with his attorney.

"You're charged with kidnapping, harboring a criminal, and resisting arrest. How do you plea?"

"Not guilty."

Karen didn't wait to be called before she took to her feet.

"I see we have a theme here today," the judge said on a sigh. "Karen Jones?"

"Yes, Your Honor?"

"I assume the remaining attorney is yours?"

"Yes, sir."

"You're charged with kidnapping, harboring a criminal, and resisting arrest. How do you plea?"

"Not guilty, Your Honor."

The judge stared at the three of them. "The preliminary hearing is set for two weeks from tomorrow," he said. "Bail is set for one hundred thousand dollars each for Ms. Jones and Mr. Gardner. Two hundred and fifty thousand for Mr. Parker."

"Oh, God," Nolan groaned.

"It's OK," Karen assured him.

"If you make bail you're to remain within the county limits until the trial. Is that understood?"

The three of them nodded.

The judge left the courtroom and the reporters fled the room.

An hour later, Karen, Zach, and Nolan were walking out of the police station only to be mobbed by the media.

Neil and Blake shoved reporters aside until the three of them were in the back of a limousine.

Karen hugged Gwen as the car left the station.

"We've booked a suite at the Hilton."

"Has anyone heard from Becky?" Nolan asked.

Karen grasped his hand.

"Not yet."

Karen's eyes met Zach's and held.

"This is it." Judy pointed to the house Becky called home. There wasn't a car in the driveway, which didn't sit well with her.

"Does she have brothers or sisters?"

"No. She's an only child."

Rick parked half a block away on the opposite side of the street.

He leaned over her and opened the glove compartment. He removed a pistol and proceeded to place it in a holster he had under his jacket.

"What the hell is that?"

"A gun."

"Well I know that. Why do you have one? Are you a cop or something?"

He smiled. "Or something."

He moved to open his door and she grasped his arm.

"You can't go in there with a gun."

He waved a finger in the air. "I promise not to pull it out unless I have to."

She tugged on him now. "Hold up. I didn't agree to this. We just need to make sure Becky's OK."

Rick tilted his head to the side. "What do you think I'm going to do?"

"I don't know, but you don't need a gun. Look at you. You could sit on Mr. Applegate and squish the man. No guns needed."

Rick's smile illuminated the car. "Glad you have faith in me, Utah, but I like a little firepower in case Mr. Appleseed has one of his own."

"Applegate. Not Appleseed."

He lifted his eyebrows and never stopped smiling. "You stay here. I'll check out the house."

She shoved out of the car right behind him.

"I said, stay in the car."

She stormed past him. "Becky doesn't know you. You might scare her."

He narrowed his eyes. "I should scare you."

"Phew. Yeah, right." The house was quiet, as was the neighborhood. Church was a serious thing most Sundays, resulting in many hours spent with the congregation. Somehow, Judy didn't think that was where the Applegate family was today.

By the time she reached the front door, Rick was beside her. Before she could knock, he picked her up as if she weighted fifty pounds and placed her behind him.

"Hey!"

He lifted a finger to her lips. "Shh!"

Suddenly Rick wasn't Mr. Hottie strapped in a body fit to fight an army, he was Mr. Annoying fit to earn a tongue-lashing.

"Stay."

"I'm not a dog," she told him through gritted teeth.

He towered over her and had the nerve to pat her head.

Judy nearly stomped on his foot.

Before she could respond, he laid his knuckles to the door. "Mr. Apple—"

"Gate," she whispered.

"Applegate?"

They waited for a few silent moments. Rick knocked again. "Mr. Applegate?"

Nothing.

Rick wiggled the handle on the door and found it unlocked.

He removed the gun he said he would leave alone and slowly opened the door.

Judy's heart kicked when her eyes fell on the mess in the living room of the Applegate home.

"Go back to the car," he told her.

She shook her head. Worry for Becky suddenly overwhelmed her. Something wasn't right.

Two lamps were in the middle of the floor, the glass in the old seventies-style end table was shattered.

"Mr. Applegate?"

"Becky?" Judy called out.

Rick glared at her now, all humor gone. His hand snapped over her lips, shutting her up.

Judy stuck to his back as he walked through the house. The kitchen was untouched; the dining room had overturned chairs. Inside the bedrooms, several drawers were opened as if someone had packed in a hurry. There wasn't any sign of anyone.

Rick holstered his gun and surveyed the room. "I don't think they're coming back."

"Oh, Becky. This is bad."

"Doesn't look good. Is there any close family nearby?"

"I don't think so. I'm not sure."

Judy stepped over the glass in the middle of the living room and noticed a dark spot on the carpet. She knelt down and touched the sticky liquid. "Is this what I think it is?"

Rick touched her finger and frowned. "Call the police."

———

The suite at the Hilton filled with people quickly. Zach recognized Karen's friends and shook Blake Harrison's hand. "Thank you for expediting the lawyers and bail."

Blake shook his head. "Don't mention it."

"I'll pay you back."

Blake waved him off. "We'll work that out later."

Zach's parents walked into the hotel room and eyed the crowed that had gathered. To his father's credit, he hadn't called him on how he and Karen were found when they were arrested. By now, their pictures were spread all over the tabloids and the media filled the lobby of the hotel, all of them hoping for a statement about the adulterous affair. Seemed they were more interested in a sex scandal about a celebrity wife than about a possible kidnapping.

A hush went over the room as his parents walked in. Zach could see his mother's torn expression as she glanced at Karen. But she seemed to get over whatever stopped her quickly.

Janice lifted her hand to Karen's face. "Are you OK, dear?"

Zach noticed Karen's hesitation. "I'm fine."

"This looks like it hurts."

The bruise on Karen's face reminded him of the police slamming her against the wall.

"It's not bad."

Before Karen could finish introductions, the door to the room opened again.

Mike strode in, his hard gaze landing on Zach briefly before he found Karen.

He walked to her side and pulled her into his arms. "Are you all right?"

She sighed. "I'm sorry."

He pulled away, looked her over. His gaze stopped at the angry bruise on her face and he cursed under his breath.

Janice kept glancing between Karen and Mike and then back to Zach. Sawyer remained silent in the back of the room.

"It's OK," Mike told her. He kissed her forehead softly before leaving her and walking toward Zach.

Zach squared his shoulders and tried to prepare for their very public confrontation.

A tick in Mike's jaw was the only motion on his brother's face. They stared at each other. When it looked as if Mike was going to walk away without a word, Zach started to relax only to have Mike's fist fly through the air and catch him in the jaw.

The room exploded as Zach fell back to the floor.

Karen jumped between them, Blake grabbed Mike's arm, and Neil stepped in front of Karen.

"Michael!" Janice yelled.

Mike waved his hand in the air. "That's for not keeping her safe. The media is going to massacre her character and for *that* I blame you."

Zach wiped the blood from his lip with the back of his hand, looked at it, then his brother. Mike wasn't hitting him for sleeping with his wife, but for being caught by the press.

Zach nodded and waved off Neil's hand as he reached to help him up.

Mike pushed forward, pressed his hand into Zach's palm, and hauled him to his feet. At first, Zach wasn't sure if his brother was going to swing again or not. One fist was fine, expected even, but Zach had no problem reminding Mike who the older brother was.

Karen moved between the two of them. "Are we good here?"

Zach looked at his brother.

"Yeah," Mike managed.

Karen turned to Zach, dabbed his lip with a tissue, and blessed him with a soft smile. "Don't we make a great pair?"

"I'd smile but it hurts."

Mike chuckled.

"Nice to know you still have a right hook to rival mine," Zach told him.

"Learned from the best." They'd fought growing up, as brothers often did, but the fight never went into the night or the next day. Seemed they were going to keep the tradition.

Sawyer cleared his throat from across the room. "Would someone please tell me what the hell is going on here?"

The room grew silent again.

Chapter Twenty-Seven

Karen was stuck, literally, between Zach and Michael. Across from the three of them sat Janice and Sawyer, both of them held their emotions in check as everyone else left the room.

"What's going on?" Sawyer said a second time after the room had cleared.

Karen placed a hand on Michael's knee, offering encouragement. The motion didn't go unnoticed by anyone.

"You were never supposed to meet Karen," Michael said. "Our marriage was scheduled to last a year. A year and a half tops."

Janice blinked several times, her eyes switching between Karen and Michael. To Karen's right, Zach watched her.

This was Michael's story to tell, however much of it he wanted. She'd offer nothing and back up whatever he said. So far, nothing was a lie and easily agreed to.

"Scheduled to last? What does that mean?"

"My life is in Hollywood, Dad. Every film in the past four years has doubled my salary every six months. Publicity, dating, marital status . . . all the graphic details . . . all of it heightens public interest and keeps my name on the lips of producers and my fans. Karen and I have had a paper marriage . . . only."

Karen glanced at Zach.

"Wait. You two have never been . . ."

Karen shook her head, looked Zach in the eye. "No. Never!"

Relief washed over Zach's face. "Why didn't you tell me?"

"I couldn't. I made a promise to Michael."

Zach took her hand in his, squeezed it.

Sawyer shot out of his chair. "But we've all seen you kissing . . . holding each other."

Michael shook his head. "I never wanted any of this to touch you. I knew you wouldn't understand."

"But—" Janice started.

"I'm an actor, Mom."

"Why didn't you tell us? Why pretend with us?" There was outrage in his mother's voice.

Michael looked at Karen. For a moment, she thought he'd open up to his parents about his sexuality. "I didn't think you'd understand."

Sawyer stood, shoved his hands in his pockets. "Well I sure as hell don't understand. And what's with you and Karen?" The question was directed at Zach.

Zach swallowed. "The attraction was unexpected."

Karen leaned into him.

"This is damn awkward," Sawyer grumbled.

"And will probably be *more so* before we leave the hotel," Michael said. "Karen's going to need the support of this family. I meant what I said about the media persecuting Karen. The world thinks she and I were happily married. With our divorce pending . . . and Zach . . ."

"I'll be fine," Karen offered.

"I don't know, babe. The media can be brutal."

"Michael, the media blows hot and then cools nearly as quickly as the match was sparked. This will blow over in a few weeks and I'll simply be your ex."

"So you were planning your divorce the entire time you've been here?" Janice asked.

It was time for Karen to come to Michael's defense. "Sawyer, Janice . . . I'm sorry. We're sorry. We'd hoped to have a brief paper marriage that the world would buy for a short time, and then move on. Hollywood is extremely flighty and right now Michael is one of the hottest things out there."

"Is the money so important that you'd sell your soul?"

Michael shook his head. "Hardly that dramatic, Dad. Karen and I are close friends. We've had a good time playing the perfect couple for the past year. But that's all it was . . . playing. Now that she's interested in someone, it's time to stop pretending." Michael shot a glance to his brother. "Chaps my ass that it's you she's interested in."

Zach was smiling, not taking anything seriously.

Janice shook her head, clearly not convinced. "Just a couple of weeks ago you and Tracey were close, Zach. What are we to think of that?"

Zach's smile fell. "Before you come to Tracey's defense, consider this. Outside the hotel last night when we were arrested on trumped-up kidnapping charges, Tracey was standing in the crowd watching."

"Oh, no."

"Oh, yes." Zach lifted Karen's hand and kissed her fingers. "I think she followed us."

Janice glanced at Sawyer and lowered her gaze to the floor. "We saw Tracey outside the courthouse."

Zach swung his gaze to his mother. "What did she say to you?"

"She apologized. At the time, I didn't understand what she was talking about. Said she thought she was doing the right thing when she heard from her cousin that you and Karen were in St. George and were keeping Becky and Nolan hidden from Becky's parents."

Karen squeezed Zach's hand. "Maybe she was hurt about the breakup."

"I doubt she has a black eye or a mark on her record that shouldn't be there. Things weren't right with Tracey and me for a while. Our breaking up had little to do with you. Now Becky is back with her abusive parents and we're forced to sit here and wait for others to watch out for the girl. Nolan is frantic, worried sick about his girl and their child. And all for what?"

"Oh, honey, I don't know what to think," Janice said.

"We need to band together," Michael told them. "Karen and I had planned the divorce before we arrived here. That will go on as scheduled. In the meantime, she's going to need our support." He waved a hand in Zach's direction. "And you're going to have to have her back. The media is vicious. They'll dig . . . more than ever before now that there is an apparent love triangle."

Zach's arm moved over her shoulders. "We'll get you through this."

"This is damn strange, Mike."

"I know it is, Dad. Be confused, yell . . . do what you have to. Just keep the truth between us."

"You want me to lie to our family?"

Michael shook his head. "No. Tell Hannah, Judy . . . hell, Rena already knows. But what business is it of anyone else? It's not like I've had any visitors in LA since I've moved away. No one else needs to know squat."

Sawyer paced the edge of the room. "Damn kids today."

Michael glanced at Zach, rolled his eyes.

"C'mon, Janice. We should get home before the press corners our daughters."

They stood with Janice. Karen watched as Michael and Zach both hugged and kissed her good-bye. She turned to Karen, pulled her aside. "If you need anything, call."

"Thank you, Janice."

"I can't pretend to understand. I just hope you know what you're doing."

Karen looked over her shoulder at the men watching her. "Me, too."

Sawyer wasn't as forgiving with his words or his actions. He stormed from the room and expected his wife to follow.

Once the three of them were alone, Karen fell into the sofa, depleted.

"Remind me to never do that again."

She expected the men to sit and laugh with her; instead, they stood staring at each other.

Karen glanced between the two of them.

"What?"

Zach crossed his arms over his chest. "What are you *not* telling me, Mike?"

Had she missed something?

Zach continued. "Karen is too amazing for a platonic relationship for over a year."

Karen swung her gaze to Michael.

Silence hung in the air.

"You're right."

Zach opened his mouth, then closed it.

"I'm gay, Zach."

Zach uncrossed his arms and dropped his jaw to his chest. "Well damn."

After the police took their statements, Judy returned to Rick's rental car and called Gwen on Rick's cell phone.

"Rick?" Gwen answered with her polished accent.

"No, it's Judy. Rick is still talking to the police."

"Oh, dear. What's happened?"

Judy explained what they'd walked in on, and how the Applegates were nowhere to be found. "I don't even know where to look."

"Perhaps Karen will have an idea . . . or Nolan."

"Are they out of jail?"

"Yes. Let me speak with them and I'll call you right back."

Judy hung up and watched as Rick walked past the flashing lights on the police car and across the street. "We're free to leave."

"I'm not sure where we should go. Seems wrong to just walk away and let the police handle what they've already mucked up."

Rick rubbed his jaw with a sly smile on his face. "Not ready to give up the adventure, Utah?"

The urge to roll her eyes was strong, but Judy refrained and gave her head a little shake instead.

"I just happen to think we're considering the entire game while the police are only picking one team. Becky's with two very misguided parents and probably scared to death. But she's not stupid. She ran away once, she'll do it again."

Rick's playful smile slid into something more thoughtful. "How might a teenage, pregnant girl run from parents who are on the run?"

Judy closed her eyes, thought of how it might feel to be surrounded by parents who might think they're doing the right thing, but weren't. "Eventually I'd make my captors think I've complied . . . became weak." Judy pictured a rest stop . . . a bathroom . . . "Then I'd use a simple task, like going to the bathroom or needing food, and then make my escape." Judy opened her eyes and saw Rick staring at her.

"Pregnant women need to pee a lot."

Judy brought both hands to her face. "God, poor Becky."

"Hey." She felt Rick's hand on her shoulder. "We'll find her."

The phone in her pocket rang. She answered to hear Karen's voice. "Judy?"

"It's me."

"Where are you?"

"In front of Becky's parents' home."

"No clue as to where they went?"

Judy sighed. "No."

"Any chance the neighbors saw anything?"

Judy glanced around at the few people that had managed to work their way to their front yards to watch the activity. "Even if they did, what could they say . . . the car drove east . . . west? All roads lead to the freeway. Where they went from there is the question."

"The hairdresser? Petra."

"Yeah, what about her?"

"She's the only person in town that I can think of to ask."

"She cuts hair, Karen."

"Oh, Judy . . . you need to know that hairdressers are the next best thing to a bartender in a small town. If anyone knows anything . . . it will be Petra."

With the phone to her ear, Judy moved from the car far enough to open the door and let herself in.

Rick jumped in the driver's seat.

Judy pointed ahead of them. "Turn left," she told Rick. "I hope you know what you're talking about, Karen."

"It's all I have."

"I'll call you back."

Judy clicked off and directed Rick to Main Street. It was Sunday and therefore quiet. They parked alongside the curb and Judy jumped out and ran into Petra's salon.

A woman sat in the chair gabbing while Petra cut.

One look and Petra lifted her scissors from the woman's hair and smiled Judy's way. Her eyes drifted beyond her to Rick and the smile grew bolder.

"Hey?"

"Uhm, Petra . . . can I talk to you a minute?"

The conversation didn't need extra ears.

Petra glanced around at those in the room and then she excused herself for a moment.

They stepped outside on the deserted sidewalk.

Judy cut right to the facts. "Karen suggested I ask you where the Applegates might take Becky."

Petra's tiny smile slid into a frown. "Is she OK?"

Judy shook her head. "I doubt it. Her parents have her . . . they have several hours' head start."

Petra looked at her shoes while the scissors in her hand tapped against her palm. "There's no family here . . . not that I've been told about. But he has a sister . . . north."

North? Great! Like the entire country was north!

"Before Salt Lake . . . I remember the name being that of a person."

"Isn't every town that of a person? Even Hilton?"

"No, not a surname. A first name. You'd remember a town of Judy."

Oh . . .

"My phone?" Rick reached out his hand and Judy handed him his phone.

A few seconds later, he opened up a map and blew up the state until he scrolled through the towns one by one.

Petra shoved close as the three of them glanced at the small screen.

"No . . . no . . . wait. There. Jeremy. That's it. Becky's aunt lives in Jeremy."

Judy squeezed Petra's arm. "Thank you."

Petra smiled as Rick and Judy jumped in the car and headed toward the highway.

Chapter Twenty-Eight

Zach would have liked nothing better than to crawl into bed and erase some of the day's images from his mind, but it didn't seem that was going to happen. After his brother's revelation, Zach had stood stunned while the pieces of their life snapped into place. It all made sense now . . . the relationship between Karen and Michael, how they appeared to be close but not intimate . . . even when they kissed Zach realized he'd seen the same behavior from his brother while performing in his films. Even Mike's exodus from Hilton, the need to alienate himself from his family to protect his lifestyle made sense now.

Zach couldn't deny the weight that had lifted off his shoulders when he learned that Karen and Mike had never been intimate. To know there would never be the wedge between him and his brother was a relief.

Karen unwrapped from his side and pushed off the couch. "I'm going to shower before everyone comes back," she said.

As much as Zach wanted to join her, he decided to use the time alone with his brother for a much-needed talk.

Karen disappeared into the bedroom suite, leaving Mike and Zach with each other.

"She really is amazing," Mike told him.

"She worries about everyone else before herself."

Mike ran a hand through his hair, stared at the floor. "I was pissed at first . . . when she told me about you two. But then I realized that I couldn't pick out a better man for her than you."

The vote of confidence warmed Zach to his soul. "I'm not sure what to say."

"Just tell me you're not fucking with her. That there's something more than a sexual itch." Mike stared at him now, all humor and smiles long gone.

"If we were only an itch, I think we would have both found someone else to scratch it. Wanting my brother's wife has torn me up for weeks. Karen knew the truth and it killed her, too."

Mike nodded. "She a strong woman, Zach . . . but there are parts of her that are painfully vulnerable. Security is important to her and the fear of being abandoned has deep roots."

"You're talking about her parents."

"She told you about them?"

"Yeah. The bastards."

Mike rubbed the back of his neck. "Makes you appreciate our overbearing relatives."

For a moment they were silent, both lost in their own thoughts.

"Mom and Dad will understand . . . about you."

Mike stood and walked toward the window. "I'm not ready to tell them, Zach. Hell, I wasn't ready to tell you. But I didn't want Karen to have to keep this from you. She's already given me so much."

"Who else knows?"

"Not many people. Rena figured it out. Karen's core friends, those you've met. No one in Hollywood."

"That has to be hard on you."

His brother shrugged. "Not really. Having Karen in my life has given me a place to vent. I'm going to miss that when she's gone."

"She's not gone."

Mike glanced over his shoulder. "You saying you're ready to move out of Hilton? Because I don't think Karen living in LA and you living in Hilton is going to work out for very long. Not to mention you can't protect her from that far away."

"I've been itching to get out of Utah for a while," Zach explained as he stood and walked to his brother's side. "If Karen wants to open a sanctuary for runaway kids, she's going to have to be close to a big city. Kids don't run away *to* Hilton."

Mike turned toward him now. "You're really serious about her."

"Yeah. Yeah I am."

Mike swiveled back to the window. "I'm going to be in Canada for weeks on end. I'll encourage Karen to stay at the house . . . hell I'd give it to her if I thought she'd take it."

"She didn't want the car." Thinking of the McLaren made Zach smile.

"Make her keep the car, would you? Such a sweet ride."

Zach smiled and nodded.

"The house is secure . . . less media can get in while we're going through the divorce. You can both stay there for as long as you like."

Zach placed a hand on his brother's shoulder. "I have your back. No matter when and if you tell Mom and Dad . . . I'm there for you."

Mike nodded and offered a sad smile. "Thanks. I needed to hear that."

The door to the suite opened behind them and Gwen, Neil, and Nolan walked in. From the expression on Nolan's face, Zach knew something was wrong.

"What happened?"

"Becky called." Nolan's hand shook as he lifted his phone in the air.

From the door to the bedroom, Karen stood with a towel to her hair. Her fresh clean scent drifted Zach's way and called to him.

"Is she OK?"

Nolan shook his head. "She was crying so hard I couldn't understand her."

"Where is she?"

Gwen placed an arm around Nolan's shoulders. "She didn't say. Something about a truck stop, hiding."

Neil had his cell phone to his ear. "Where are you?"

"Is he talking to Rick?" Karen asked.

Gwen nodded. "I think we should notify the police. They must realize the danger Becky is in by now."

Karen nodded at Zach's side. "I think so, too."

Neil moved away from them as he told Rick what they'd learned. "She's hiding in a storage closet of some sort. I have no idea which truck stop. No, she won't. Call . . . right." When Neil hung up, he addressed them.

"Rick and Judy are en route to Jeremy."

"She could be at any truck stop."

"Becky didn't give you any hints?" Karen asked Nolan.

"Just that they'd been driving for a couple of hours."

Zach looked at Neil. "We need a state map."

————

Judy and Rick circled the lot of the second truck stop twice before pulling the car into a parking spot.

They walked side by side into the convenience store that accompanied the gas station and restaurant portion of the truck stop. "I'll check out the bathroom first."

Rick scanned the patrons as they walked by and said little. The man had a strange way about him, Judy decided. He had this perpetual smile when he was talking to her, and a look of killer intensity when he was concentrating.

He walked her to the door of the ladies' room and turned his back to the wall to wait for her. *He must be a bodyguard of some sort.* The man had the expression *don't fuck with me*, glaring at anyone who looked. And who would? Only the completely stupid would mess with the man.

Judy checked each empty stall and waited until every woman had left the room before moving on.

"Not in there."

"Neil said a supply closet."

"Let's take a look around for her parents. If we see them, then we know she has to be here somewhere."

"Or they may have left her," Rick said.

They started in the restaurant, telling the waitress they were looking for friends. The search came up empty and they moved to the back of the truck stop. There were services for drivers ranging from an on-staff chiropractor to shoe shining. Not that Judy could think of truck drivers wearing shoes that needed shining. But that's how these stops rolled. There were places for a girl the size of Becky to disappear everywhere.

Across from the bathroom, Judy scanned the store. Like her own personal shadow, Rick stood beside her. From the corner of her eye, she noticed someone who looked a lot like Mr. Applegate ducking behind a bookcase. Instead of being obvious, she moved in front of Rick, hiding her face and pretending to pick lint off his jacket.

His stellar smile took her breath for a moment as he looked down at her.

"Over my right shoulder, behind the bookcase . . ." she whispered.

He leaned down to hear her.

Rick lifted a hand to her hair and played with it while looking where she suggested.

"Tall, skinny . . . wearing a plaid long-sleeved shirt."

"Dark brown hair?"

"Yeah."

She lifted her purse from her shoulder and removed a compact. "Is he watching us?"

"He's glancing this way, but seems to be reading a book."

Judy lifted the mirror until she was able to locate the man in question. When he lifted his head from the book in his hand, she froze. "That's Becky's dad."

She snapped her compact shut, looked into Rick's green eyes. "She's here somewhere."

"He keeps looking over here."

"He probably recognized me."

Rick jolted suddenly, moved Judy to the side. "Call the police." Then he was gone, running into the store.

She turned in time to see Mr. Applegate run through a back door and Rick follow.

She dialed 911 and ran toward Rick.

"Nine one one, please state your emergency."

"I need the police. I'm at the Millroad truck stop and there's a man here holding a girl against her will." Judy wasn't sure what else to say to the woman on the phone. "Hurry."

"Is this man armed?"

"I don't know." Judy burst through the back door to see Rick tackling Mr. Applegate to the ground. As she thought, Rick only had to sit on the man to get him to comply. "Hurry."

Judy lowered the phone from her ear. "Becky?" she called at the top of her lungs. "Becky?" The people in the store looked at her as if she were crazy, but Judy kept poking her head into back doors and calling Becky's name.

"Hey, you can't go back there." An employee tried to stop Judy from walking into the storage room but she walked through the employee-only door anyway.

"Becky, it's Judy . . . you can come out now."

"Hey, miss. You can't be back here."

Judy looked at the fiftysomething man and frowned. "Becky?"

The room was small and didn't have a scared teenage girl hiding within the boxes, so Judy kept moving.

By now there were people gathering around watching her while others watched through the windows at what Judy assumed was Rick making sure Mr. Applegate didn't get away.

Judy retraced her steps toward the rooms in the back where the truck drivers managed their haircuts and midstate back cracking. "Becky?"

She was about to turn back into the restaurant when she heard a door open behind her. Huddled in a sweatshirt, Becky poked her head out.

The swelling around Becky's right eye and the way she held her arm stopped Judy from breathing. "Oh, Becky."

Judy reached the girl before she fell. "Call an ambulance. Someone call an ambulance."

She crumbled to the ground with Becky and held her. "It's OK. You're safe now."

———

Karen, Zach, Michael, and Nolan sat in the hospital waiting room, while Rick and Judy were still held up with the police giving statements. Samantha and Blake had already flown back to California, and Gwen and Neil had returned to the hotel once they knew everyone was accounted for. Well, everyone but Becky's mother. She'd yet to be found and it didn't seem that even Becky's father knew where she could be hiding.

Outside, the media swarmed, all searching for the story buried in the gossip.

Although the charges against her, Zach, and Nolan had yet to be dropped, it was only a matter of time.

Karen was going on forty-eight hours with virtually no sleep when they arrived at the hospital.

"What's taking so long?" Nolan paced the small, private room like a caged animal.

"I don't know."

They all thought the worst. They knew Judy had found Becky, and that the girl had been bruised and hysterical. It took the hospital some time before they'd even talked to them.

Judy and Rick arrived thirty minutes later, looking tired and wrung out. Karen hugged Judy and thanked her for her help. "Have we heard anything?" Judy asked.

"No. Nothing. How was she when you saw her?"

Judy glanced at Nolan.

"She was beat up pretty bad. I think her arm was broken."

Nolan's hand curled up into a fist.

Zach took hold of Karen's hand.

Judy watched Karen and Zach with a frown. "Uhm? I know I probably shouldn't ask . . . but aren't you married to Mike?"

Michael laughed and swung an arm over Judy's shoulder. "C'mon, sis. Let's go for a walk and I'll explain."

Karen couldn't help but notice how Rick's eyes followed Judy when she left the room.

Rick was a good guy . . . maybe a little hard for someone like Judy, and probably too much of a player.

Zach stood, shook Rick's hand. "Thanks for your help."

Rick shook Zach's hand. "I'm Rick Evans."

"Zach Gardner."

"Oh, that's right you haven't met. I'm sorry."

"It's been a busy day, sweetheart. You're allowed."

"Rick works with Neil . . . or does Neil work with you now?" Karen asked teasingly.

Rick shrugged. "I help him out when I can."

Nolan shot to his feet when two men in lab coats walked into the room. "We're looking for Nolan Parker."

"That's me."

Karen moved beside him, Zach moved to his other side.

"Is Becky OK?"

The doctors exchanged glances. Karen felt her heart drop deep in her chest.

"Becky is going to be fine. She has a fractured arm, a few lacerations that required stitches."

Nolan swallowed. "Then I can see her?"

The doctors glanced at each other again. "About the baby."

Karen looked over Nolan's head and into Zach's gaze. She knew what the doctor was going to say before the words came from his lips.

"She started bleeding in the ambulance. There's nothing we could do this early in a pregnancy to keep her from having a miscarriage."

Nolan's eyes searched those of the doctors. "We lost our baby?"

The doctor who did all the talking nodded. "Yes. I'm sorry."

Zach gripped Nolan's arm while tears ran down Karen's cheeks. Even Rick had to look away.

"How is Becky?"

"Understandably upset. She's asking for you."

Nolan pushed away from Karen and Zach and walked out of the room without a backward glance.

Zach pulled Karen into his arms when the tears started to fall.

"I'll go find Judy and Michael," she heard Rick say before he left the room.

Tears soaked Zach's shirt as she gripped his arms. "Why?"

"I don't know, baby. I don't know."

Chapter Twenty-Nine

Four days later, Nolan and Karen were helping Becky into the Gardner home, setting up Michael's old room for her to stay.

Becky and Nolan decided to wait to get married, at least until she reached her eighteenth birthday. The Gardners insisted on helping her get through her last year of high school.

Samantha and Blake's fancy lawyers were on the court steps twenty-four hours after Becky was found, demanding the charges against Zach, Karen, and Nolan be dropped. At the same time, they were asking that Mr. Applegate be charged with murder because of Becky's miscarriage. It was a long shot to expect a conviction on anything other than kidnapping and assault, but Karen held hope that the man would be in jail for a very long time.

Karen said her good-byes to Becky, assuring her she always had a place with her if she needed it. Not that Karen thought she would. Nolan did not intend to let Becky slip through his fingers.

"They have been through so much," Karen said to Janice as they stood in the living room surrounded by Karen's bags. She'd been away from home too long and it was time for her to finally leave Utah. She'd spent time with Zach, but not in the way she would have liked. Between hospital lobbies and police stations, intimacy wasn't an option. As much as Karen would have liked to say the looks and comments of others didn't bother her . . . they did. In the eyes of many, she was a married woman fooling around with her husband's brother. Karen owed it to Michael and to Zach to keep her distance.

"Have the police said anything about the mother?" Sawyer asked.

"Nothing. Apparently she's the one who distracted her husband long enough for Becky to hide. She's still missing." Becky's dad gave up on making his wife beat their daughter, and instead took on the task himself. Karen hoped that with enough help, Becky would heal and move on with her life.

The door to the house opened and Zach stepped in to grab Karen's bags. "Is this everything?" he asked.

"Yeah."

Karen hugged Janice and then Sawyer. "I'll call you with details about the party." Michael was serious about a divorce party. Unlike when they were married, he wanted everyone there.

Watching Sawyer roll his eyes made Karen chuckle. "How am I ever to believe my son is getting married for real after this fiasco?"

Karen glanced at Zach and chuckled. "If and when Michael ever gets married for real . . . you'll know it!"

"I'm glad someone's sure about that," Janice mumbled.

They walked out to the driveway and Zach tossed Karen's bags in the back of his truck. But before they could climb in, someone pulled into the driveway behind him. From the car, two couples emerged, both women holding large baskets.

"Who are they?" Karen whispered to Zach.

He shook his head. "I recognize them, but don't know their names," he whispered.

The man who drove walked toward Sawyer, and reached out his hand. "Sawyer. Good to see you."

"Hi, Ben." The men shook hands and Sawyer proceeded to introduce Ben and his wife and the couple with them.

"I understand Becky Applegate is staying with you and your family," Ben said.

Sawyer glanced at Janice and then pulled her close to his side. The gesture was one of unity, and something Karen hadn't seen between the two of them before. They were standing behind their decision to bring Becky in and nothing could have warmed Karen's heart more.

"That's right."

Ben nodded and smiled. "We've heard what everyone else has and our congregation wanted to do something to extend a hand to her . . . and to you."

Karen paused and looked at the four people standing in the drive.

Ben's wife handed Janice one of the baskets and set the other one beside them. "Most of this is handwritten notes of thought and prayer for Becky. A few things to let her know she's loved."

Janice took the offering. "I don't think she's ready for visitors right now."

Ben's wife shook her head. "I can't imagine she is. We just want her to know we're thinking of her . . . praying for her."

Ben handed Sawyer an envelope. "A monetary contribution."

Sawyer tried to hand it back.

"Please. Use it, or put it away for Becky for a future time. We've set up a fund that we will add to monthly on her behalf. So that she might have the ability to go to college or whatever it is she chooses to do in the future."

Ben then turned to Karen and Zach. "Thank you both for the sacrifices you've made."

Karen hadn't expected Becky's church to be so willing to stand up for her. She'd have to ask herself why later . . . for now she felt overwhelmed and humbled. "We did what anyone else would have in the same situation."

Ben shook his head. "Not everyone. Or this world would be a much better place."

Karen couldn't argue that.

Ben shook Sawyer's hand again. "If you need anything, please ask."

The four visitors returned to their car and drove away.

"That was very nice of them." Janice glanced into the basket and sighed.

"I'm sure Becky will appreciate their support." Karen hugged Janice again. "I'll call."

"Bye, dear."

When Zach pulled out of the drive, Janice and Sawyer were walking into the house carrying the gift baskets meant for Becky.

Karen watched the town of Hilton fade as they made their way to the freeway. "This has been the longest and least restful vacation I've ever had in my life," Karen uttered with a laugh.

"Oh c'mon, this can't be the first time you've been arrested and made the target of a statewide search."

"Life in front of the paparazzi has nothing on Hilton, Utah."

Zach's shoulders folded in while he laughed. "They'll be talking about this for years."

"So long as they're talking about me and not Becky. She's going to be OK, here, right?"

"If you think she's the first teenage girl to get pregnant and run off, you'd be wrong. Some actually stayed and raised their kids here. She'll be fine."

They eased onto the freeway toward St. George and her flight home.

"Is Rick or Neil meeting you at the airport?" Zach asked.

"Rick. But I think he's bringing a few of their friends." Karen expected the paparazzi and their cameras as word of her return broke. The day before, Michael had filed for their divorce and word was everywhere. She knew the entire story would follow her for a few weeks.

"I still think I should be with you."

"We've been over this. The public will forget me in a few weeks. Michael is already setting up a few photo ops with other women to take the focus off me. Once those pictures hit the tabloids, I'll be yesterday's news. Movies are less than two hours long for a reason, Zach. The attention span of Michael's fan base is limited. Trust me."

"I don't know."

"Zach, you have a life here. You can't just leave." She'd thought a lot about their relationship and what it would mean to keep it going across state lines. Instead of thinking the worst, she wanted to give them some time to see what would happen when they weren't seeing each other every day.

The airport parking lot was full, forcing them to park off-site. Because of security, they had to say their good-byes long before the plane was due to leave.

Karen didn't want this moment to be ruined by tears, but she felt them crawling up her throat as the moments they had left together closed in.

Zach held her hand, tugged her away from the line leading to her plane. "Call me when you land."

She nodded, not trusting herself to speak.

Zach placed his palm to the side of her face and forced her eyes to his. She didn't want to leave him. Maybe living in Utah was something she could do.

"Hey . . ."

He swiped the tear that drifted down her cheek. "You feel that ache?" he asked as he pointed to her chest. "I have the same one right here."

She choked when he pointed to his own heart.

"You know what that means?"

"It means we're both saps."

Zach smiled. "No, it means we can't stay away from each other for long. So tears aren't necessary."

Karen choked back a sob and lifted her lips to his. The tenderness behind his kiss brought more tears. The ache grew wider. Zach was wrong. The pain in her chest told her she loved him. Saying good-bye to someone you loved always hurt.

He ended their kiss and hugged her like a starved man.

As expected, the paparazzi met her at the airport, but not before Rick and three suit-wearing men surrounded her. Only once she was sandwiched between them in the back of a limousine did Karen remove her sunglasses.

"Thanks for your help, Rick."

He sat to her left and shielded his eyes from the flash of a bulb that filled the inside of the car.

"My pleasure. How's everyone in Utah?"

"Settling. Becky is staying with Michael's parents. Nolan is rooming with Zach. It's all good."

"How's Judy?"

Karen smiled. "Good. She really came through."

"Tough kid." Rick didn't meet her gaze when she lifted her eyes to his.

"She's not a kid."

"Close enough." OK, so he had seven . . . maybe eight years on Judy. But they weren't that far apart in age.

"I'm sure the men on campus would disagree with you."

"Hmm."

Karen grinned . . . and waited.

"I forgot where she said she was going to college."

"Boise State."

"Oh, yeah, that's right."

Karen couldn't help but laugh out loud. Judy wasn't going to Boise State, she was at the University of Washington . . . and it was obvious that Rick was just fishing for information about the *kid*.

"What?" Rick asked.

"Nothing." Watching this unfold would be worth the wait.

The gates to the Beverly Hills home opened and the city lights behind the house reminded her of the millions of people who surrounded her. Rick and his security helped her inside with her bags, and swept the interior and exterior before leaving.

She flopped on the couch and pulled her cell phone from her purse. She dialed Zach's number and waited for him to pick up.

"Hey, babe."

She liked that. "Hey."

"You made it home OK?"

She glanced around Michael's empty house and smiled. "I did."

A knock on the front door brought her to her feet. Rick must not have left yet.

"How is Nolan settling in at your house?"

"I'm sure he's fine."

Karen held the phone with one hand and opened the door. "What do you mean? You don't know?"

Expecting Rick, Karen gasped when she opened the door to find Zach standing there.

He dropped his phone from his ear. "I don't know because I'm not there."

After the shock of seeing him waned, Karen jumped into his arms. She was sure one of them dropped their phone. She wrapped her legs around him as he carried her into the house. He kept his lips pressed to hers.

"I can't believe you're here."

He kicked the door closed, kissed her again. "I can't keep you safe if you're miles away."

She couldn't stop smiling. "You're crazy."

Karen's feet slid to the floor and she stared at him.

"Crazy? Maybe . . . you have to be crazy to fall in love with your brother's wife."

Her jaw dropped as his words sank in. "Your brother's *fake* wife."

"I mean it, Karen. I love you and the paparazzi will just have to get used to taking our pictures. I'm not leaving you to face anyone alone."

"Oh, Zach. I love you, too."

When she kissed him, their lips sealed their words.

"What about Utah . . . your job?"

"Utah can do without me. And my foreman can run my job site. They can do without me, but I can't do without you."

"Oh, Zach." She tilted her head, kissed him again. He was here . . . in her arms . . . without anyone knocking on the door, any family calling . . . anything to break them apart.

Karen pulled away only to tug him to the room she called her own while living in Michael's home.

He lowered her to her bed, pulling the shirt from her shoulders before pressing her into the mattress. Her legs tightened around his waist, her hands trailed down his back and up again. "It's been too long." She tossed his shirt to the floor.

"Less than a week."

"Too long," she said between kissing and tasting his moans.

"I won't make you wait again."

She laughed, pushed him onto his back, and worked her lips down his chest. The clasp of her bra popped free. "Getting better at that," Zach said before he sat up and tasted the flesh hidden by her bra.

"Practice is a good thing."

Zach rolled her onto her back, held her hands aside, and sucked her nipples into tiny beads of need. She shivered, called his name.

"I love hearing my name from your lips," he confessed. He slid down her body, wiggled her pants from her hips, tasting his way down her belly, her thigh. He opened her, tasted her until she exploded with his name on her lips.

The earth under her barely came to rest and he was inside her, taking her with him on a never-ending journey of passion.

He rode her, told her how much he loved her as they came together.

She smiled into his shoulder as their hearts slowed their wild pace. "I love you, Zach."

Epilogue

Scaffolding wrapped around the entire north side of the five-thousand-square-foot Victorian that overlooked the Pacific Ocean. The winter breeze had Karen wrapping her arms around the sweater she'd tossed over her shoulders to ward away the cold.

Construction on the old home had been nonstop since she and Zach had found the abandoned property two months after their return from Utah. It was perfect. The two acres of property afforded them privacy and the ocean view allowed time for reflection and healing. Something every teen would need during their stay.

At the current pace of construction, they would be open to needy kids by spring. Her dream of helping others was finally coming true. She and Zach were living out of an upstairs suite during the construction, all of which he was overseeing. He'd flown back to Utah a few times to finish the work he'd started there. It didn't take Zach long to make contacts in LA, and already he had a small team of men working on individual spec homes instead of the big housing jobs. Apparently, custom work appealed to Zach more than the cookie-cutter homes that had popped up all over the nation before the recession. With the economy bouncing back, spec houses were becoming more popular.

Karen didn't need to turn around to know who walked up behind her. Zach's arms, the scent of his skin, wrapped around her. "What are you doing out here?"

"Just thinking about how happy I am," she told him.

He kissed the top of her head and held her.

"Aren't you going to pick up your parents?"

"Not yet."

The divorce party was the coming Friday and the entire Gardner clan would be arriving over the next couple of days to attend.

"I wish everything was done here so they could stay with us."

Zach nuzzled her neck. "Next time."

"Maybe we can have a grand opening ... or housewarming something or other."

"I think you like to throw parties as much as my brother."

Karen laughed. "Yeah. We have that in common I guess. Did we get confirmation that Nolan and Becky are coming for the party?" The young couple were still very much in love and even stronger after losing their baby. Secretly, Karen hoped that if they did decide to get married right after Becky finished school in the spring, that Karen could convince them to have their wedding on the very spot she and Zach stood now. The kids deserved nothing but good things after all they'd been put through.

"My mom said they will be on a flight tomorrow. Becky had a final or something."

"Good."

"Oh," Zach unwrapped his arms from her. "I almost forgot."

She sent him a questioning look.

From his pocket, he removed a small box. She looked at him with a coy smile. The last time he'd handed her a small box it held the key to the house they now stood next to.

"What's this?"

"Open it."

His beautiful eyes watched her as she lifted the small silver lid.

The two-carat round diamond sat in a cluster of smaller stones in a setting that matched the era of the home they'd picked out together.

"Zach," she whispered.

He bent down on his knee and Karen lost it. Tears instantly sprang to her eyes.

"I want you forever, Karen. I want to spend every happy and every sad memory with you by my side. Will you marry me?"

She dropped to her knees beside him. "Oh, Zach. You know I will."

He kissed her, briefly, then slid the ring on her finger. "I love you."

She reached out her hand, and smiled at his choice of rings. "I shouldn't be this happy days before my divorce."

"You should when you're married to the wrong person."

"It doesn't feel like I've ever been married to anyone."

He smiled, kissed her again.

"When should we plan a wedding?"

"Anxious?" she asked, smiling at the thrill in his voice.

"You have no idea. Waiting for this divorce has taken years off my life."

Karen stared into the eyes of her future and fell in love all over again. "Well, the divorce will be final by Friday. I'll be single by Saturday."

He blinked. "This Saturday? You want to get married this Saturday?"

She bit her lower lip. "Why not? Your family will be here. Michael isn't off on location . . . my friends are all in town. Why not?"

"Can we do this by Saturday?"

Karen tossed her head back and laughed. "Remind me to tell you how quickly all my friends have tied the knot. So what do you say, Zach Gardner . . . will you marry me on Saturday?"

He brought her to her feet, lifted her up on her toes, and kissed her.

"I can't wait to make love to Mrs. Karen Gardner."

"I can't wait to make love as Mrs. Karen Gardner."

"So you'll take my name?"

"You can't keep it from me. Now come on . . . we have a lot to do and less than four days to make it happen."

Before she could pull him away, Zach stopped her. "Wait."

He stared at her, through her.

"What is it?"

"I just want to savor this moment. Remember it forever."

Her heart melted as they stood there, both holding the moment and knowing that they would have many more like it to come.

Acknowledgments

There are many things that spark a writer's muse . . . a vacation, an interesting person . . . a place. Utah is one of the most beautiful places with which God graced this world.

I was first, enamored with the beauty of the landscape and second, thankful for the hospitable people. My small town of Hilton, Utah, may only exist in my mind, but small towns everywhere will relate. They truly have little graffiti and do seem to roll up their sidewalks by eight p.m. . . . but for some strange reason this city girl can only imagine, they claim a populace that is loyal to the bitter end.

For Manuela, who certainly doesn't gossip, but surely knows what everyone is up to!

For Tammy and her family, who opened their home and hearts to ours.

For my critique partner, Sandra, who inspires all my Michaels.

To Mr. and Mrs. Hart and Mr. and Mrs. Halstrom . . . who took me in as a young, scared teen and offered me a safe home so I could finish high school.

A special thanks to Judy, who taught me firsthand that faith went beyond what one learned in church and extended to others beyond her own religion.

As always, to Jane, Lauren, Miriam, and everyone at Dystel and Goderich Literary Management.

To Melody, for her editorial flair and tearing up at the right times, and everyone at Montlake for all you do.

Once again to David and Libby. Nearly every holiday picture I have captures yet another person you've taken into your home. It's people like you who find it in your hearts to help others, regardless of the hardship it may place upon your shoulders. Though I can't say this book was written with you in mind . . . I can't think of any others to actually dedicate this book to. You would be Mr. and Mrs. Gardner welcoming Becky into your home. You wouldn't even think twice. The world would be a better place if more people like you existed.

I love you!

Catherine

About the Author

New York Times bestselling author Catherine Bybee was raised in Washington State, but after graduating high school, she moved to Southern California in hopes of becoming a movie star. After growing bored with waiting tables, she returned to school and became a registered nurse, spending most of her career in urban emergency rooms. She now writes full-time and has penned the novel *Not Quite Dating*, as well as the Weekday Brides series. Bybee lives with her husband and two teenage sons in Southern California.

STAND YOUR GROUND

CPH.
SAINT LOUIS

Devotions for Teens by Teens

Acknowledgments

Special thanks to
TKD, Jeannette, Mark,
Rich, Marge, Cindy,
and the many people
who helped along the way.
Special thanks to the teen authors
who poured out their best.—Ron

All Scripture quotations from THE HOLY BIBLE, NEW INTERNATIONAL VERSION®.
NIV®. Copyright © 1973, 1978, 1984 by International Bible Society.
Used by permission of Zondervan Publishing House.
All rights reserved. Cover Illustration © Jon Berkeley.
Excerpts from *Luther's Small Catechism* © 1986 Concordia Publishing House
are used by permission.

Copyright © 2001 Concordia Publishing House
3558 S. Jefferson Ave. St. Louis, MO 63118-3968
Manufactured in the United States of America

Library of Congress Cataloging-in-Publication Data
Stand your ground : devotions for teens by teens.
        p. cm.
    ISBN 0-570-05291-2
    1. Teenagers--Prayer-books and devotions--English. 2. Teenagers'
writings, American. [1. Prayer books and devotions. 2. christian life.
3. Conduct of life. 4. Youths' writings.]
    BV4850 .s73 2001
    242' .63--dc21
                                    2001001367
1 2 3 4 5 6 7 8 9 10   10 09 08 07 06 05 04 03 02 01

Our thanks to our teen authors

Matt Augustine
Erin Baker
Heather Boyd
Eric Cannedy
Jacob Carr
David Cecil
Megan Corson
Erica Demel
Ross Engel
Nate Farber
Donine Fink
Scott D. Whitehouse-Gercken
Kristen R. Heimsoth
Justin Hoag
Laura Joyce
Kristina Johnson
Tim Kassouf
Christel Kopitzke
Steven T. Lessner
Justin C. Lohr
Terry Lucas

Brittany McIntyre
Katie Maske
Katie Moehrig
Amber Morris
Kristina Neumann
Kim Niehaus
Ashley E. Oliver
Lisa Olson
Kristen Reeb
Tom Roma
Alissa Smelser
Michelle Lynn Sperberg
Annie Tiberg
Bethany Tweeten
Emily Vance
Lisa Widlowski
Amanda Wilhelm
Allison Wilson
Amy Zepp

Preface

My office is full of surprises: the unusual and usual; joy and sorrow; tears and fears; complaints and praise; confessions and forgiveness; pleas and thanks. Name the situation or the emotion, and it's been in my office. In the years I've spent as a school chaplain, nothing has touched my soul like watching a young person reach beyond mud-stained trouble to stand, by God's grace, on higher ground. As faith grows and feet become steady, I know it's a blessing of the Holy Spirit. It's a metanoia—a change of heart, soul, words, lips, feet, hands, attitude, and latitude. It's receiving Christ's forgiveness offered in love. It's standing your ground through Christ's stand-alone mercy. It's helping one another—teen to teen, parent to teen, teen to adult. It is God's Word—active and living.

During this time when teens break free of childhood and dependency on parents to enter adulthood, you need a perspective on life that reveals its deeper purpose and its deeper hope, which extends far beyond the promise of tomorrow. At the heart of such a life-shaping perspective is faith in Jesus Christ as Lord and Savior. These devotions affirm that God is alive and working in the lives of His chosen people.

These devotions were written by teens to whom God is a reality. These writers don't know you personally, but as you read their words, you will come to

know a little about them and their understanding of who God is, what life is about, and what faith means as we each live out our God-given purpose. The teen authors have written about real problems, real dreams and joys, and real events. They have written in love and seek to reflect a confidence in God's forgiveness and acceptance in Christ. Each writer shares, in his or her own way, a trust that our heavenly Father's plan for His children is good and will bring us ultimately to be with Him in heaven.

As I sat in my office and selected these devotions, I experienced many more surprises—at the talent demonstrated in the writing; at the insights of the young contributors; at the faith walks shared; at the ways these teens have, through faith, stood their ground. I pray that these words will surprise you, delight you, help you, and affirm your faith in God for years to come.

Use these devotions in the privacy of your room, with a friend at a favorite place, or with a group. Read them in times of joy, crisis, sorrow, or uncertainty. And if, by the power of the Holy Spirit, these reflections on God's Word, His faithful promises, and His work in your life help you to stand your ground, this project was a success.

Ron Roma
General Editor

Introduction

Have you ever had a "mountaintop experience"? You know, when you have that euphoric
feeling? It's like you're on top of the world and
things couldn't possibly get any better. Everything
is wonderful, and you know that God is the reason
things are so great. It's just God and you, and you
sing with the psalmist: "Great is the LORD, and most
worthy of praise, in the city of God, His holy
mountain" (Psalm 48:1). At times like these, it's
easy to stand your ground—and the view couldn't
be better.

But there are low times, darker times, more
challenging times as well. Everybody experiences
valleys. At these moments, the footing seems shaki-
er, less firm. It's harder to stay standing, to maintain
balance. But we're not left alone in the quicksand.
As God's people, we also can confess with the
psalmist: "I lift up my eyes to the hills—where does
my help come from? My help comes from the
LORD, the Maker of heaven and earth" (Psalm
121:1–2). And with God's help, we are enabled to
"stand our ground," even when everything around
us seems to be sinking sand.

No matter life's circumstances, as God's people, we are invited to "set [our] hearts on things
above, where Christ is seated at the right hand of
God" (Colossians 3:1). In Christ, we have hope and

love, forgiveness and encouragement. We experience the generous grace of God and His powerful presence in our lives. God's Holy Spirit enables us to stand our ground in the valleys, even below sea level, as well as on the mountaintops. These are God's sure promises to us!

These devotions express the faith of these Christian teenagers—a faith they want to share with you. In these pages, teen writers describe what it means to them to "set your heart on things above." They offer you encouragement even as they express Christian joy and confidence. Each devotion contains thought-full words that say, "Take heart. Stand your ground. Trust the Lord to help you do it!" These are mountaintop words for teens by teens—words by which God empowers young people to claim the higher ground.

May these pages be a blessing to all who read them, and may God be glorified through them.

Terry K. Dittmer
Interim Director, LCMS Congregational Services—Youth Ministry
The Lutheran Church—Missouri Synod

Reaching Higher Ground

Read: Matthew 19:21–26

In Matthew 19, Jesus speaks to a rich young man, telling him what he must do to enter the kingdom of God. Jesus said, "If you want to be perfect, go, sell all your possessions and give to the poor, and you will have treasure in heaven. Then come, follow Me" (Matthew 19:21).

When Jesus tells this man he would "be perfect," He wasn't speaking in the human, temporal sense. He was explaining how the young man could remove some of the distractions in his life. Does this mean that believers should give up everything they own? No, we still have the responsibility to care for the needs of our families and ourselves so we are not a burden on others. The point Jesus was making is that nothing on this earth should come between ourselves and God. With God's help, we willingly can give up anything, at any time, so we will be able to serve God and His people better. When Christ is above any possession, earthly relationship, or material goal, our focus is on the life that God intends for us.

Last July, my youth group from Menomonee Falls, Wisconsin, took a servant trip to West

(Matt Anderson

Virginia. We spent an entire week in a small mountain town fixing old houses to make conditions more livable. We paid our own way to get there, slept on a crowded floor, and worked in 100-degree heat every day. Despite the things we gave up, most of us came away saying it was one of the greatest, most faith-building, experiences of our lives.

Think of the one thing that you love the most in your life. Would you be willing to give it up if God asked you to do so?

Prayer: Dear heavenly Father, thank You so much for sending Your Son, Jesus, to die for me so I can be with You. I want to be closer to You, Lord. Help me not to make excuses when asked to serve Your people. Make me willing to give up anything to follow You. Help me to let nothing come between myself and You, God. Guide me to that "higher ground" by Your side. In Jesus' precious name I pray. Amen.

Temptation

Read: 1 Peter 5:8–11

Every day we are confronted by the temptations of this world. We are surrounded by a world that continually sins. Someone might try to get us to do something that we know is wrong, and these situations can be very frustrating. As Christians we are called to live for God and Him alone, not in the temptations of this world. Sometimes the devil tries to persuade us that giving in to temptations seems right. With God's help, we can resist the devil and keep our eyes on Christ, who saved us from all sin.

Job, in the Old Testament, was a Godly man who followed God's commands, and God blessed him. So Satan said to God, "But stretch out Your hand and strike everything he has, and he will surely curse You to Your face" (Job 1:11). Satan was trying to prove that Job would curse God. Strengthened by his faith, Job never cursed God. God blessed him, and he regained all that he had lost and even more.

Sometimes things might not go our way or something terrible might happen. Our faith in God reminds us that He will never leave us or forsake us. God uses these times of testing to "perfect, estab-

lish, and strengthen" us so when we overcome temptation we are restored, made strong and firm in Christ. (See James 1:13 and 1 Peter 5:10.) As children of God, we are called to fear and love Him and put away temptations and be holy before Him. We all fall short of the kingdom of God, but Christ came and took our punishment so we can have eternal life.

We were bought at a price so by God's power we can resist all the temptations of this world. As we put our focus on Christ, we have great rewards in heaven.

Prayer: Dear Lord, sometimes temptations seem to be too large to handle, and I feel helpless. Help me to trust in You, to focus on Your will for me, so I may overcome temptations and take the "higher ground." Amen.

In the Hands of God

Read: Psalm 34:15–22

There is a vicious infection that plagues millions of Americans, young and old. It can be a killer or a crippler of the emotional senses. Almost everyone has it, and there is a simple, yet miraculous cure that often is overlooked.

The infection is called "stress," and the miracle cure is God. Psalm 34:19 says: "A righteous man may have many troubles, but the LORD delivers him from them all." This promise is stated again in Nahum 1:7: "The LORD is good, a refuge in times of trouble. He cares for those who trust in Him."

This promise of God is something that often is forgotten amid the term papers, relationships, gossip, heartbreak, and other hardships that plague us teens. We spend night after night tossing and turning, worrying about how we will handle everything when we wake up. What things in your life cause you to be stressed? How do you usually deal with being stressed?

What we often don't realize is that God will take those troubles out of our hands and into His own so we don't have to worry about them any-

more. He loves us that much! All it takes is a few moments spent in quiet prayer.

At your Baptism, God took you into His family. You became a forgiven child in His kingdom. He promises to care for you forever, to help you carry the overwhelming burdens of life, to love you, and to give you eternal life.

When you spend less time worrying and stressing, you will have more time to enjoy the gift of life that God so graciously gave to you. Thank Him for relieving your burdened shoulders. Let God take on your stress. He can handle it!

Prayer: Lord, thank You for taking my burdens on Yourself. Thank You for making me part of Your family and promising to care for me forever. Amen.

LIFEguard

Read: Psalm 68:19-20

This past summer I took a lifeguarding course. I learned many things: the proper techniques to rescue different types of victims, how to spinal board someone, how to perform CPR and rescue breathing, and countless other things. One of the most important things brought up time and time again was the fact that when you sit up in the chair on duty, you are responsible for the life of each person in your zone. When you lifeguard, you care for each person in the pool and desire everyone to be safe.

In a sense, God is a lifeguard too. However, He's not just any lifeguard—He is the Great Lifeguard. While I might guard people for a few hours a day at a pool, God watches over us every moment of every day. While I have the skills to rescue a drowning person, God rescues our body and soul. While I am taught that I should be willing to put my personal safety on the line for the patrons I serve, God did a lot more than putting His personal safety on the line. God sent Jesus to die for us so we could have eternal life! When there was no way to save our drowning souls, God sent Jesus to rescue us from eternal death. It is certainly true in Psalm

(Heather Boyd)

68:20 where the psalmist writes that "our God is a God who saves; from the Sovereign LORD comes escape from death."

God made the ultimate sacrifice for us in Jesus! Whenever we experience those times in the "low ground" of life, when it seems as though we're drowning, know that Jesus is your rescue and salvation. He always will be watching and guarding you.

Prayer: Dear Lord, thank You for coming and rescuing me. You put everything on the line for me, and You made the ultimate sacrifice—You gave up Your life for me. Help me always to remember that You are watching over me and that You will never fail me. Amen.

Earthquake!

Read: Isaiah 40:9–11

August 8 was the most terrifying day of my life. While worshiping at an evening service, an 8.2 earthquake rocked the ground where I stood. I watched the candles sway as the building itself seemed to be walking! It seemed like an eternity. As I looked into the faces of my parents and the other adults around me, I saw fear in their eyes. It struck me that they all thought we were going to die. As suddenly as the shaking began, it stopped. All of us had survived the longest minute of our lives.

Seven years have passed since that night. Although I do not recall every detail, every minor shake, small rumble, or loud noise sets me on edge and gets my heart pounding. But God has given me His Word in Isaiah 40:10 to dwell on instead of the fear. God says in this verse that we need not fear because He is our God and He will strengthen and uphold us with His righteous hand. Now whenever that familiar dread comes back to haunt me, I remember this verse and know that no matter what happens to me, I am not alone. God will never leave me. His power is greater than anything.

What are you afraid of in your life? What mem-

ories do you have that make you shudder, even if only on the inside? Whatever they are, think about them when you read this verse and know God's power and strength are far greater than anything on this earth, under the earth, or inside of us. The next time you are tempted to give in to your fears, remember God will uphold you with His righteous hand. He will strengthen you, protect you, and be with you always!

Prayer: Dear God, thank You for being with me always and for upholding me when I am in distress. Help me never to forget that, even in my fear, You are there and gladly will take fear away from me. In Jesus' name. Amen.

Free Time

Read: John 2:1-11

It was a Friday night during football season, and everyone had gone to Brian's house after the game. Nothing very interesting ever really happened at these postgame events; people messed around and talked about who had kicked the winning field goal at the game. Things were getting pretty boring this particular evening, and most of us were thinking of leaving.

Some people, however, wanted the party to last a little longer, so someone suggested that we play Truth or Dare. No one could resist the temptation of seeing someone act out a dare or admit to a secret in front of the group, so we decided to stay a while longer.

Have you played Truth or Dare? Games like it are designed to make people uncomfortable. Often the dares can cross the line and embarrass people. Few people feel comfortable revealing a truth about themselves to a group. If someone refuses to answer the question or perform the dare, he or she is excluded from the group. When you try to confront people about situations such as these, the response often is, "It's just a game. We're just trying to have fun."

It's usually during innocent fun that things can go too far. Should we separate the things that we do for fun

from the rest of life? Does God care about what we are doing for fun?

In the Bible reading, Jesus shows us that He truly cares about all aspects of our lives. Whether we are in church, at school, at home, or at a party at a friend's house, Jesus is there, caring for us every day. When we are faced with situations that make us uncomfortable, we can stand our ground because our Savior strengthens us to do so. God wants us to have fun, but He also would have us honor Him with our lives.

The next time you find yourself in a situation like the one I described, ask yourself
- What can I do or say as a Christian when faced with situations that make me uncomfortable?
- How can I have fulfilling free time while lifting others up?
- How can I use a difficult/uncomfortable situation to witness my faith to others?

Prayer: Thank You, Jesus, for showing Your care for me. Help me to be an example for others and to stand my ground in faith when I am faced with difficult situations. Thank You for being there with me all the time. Amen.

Goals

Read: Philippians 3:12–14

There once was a man with a goal in life. We'll call him Mr. Jones. His goal was to teach in a Christian school. He was working at Safeco when he received a phone call to give a chapel presentation at a small Christian school on the north side of Indianapolis. His message impressed the leaders of this school. Little did Mr. Jones know how God would fulfill his goal. After the chapel presentation, Mr. Jones was asked to be headmaster at this small Christian school. The salary was low, but Mr. Jones had saved enough money so he could fulfill his dream and still support a family.

About halfway through the year, Mr. Jones developed pain in his lower back. He went to the doctor and found out he had a tumor on his back and shoulder blade. He also had prostate cancer. Mr. Jones would have to undergo treatment to keep the cancer under control. This made him tired, but he continued to lead the school, earning the respect of the students. If the health problems were not enough, Mr. Jones started receiving nasty letters from the former headmistress, telling him she disliked how Mr. Jones was running the school.

Mr. Jones left a lasting impression on me as well as on others. He never fought back at the former headmistress. He never complained. He kept pursuing his goal and setting an example for the students because the students knew what he was going through. He showed us how we could focus on Christ and persevere through rough times.

Our ultimate goal is heaven. God guides everything that we do as we attain that goal through faith in Christ. We are blessed to have many role models who help us along the way to achieving our goals. Role models like Mr. Jones persevere in the face of obstacles and help us to rise above as we stand firm in our faith and await the prize God has for us in heaven.

Prayer: Dear God, help me use the talents You have given me to reach my earthly goal. Keep my eyes focused on You, no matter what anyone says or does. Thank You for the gift of heaven, which is mine because of Your Son, Jesus. Thank You also for the role models in my life that help me along life's path. Continue to bless and keep me. In Jesus' name. Amen.

Through His Grace

Read: Mark 8:22–26

So many times in my walk of faith I question if I'll ever get to where I'm headed. It seems as though the second I get started, my sinful self trips me up again. In Mark 8:22, it says:

> They came to Bethsaida, and some people brought a blind man and begged Jesus to touch him. He took the blind man by the hand and led him outside the village. When He had spit on the man's eyes and put His hands on him, Jesus asked, "Do you see anything?" He looked up and said, "I see people; they look like trees walking around."

Jesus wasn't finished with the man though. Mark 8:25 says: "Once more Jesus put His hands on the man's eyes. Then his eyes were opened, his sight was restored, and he saw everything clearly." The man was washed in the miracle of God's healing love and able to see clearly.

We can't expect to be perfect in our walk of faith. Each and every day, though, God offers us for-

giveness for all of our stumbles. He picks us up and helps us to take a few more steps. If we never tripped, we would never know how it felt to be picked up in the hands of the Savior, brushed off, and washed clean in a flood of grace. The only thing making that possible is God's unfailing love in Jesus Christ. He loves us so much that He takes time to continually mold us, shape us, and form us into the beautiful children He created us to be.

Prayer: Dear God, please send the power of Your unfailing love in my life. Forgive my sin, and shower Your grace on me. Thank You for the love I have in Your Son, Jesus. In His name I pray. Amen.

Hiking in His Presence

(David Cecil

24

Read: Ephesians 3:14-21

One of my favorite places in the world is Colorado. I love the mountains, streams, and the wildlife. And one of my favorite things to do in Colorado is to hike into the mountains and experience God's creation from a new perspective. One time as I was hiking, a member of the group commented that of the countless tourists that came through this particular town, almost 90 percent never actually went into the mountains. They were content to stay on the flat ground and admire the beauty from afar.

How much is that like our relationship with God? So many times we are content to stay back and admire God's greatness from afar. Sure, we are aware of His presence, but God wants more from us. He calls us and brings us to Himself to experience firsthand His mercy and grace. He wants nothing short of the best for us, and that means being completely wrapped up in His love. No more viewing God from a distance—God brings us into His very presence.

Sometimes we need to see God from a new perspective and from a new challenge. That new

perspective may mean we have to come out of our comfort zone and go to places we've never been. It may mean going on a servant event or visiting someone who is a shut-in or in the hospital. It may mean starting a new Bible study with your youth group or at your school.

We may never fully understand God's care for us. Yet Ephesians 3:18 reminds us that we "have power, together with all the saints, to grasp how wide and long and high and deep is the love of Christ."

Prayer: Dear Lord, You bring me to higher ground in the mercy of Your Son, Jesus. Help me to grow in love for Him and other people by Your Holy Spirit. Even when I don't understand Your ways, help me to see how much You care for me. In Jesus' name. Amen.

Well Watered

Read: Ecclesiastes 3:11

When I was in third grade, my class did an experiment with plants. We planted seeds and waited to see who could grow the biggest plant. We put them by the windows so they would have sunlight, and we faithfully watered them. They were growing so well!

About three weeks into our experiment, we had Christmas vacation. The plants were left in the care of the janitor, and we enjoyed the time off from school. When we came back, we found all our plants dead. They had not been watered; the janitor had forgotten. If only I had cared more for my plant!

Now imagine your heart as a seed or a plant and God as the gardener. God has planted faith in our hearts. He wants us to have a spiritual thirst. Like plants, our hearts need nourishment. Our hearts need the life-giving water of Christ and the filling Word of God. Nourishment from any other source is like contaminated water or rancid food— it takes the place of real nourishment only for so long.

We never can be satisfied completely with things of this world. Do not let earthly desires take over your heart. Water your heart! Protect what God has given you by immersing yourself in God's Word. Grow in the Lord. God has planted a special gift in your heart. God has not left you without the tools and nourishment needed!

What are you using to nourish your heart? Are you leaving your heart in the care of somebody other than God?

Prayer: Heavenly Father, thank You for loving me so much that You gave me the gift of a Savior. Help me to live for You and to grow in You. Help me to use all the gifts You have given me. Thank You for loving me. In Jesus' name. Amen.

Warming the Bench

Read: Luke 14:10-11

What part does God play in athletics?

I asked myself this question the summer before my junior year, the year that I hoped to make varsity volleyball. Frustration led me to ask that question—frustration with God and frustration with the physical preparation needed to try out for a varsity sport. Although I made the volleyball team, my question was not answered immediately. It was not until softball season that I finally understood. The reason it took that long for me to see the answer was because I was not listening to God.

I was trying to be a star, a person who wanted to take care of my future. I felt that my junior year was the time to be noticed in athletics, and I prepared to do it all myself. Going into the softball season, I decided that I would play for fun and stop thinking about being a star. Then God could use my talents. It was at that point when I realized the answer to my question: *What part does God play in athletics?* I needed to humble myself. The word *humble* means "to not think too highly of oneself; to bring low or prostrate." In trying to be a star, I was not giving glory to God. Only when God came first

in my life could I clearly see His plan for me. I had the best softball season in my 12 years of playing. Pride separates us from God.

What things in your life may be blocking your sight of God? How has God lifted you up?

Prayer: Lord, thank You for my triumphs. Please humble me today so I can see You in all I do. Use my talents for Your will. In Your precious Son's name. Amen.

Change

Read: Hebrews 13:7–8

Change—what a big impact it can have on a person's life. I sure had a big change in my life. My dad is a pastor, and one November he received a call to a church in California. At the time, my family and I were living in Nevada. We belonged to a wonderful, growing congregation, and we kept busy with school, sports, and music. I had just started high school. I, for one, did not want to move.

The night that I was hit with the news that my dad had accepted the call, I cried myself to sleep thinking life was not fair. The move would mean a huge change in my life and in the lives of others.

The following March my dad moved to California, leaving the family behind to finish the school year. The next few months were hard on the rest of us as we prepared to leave Nevada. In June, we joined my dad in California to start our new life.

That fall I had to start a new high school and meet new friends. But I made the volleyball team and started attending youth group at my church. Some of the girls at my church helped me out by showing me around school and by being my friends. In October, my family moved into a brand-

new house. I had my own room. All those changes began to look much more positive.

Hebrews 13:8 tells us "Jesus Christ is the same yesterday and today and forever." No matter what changes occur in our lives, Jesus Christ will not change. He always will be our Savior. His love and compassion can overcome any doubt that we have. He will remain faithful to His Word.

I have now lived in California for more than a year, and I really enjoy it. Jesus has been with me every step of the way. When changes occur in your life, remember that the one thing that won't change is Jesus Christ and His saving love that He gives to all who believe.

Consider these questions the next time you face change in your life:
- Why does God allow change in our lives?
- Can good things come out of change?
- What reassurance does the Bible give to us about change?
- What change for the world occurred when Jesus died for our sins?

Prayer: Dear God, thank You for Your never-changing love. Thank You for Your Word and the hope that it gives to me. Please help me through the tough changes, and help me always keep my focus on You. In Jesus' name. Amen.

Love with Christ

I started dating a girl the end of my senior year of high school. At that time I thought she was "the one." We spent a lot of time together doing the things most teenagers do on dates, each of us believing that we would be together forever.

However, something was missing in our relationship. My girlfriend had been baptized, but she only had been to church a half dozen times in her life, mostly for weddings and baptisms. She did not really know much about Christ and His great love for us or what faith is. She did not know God and was set on not bringing Him into our relationship.

As a Christian, this placed a great strain on me. Getting my girlfriend to come to church with me often meant I had to bribe her. I would buy her gifts to make her happy. It seemed like a worthwhile sacrifice because she was going to church and maybe was learning about the love of God. Gifts were not the answer, though; her heart was not open to Christ. Every opportunity I took to talk to her about my faith was met with indifference and a closed mind and heart.

A relationship without Christ at the center is

difficult. As young adults, many temptations come into a relationship. Overcoming these temptations can be done only with the strength Christ gives. Most important, sharing the same faith and the love of Christ strengthens a relationship.

True love is a gift from God. It was displayed when He created human life in a perfect world, demonstrated again when He sent Jesus to die for us (1 John 4:9), and is seen every day as we build relationships with family members and with others, even in dating situations. Christ demonstrated His love for us so we can share love with others.

Put God and His love into your relationships. His love will strengthen the love you share and can make it last. Find someone with whom you feel comfortable talking about Christ, someone who will share your faith in Christ. The relationship will grow and be strong with the help of God! Remember, love and relationships are gifts from God.

Prayer: Heavenly Father, thank You for the gift of relationships. Help me always to place Christ at the center of my relationships. Let them grow with Your love as the center, and help me always to remember that relationships and the love shared between people are something You designed. In Jesus' name. Amen.

A Shot of the Holy Spirit, Please!

Read: Ephesians 5:15-18

College! Finally I was getting out of the house and getting out on my own!

In college, learning takes place both in and out of the classroom. I figured that with the sheltered life I had led for the past 18 years, I had a lot to learn. My knowledge of alcohol was limited to TV commercials and college stories. However, everyone around me seemed to know how to drink—what was good, and what was bad. For the first month or two, I was able to come up with excuses for not going out to drink and party, but my reasons eventually started sounding weak. Finally, I gave in and went out. That night I stumbled home feeling something I had never felt before. Everything seemed funny, and I felt like I had the courage of 10 men. I had learned a new way of life, but this learning came with a headache.

The next couple of weekends, I went out with friends, each time partaking in more kinds of drinks. Then one night I watched a team of paramedics take a friend out on a stretcher. I decided that going out every weekend and getting drunk wasn't the life I should be leading. I realized that in my "par-

(Ross Engel

tying," I had pushed God out of my life. It wasn't that I didn't need Him, it was the fact that I felt guilty for my actions every time I thought of God.

That night after the ambulance left, one of the guys who lived on my dorm floor, whom I didn't know well, invited me to a Saturday night worship service. I went with him the next weekend, and the pastor talked about the temptations of alcohol. As he quoted Ephesians 5:18, I remembered that having the Holy Spirit in me was better than any kind of frosty beverage. The Spirit didn't leave me feeling empty the next day, and He certainly didn't cause any headaches. Being filled with the Spirit rather than with alcohol allowed me to feel the grace and love of God rather than the false courage and guilt that alcohol had granted me.

As I became more involved in church, I realized that college is not all about partying and getting drunk. Many people don't drink and don't go to bars. There are many better things to do at school than drink. Fill yourself with the Holy Spirit! It's the best thing to fill up on when living on your own.

Prayer: Heavenly Father, being out on my own can be difficult. The world has so many temptations—and drinking is one of them. Fill me with your intoxicating love and the Holy Spirit! In Jesus' name. Amen.

Just Another Worrier

Read: Matthew 6:25–34

Ross Engel

> If you want to make God laugh, tell
> Him your plans for the future.

Like most people, I worry about my future:
How will I pay for school? What will I be when I get
out of school? As a student, I worry especially about
making the right choice for my career. I guess my
biggest fear is that I'll do something wrong and really screw up my life. In my struggles, I have changed
my career focus six times.

I really don't want to make the wrong decision
with my life. Of course, I know that I have made
wrong decisions, and sometimes that causes me to
worry too. I worry that because of my mistakes,
someone might love me less or think less of me as
a person. As I was growing up, I worried about
dressing right and being popular with the in crowd.
But now I've come into my own, though, and I realize that worrying about things such as clothes is
pretty worthless. There are many more important
things that deserve to be worried about. Or are
there?

Jesus has something to say about this. In Matthew 6:25, He tells us not to worry. The birds of the air do not worry, and God provides everything they need to live. Jesus also tells us not to worry about the future. In verse 34, He tells us that "tomorrow will worry about itself." Basically, He is comforting all of us who worry about our futures. God has a plan for each one of us, and worrying is useless. By worrying, we don't change God's plan for us or make things any easier on ourselves. Worrying only adds stress and does not add a single hour to our lives.

Rather than worry about what tomorrow will bring, we can thank God for today and make the most of whatever God gives to us. Only He knows the future, and knowing that is enough for us not to worry.

Prayer: Dear God, You hold my future in Your hands. You have the ultimate plan, yet I still worry sometimes about what tomorrow will bring. Please grant me the assurance I need to put my fears to rest and to trust in Your plans for me. In Jesus' name. Amen.

Letting God Guide

Read: Romans 5:1-2

Josh lived in California. He loved to hang with his friends and chat with girls at the beach, but most of all, he loved tennis. When he became a freshman, he went out for the boy's tennis team. His high school had just come off its fourth straight state title. Despite his uncertainty, Josh made the team.

Josh arrived at practice to find himself matched against Matt, who was a senior, the team captain, and the number one singles player in the state. Josh felt his entire body go numb as he slid onto the court and prepared to play. The coach sat down on court one as Josh began to practice across the net from the state's premier player. Matt hit every ball with ease, but Josh struggled to hit the ball at all. This pattern continued for the first week of practice. Josh went to the coach's office at the beginning of the second week of practice. He thought that the coach had made a mistake picking him for the team.

"I'm sorry, Coach," Josh said. "I don't know what's wrong. Please let me stay on the team. I'll try harder, I promise."

"Josh, nobody is taking you off the team," his

coach said. "You earned your spot, and you don't have to try to be like everyone else. Relax and play tennis like you know how. Okay?" Josh nodded his head and left.

The next week of practice went much smoother for Josh. He began to hit the ball better and soon found himself back in his rhythm. He was himself—part of the team.

Many Christians find it hard to believe they are new creations in Christ. They think they have to try harder and do better to gain the identity they've been freely given. Do you find yourself trying harder or "performing" so you can feel valuable or loved by God?

Sometimes when we become part of His team, we strive to be the perfect Christian. But since perfection is impossible, we find ourselves discouraged. When we try to be a perfect Christian on our own, we can never succeed without the help of God. When we fail, we can realize that no matter what we do, God freely offers forgiveness through Jesus Christ and sends the Holy Spirit to guide us in our daily walk.

Prayer: Dear Jesus, I ask for Your guidance and direction. Help me to see Your leading in my life. By the power of the Holy Spirit, strengthen me for my daily walk of faith. Amen.

Where's Your Treasure?

Read: Matthew 6:19-21

My youth group participated in a servant event in Little Rock, Arkansas. Our project was to paint and do light yard work for elderly people. When my group reached our first house, we realized that we had our work cut out for us: The yard was an absolute jungle, the paint thick and dirty on the brick house. Our group got right in there, busily chipping the paint and cleaning the porch. By the end of the day, it appeared we hadn't made much progress.

We talked to other groups who said they were almost done with their first house. Then I realized that the best we could do was to make this house look livable. Before the trip, I had envisioned making the houses look new and classy. I had a mistaken idea of what beauty was and how the house should look.

Although we couldn't give the owner of the house an elegant home, we could give this woman something she wanted and needed. On the last day of work, I left a card that had a personalized version of John 3:16 on it. She may never have fame or wealth, but she could be offered an even greater

gift—the great gift of the Gospel. Jesus died and rose for her!

In Matthew 6:19–21, Jesus reminds us of what is really important. All worldly goods and advantages are meaningless. Even all the hard work done on that house would surely rot again, but the gift given to us through Jesus' death and resurrection will never pass away. God would have us look toward our heavenly goal with Christ, our priceless treasure, leading us there.

Even if you feel unable to help someone in any other way, what does Jesus always want us to share with others?

Prayer: Dear God, in this sinful world, help me to focus on storing up treasures in heaven. Help me to share the Gospel so others can enjoy the treasures of heaven also. In the name of Jesus Christ, my Lord. Amen.

Trust Him with Your Future

Read: Romans 8:28

As teenagers we are stuck in that awkward space between childhood and adulthood. Many teens either try to grow up too quickly or are apprehensive about the future. Personally, I fall into the apprehensive category. As a rather indecisive person, the future always appears a bit uncertain. "Will I pass the test?" "What college should I attend?" "Will I have enough money?"

No matter what category you fall into, as you think about your future, God speaks to you through His Word. God continually reminds us that He loves us and wants the best for us. So our lives always will be fantastic, right? We know this is not true. God uses tough situations in our lives to mold us and to prepare us for the future. During these times, we rely on God's perfect timing and plan for our lives.

We don't have to rush growing up or to be anxious about the future. God is in control. Trust Him. Trust our God who was willing to live on the lowly sinful soil of this earth and die to redeem us. Jesus died and rose so we will gain entrance to higher ground one day. Jesus paid the unfathomable

Donine Fink

admission price to heaven for you and me. Proverbs 3:5–6 says: "Trust in the LORD with all your heart and lean not on your own understanding; in all your ways acknowledge Him, and He will make your paths straight." God directs our future paths.

- Do you find yourself trying to rush to the next phase of your life too quickly? If so, how could you better use the stage you are in right now?

- Are you nervous about the future and all the changes it inevitably brings? Name some concerns you can take to the Lord in prayer.

- Do we have any reason to worry about the future? When does God work for our good according to Romans 8:28?

Prayer: Heavenly Father, forgive me for those times I worry about the future or try to take it into my own hands. Remind me that You will guide me in the future. Thank You for always working for my good. In Jesus' name I pray. Amen.

Cult Anxiety

Read: Psalm 55:22

Cults are becoming more prevalent in society as people are brainwashed into believing lies and blindly following false leaders. On the news we hear of extreme mass suicides occurring within cults. There also are less extreme cults that try to mask themselves as churches or even Christian cults.

The issue of cults has weighed heavily on my mind since I was a young child. Some of my dad's relatives are Mormons. They claim to be Christian, but they aren't. They are relying on their own good works to get them to their own version of heaven. They add things to the Gospel of Jesus and have created "another" Bible. It pains me to know that some of my family and friends don't know Jesus Christ as their Savior from sin and death.

My witness to people in cults seems to fall on deaf ears. This past summer I had the privilege of talking to a Jehovah's Witness. This woman was very knowledgeable of Scripture passages. She had as strong a faith in her beliefs as I do in Jesus Christ. Unfortunately, we had two completely different interpretations of the Bible. As a result, I felt that no headway had been made. She was as concerned for

my spiritual well being as I was for hers.

When feelings of frustration and discouragement abound as we witness our faith in Jesus, we can look to higher ground. We are not alone, and our attempts in Jesus' name are not futile. God is with us.

Jesus invites us to lay our burdens at His feet. Psalm 55:22 reminds us to "cast your cares on the LORD and He will sustain you; He will never let the righteous fall." All I could do after speaking to that lady was lift her up in prayer. I prayed that the message of salvation through Jesus had been sown in her heart by the power of the Holy Spirit. Cults always will be a special concern that I will take to higher ground through prayer.

- Do you have friends or family members in cults?
- Have you ever talked to them about their beliefs?
- What is one way you always can help that person?
- When is the last time you prayed for that person?

Prayer: Heavenly Father, the issue of cults is so difficult that I often feel helpless. Remind me to come to You in prayer so the eyes of those who follow cults may be opened to the Gospel message of love of Jesus Christ, my Lord and Savior. In His name I pray. Amen.

Where Do You Stand?

(Scott D. Whitehouse-Gercken)

Read: 1 Corinthians 1:18

When people are asked to define *Christian,* the most common responses I get are, "They're nice people." "They go to church." "They're concerned about school prayer."

Many people attend a church, but this does not necessarily mean they are Christians. If you are sitting in a garage, does that make you a car? Then again, where is the best place for a car to pause and get fixed up for another go around in the world?

Many people are concerned about the posting of the Ten Commandments in schools and whether God is present in our schools. But if you listened to conversations at my school cafeteria, you wouldn't need directions to Sodom and Gomorrah. You'd be there. The Ten Commandments are God's Law, not 10 good suggestions. My school friends seem far away from following God's Law; they follow their own rules.

But there is good news. The Ten Commandments aren't the only things God has shared with us. The Gospel may be foolishness to the world, but it is the message of salvation for those who repent. Jesus gets us out of the low places of our sinful lives

and the destructive attitude of "live and let live." The Gospel shares the power of God against destruction by persecution or rejection. "The LORD is my light and my salvation—whom shall I fear?" (Psalm 27:1).

Whom, indeed! Christians need not fear rejection. What is that compared to Christ's love for you? His love is so great that He promises, "Blessed are you when men hate you, when they exclude you and insult you and reject your name as evil because of the Son of Man" (Luke 6:22).

Being nice, going to church, or being concerned about prayer doesn't make you a Christian. Other people fit that description too. You are a Christian because of God's free gift of faith for Christ's sake! Jesus died and lives for you and me. How can we not boldly live and die for Him? How can we not proclaim His Gospel?

Prayer: Dear God, thank You for the gift of faith in Your Son as my only Savior from sin. Help me to share Your Gospel with the people I see every day. In Christ's name. Amen.

The Perfect Prom Party

Read: Ephesians 6:1–4

Kristen R. Heimsoth

Prom. One of the most exciting times in the life of a high school boy and girl. We can dress elegantly, eat wonderful food, and have fun with others our own age. Although it can be an enjoyable event, it also can be dangerous. Some after-prom parties include pressure to drink and take drugs.

As a junior in high school, this past spring was my first prom. The day before prom, our school, along with the local police and fire departments, demonstrated a car accident caused by teenagers driving under the influence. Guest speakers told us how drunk drivers had killed their children, family members, or friends. These speakers encouraged us to have a good time but to make the right choice.

Prom night came, and I had a good time. After the crowning of the king and queen, a few of my Christian friends and I had our own party at one of our houses. We had a great time watching movies, eating popcorn, drinking soda, and talking. In my eyes, this was the perfect prom party.

Our parents and other authorities don't want us to drink or take drugs because they care about us and don't want anything bad to happen to us. God

tells us in the Fourth Commandment that we should respect people in authority. As Martin Luther put it in his catechism:

> Honor your father and your mother. *What does this mean?* We should fear and love God so that we do not despise or anger our parents and other authorities, but honor them, serve and obey them, love and cherish them.

In Romans 13:2, Paul reminds us: "He who rebels against the authority is rebelling against what God has instituted, and those who do so will bring judgment on themselves."

Paul notes the promise attached to the Fourth Commandment in Ephesians 6:3: "that it may go well with you and that you may enjoy long life on the earth." As God's Spirit guides us to obey our parents and make the right choices, we enjoy the blessings of new life in Christ. When we sin, His love and mercy reaches out to us and we receive His forgiveness and the promise of eternal life with Him. In Christ we are guided in love and directed by His Word.

Prayer: Heavenly Father, help me to know Your love and forgiveness in Jesus. Guide me in the right path through Your Son. In His name I pray. Amen.

Bringing Home the Trophy

Read: Luke 9:22

Anyone who participates in competitive sports knows that you have to endure pain and suffering. The pain of sore, tired muscles, the suffering of running until you're physically sick, the fatigue of pushing your body to its physical and mental limits. I have spent many days running several miles before breakfast. I go to practice and run some more, pushing my body to do everything the coach asks of me as I try to make the team. I run sprints and long distances, lift weights, do push-ups and pull-ups, and more until I can no longer convince my body to keep moving and collapse in exhaustion. All this for a chance to win, to take home the trophy, to be the best.

Luke 9:22 says Christ would have to endure suffering and rejection, and even death, to save us. His body was physically beaten and whipped. He endured the pain of the crown of thorns and the nails driven through His flesh. Jesus was spit on, made fun of, called names, and rejected by the people He came to save. Could you endure that kind of pain and suffering? Would you be able to keep going, knowing the crowd was against you? Would

you continue to compete, or would you quit?

Jesus didn't endure this pain and suffering so He could win first place and a trophy for Himself. He did it so we could have the prize—the treasure of heaven. Jesus didn't stop after the suffering and His death. He kept on going, exceeding the limits of His physical body. He rose from the dead. All this so we can live forever with Him.

When I push myself to excel in sports, I try to be mindful of how Christ pushed Himself and His body for me. Keeping this in my mind helps me to remember where I get my strength for doing everything. I tell myself, "Do your best, and let God do the rest." Christ did the rest. He rose again. We can be certain that the trophy of heaven is ours.

Prayer: Lord, thank You for the pain and suffering that You endured for me. Because of Your sacrifice, I win the prize—the trophy of heaven. Amen.

A Day in My Life

Read: Philippians 4:11–13

You wake up at 6 A.M., shower, pick out something to wear, eat breakfast, brush your teeth, then run to catch the bus at 7 o'clock. After a noisy bus ride, you arrive at school where you quickly go to your locker to drop off and pick up books. Then it's off to catch your friends before the first bell rings and you have to go to class. You make it through your classes, and the last bell rings at 2:45.

After a quick locker stop, you're off to practice. After practice you catch the end of your brother's soccer game. It finishes shortly after you arrive, and you head home to tackle homework and eat something. Oh, don't forget about your two best friends who are in a fight, which you have to referee. And there's that report you really should start writing. And who knows what else the next hours might bring! All you want to do is go to bed, but there's still so much to do ... ahhhh!

Do you ever feel like your schedule is overwhelming, and there's just too much to do? Whether it's sports, clubs, church and community activities, or even just a heavy load of homework, high school is an incredibly busy time for all of us.

We have to balance schoolwork, extracurricular activities, friends, family, and church while meeting the expectations of parents, teachers, coaches, pastors, and friends. It sometimes seems impossible to do.

Knowing God is with me helps me to deal with all the things I need to do each day. A quick prayer for patience or guidance is comforting, and I am reassured that God is always ready to help. Philippians 4:11–13 says:

> I have learned to be content whatever the circumstances. I know what it is to be in need, and I know what it is to have plenty. I have learned the secret of being content in any and every situation ... I can do anything through Him who gives me strength.

What a great reminder these verses are to me. God is there in everything I do, and He's ready to give me just what I need. The next time life becomes a little overbearing, call on God. Ask Him for strength. He's always there to help.

Prayer: Dear God, thank You for being with me always. Please give me the strength to accomplish everything I need to do each day in a way that is pleasing to You. Thank You for being the one whom I can look to for help and guidance. In Jesus' name. Amen.

God Is with You , Even in Tragedy

Read: Psalm 98:3

Kristina Johnson

A year ago, the pastor of my church, Rev. David Brabender, was killed in a car accident. Pastor Dave had been our pastor for years, and he was loved by all. He wasn't just our pastor—he was a friend and our shepherd in the Lord. He was young, and no one in our congregation was prepared for his death. It was a terrible tragedy.

I couldn't keep from asking why God let it happen. Why had God allowed our pastor to be taken away? What would we do without him? How could something so bad happen to someone so good? Hundreds came to Pastor Dave's funeral. He had been loved and respected in our community and had many friends. Everyone was sad.

For a long time I struggled to understand why God had let this happen. But as months passed, I began to realize that God's hand was in all of it. Pastor Dave's death had brought many people to church for his funeral—people who hadn't been to a service in years. Some heard the Gospel for the first time. Because of our pastor's death, many of these people realized how short life is. Many people were strengthened in faith in Christ. Because of this

tragedy, our congregation's members grew closer to one another as we comforted one another. God brought us closer to Himself as we looked to Him for comfort and guidance.

A few weeks ago, my church called a new pastor. All of us still mourn Pastor Dave, but it is easy to see now that his tragic death helped us to rely on Christ.

In Romans 8:28, God promises to work through all things, even tragedies, for the good of those who love Him. If there has been a tragedy in your life, remember God's promise to you. God will be with you in all things; ultimately, He will work for your good. He sent His Son to give us forgiveness, life, and hope. Jesus is the only way, truth, and life when tragedy strikes.

As you think about the tough times in your life, consider these questions:
- How have you seen God's hand at work in tragedies?
- Have you trusted in God to work for your good, even when things seem to be going wrong?

Prayer: Heavenly Father, help me to remember Your promise to work for my good in all things. Reveal Yourself to me so I can see You at work in my life every day. Thank You for calling me by faith in Christ Jesus, and help me to do Your will. In Jesus' name I pray. Amen.

Continuously

Read: 1 Thessalonians 5:17

"You guys gotta push yourselves," barked the coach. "You'll never be champions like that."

The team was finishing a strenuous practice that had become part of its daily routine. The coach was demanding, but he cared immensely for his team. Each player was crucial and valued. Every day this dedicated group of athletes pushed themselves to the limit in practice, and for what? To get better—to be the best.

Our world is fast-paced. Most of us find ourselves running here and there, trying to fit everything into our already packed schedules. A few months ago, I found myself crossing off "youth group" on my calendar and replacing it with practices or even hanging out with friends. It was when I went to replace "church" with wrestling that I caught myself. I looked again at my calendar. Where was God? It had become so easy to go to wrestling practice and push myself to physical exhaustion, yet so hard to find five minutes each day to spend in God's Word. If you had asked me, I would have said that my faith was my number one priority, but I certainly wasn't reflecting that in my life.

Christ should have been my first priority, but I was slipping. As a Christian I wanted to set aside time to focus on God and find strength in His Word. The Bible instructs us to "pray continually" (1 Thessalonians 5:17). Everything we do can begin with prayer and be done in praise and thanksgiving, all to the glory of God.

"Pray continually"? I slip up so much—God doesn't want my praise. He won't hear my prayers, I thought. Despite all of your sin, God's always focused on you. God provides undeserved forgiveness through Jesus Christ. He's always there to help you through the rough times in life.

In the midst of your busy life, give glory to God. If you can't meet a set prayer time every day, then find time to focus on the Lord whenever you can.

Prayer: Dear God, thank You so much for the gift of faith, forgiveness, and eternal life in Jesus Christ! Remind me of Your everlasting love, and by the power of the Holy Spirit, keep me focused on You. Father God, I'm sorry and ask forgiveness for my sin. May everything I do be in praise and thanks for Your undeserved gift of salvation. In the name of Your Son, Jesus Christ. Amen.

Whose Story Is It Anyway?

Read: Mark 16:15–16

Have you ever been to a movie and found yourself wishing you could have the same thrill of adventure? Even when it seems there is no way out, there is a happy ending. Unfortunately, we have learned that adventures like these are only the creation of talented screenwriters—or are they?

When Jesus sent His disciples out into the world to preach the Gospel, they did not know what lay ahead for them. They had been granted miraculous powers to heal and cast out demons. They had to face the mighty forces of sin and evil with no help from the Romans or the leaders of the Jewish church. Eventually, they would experience gruesome deaths. Is this the story line for this year's summer blockbuster? No, it is the story of the New Testament church as recorded by the apostles themselves in God's inspired Word.

"What does this have to do with me?" you ask. This adventure is our story as well. What!? An adventure for us, here, in the 21st century? It is up to us to continue the mission of the Lord—it is our turn to face the challenges. There are many things we can do in our everyday lives: talking to a friend,

giving some Bible-based guidance to someone in need, going on a mission trip. By living a Christian life and setting a good example for those around you, you actually are doing more than just working. When things get tough, we have the ultimate happy ending to look forward to—heaven. Our adventure is the challenge that God has called us to be lights to this world! Consider how you can fulfill your "assignment" from God to spread His Word. May the Lord help you to see the adventure in serving Him.

Prayer: Dear Jesus, thank You for giving me the opportunity to have adventures in my own life as I serve You. Please give me the strength and guidance to do Your will. Amen.

Lockers

"If you believe, you will receive whatever you ask for in prayer" (Matthew 21:22). Does this include opening lockers? I sure hoped so when I realized I could not open my gym locker in sixth grade.

While in elementary school, I couldn't wait to get to junior high so I could have lockers and more than one teacher. Naturally I was disappointed when I found out that I was "combination lock challenged." After seeing me struggle for what seemed like 20 years, my friend offered to open my lock for me. Six months and four days later, she was still opening it for me—saving me from the embarrassment of using the "I couldn't open my locker" excuse yet again for being late to gym class. (To this day, all sixth-graders at my junior high are required to take home their locks and practice opening them.)

By May of my sixth-grade year, I had decided I had had enough. I started in on the lock. "Six right," I mumbled and began to close my eyes; "36 left," I whispered as I asked God to please help me open my locker; "10 right," I intoned. *Click!* I had opened

my lock for the first time!

My friend appeared around the corner to help me and was surprised to see me dressed. "How did you ...?"

"I said a little prayer."

To this day (and I am now a senior in high school), I cannot open my locker without prayer. Believe me, I've tried. Sometimes I feel like Gideon and the fleece: "Okay, God, I'm not going to ask for Your help now." (Locker doesn't open.) "All right, now can You please help me open it?" *Click!*

It's a great witnessing tool (or a good way to get the cute guy next to me to say hi). I think God keeps me in check this way—it's as though He's saying, "Christel, come to Me—even for the small things." Christ is our Savior, and He invites us by His love and sacrifice on the cross to find comfort and hope in all things. May the Lord help you to go to Him for the small things too.

Prayer: Dear heavenly Father, thank You for the assurance that I can always come to You in prayer. It is so good to know that I can go to You for everything, no matter how small or how much I think I can do it without You. Please help me to remember to come to You in every time of trouble. In Jesus' holy name. Amen.

Knowing God Is Always with You

Steven T. Lessner

Read: Psalm 16:8

It had been an absolutely horrible day for Scott. It all started when a blurry vision of his mother appeared above his face at 6:15 A.M. As his eyes opened from a peaceful slumber, his mother's irate face pressed down toward his with the lovely greeting, "You overslept! Get up. Now!" Looking at the clock, the reality of the situation dawned on Scott, and he hurriedly threw back the covers and stumbled out of bed.

Scott made it to school just before the late bell. He hadn't had a chance to brush his unruly hair, and his friends and homeroom teacher stared strangely at him when he entered the classroom. Scott told himself that things could only get better. Unfortunately, they didn't.

During first period—algebra, a class he was having trouble with—Scott got back a test for which he had studied extremely hard. Scott sat silently while the tests were handed out, hoping he had at least gotten a C. The ugly red F stared up at him from the paper, as if taunting him.

At his locker, looking in his mirror and trying to fix his hair, Scott heard his girlfriend's voice.

Sighing with relief that he could have a talk with her, Scott turned to speak to her. The sight that met his eyes caused his mouth to drop open and his eyes to bulge. His girlfriend, Sarah, was kissing some guy from his science class! Overcome with emotion, Scott slammed his locker shut and ran all the way to his next class.

Every teen has a day like Scott's. It seems as though nothing turns out right and everyone is against us. During one of these frustrating days, have you asked God for help or thought about opening the Bible? Do you wonder if God is with you through these times or if He cares what happens to you? The answer lies in Psalm 16:8. Saying this verse to yourself in times of turmoil can give you peace in the midst of a troubled day.

God sent His Son, Jesus Christ, to walk the way with us, especially in the middle of a terrible day. Christ knows what we face because He faced it too. He brings us hope and strength when we need it most. Knowing that God is always with you is something that can get you through anything.

Prayer: Heavenly Father, let me always remember that when I have a problem, You are always with me. No problem is too great for me to face and conquer because You are by my side. Through Jesus Christ, my Savior. Amen.

A Beautiful Picture of Death

Steven T. Lessner

Read: Psalm 23

The phone call came late one evening. I heard my father's voice say the usual greeting upon picking up the phone. Suddenly, the cheerfulness in his voice vanished. He grew melancholy as he asked the questions: "When?" and "How old was she?" My mind began to race over the list of close relatives. After hanging up the phone, my father sadly told me that my aunt had passed away.

After the initial shock had worn off, I began to think about my aunt. An extremely caring person, she had been a constant blessing to our family. Helping family members in times of trouble or illness, she was like an angel in disguise. She had been sick for a long time with a blood problem. During her illness, she had maintained a positive attitude and drew on her steadfast faith in the Lord to help her through this difficult time. Calling and visiting her, I found her to be a wonderful friend who always listened and gave a warm hug.

Looking down at her peaceful and familiar face at the funeral, I realized that this would be the last time I would see her for a long time. Saying good-bye to a friend as dear as this was not easy. I

would miss her laugh, her smile, and her words of encouragement.

Losing a close relative or friend is especially trying for us teenagers because we have a limited experience with death. Do you ever think about how friends or family members felt when they died or what they are doing in paradise? Psalm 23 paints a beautiful picture of death and lets us know that our beloved friends and family members who die in faith experience the complete peace of God as they enter the gates of heaven. I found solace in knowing that Jesus had taken my aunt's hand and led her into heaven where pain and sorrow could never touch her again.

It was as though God gave me this psalm when I needed it most. It was printed on the back of my aunt's memorial card. Christ has won the victory over sin and death for us. We have eternal life with Jesus.

Prayer: Lord, please help me remember that my loved ones are with You in paradise where pain and sorrow will never touch them again. Amen.

In loving memory of Angela V. Rice

Love and Courage

Read: 1 Corinthians 16:13–14

The big school Christmas Dance was coming up, and everyone was going to have a date—except me. While everyone else would be dancing in the gym with their boyfriends and girlfriends, I was going to be watching them have a great time and hating myself for coming.

It wasn't that I couldn't ask someone to the dance; it's that I was too scared to ask anyone. I really wanted to ask a certain girl, but I couldn't seem to gather the courage to invite her. Every day in English, I wanted to turn around and ask Stephanie if she'd go to the dance with me, but when I tried to ask her, I got panicky that she'd say no. Why couldn't I do this?

I know God is there for the big things, but does He care about this particular situation in my life? I asked God to help me gain the strength and courage to confront my fears and ask Stephanie, but I still couldn't do it. Why wasn't God helping me?

I learned that God was helping me, just not in the way I expected. While I was walking to my locker to get something, Stephanie was at her locker. Instead of me asking her out, Stephanie asked me to

the dance! At first I couldn't believe my ears, then I realized God was right there with me with my little situation.

I had so much fun with Stephanie at the dance. It was simply wonderful! Thank You, God, for helping me gain the courage, though not in the way I expected. Even in a simple situation like mine, I saw God work wonderfully and perfectly. He knows our every need, whether great or small.

Have you encountered a moment when you couldn't seem to overcome one of life's many obstacles? God always works in your best interest, though maybe not when or how you expected.

Prayer: Lord, I get scared at times when I'm trying to overcome a difficulty in my life. I need You to strengthen me and give me the courage to defeat this obstacle. Only with Your help, Jesus, can I conquer these barriers and continue to live in Your love. Amen.

Stress

Read: 1 Kings 19:4-8

We work, we strain, and we sweat every day to achieve our many goals. These little battles take a toll on us physically, mentally, and spiritually. Stress is evident in everyone's life. We all deal with it. Whether we stress over our finals or peer pressure, stress is no fun.

In 1 Kings 19:4-8, Elijah deals with stress and the pain of doing God's work. Working for God was no easy job. The pay wasn't too good, friends were hard to come by, and there was the fear of others wanting you dead. Elijah was fed up, tired of work, and stressed out because he feared for his life. Elijah wished he were dead. Out in the desert, he fell asleep. Suddenly, Elijah was awakened by an angel, who gave him bread and water. Elijah ate and was full, then he went back to sleep. The angel returned and gave Elijah more bread and water. Once again he ate and was full. Elijah walked for 40 days in the desert on those two meals. God sustained Elijah as he relied on Him.

Isn't it amazing how God gives us everything we need? In His love, He sent His only Son to offer forgiveness and hope to all who believe. Christ

Terry Lucas

became sin for us and was the sacrifice for our sin. When we get stressed, we can trust and rely on God's power to get us through anything.

As you face stress in your life, reflect on these questions

- What stresses in your life can be avoided or prevented by planning ahead and praying?
- Have you ever felt so stressed that you have wished, like Elijah, that you were dead?
- Who can you talk to about stress and pressures in your life?

Prayer: Dear Lord, I realize that I need Your help daily in my life. I cannot make it through an hour without You. Lord, be present in my life and feed me on Your spiritual bread of life. Amen.

Sin

Read: Romans 6:20-23

Sin. Everyone does it, right? I do it, you do it, and your friends do it. No big deal, right? Well, that's what the world teaches us, but God teaches us differently through His Word, the Bible. The Bible teaches that the wages of sin is death (Romans 6:23). In fact, sin is the *exact* reason Jesus Christ, our redeemer, our ruler, our *God*, stepped off His throne and came to this earth. He was humiliated, persecuted, beaten, spit upon, betrayed by a kiss from one of His friends, and murdered! Our awesome God went through things that I can't even imagine or comprehend so you and I could live with Him eternally! WOW!

God gives us the gift of grace to live with Him in an everlasting paradise where "He will wipe every tear from [our] eyes. There will be no more death or mourning or crying or pain" (Revelation 21:4). Just imagine! We will be perfect, and everything will be perfect! God even has prepared a perfect place for us! AWESOME!

We have a faithful God who promises that we will not be tempted beyond what we are able to endure (1 Corinthians 10:13). In addition, God has

given us the gift of prayer so we can ask Him to develop in us a stronger and deeper faith in Him. We also can ask God in prayer to send His Holy Spirit to help us fight sin.

Revelation 20:10 tells us what will happen to Satan because he has deceived God's people.

> And the devil, who deceived them, was thrown into the lake of burning sulfur, where the beast and the false prophet had been thrown. They will be tormented day and night for ever and ever.

I think everlasting life in heaven sounds quite a bit better than spending eternity being tormented day and night in hell. Of course, we will sin, but God freely offers His forgiveness and salvation for Christ's sake.

Prayer: Father, thanks so much for sending Your one and only Son to this earth to be crucified so my sins may be forgiven and I can spend an awesome eternal life with You in paradise. Thank You so much for Your amazing love. Please be with me, guide me, and give me strength so I will not give in when temptation comes knocking on my door. Thank You in Jesus' name. Amen.

Judging Others

Read: James 3:13 – 18

Finally! Camp is here, and I'm totally pumped for this upcoming week. I look around and see nothing but familiar faces. Then, I see her. With her blonde hair, perfect body, and nice clothes, I can't help but envy her. We weren't really enemies or friends last year (or so I thought), but I had been sure that she was truly a snob. She had been in my cabin last year, but I hadn't really gotten to know her.

At dinner, I found out that she was in our group to go rock climbing and rappelling. I didn't know it at the time, but God had a wonderful plan in store that involved both of us. When we went rock climbing and rappelling, we discovered that we had a friend in common, and we hung out. At first I was uncomfortable because I didn't know whether she was judging me, but I figured, *I'm at camp, and I should just be myself.* So I was.

Later that night, she sat with me and some other friends for dinner. It was awesome to see God at work! Within the few hours that we had spent together, a friendship had formed. As the week went on, we got to know each other better, and I let go of

the envy and jealousy that had made me perceive her as an enemy. Instead, I had gained a friend.

As I look back on that week, I realize Christ gives us the power to go beyond our sin and seek forgiveness and reconciliation. My envy and sinful pride almost destroyed the opportunity of friendship.

God's Word reminds us that envy is a sin. It separates us from God. However, we can ask forgiveness for the times we envy others and trust that because of Christ's death God does forgive us. And He will help us to see the good in others and become peacemakers. God will work in all things for our good—including showing us friends where we thought we had enemies.

Prayer: Heavenly Father, I'm sorry for the times I envy others. Thank You that through Jesus' death, all my sins are forgiven. Help me not to pre-judge, but instead to look at the unique gifts You have to given to those around me. Thank You for the unexpected ways You bring friends into my life. In Jesus' name. Amen.

The Rescuers

Read: Proverbs 24:11–12

Abortion has become a remedy for ignorance and irresponsibility. For many people, abortion has become a way to preserve the economic, emotional, and social integrity of all parties involved. They feel that a "quiet" abortion is a better alternative than bringing a child into the world. They are blinded by their own selfishness so they cannot see that their relief is pain for the child they are killing. As a result of these selfish acts of irresponsibility, millions of children will be killed.

We scorn cultures where barbaric acts of genocide are being carried out. We fight to save those dying of hunger and AIDS in Africa, and we send troops to Bosnia and Kosovo to save the innocent people who are victims of social injustice. We speak out against concentration camps and gas chambers, yet we allow millions of American children to be savagely slaughtered. Accountability and responsibility should never be overshadowed by trends or pop culture. When we allow ourselves to succumb to those ideas, our integrity no longer has any validity.

As Christians, we have been given new lives in Christ, and we can strive to protect those on the

verge of becoming victims of abortion. We can approach this tender issue with hearts full of the compassion and forgiveness Christ has demonstrated toward us. And we can educate those "staggering toward slaughter" about how precious the gift of life really is. In Deuteronomy 30:19–20, God reminds us about the importance He places on life: "Now choose life, so that you and your children may live and that you may love the LORD your God, listen to His voice, and hold fast to Him. For the LORD is your life."

Just as the Spirit of God pleads on our behalf, we have a responsibility to "speak up" for the helpless. From newborn cries to tottering first steps, we can celebrate that life truly is precious in God's eyes. With the light of Christ illuminating our lives, let us witness with courage and conviction about the gift of life.

Consider these questions about the sanctity of life:

- What measures can we take to encourage those considering abortion to seek a different solution?
- How can we be witnesses to others about the sanctity of life?

Prayer: Dear God, illuminate my heart with the light of Your love as I witness to others about the gift of life. Thank You for sending Your Son to rescue and save all the children of the world. In Your Son's name. Amen.

Off the Beaten Path

Read: Mathew 7:13-14

There are times in life when people are confronted with difficult choices. These choices require setting off on paths that lead in different directions and that end with contrasting goals. Sometimes these goals are not easily recognized. Many times the most fruitful rewards are hidden beneath the snares and pitfalls of everyday life. Likewise, many destructive endings are camouflaged beneath the glitter and shine of fame and popularity. It is easy to choose a path with no visible pitfalls at the beginning, but that first step could be toward drug and alcohol abuse, sexual immorality, or any other questionable display of character. It is much easier to accept a worldly position because that position brings acceptance.

It is more difficult, however, to accept positions of moral integrity and honesty. Few people are likely to jump on your bandwagon to promote your positions in life. As Christians, we have been given the eyes to see these errors and sinful behaviors. God's promises propel us beyond the jungle of human desires and into the security of His kingdom.

The words of American poet Robert Frost accu-

Katie Maske

rately describe this inner struggle when dealing with choices and considering the ultimate reward for blazing a new trail. Taking the path less traveled in terms of our spirituality is eternal life in heaven with Jesus. We realize that our faith in Christ while on this seemingly treacherous trail makes the difference. Jesus walked the same path. His path brought Him to a wooden cross on a hillside where He was crucified for us. Christ has taken the journey for us. Because of Christ's steadfastness on His journey to Calvary, we are assured an unbelievable reward. Heaven is ours!

Prayer: Dear God, thank You for Your wonderful promises that reassure me every day of the goal awaiting me at the end of my path. Help me to encourage others on their journey of faith. In Your Son's name. Amen.

One Wardrobe, Many Hats

Read: 1 Corinthians 12:4-6

There is a lady in my congregation who has a hat for every occasion. She wears a red, white, and blue hat to celebrate Independence Day while sprigs of flowers adorn her Easter hat. No matter the day, whether it is a celebratory day or an ordinary one, she always has a hat to signify its importance. In doing this, she shows her enthusiasm for living.

In the life of a Christian, we are called to "wear" a variety of hats. This could be wearing a hat of compassion when consoling someone who has lost a loved one. It could be wearing the hat of forgiveness when showing others the forgiveness we, as redeemed Christians, have received from Christ's death on the cross. It could be wearing the hats of optimism and enthusiasm when sharing the Gospel with someone for the first time.

We have an important responsibility as Christ's ambassadors on earth: to exemplify His love in all areas of our lives. At times it may seem difficult, but Christ has assured us that we are not alone in our pursuits. He is there to guide our every action and encourage us with His promises. He gives us the strength to take a new "hat" off the rack

each day as a witness to others. It does not have to be a festival day to witness to others. Our promised eternal life in heaven is reason enough.

So take your hat off of the rack. For some, it may be a bit dusty, and still others may find their hat quite used. Whatever its condition, wear it with pride and conviction for Christ.

Prayer: Dear Lord, grant me the strength and courage daily to wear my hat for You. May my witness always be a reflection of Your love and forgiveness. Amen.

Putting It Off

Read: 1 Kings 1:11-27

Ever heard the cliché: "Why do today what you can put off until tomorrow?" I received a letter inviting me to participate in this devotional project a few months back. I had grand ideas of what I would write. Then, life got a little hectic, and here it is, a day before the deadline and I'm just starting. Sound like you?

Procrastination is a pretty easy trap to fall into. It can be difficult to stop the cycle. So what does the Bible say about it? In today's Bible reading, King David put off announcing his successor, and look what happened. Another son tried to steal the throne. Not good, considering all the things that we know God had planned for Solomon. Eventually, Solomon would be revered as the wisest king ever, simply because he asked the Lord for wisdom to rule. He even built a beautiful temple to the Lord. That's pretty important stuff!

So how does that story affect us in the 21st century? If it's in the Bible, God put it there and it is important. This story may be God's way of alerting us to the danger of procrastination. Why should we do everything in a timely manner? Consider what

happens when you procrastinate. Do you do your best work? Or could you have done better if you had spent more time on the project? Do you feel like you are cheating yourself and God out of a chance to show what His creation can do? How might this affect the plans God has for you? How can you stop putting things off?

Even when we sin, God calls us by the Holy Spirit to seek His forgiveness in Christ. We may "put off" getting things done, but God didn't "put off" giving us His Son for life.

Prayer: Father God, I know that You have made my body and mind in Your image. I ask You to help me use them to the best of my abilities so I might praise You through my actions. Guide me to make wise decisions in my life that follow Your plan. In Jesus' name. Amen.

Jealousy

Read: Romans 13:11–14

Alexandra's always getting new clothes, why can't you buy more? Brian excels in sports while you warm the bench. Jason gets better grades than you, no matter how hard you study. Instead of being happy for them and trying harder, you're jealous of their success.

Sound familiar? Envy is a feeling with which we all struggle. I remember when I invited Katie, a friend of mine, to youth group. My friends in the group quickly accepted Katie, which made me happy. But soon, Katie became *good* friends with my friends in the group and the guy I liked started liking her! I became jealous and didn't want her at youth group anymore.

My jealousy got in God's way. I could have been happy that my friends liked Katie so much. Just because they liked her didn't mean I was less of a friend to them. All my sin did was drive Katie and me apart. I apologized to her, and we've resumed our friendship. I needed Christ's forgiveness and His help to fight this jealousy.

Jealousy is a horrible thing. It can tear a whole community apart if you let it. In Proverbs 14:30, God says: "A heart at peace gives life to the body,

but envy rots the bones." Jealousy not only hurts others, it hurts you as well. God asks us to give up our jealous feelings with His help. The next time you feel the jealous green-eyed monster creeping in, pray for the strength to resist it that only God can give. Pray also for the person of whom you are feeling jealous. It's hard to be jealous of someone for whom you're praying. Thank God that He sent His Son to cover the sins of the whole world, especially those that trouble us. Trust that God will bless you and keep you.

Prayer: Heavenly Father, help me to be happy when You bless others! Give me a heart that is at peace. Help me to overcome any feelings of envy toward others by the power of Your Spirit. In Jesus' name. Amen.

Gossip

Read: Proverbs 26:20–23

Psst! Did you hear about Todd and Sheila?!?

How many times have you been in that situation? Whether you are giving out the latest tidbit of news or receiving news, you're gossiping. Sometimes it's a harmless secret about a surprise birthday party, but most times, gossip hurts someone. Sometimes the story may be true, sometimes not. But few people stop and ask, "Is this true? Would it hurt someone?" Reputations and friendships can be ruined by spreading stories.

There is a parable that illustrates what I'm trying to say. A man had sinned against his pastor by spreading a story about him that wasn't true. He came to the pastor to beg his forgiveness. The pastor said, "All right, I will forgive you, but first I'd like you to do something. I'd like you to take a pillow filled with feathers and climb way up to the top of the church steeple. Rip open the pillow, and let the feathers fly to the ground."

The man was confused, but he fulfilled the pastor's request. He came back after completing the deed and said, "I've done what you asked. Will you now forgive me for spreading that lie about you?"

The pastor said, "Certainly. But one more request. Gather up all the feathers that you just let go."

This parable illustrates for us the fact that once our words are out, we never can erase their impact. Gossip is sin, and it can hurt. It breaks God's commandments and destroys relationships. We find forgiveness for the sin of gossip and all our sins in the cross of Jesus. He died to win forgiveness for us. He gives us strength to resist temptations, including the temptation to gossip.

If you have been the object of some form of gossip, seek God's strength in Jesus to be restored. If you have a problem with gossip, you can go to the cross for forgiveness and ask God to help you change this behavior.

Next time a person approaches you with the latest gossip, don't believe everything you hear! And be careful not to add to the harm by spreading it.

Prayer: Heavenly Father, help me not to gossip about others. Let me look for the good in people and build them up instead of tearing them down. Help me set a good example for others. I ask this in Jesus' name. Amen.

Sheep Thrills

Read: Psalm 100

This spring I got to chase sheep. I was at a country graduation party that was nearing its end when I spotted two adorable sheep grazing in the pasture. I suddenly got an overwhelming urge to catch one of them. I am a "city" kid, but I figured my chances were as good as anyone else's, so I gave it a go.

I climbed over the two fences and sauntered toward my two unsuspecting victims. As I neared them, the ground started to rumble. I turned and saw the remaining 25 sheep stampeding straight at me. The farmer thought he'd have a little fun with me. He had chased the sheep out of their shelter toward me. I've never been so scared in my life.

As soon as the sheep saw me, though, they headed in a different direction and the chase began. I pride myself on being an okay runner, but no matter how hard I tried, I couldn't catch a single one. They kept bolting every time I came hear.

The farm family was having a ball watching me. They started chanting, "Baa! Ram! Ewe!" And the farmer's wife yelled, "Go, Babe!" I wouldn't give in though. I had to get one. Little did I know how

Kristina Neumann

stupid sheep are. The sheep couldn't understand that I wasn't going to hurt them. Finally, I gave up.

That night, I started thinking. Jesus called us His sheep. Psalm 100:3 says that we are "the sheep of His pasture." After reading that, I thought, *Are people really as stupid as sheep?* Then I realized that we are. We murder, destroy, and—well, the list goes on and on. Yet, Jesus still loves His sheep.

I then was hit by a moment of clarity. Jesus, the Good Shepherd, loves us, and He died for us in our deserved place. He paid the price on the cross so the stupid, ignorant sheep could live. Isaiah 53:6 says, "We all, like sheep, have gone astray, each of us has turned to his own way, and the LORD has laid on Him the iniquity of us all." This means that Jesus took our sin on Himself and died to give us life! We can run, bolt, or hide, but He's never, ever going to give up on us. He did it for the sheep.

The next time you think about sheep, consider these questions:
- How did the Good Shepherd come and find you?
- What assurance do you have with Jesus?

Prayer: Dear Lord, thank You for not giving up, even when I am stubborn. You are always there for me, to forgive, to comfort, or just to listen. Please forgive me and keep me safe and secure. Thank You for making me Your lamb. Amen.

For I Am Convinced

Read: Romans 8:38–39

Kim Niehaus

It all happened on April 3. I was sprawled out on the living room floor, watching a movie with my parents. It was my little brother's 13th birthday. He was busy entertaining his birthday guests. Dad had come home early to see Ryan before his guests came. Usually, Dad worked late in the shop with Grandpa, so it was highly unusual for him to be home.

After we were well into the movie, the phone rang. Dad grumbled as he reached for the cordless phone on the floor. Then, his expression changed to one I had never seen before.

"Dad? What happened? Where are you?" As he spoke, my father started to sob and scream, "Get my shoes! I have to go! HURRY!"

I ran as fast as I could to the back door and fumbled through the shoes until my hands ran across his. Mom and I kept asking what had happened as we helped him. All he could say was, "It's Dad. Keith found him. I have to go *now*!"

My mom wouldn't let him go alone. They immediately left, and I sat at the top of the stairs, dumbfounded. Later that evening, my brother, his

friends, and I waited at my cousin's house for my folks to return from the hospital.

My mom and our vicar walked through the door at about 11 P.M. She sobbed, "Kim, he's gone."

I froze in terror and screamed, "What are you talking about?!? I saw him yesterday!" Tears ran down my mother's face. My legs turned to jelly, and I collapsed in my mother's arms.

The inevitable face of death was looking me straight in the eyes. The night before the funeral, my grandpa's pastor brought us together for prayer. It was then that I was reminded about grandpa's faith in Jesus and started to feel calm. In Jesus I found a peace despite the death of my grandpa. Jesus rose again from the tomb so all who believe in Him would be with Him forever!

This shocking experience became a celebration of life—the life that is only found through Christ Jesus. God has prepared a special place for us in heaven. I can be sure that grandpa is in good hands.

Prayer: Dear heavenly Father, I thank and praise You for Your amazing love! Thank You so much for conquering death and giving me the gift of everlasting life. Help me to turn to You in the best and worst of times. In Jesus' name I pray. Amen.

Let's Live It

Read: 1 Timothy 4:12

My friend, Chris, had smashed his finger in the door. He decided to see a doctor. So I jumped at the chance to take him to the emergency room.

As we waited, Chris struck up a conversation with the teenage guy sitting next to him. I decided to find a restroom. When I came back, I asked Chris about the guys situation.

"He's here for his girlfriend," Chris replied.

Chris finally was called to see the doctor. As I waited for him, my thoughts kept drifting back to the guy.

So I walked over and sat down next to him. "May I ask what your name is?" I said.

He looked at me with a tear-stained face. "Caleb. It's Caleb," he replied.

"Hi, Caleb, my name is Kim. Why are you here?"

"I'm here for my girlfriend. She swallowed a bunch of pills," he said and stared straight at the floor. I paused, not exactly sure what to say.

"Can I pray for her?" I asked.

"Go ahead," Caleb replied.

As I finished praying, Caleb joined in with an

amazing prayer of his own.

The nurse soon came to take Caleb to see Deborah. "I'll be praying for you, Caleb," I said as he got up to leave.

"Thank you so much," he said as he left.

Shortly after Caleb had left, Chris came around the corner. He seemed upset. "Let's go," he said.

"We just made a wasted trip. The doctor said that there is nothing he can do for my finger. It's perfectly fine."

"But, Chris, this trip wasn't a waste," I answered. I told him about Caleb.

As we talked on the way home, we realized that we were in that emergency room for a purpose that day.

God calls us to go and make disciples. We don't have to be afraid of what to say because we will be given the right words to say at the proper time. Christ assures us of power through the Holy Spirit to be His witnesses. There are opportunities all around that God gives us to share our faith with others and to proclaim the Good News of Jesus.

Prayer: Heavenly Father, thank You so much for providing for all of my needs. I pray that You would strengthen me and give me the right words to say when I am witnessing. Use me to show others Your love. Thank You for being such an awesome God! In Jesus' name. Amen.

Has God Forsaken You?

Read: Deuteronomy 4:31; 31:6

Not long ago, my Aunt Ola was diagnosed with a type of cancer called lymphoma. She had received chemotherapy and radiation treatments. Ever since she was diagnosed, Ola has thought that the Lord was punishing her. She thought that the Lord had forsaken her. My mom and I started going through the Bible, looking up verses to help her see the faithfulness of God. We shared some powerful words of God, words of comfort and promise, hope and strength in Christ. Eventually, my mom and I saw a change in Aunt Ola, and we encouraged her to continue to see the promises of God in Jesus and His love for her.

Moses wrote in Deuteronomy that God would never forsake us or leave us. In John 14:16, Jesus promised the presence of the Holy Spirit in our lives to carry us through all circumstances. The Bible is a book filled with promises for life. It's a book of comfort and hope. I saw a wonderful change in Ola's life through God's Word. I know His Word will give you hope and power as well.

Prayer: Dear heavenly Father, keep me in Your arms and be with me through everything going on in my life. Protect me and keep me close to You so when I face trials, You will be the one on whom I call. In Jesus' name. Amen.

Friendship

Read: Ecclesiastes 4:9–10

Friends always have been a big part of my life. There are rough times with my friendships that have made me more aware of what a true friend is.

When I was in second grade, I attended a local private school. At this school I was a "nerd," and no one really liked me. At the time I had only two friends (or so I thought). After leaving this school in sixth grade, one of my "friends" told me that it was my fault that she didn't fit in and it was better for her in school without me. Needless to say, she was not really my friend. The other "friend" I never saw again. I thought these two people were my best friends at the time.

In seventh grade, I went to school where I had gone to church all my life. That year there was another new girl in my class, and she and I immediately "clicked." Like my previous "friends," she put on a mask for me. She would go out on the weekends. She started meeting people off the Internet for dates and became sexually active. She left the school, and I never saw her again.

In eighth grade, I began to realize the right and wrong people to choose as friends. My friends from

eighth grade are still my friends today.

Through all the trials with friends, I have learned that friends come and go, but there is only one friend you can trust—my best friend, Jesus Christ. I know Jesus is my friend because He loves me, forgives me, and comforts me. He helps me to strengthen my relationships with friends through my relationship with Him. God gives us earthly friends to help us along the way. I encourage you to be the best earthly friend that you can be, encourage people in their faith, and help them in their walk with Jesus.

Prayer: Dear gracious Father, I ask You to be with me and my friends. Help us to build healthy relationships in Your name. Jesus, help us to know that You are the ultimate friend. Help me to grow in faith by the power of Your Spirit. Amen.

Trust Me

Read: Proverbs 3:5-6

Many things happen in this world that do not seem to make sense, and we often find ourselves asking God why. Why does it seem that just as you start to put the final piece in place, the puzzle falls apart and the pieces scatter everywhere?

I recently watched my puzzle break into a thousand bits and take my heart with it. Charlie and I always had been a couple. He was not only my boyfriend, he was my friend. We had spent every moment we could together. Everything about him seemed right, but with just six little words my clear-cut picture of life was thrown out of whack! "I want to see other people." I would hear those words play in my head over and over again, making me feel worthless and confused. Why? I just did not understand.

I tried to preoccupy myself with other things, hoping to keep my mind off of Charlie. I put much effort into making new friends and hanging out with my best friend. I also spent my time talking to God and asking Him for strength. My mom has a very strong faith, and she reminded me to talk to God in prayer, claiming it would help when I was down.

Eventually, I started to understand why it all happened. God drew me closer to Him and to my family. It made me aware of the separation between my best friend and myself, and it helped save our friendship. I learned so much about relationships that I can apply to the future. I would never change what happened because I definitely gained more than I lost.

I know sometimes it's very hard to see the reasons behind the pain and suffering we endure, but God has a plan for us. We can trust God to know what's best. We can trust that He has something better in store for us.

Prayer: Dear heavenly Father, Your plan is greater than anything I can comprehend. Consequently, at times it is hard for me to understand why things happen the way they do. Remind me that after every low there is a better time to come. Take my hand and guide me, God, and when I can walk no more, carry me in Your loving arms. In Jesus' name. Amen.

A Flood of Sin

Read: Psalm 119:105–112

One day as I left for school, it was a wonderful sunny morning outside, but not for long. The sky darkened, the sun hid in the overwhelming clouds, and it began to rain. It started raining and didn't stop for days. (This would be the start of the worst flooding in Missouri history.) Later in the week, the creeks and rivers around our house began to break over their banks. It continued to rain. We were actually sandbagging around the doors and windows to keep water from coming into the homes.

After an especially bad rain, I noticed that the sewers in the street were filling and overflowing into neighbors' yards and driveways. As I came into my house, my heart sank. We had been working so hard on the outside that we hadn't noticed that the house was filled with water. It smelled horrible. The sewer had backed up. Our basement had almost two feet of sewer water in it—gross!

After about five hours of moving everything, trying to salvage all the items that had not been touched, the rain stopped. As the water receded, we found stains, dirt, and muck everywhere. Many valuable things had to be thrown out because of the

contaminated water and the odor. The whole family was upset.

What an example of what sin does to our lives and our families. This was a real-life illustration for me about the contamination of sin. But sin comes into every home and touches every family. It reaches into everyone's life. Sin consumes everything vulnerable.

It wasn't until clean water power-flushed out the contaminated sewer that we could start rebuilding our basement. God can clean up the sin in our lives. The Holy Spirit works through the "power-cleaning" of our Baptism. By God's Word and sacraments, we are made new.

Ask God to open your eyes and heart to the needs of those He has placed in your life. As you see those needs, pray for an opportunity to present the life-changing words and work of Jesus Christ. Only He can meet your deepest needs, clean you "to the foundation," and bring refreshing forgiveness. Even in a flood of sin, He brings us to higher ground!

Prayer: Dear heavenly Father, forgive my sin and wash me clean in the love of Your Son, Jesus. Open my eyes and heart to Your mercy and Your saving grace every day. Let me share Your power with others so we may be closer to You. Through Christ my Lord. Amen.

A Second Chance

Read: Matthew 18:21-22

You start school with a clean slate. Everything is going well for you for the first half of the year. Your test scores are rather magnificent. Your daily work is fantastic. You get that date to homecoming, and it all seems great.

But as the second half of the year comes, things start going wrong. Your quarter test scores begin edging down by nearly 25 percent. Your daily work grades are dropping. Your former girlfriend and her friends won't talk to you. You get your report card and nearly die. You get an F in English, and your parents ground you indefinitely. It seems all those opportunities, all those good intentions, and all those good times are gone.

Will you get a second chance? Feeling hopeless?

Isn't it amazing how hopelessness makes rescue seem all that more miraculous? When we're at our most vulnerable point—certain that we'll never get a second chance—it is that much more of a comfort when rescue finally comes. Is anyone ever more hopeless than those people without that second chance from God in Jesus?

God is on your side! He will give you another chance 100 percent of the time. If everything in the world goes wrong, if you get in major trouble, God will give you a second chance.

No one else but God could help us. God loves us, and He cares for us. He sent His Son, Jesus Christ, to die on the cross so our sins could be forgiven and we could be born again to a second chance at eternity. How does God give you a second chance in daily life? Think of someone with whom you can share a second chance.

Prayer: Dear heavenly Father, thanks for giving me a second chance every day. Help me to depend on Your love and mercy in everything that I do. I know You want me to share the love of Your Son, Jesus, with those around me—give me the strength to be Your second-chance witness. In Jesus' name. Amen.

Change/Changeless

Read: James 1:16–18

Alissa Smelser

I was thinking the other day about how much life changes. When I was 2 years old, my parents had my brother. After being the only child, I became the big sister. I continued to grow and went to preschool and to elementary school. Each year, I changed to meet the new situation.

My life really changed when my dad got a job in North Dakota, and I had to leave my friends. As I was adjusting to this change, my mom had my little sister. Besides these changes in my life, I've seen changes in my friends' lives too. A close friend had a major change in her life when her father died unexpectedly.

Over the years, my choice in friends has changed. I have changed in what I like, in what I don't like, and in what I want to do in my life. In high school, changes come a lot faster and are more drastic, including getting my driver's license, having my first real boyfriend, and having a lot more freedom. Some changes are brought about by my sin, and in the end, they only hurt me.

Amid all these changes, I feel comfort knowing that Jesus' love for me will never change. From the

time that I was changed in Baptism to the time I die, I can be assured that God will love me forever. Christ continually washes me clean of all the sins that change my life. I can have peace in knowing that God is always with me when it's time to make a big decision that will change my life. I know that Jesus will guide me through the changes and will be the same loving and forgiving Savior today and forever.

Prayer: Dear Jesus, thank You for dying on the cross for my sins. Thank You also for always being there for me through all the changes in my life. Amen.

Doves and Pigeons

Read: Genesis 8:6–11

Michelle Lynn Sperberg

104

I am 14 years old and recently was diagnosed with osteosarcoma, which is a type of bone cancer. During my stay at the hospital, my mother and I prayed for strength to help me make it through the rough times with chemotherapy and the surgeries that followed.

One day a pigeon flew outside my window and sat as pretty as ever with the bright sun shining down on him. At first we didn't think too much of this bird, but then we noticed that he would leave and return again each morning and each night to sit by my window.

As time went by, my chemotherapy was getting a little easier to handle. My mother and I continued to pray together. The pigeon became a symbol of God's peace in my life. In a way, this pigeon reminded me of the dove Noah sent out from the ark. Noah's dove left the ark to find land and returned again to its temporary home. Noah's dove lifted his spirits when it returned with the olive branch. The daily visits from the pigeon reminded me of God's care for Noah and helped keep my spirits high.

God's Son left the comfort of His heavenly home to stand by my side. Jesus became the sacrifice by which my sins are forgiven. In Christ's resurrection, I have the hope of heaven. I found strength to endure through the love of Jesus. I have had major surgery to remove the cancerous tumor. With God's help, I will walk again one day. Through the promises in His Word, God keeps me growing stronger with each passing day.

Prayer: Dear God, thank You for the strength and wisdom You have shown to me in a time of need. Help me to trust in You so I may leave all worries with You. Please keep me in Your loving arms today, tomorrow, and always. In Christ Jesus I pray. Amen.

Waiting for Dating

Read: 2 Corinthians 12:9

Do you ever feel like you are missing something by not being in a serious relationship with a member of the opposite sex? I do sometimes. I read romantic fiction, which used to influence what I thought about relationships. I was 16 years old, had never been kissed, and had never been in a "real" relationship. I was jealous of people that were in those relationships.

I used to think it was my fault. I felt I wasn't pretty enough, skinny enough, or my personality wasn't what guys wanted. I couldn't measure up to the "ideal." But I knew above everything else that I didn't want to be ashamed of my faith.

But I have changed my perspective on dating and relationships. If a certain guy that I like doesn't like me, it's his loss, not mine. I'm not going to stress over it. I still look for a guy to talk to and really get to know. But I've learned to appreciate the words *wait, patience,* and *prayer.* I've learned to see these as gifts from God.

Every night when I have my personal prayer time with Christ, I always pray for my future spouse. The song "Someday" by one of my favorite bands,

LaRue, talks about how hard it is to wait for that special person to come along. As it describes the waiting process and the hope that someone special is waiting for me, it reminds me to pray for my future spouse. That song helped me to turn my dating life over to God. It helped me to accept that I would rather have my love life in God's hands, not my own. He knows who's perfect for me, and I can trust the Lord.

Prayer: Dear heavenly Father, help me to accept that You hold every aspect of my life, including my dating life, in Your hands. Help me to pray for and about my future spouse. Please take this burden of stress and worry about dating off of my heart. Thank You for always being there, Father. In Jesus' name I pray. Amen.

Liar, Liar

Annie Tiberg

Read: Revelation 21:7–8

Lying is a common problem. We lie to get out of situations, to help ourselves look better, to make another person look bad, or to help someone. So when is lying right? Never. Lies always will get you in trouble.

I have this problem with lying to make it seem as though I know a lot. I'm not saying that I'm not smart, but I lie to make people like me. That's wrong. One time as I was talking to a couple friends about popular movie stars, I told them I had met the cast of one of my favorite shows. Actually, I was only in the studio audience of a taping while one of the show's stars was being interviewed. One friend then replied, "Well, I have been on the set, and I talked to the cast of *Dr. Quinn.*" I knew she had done it because she has pictures to prove it.

Many people spice up their stories to make others like them, or they want people to think better of them, or they want to feel superior. Any sort of lie, whether it's a plain falsehood or a spruce-up-the-story kind of lie, is still wrong.

After I lie, I feel guilty because I have been untrue and disobeyed God. I hate when I do that,

but we all do it. We are all sinners and need to repent. God gives us His free gift of forgiveness. Christ was sent by God to win forgiveness for our sins and to bring us to life and strength in Him. By the Holy Spirit, we are placed in a wonderful relationship with Him through faith given in Baptism. Through the Holy Spirit, God strengthens us to be like Christ in our actions, thoughts, and words. God calls us to be honest with Him, with ourselves, and with others.

Prayer: Heavenly Father, You know I love You and hate to disobey You. I don't like it when I lie. Please help me to stop deceiving myself, and others around me, with my lies. Forgive me. Help me to do Your will by telling the truth. Thank You for helping me realize my mistakes. Give me the strength to be truthful. In Your Son's name. Amen.

What Do You Want to Be?

Read: Matthew 9:35–38

I'm sure that you've been asked what you want to be when you "grow up." Maybe you already know. Or maybe, like me, you have no idea.

But I don't think you need to be "grown up" to do your work for Jesus. Sometimes I'm afraid and think, "What can I do? I'm only one person!" It's at those discouraging times that I need to remember that Jesus was one person also. Through His life, death, and resurrection, He saved the entire world. Although He was fully God, He was fully human too. What if Jesus had said, "I'm only one person. What can I do?" We can get so easily distracted by other things, but it's important that we remember what God has called us to do—to spread the Good News of Jesus Christ.

Jesus went through towns and villages, teaching in synagogues, preaching, and healing. Matthew 9:36–38 says,

> When He saw the crowds, he had compassion on them, because they were harassed and helpless, like sheep without a shepherd. Then He said to His

disciples, "The harvest is plenty but the workers are few." Ask the Lord of the harvest, therefore, to send out workers into His harvest field.

This past summer, I was, in a way, sent out into the field. I spent a week on a backpacking trip in Upper Michigan. Of the 10 people on the trip, I was the only Christian. As we learned more about one another and grew as a team during our long campfire talks, I tried to be a witness to each of these people. During one talk, one of the counselors asked what inspired us. I told everyone of my faith and how Jesus inspires me. I don't know if I made any impact on any of the people that night, but it definitely helped to strengthen my faith.

We are to be workers in the field. Although we're not "grown up," God provides opportunities for us to serve. As we seek to find ways to serve Him, we can ask ourselves these two questions: How is God calling me to be His servant today? How will Jesus help me to trust Him fully and to offer myself as a witness to people I meet today?

Prayer: Dear Jesus, I pray that You would give me the strength I need to be Your witness. Give me a heart of compassion, and make me willing to serve You. Thank You, Lord, for using me. Amen.

Click "OK"

Read: John 14:1-3

My childhood has been different from most teenagers. You see, I've been through two divorces. I have a biological mom, a mom who's pretty much raised me, and my dad. They've all remarried in the past three years.

Life with six parents gets pretty rough sometimes. I have to battle schoolwork, an ever-changing social life, and I have to try and make good decisions about peer pressure. Trying to do all this and keep all six of my parents happy is a lot to handle; sometimes I get really stressed. Lately, I've also started to wonder why my life has been so different and why God picked me to live this life.

Last November, I went to a youth gathering in Columbus, Ohio. My youth group got there late on Friday night and we'd already missed one of the keynote speakers, so we took a seat on the floor in the back row. The next speaker began to talk about all of life's challenges and how crazy our world can get at times. The speaker started talking about computers. He was rattling off all these technical names and problems that could go wrong with a computer that, obviously, none of us teens understood. He

then said something I'll never forget. He reminded us that when all those crazy messages that we don't understand appear on our computer screens, we usually just click "ok" and trust that everything really is okay with our computer. He said that our relationship with God should be similar to those frequent incidents with our computers. When things go wrong and God gives us a problem we don't understand, we can "click 'ok'" in our prayers and put our full trust in God that everything in our life will turn out according to His plan. We can trust God with all our heart and let Him care for us.

The words of John 14:1 remind me of the youth gathering speaker's message. I am reminded to trust God with all my heart, and I know that God does not want me to worry about why my life has turned out as it has. God has a reason for everything, and I've learned to "click 'ok'" in my life. I am assured that God is taking care of everything.

Prayer: Dear God, thank You for today. Thank You for reassuring me that even though life gets crazy and I might not understand why things happen to me, I can put my trust in You. Thank You for taking away my worry and confusion. In Jesus' holy name I pray. Amen.

I Do

Read: Matthew 7:7-8; 2 Corinthians 6:14

As teenagers, we definitely think about the opposite sex, but how often do we actually think about marriage? Don't assume you are too young to think about marriage. Many married couples met very early in life. My mom used to tell me to think of every boy I date as a future husband. That's when I started to realize that, as a Christian, there are certain qualities essential to a God-pleasing relationship.

Apart from the obvious traits such as honesty, faithfulness, and respect, it is of dire importance that my future mate is a Christian. God should be most important in our lives, and how awful it would be not to share Him with the one we love.

So start looking for these qualities now. The best way to get started is to pray. Our Lord can be pretty creative in His work; you never know what's going to happen. Pray for your future spouse. Ask and it will be given to you. God wants you to be happy and to keep growing in Him. Don't worry; He'll put the right person in your path.

Lisa Widlowski

114

I Do

It may seem like ages before you are wed,
But it comes sooner than what's in your head.
It's scary to think of the vows that you'll share,
To have and to hold, to cherish, love, and care.
God's got a person lined up just for you;
Keep your eyes open in all that you do.
It could be your neighbor, classmate, or friend—
Only God knows your spouse in the end.
Whoever it is, wherever they are,
You can start praying for them, right now!
Hope that they remain pure in the Son,
That their journey in faith has just now begun.
You can do nothing but wait, hope, and pray,
God will show you the one who will stay.
Pray for your soul mate each and every day,
Just to make sure they believe He's the way.
So though right now you don't have a clue,
He'll make you certain before the "I do."

Prayer: Dear Father, please help me to find the one
You chose just for me. Bring me somebody
that I can grow with in Your Word. Please
keep both of us faithful to You. In Jesus'
name. Amen.

He Has Plans for You

Read: Jeremiah 1:5

Once there was a baby abandoned in a faraway country. She was left to die in the town's garbage dump. But while this infant was dying of hunger and rats nibbled on her bare skin, by the grace of God, a nurse happened to walk past. Seeing this poor child so close to death, the nurse brought the baby to the local orphanage.

Meanwhile, in another country, a family was moved by God to adopt a child. They were blessed to receive that abandoned baby—rat bites and all. God had a special place for this child. The family raised the little girl in the church, and she grew in stature and in faith to be an amazing woman of God.

Today, you can find this woman doing missionary work in Guatemala, raising her own family, and spreading God's Word. This wonderful lady is my aunt. When I think about how her life began and where she is now, I can't help but be proud. Being related to such an awesome lady has truly inspired me.

God has a very special place for each one of us. And even though God's call to you may not neces-

sarily be foreign ministry, it doesn't have to be. You can be a witness for Him anywhere you go or in whatever He wants you to do. Whether God wants you to be a Sunday school teacher or a repairperson, there always are opportunities to shine your Gospel light.

I love telling that story about my aunt. It shows that God works miracles in our lives, even when we may see the situation as hopeless. God gave us Jesus, who died on the cross to show the greatest love that ever existed. In Christ we have the gift of forgiveness and eternal life. He gives us faith to be His witness and to proclaim His amazing grace. God sees potential and promise in each one of us. We were created to do His will.

The Lord will fulfill His purpose for me. (Psalm 138:8)

Prayer: Dear heavenly Father, please help me to realize that You have plans for me. Help me to live for You and to touch the lives of others through my words and actions. I want to be Your instrument; use me as You planned. In Jesus' name. Amen.

Friends May Fail

Read: Job 19:19; Hebrews 13:5

"What happened to all my friends?" I often wondered this summer. The group of girls I seemed to have spent the majority of my high school years with had practically vanished. They were all still here, just distanced now. These were the girls I went to every dance with, shared secrets and problems with, and now it was as though we were no more than acquaintances.

We all had graduated in June, with the whole summer ahead of us. Plans of road trips, graduation parties, and college preparations stretched as far as the eye could see. However, only a few weeks into the summer, it was quite clear that none of these friends were going to make an effort to stay in touch. They started to hang out with another group who did not exert a good influence. Before I knew it, my friends were getting drunk and engaging in other dangerous activities almost every single night. They had really changed.

Although I knew what they were doing, I was still hurt at not being invited. I felt betrayed and frustrated. I did, however, find a little hope that maybe they didn't invite me because they knew I'd

say no. Maybe my convictions had rubbed off a little.

This summer helped me figure out who my real friends were. I went on a few church trips, got back in touch with some old friends, and even started a little "support group" with some close friends from church. I also think I've gotten a lot closer to God this summer. He is a friend who will stick closer than a brother. I know my friends are not perfect, and we will all make mistakes. But I know God will be there even if everyone else fails. Through the Holy Spirit, I learned to put my faith in Jesus. Jesus gives us forgiveness for our sin and calls us to live a life guided by God's Word. Even when I—or my friends—wander from His path and make mistakes, His Word calls me back to seek the love and comfort of Jesus Christ.

Prayer: Dear Father, please help me to find the friends who are true. Help me to be a good friend and an example to others. Please bless all my friends and keep them in Your arms. In Jesus' awesome name. Amen.

Voice of God

Read: Proverbs 2:9–15

How often have you prayed and waited for an answer? Many times I pray for days and still never seem to get an answer. I often wonder if I'm just looking too deep into what God is trying to tell me. Sometimes it can be right in front of my eyes, but I spend too much time looking into the details, making it hard to see the actual picture.

One night four years ago I decided to pray for God to lead me in the right direction, help me with school, and help me to focus on important things in life. I said my prayer without expecting an answer. Then I flipped open my Bible and read Proverbs 2:9–15:

> Then you will understand what is right and just and fair—every good path. For wisdom will enter your heart, and knowledge will be pleasant to your soul. Discretion will protect you, and understanding will guard you. Wisdom will save you from the ways of wicked men; from men whose words are perverse, who leave the straight paths to

walk in dark ways, who delight in doing wrong and rejoice in the perverseness of evil, whose paths are crooked and who are devious in their ways.

My mind was blown away. Everything I'd prayed about was summed up in these verses. From that moment on when I pray, I don't pray for quick answers. I know that God has an answer, and in His time, He will make it known to me. Christ is my Good Shepherd and guides me on His path of righteousness.

Is it possible that God will talk with us in such simple situations and that the answers to life's problems are no further than our Bible? Yes! As Romans 12:12 says: "Be joyful in hope, patient in affliction, faithful in prayer."

Prayer: Dear heavenly Father, open my ears, my eyes, and my mind to the words You so clearly send to me through Your written Word. As I lift up my troubles to You in prayer, help me to know that You love me and will protect me. In Jesus' name. Amen.

Kiss the 'Beener

Allison Wilson

Read: 1 Corinthians 10:12-13

Burning sweat, throbbing pain, wet palms, and only one thought going through my mind, "I have to kiss the 'beener!" While rock climbing, there's only one goal in sight—the carabeener at the top.

Our lives can be compared to rock climbing in many ways. The rock face is our whole life. There are many obstacles—some are harder than others on the journey to the top. Sometimes there are good footholds and handholds, while other times there are none. There will be hard times in life when we feel God is not there and there's nothing to hold on to. But the truth is, like the rope that connects me to the carabeener, God is always there.

Sometimes you have to use all the strength left in you to jump and reach to touch the 'beener. In life, sometimes you have to take a leap of faith, put all your trust in God, and ask Him to help you fully rely on Him, even when it feels as though you're hanging on to nothing. As you climb, someone is always on the ground below you, belaying you up the rock. In the same way, God's Spirit dwells within us, always strengthening and building up our faith. When rock climbing, the rope that is holding

you up is your only lifeline to catch you when you fall. Jesus is your lifeline. He is there when we stumble and fall to sin. In 1 Corinthians 10:13, we are reminded of God's promise to lift us up and strengthen us for our walk.

Prayer: Dear heavenly Father, our only lifeline from whom all our strength comes, be with me on my journey up the rock of life. Help me to stay strong in You and always trust in You so I will come to You when I feel as though there's no one to turn to. Remind me that You gave me Your Holy Spirit that dwells in me! When I think I can't bear any more trials, show me the way! All this I ask in Jesus Christ's most precious name. Amen.

Worry

Read: 2 Corinthians 4:16-18

Do you feel stressed out? I sure do because I'm involved in so many things! Sometimes I get so worried about something that seems like such a big deal at the time that my focus strays from God.

The truth is, I worry about everything and get stressed way too often. There are so many trivial things that go on in my life, and it seems as though they are so important, but they aren't! When I get to heaven, God is not going to ask me how many hits I got during my high school softball career! He's not going to say, "I'm so proud of you, Allison, for being elected secretary of your class your junior year of high school!"

I don't need to worry about those things as much as I do. What matters is how my faith in Jesus is and how I live for Him every day! In 2 Corinthians 4:17-18, we read:

> For our light and momentary troubles are achieving for us an eternal glory that far outweighs them all. So we fix our eyes not on what is seen, but what is unseen. For what is seen is temporary, but what is unseen is eternal.

One of the many things I worry about is my appearance, but I can remember that I'm beautiful in God's eyes! When I worry about not having a boyfriend and wondering if I ever will, I know that God may be preparing someone as my spouse already and I will know who it is in God's own time. He may be preparing something else entirely—even being single—for my future.

Jesus says in Matthew 6:34, "Therefore do not worry about tomorrow, for tomorrow will worry about itself. Each day has enough trouble of its own." Don't be anxious about the future because it's all in God's hands. Don't waste your precious time here on earth worrying about temporary things. Instead, focus on things that are eternal!

Prayer: Eternal Father, You are the only one who matters, and You hold my future in Your hands. Guide and direct me to understand what things in life are of real importance so I may do Your will and keep my focus on You. In Your Son's amazing name I pray. Amen.

DATE DUE